VICTIMS of CONSCIENCE

Especially for Hannah + Holland,

Enjoy!

Neil
Wilson

By
B. NEIL WILSON

ISBN: 1460904389
ISBN-13: 9781460904381

HONORS:

I'm forever indebted to members of High Country Writers for their help and encouragement over the years. Finally the book is finished due to the aid and patience of my bride of fifty one years, Frances, my partner who suffered with me during many confusing moments – especially with the computer. And I would still be struggling with corrections were it not for our good friend June Bare. Much of the credit for the finished product should go to June. Then there is Bill "Eat Desert First" Dacchille and son Stephen that kept my sick desktop going. It was getting to the point that if I needed to use my computer it would have to be done at Bill's house.

I appreciate all the encouragement from relatives and friends. It is for them whom this was written. I'm pleased my dear friend Pastor Bob Wolf, a fellow Civil War buff, consented to critique my material and include the effort in his busy schedule. I should mention Steve Frank who encouraged me to keep going and his wife Susan that told me of a distant cousin that had been a guard at the prison. So now Susan, you can show this to your doubting cousin. With friends like these, how could I go wrong? There are so many acts of kindness on the part of HWC

(High County Writers) and friends it could be another story.

This story should be dedicated to Pastor Bob Wolf whose encouragement has meant so much to me.

If I have left out any one that should be recognized my apologizes. I can blame it on old age that has caught me.

It is hoped that the reader will enjoy this story as much as I have enjoyed writing it.

B. Neil Wilson

NEIGHBOR – FRIEND OR ENEMY

Tom Gentry stopped in his tracks. The sudden change upset the chickens in his gunnysack. A young girl that followed too close, bumped into him. He turned to face his sister. "Sue, the rumor must be true. And that crowd at the store appears none too happy. That's Sheriff Brown with them men. There's been a killin'."

"Not necessarily so, Tom. You believe every rumor you hear? We got to get on to the store. You almost upset my basket of eggs and butter."

"Sue, Lem would never lie to me. He just said it was likely."

"Why was it likely, Tom?"

"He said there was too much excitement and fuss. That was down at the sawmill. Lem heard a few words that sounded like a knifin'. We better get on to tradin' our goods. Ma wanted coffee and flour you know."

Tom grumbled before moving. "We could avoid that gatherin' except for the butter. Would be better to come tomorrow."

Sue looked at Tom in disgust. "You know you're curious about the gatherin'. Just because you don't see Mary Ellen father's buggy you're disappointed. Let's get closer so we can hear somethin'."

Sue complained, "These petticoats sure make this old blue dress hot. I expect Ma is right. I need to start being a lady even if it don't feel right. Sure is hot for March."

Tom saw Sue fingering her dress and remembered that she had made the same complaint to their mother. This prompted him to look down at his shoes.

I'm glad you fellers are finally broken into walkin'. Makes me feel good all over, and with the sun on my back I'm most comfortable. Women folks fuss over clothes. It matters little to me that my brown trousers and shirt are faded and patched. I could use a new pair of suspenders.

"Sue, if this ain't ... I mean isn't Saturday, why are there so many at the store? What further proof do we need? So, we can go find out who and why."

Virgil Mason, the storeowner, shouted, "I tell you sheriff, it has done went and started. Yancey Cagle was for separatin' from the Union and some don't like it. That was why he was murdered ... stabbed to death like you said."

Sheriff Brown puffed out his chest and stared Virgil down. "I said nothin' bout him bein' a separatist. I just said he had been stabbed, and with his own knife. Besides, he was more neutral bout the subject in public. I knowed him better than you. To tell the truth, he is for this State, but he was for stayin' in the Union."

Old man Wiggins had been sitting quietly just listening. He noticed Tom and his sister Sue. "Tom, your paw and Yancey is, or was good friends. Would you say he was mouthin' about separatin' or stayin'? Don't sound like much of a reason to fight."

Tom suddenly found himself the center of attention. "No sir, I mean he never talked politics at church I knowed of. He and Paw saw things pretty much the same. Both wantin' what's best for North Carolina but mostly Unionists, I think."

Mason's eyes bored into Tom. The storekeeper's friend Dandy Buchanan didn't look too happy either. It appeared the two men didn't like Tom's comment.

Tom thought to himself, *I've done said it now. Those two won't be too friendly from now on, I would reckon. It's time to do some swapping and get on back to the house. I want to tell Paw about the murder.*

Virgil Mason didn't like the way the conversation ended, but he was happy to get the eggs the youngsters brought. He dismissed Tom and Sue as fast as he could so he could listen to the murder discussion. Virgil started to say something but the sheriff and the others continued to argue.

"What is to be done about finding the killer?" a by-stander shouted at the sheriff. "There were a lot of foot-prints around the body. The trampled weeds look like a fight."

Tom nudged Sue and motioned toward the door with his head. He spoke loud enough for her to hear. "Sis, let's not hang around. We've heard enough, and folks here are getting upset. We don't need to be around all this anger."

Halfway back to the house, Tom noticed something curious. Someone had made a trail through the family cornfield. "Sue, nobody but a stranger would go through there. Why would they leave the road here? Take the goods with you. I want to follow this trail."

"All right then. You just go on playin' detective and get yourself in trouble. Might be more than you can chew, brother."

Tom had not gone far when he discovered two sets of footprints. One walked fairly straight. The other's left foot made a deeper imprint. *He must be crippled up some. Would be easy to follow on plowed ground. When he gets to the woods I might lose him … walkin' on leaves and such.*

There were voices ahead that made him hesitate. *Somebody's talkin' down by the creek. It would be funny if I found the killers. The look on sister's face … I can just imagine.*

A loud voice stopped Tom in his tracks. "You had to kill him too? You'll have the whole county down our necks."

"I didn't kill him. Just found him like that. Somebody broke his neck. See how it's twisted sideways like that. If'n it was me, I'd a-used a knife or clubbed him good. I'm a goin' to take his coat with all them buttons. He ain't goin' to need hit no more."

Tom crept closer until he could stand up straight. He leaned against a large oak. *Another killin'? Knees, don't you fail me now. This is important enough to stay close, and if I run now, they might see or hear me for sure. I hope the sheriff's still at the store.*

The first man voice spoke again. "If'n I was you, Cousin Slim, I would leave that coat be. You want to mark us by wearin' that dead man's coat? We better make tracks. Won't be long for them to get a lot of men and start lookin' because of that first killin."

The other man responded, "Reckon you're right. We need to find another pair of fast hosses. Wish the bunch had let us keep the ones we had."

"Don't mean to rile you, Slim, but you was just too blood thirsty for the bunch. You got us into trouble twice. They didn't want us around no more."

Tom shifted his left leg that was getting cramped. His foot slipped off the damp tree root only a few inches, but the contact with the ground made enough noise to attract the men's attention.

"Junior! You hear that? Take a look over yonder beside that big oak."

"I heared nothin' cept'n this creek. You getting jumpy?"

"Junior, I see a britches leg beside that tree. We got company. Go get him. We don't know what he done heared."

Tom bolted for a line of trees that hid the family springhouse.

It's time to make for the store and find the sheriff.

Fear and excitement propelled him faster than he ever remembered running. Something whizzed by his right ear followed by a pistol shot. The gunshot prompted him to dive over the fence. He landed on his belly, flipped over and slid down a shallow bank. His shoes stopped short of falling into the little stream that led from the spring. He took a quick look over the fence and saw two men moving back into the neighbor's patch of woods.

One of the fugitives let out a puff of air in exasperation. "Junior, who is the fool now? Tell me. That shot will bring the whole bunch from the store."

"Oh, they'll just think somebody shot at a rabbit or somethin'. Let that boy be. He is too fast for us, and you with your game leg. We better find a mule or somethin' and head fer the mountains and your kin like we planned. You or me don't know this country enough to get shed of that boy." Junior chuckled. "That boy sure could run. Never seed a deer run like that."

"Junior, that boy can put us at the killin', and now this dead man. We got to get that feller. If we come back this way he could be trouble. I might have business in the east again soon. I aim to get rid of him the next time I come back this a-way … skin him good. I hate smart younguns like him."

"What chance we got of that, Slim? Too many people at the store and a-bouts."

"Not now, Junior. We'll wait till next time we comes this a-way."

Tom ran by the little stream that ran from the spring-house. The bank on each side gave him cover. He yelled at the house before leaving the stream.

"Ma, Sis. Grab the shotgun or musket and don't let any strangers near the house till I get back … explain later."

Tom ran up to the store out of breath. The sheriff, deputy and several men were gone. Three men were still hanging around. Old man Wiggins watched Tom as he tried to catch his breath. He removed the pipe from his mouth, stared at Tom for a second or two before speaking.

"Tom boy, why you runnin' on so? You're goin' to make your self-sick again like you was back in the winter. Your face is as red as a pickle beet. What is so all fired important?"

"Mr. Wiggins," Tom paused to catch his breath. "I followed a trail through our corn field, saw and heard one of the killers admit to killing Yancey …" (Another breath,) "… and the killers found another body. It was Buttons."

A bystander jumped in his wagon, snapped the reins and shouted at his mule. "I'm a-goin' to fetch the sheriff back."

By the time Tom caught his breath he spotted the sheriff. He spoke to no one in particular, "The self-appointed lawmen will take too long to reach me. I'm gonna back-track to the body. I know the sheriff will soon catch up."

He noticed his father hurrying from the direction of the house carrying a musket under his arm. Tom stopped near the body to wait for the men and his father. It was an excited group of men that returned with the sheriff.

Mr. Gentry was soon close enough to speak. "What's the trouble, son? You scared the women folk … That's Buttons a-layin' there. What happened? If there is danger a-foot, you shouldn't come out here by yourself."

Mr. Gentry observed Tom's stern features and his face glowed with pride in his son. "I'm about to forget you're a responsible young man."

Sheriff Brown trotted up to Tom and his father. "Tom, did one of them fellers you saw kill Buttons?"

Brown didn't wait for an answer before giving orders. "Two or three of you men see if you can find them in the woods. The rest stay back until I'm through investigatin'."

Tom wiped the perspiration from his forehead with his sleeve. "Sorry, Paw, for scarin' folks. I must've got excited. I'm about to forget them two that found Buttons… Mr. Dempsey. The way they talked they found him like that and decided to head for the mountains. That was before they saw me. I expect they made tracks when they saw everybody headin' this way."

Tom then told of the conversation he had heard for the benefit of all present.

The storekeeper, Mr. Mason grunted in disgust. "You're just sayin' that to protect your paw. Buttons was fer pullin' out if South Carolina does. They've had words about this. Everybody knows Buttons was fer separatin' from the Union."

It was Tom and his father's turn to be disgusted. Mr. Gentry remained quiet and let Mason talk himself into a corner.

Tom hooked his thumbs in his galluses, a habit he picked up from his paw, and interrupted, "And I suppose we drug the body across the creek from Button's property into ours. You can see he was drug out of the creek. Then I suppose I shot at myself when I ran for the trees next to the house. Everybody, including yourself, heard that shot and I got nothin' to shoot with."

Tom thought, *Mason looks like he swallowed a not-too-ripe persimmon.*

"Hey sheriff!" a man shouted. "I see where them two took off for Button's place. You want us to take after them? They get hold of his horses and they'll be hard to catch."

"You do that, but don't get too close cuz they be armed. Keep me informed. I expect them two won't stop till they reach the hills."

The sheriff turned to appraise Tom for a bit. "Tom, I appreciate what you done. But now I got two murders on my hands. If those two didn't kill Buttons and most likely killed Yancey, we got to catch them to prove they is Yancey's killer. That ain't too hard to accept, but who killed Buttons if they ain't done it?"

Mr. Gentry slapped Tom on the shoulder. "Let's go home to supper and see if we can calm the women down. We elected the sheriff to take care of troubles such as this."

Tom felt good about his part in the days' excitement. *Except for some of my school friends, the folks here about are accepting me as a man.*

Tom's mother, Nell Gentry and Sue stepped onto the porch. The father and son's casual approach erased some of the worried for the women. Nell shouted to the two before they reached the springhouse. "From the looks of you two, I'd say we have nothing to fear anymore."

Will Senior shouted back. "We'll tell you all about it over supper, Ma."

LIFE'S DISAPPOINTMENTS

It was not unusual on Sundays to see the Gentry family filing into their pew. As was their custom, sister Sue and Tom led the way into the fourth pew on the left, followed by brothers Willie and Homer, mother Nell and father William, Sr. In fact, they and their kin filled the entire fourth row. As usual, Uncle Casper and Aunt Jane were late.

Tom adjusted his long legs under the pew in front. Glancing around he noted there was a larger number than usual.

Most of the Tyro community is in attendance this Sunday. I suspect dinner-on-the-grounds in honor of the new minister contributes to the numbers. Hope he won't preach too long.

The minister motioned to the organist to start the hymn. One of the Bell twins, Herbie, took his turn to pump the organ. Following the introduction, most everyone joined in the hymn. Ma Gentry, Sue, and Homer typically led the congregation in singing. Their strong voices motivated the rest of the worshipers to sing out

After the hymn the preacher leaned over the rough old pulpit. "Please be seated. That was a resoundin' amen to this old hymn. Always one of my favorites. Bow your heads and join me in prayer."

Tom wondered how long the man could pray. He was startled when the preacher launched right into the sermon without losing a breath.

It's time to sit back and hear about my sin.

Even though it was the first of March, the weather had turned warm, much to the delight of the little congregation. Most of those that attended had dressed for the usual colder days they had been experiencing, which meant the crowded little church was going to get warm. Before the service, a couple warm bodies took it upon themselves to open the windows. This allowed a pleasant breeze from the southwest to enter. With the breeze came the smells of food that had been placed on boards laid across sawhorses, tantalizing young and old. The adults tried to concentrate on the sermon or at least make a show of listening to the new pastor. Wonderful odors became a great distraction for everyone, especially the young people.

Willie leaned over and whispered to Sue, "The children and courting age folks are getting restless, and want the service to end."

The children in front of the Gentry family were getting impatient with the preacher's long-winded sermon. The scent of the food coming in through the open window was a distraction to both children and adults.

There was one notable exception. Young Tom Gentry was distracted by something else. He was only aware of Mary Ellen Green who sat in her usual spot with her parents and younger brother. Tom counted the heads of the Green family and stopped when he again reached Mary Ellen. *As usual, there they are, in the pew on the right, two rows from the front. This always places Mary Ellen next to a window.*

The window allowed light to fall across her blond curls, making them glow. An occasional breeze made her hair shimmer adding to his discomfort.

His fantasy allowed him to imagine running his fingers through her hair and playing with the curls. He tried not to stare, but when he looked straight ahead her presence was still painfully near.

Tom thought to himself. *How can a young man like me concentrate on a service when such a pretty girl is in front of me? And the minister's high-pitched voice is irritating. I sure miss my good friend, Pastor White. He would understand my feelings and perhaps shorten his sermon. Always said I had a good understanding of things for my age. If he should see me now I wonder what he would say.*

Mary Ellen placed her hand behind her neck and fluffed out her curls. Tom didn't know if this was a conscious act to attract attention or an unconscious movement born out of habit; however, when boys were around she knew the effect it had. Any movement she made attracted Tom's attention. This action captivated him; it was always a wonderful experience.

Suddenly the preacher pounded on the pulpit and shouted. "Repent and be baptized." Tom jumped in his seat. When he looked back at the preacher, the anger in the man's face so startled Tom that he gulped, getting strangled. This made him start coughing. He quickly reached for his handkerchief in his hip pocket, placed it over his mouth and made for the door, pretending to be much worse.

"It's a chance to escape that preacher", Tom whispered under his breath. "That man will never replace my friend, Preacher White."

Tom stopped at the bottom of the three steps, took a deep breath and hastened to look around. He felt like someone was watching him and turned quickly to find his old friend Lem smiling at him. Tom's former playmate observed him from across the boards of food, which were lined up beneath two huge oak trees.

"Lemuel, what in tar-nation are you doing out here instead of your usual place in the balcony listening to the new preacher carry on?"

"Well Mister Tom, you don't have to listen too hard or be in that balcony to hear dat preacher. I can hear him right good where I stands. Besides, my master done told me to watch the food so's the dogs don' get into it. You knows I likes to be inside dat church. When you calls me Lemuel instead of Lem, I knows you is displeased wif me."

"Why would I be displeased? I was just surprised to find you out here. Lem, it's a good thing the boards are covered with that white cloth or you would be fightin' the flies too."

Tom thought to himself, *this slave-master business just don't feel right with Lem. We can be friends in private! This is hypocritical after practically growing up together. I wonder if I'd have the gumption to hide him or protect him if he decided to run away.*

"In fact Lem, I'm especially glad you are protecting the food. You know how much I like to eat. There is always too much food, but it is always good. I can't wait to see what's in some of those baskets still in the wagons. Some of the ladies wait until the last to put out their best. Reckon it's some kind of contest?"

As the church doors opened, the new minister emerged, ready to greet each person as they passed.

The ladies hurried ahead of the men folk to unveil their favorite recipes, so that their dishes were placed with care and pride. The men formed a group to themselves while the school age youth watched for the signal to grab a plate.

Beemer Green, Mary Ellen's younger brother, was the first to reach the plates of fried chicken. He looked back at Mary Ellen. "I'm goin' to get some of this pork too. Be glad when summer comes so we can bring fresh garden vegetables, but for now we got to be satisfied with dried vegetables and preserves. I ain't complainin'."

Everyone eyed the pies and cakes at the end of the line hoping there would be some left for themselves. Mothers and older sisters were kept busy herding the little ones while the older school age children kept pace with grownups.

Tom was one of the next to fill his plate and quickly moved to the side to observe Mary Ellen. She filled her plate, turned, smiled at Tom and moved to a stone bench under a budding maple tree. The look on her face appeared to be an invitation for him to join.

When the two young people eyed each other, she would look down demurely. Tom was captivated. They ate quietly and watching the others file past on their way to find a place to eat. He could tell she was uncomfortable and preoccupied. Mary Ellen frequently glanced over the crowd as if looking for someone.

After taking a bite, Tom remarked, "That sure was good pumpkin pie. Do you suppose it was canned like I heard tell?"

"It wasn't dried Tom, I can tell. Of course they can last a long time in my mama's cellar."

Her attention was suddenly drawn to a new arrival on horseback. Without looking, Tom knew it was Walter Buchanan. Her eyes revealed her interest in him. Tom's stomach turned into knots, his face burned hot. He wanted to disappear into the woods behind the church.

Walter spoke loud enough for all to hear. "I'm sorry preacher for missin' preachin'. Our cows got out and it took a while to fetch them all back. I could sure use some of that food right now after all that cow chasin' and such."

He made a big show of throwing a leg over the side of the horse. When his feet hit the ground, he carelessly threw the reins over a wagon wheel. The next move was in the direction of the food.

Mary Ellen smiled at Tom and patted him on the knee before rising from her seat. "Tom, you have always been like a brother to me. I always enjoy your company. Please excuse me." She then pranced off with her plate to join Walter.

Tom forced a smile and nodded. His thoughts turned to revenge. His long time competition with Walter's fine horse and family's large farm focused in his mind. Tom thought he'd like to block Walter's right fist while punching him in the gut.

Over the year's Walter has bullied me. But now I'm almost as big, and I feel the time is fast approaching to get even.

His thoughts turned to Mick Mason, another bully of sorts. *Those two, Mick and Walter have always been a thorn in my side. Thinking on them right now makes me angry and that would bring on a lecture from Ma if she knew.*

Mick was small of statue but made up for his size with his mouth. Like Mary Ellen, he could be a friend when it was convenient for him. Mick desired to be bigger in the eyes of the other classmates, so he chose to pick on

Tom when Walter was around. He often started trouble between Walter and Tom.

"Tom, there is only one more week of Mrs. Fortner's special class, and you won't have to put up with Walter and Mick, especially that Mary Ellen."

Tom turned around slowly to face his sister Sue, getting angrier by the second. He expected to see her mocking face. Instead he read real concern for him. It was as if she could read his mind. His anger turned into a deep hurting in his chest.

Sue continued, "Tom, I don't enjoy saying this, I really don't. That is the third time she has thrown you over for Walter, and she has done this for a wealthier cousin from Salisbury too. Sometimes it is to make you jealous, to tease you or to torment. How long are you going to take this abuse, big brother?"

His hurt turned to real anger, but not at Sue. *Sue is saying the same thing I have said to myself lately. Little sister of mine, you sure can see the fly-in-the-ointment. You are growing up. The people at school and church don't know how to appreciate you. And it's a pity that if she or I talked educated in front of most folks, they would say we were putting on airs.*

"Sue, you put the last nail in the mule shoe. Neither you nor Ma will have to remind me anymore. Like Ma says, there are other fillies about."

Tom decided to spend the rest of the afternoon listening to the men talk politics. His father, he noted, remained calm, but Mick's father, Mr. Mason was adamant about something. The closer he got the less he liked his decision to listen.

Mr. Mason slammed his right fist into his open left palm. "Mr. Gentry, I tell you we can't let the North tell us how to live … change our way of life. South Carolina's got the right idea."

Tom's father shrugged. "You know Mason, I don't judge y'all for ownin' slaves just because I don't. We need to keep this country together. How can our country long survive if we begin to split up into small fragments of states or countries? Do you think a confederation of southern states, if allowed by our government, could survive without itself splittin' into other smaller countries, sir?"

"Will Gentry, we just have to let the North know they will have to let us alone. The southern states will have to stick together and let the North know what's what."

Tom decided he had heard enough, and wandered aimlessly toward home.

TIME TO LEAVE HOME

The month of March had its cold and warm days; however, the weather was of little concern to the students of the Special Class. These were eager young writers and prospective law students. The teacher, Mrs. Fortner's deceased husband had been a lawyer of some repute. He had often included her when instructing young lawyer hopefuls. She knew Blackstone's book on law as well as her husband. Therefore she was regarded highly by the community and students.

Normally Tom and the other students would have been judged to be too old for further schooling. It was time the girls were getting married and the boys working.

Monday, students were to read a portion of their work before the class. Tom and Mick had chosen a particular point of law they wish to defend. Mary Ellen had written poetry and Walter had completed a study on Morgan horses. The Bell twins had chosen to write stories that were scientific in nature. Herbie wrote on honeybee keeping and Hector on the different shapes of Indian arrowheads.

Mrs. Fortner and the class had decided to grade one another papers. Tom decided he wanted to grade Hector Bell's work on arrow heads and decided Hector should receive an A.

Mrs. Fortner stood to address the class. "As agreed, we shall give our opinion on the grade you think your class mates should receive. It is now time to vote, so to speak."

Each student received an A, A minus or A - plus. It was time for the class to vote on Tom's work. Every one voted for Tom to receive an A. However, Mick stood and shouted. "Give him a D. He only deserves a D. What do you say, Walter?"

Walter looked around at the rest of the class before making a comment. "Aw, I know I said an A at first. Just give him a C, I reckon."

The rest of the class shouted in unison. "Give him an A." Mick yelled louder. "No! Give him a D or a C minus"

Tom began to see red.

Finally Mrs. Fortner held up her hand for quiet. "Let's at least give Tom a B plus."

Tom seethed with anger. *If it were not for Mick, I would have gotten an A. The rest of the class thought so. He is nothing but a little sawed off peep-squeak, letting Walter do all his fighting for him. The only reason Walter's in the class is because of Mary Ellen. I never figured why Mick the Mouse... Say! That is a good nickname for him. Never figured why he wants to torment me. I've never done anything to him.*

Mrs. Fortner looked over the class with a pleased smile. "Friday, as you know, is our last day. It has been a blessing and a pleasure to work with such a mature group. You have done well. You should go far in life and I pray that you do. We will use the rest of the week for questions you might have ... question and answer week. If the weather permits we can celebrate with a picnic Friday. Go home now and enjoy the evening. Hector, I would like to see your arrow heads out in the sun light."

The twins were the first to exit followed by Mrs. Fortner and Mary Ellen. Walter was about to wait on Mick but decided he had rather follow Mary Ellen. Tom slowly put his papers in order before picking them up.

Mick turned to Tom with a smirk. Twisting his body smartly to confront Tom and spouted. "You didn't get an A and Walter's got your gal. You ain't so smart."

Tom's pent up anger exploded with a backhand across Mick's face, sending him backwards through the desks and against the wall.

Mrs. Fortner ran back into the room. "Boys, boys! Stop this before you completely wreck the room. Mick, go home now. Tom, remain here. I need to talk to you."

Mick stopped at the door and turned to give Tom a rather crooked smile out of his red, swelling face, as if to say, "I got the best of you again."

Tom rested fearfully on his heels, dreading to hear what his favorite teacher had to say. He tried to read the expression on her face but it was impossible. She always looked serene. Displeasing Mrs. Fortner in any manner was beyond his comprehension. Most all of the students strove for her approval, especially Tom. The kind and gentle efforts she exhibited with her class were an inspiration to all she taught. Firm but fair was one of her unwritten rules.

After Mrs. Fortner put the several desks back in place, she turned to look at him. "Tom, Mick might be the same age but he is too small to knock around. He is small in stature, and sometimes small in mind. Next time, turn him over your knee." A slight smile made the corner of her eyes crinkle and shine.

The compassionate teacher looked Tom in the eye. "I should have foreseen what could happen if I let the class decide the grades. It is supposed to be a tight-knit, friendly class. As it turned out I was wrong. For that I apologize.

"Tom, you are intelligent and have a quick mind. I'm going to speak to your parents. I think you should continue to study law. Go and enjoy the rest of the day. You deserve a rest from this room."

Tom felt uncomfortable and could feel his face getting warm again but for a different reason than before. He was thrilled and embarrassed at the same time, barely aware of walking out the door. The elation he felt as he walked down the school steps would stay with him the rest of his life. Even the shout from Walter didn't put a dent in his mood. Walter stood up from where he had been sitting with Mary Ellen and advanced toward Tom. "Why don't you try pushing me through a seats, farm boy?"

Before responding, Tom rehearsed in his mind how he would block Walter's blow. Now was the time to test Uncle Casper's boxing lessons. He couldn't help grinning when he spoke.

"I knocked Mick through at least two rows of desks before the wall stopped him. Now I'm ready to take on you … and Mick. It won't be a short little scuffle like before. I've got several reasons to bloody you, Walter."

Mary Ellen ran in between the two boys. "Walter, if you are going to walk me to the store before Paw comes, you better stop. There is no time for fightin'. Besides, I heard Sue say she would jump on your back the next time you got him down. You know how that tomboy can fight."

As if summoned, Sue ran up half out of breath. She quickly grasped the situation by the expression on the boy's faces. "Tom, hurry home. Uncle Art and Aunt

Eleanor just pulled into the yard with three wagons. Uncle Art wants to have a talk with you."

Walter and Mick laughed. Mick was determined to have the last word. "Saved by his sister again."

Sue stared hard at the two boys. "Fellers, I reckon Tom don't need my help. Our Uncle Casper, an old sea captain's been teachin' Tom how to take care of himself all winter."

Walter stepped closer, knocking the papers out of Tom's hand. "We'll just see about that."

Tom pretended to reach for the papers with his left hand, threw a right into Walter's stomach, and another quick left jab to the ribs with his left. Walter tried to cover his midsection and left his face open. Tom finished the attack with an uppercut to the jaw. Walter took a step back and sat down hard. The look on his face was total surprise.

Tom pivoted around expecting Mick to jump him but he need not to have bothered. Sue stared Mick down.

Tom squatted to speak into Walter's face. "Come on Walter, I'm just getting warmed up. Don't sit down on me now."

Mary Ellen turned her back on the group and started sobbing. "I'm going to meet my paw at the store without you. I don't want to talk to either of you again."

Walter staggered to his feet. With some effort he ran after Mary Ellen. He wiped his bloody lip on his sleeve and made an effort to catch up. "Aw, Mary Ellen. You've seen us fight before. It's not like we never got into no scuffle afore this. I'll walk you to the store. It ain't that far."

* * *

The three wagons were longer and held more freight than Sue had led Tom to believe. He had pictured the wagons to be like their own farm wagons. Each of these wagons was hitched to two large mules. A cow was tied to the back of one wagon and a calf to another. The last wagon must have held the family's belongings. Tom was so preoccupied with the wagons he had not noticed a young black boy sitting on the second wagon seat until the boy moved.

Tom's mother called to him. "Come say hello to your uncle and aunt. Uncle Art has a proposition for you." The rest of the family, who included Tom's mother, father, Uncle Casper and Aunt Jane, surrounded Uncle Art and Aunt Eleanor. To complete the scene, the family dog, Herkimer, stood to one side, slowly wagging his tail.

Tom and Sue hurried to join the rest of the family. Uncle Art turned to appraise Tom.

His uncle moved out of the circle of relatives to extend his hand. "Tom, you've growed up considerably. I know your folks here are real proud of you. I've been talking to your brother Willie here, your paw you know, and he says it's up to you."

Tom could only imagine. *I'll bet he wants me to travel with them ... handle one of the teams. What else would he want of me? I wonder where they plan to go.*

"I see you are properly puzzled." Uncle Art grinned and shook Tim's hand. "Well, here it is. We started out with Ned here ..." He pointed up at the young black boy who gave Tom a toothy smile. "... and another lad we had to let go home cuz he got sick. That leaves me, Ned and your Aunt Eleanor to handle the teams."

Uncle Art hesitated a moment or two to watch the wheels turn in Tom's head. "I'll give you fifty ... no, seventy five dollars since you are family, to drive one of the wagons and help set up the store when we get there."

"Now Art," interjected Aunt Eleanor, "we can do better than that. You ain't told him where we are a headin'.'"

Art scratched the stubble on his chin as if contemplating what he was to say next. We're headin' into Cherokee country. We got a lease from Chief Will Thomas, the only white chief I ever hear tell of, to be partners like, in a store near Cherokee. We got the option to buy or we wouldn't have agreed. Besides, there is just too much unrest caused by this see-session talk back home. We want to get away from that talk and hard feelin's."

"You can help me set up the store, Tom. The wagon in back got our house goods and the other wagons got shoes, cloth goods, flour, salt and such for the store. What do you think of that?"

Tom looked first at one parent then the other, waiting for their advice. They only stood watching him, knowing he had to make the decision. Tom spouted out the question that was on his mind from the beginning. "What about Willie or Homer, Paw? They are older. Wouldn't you want one of them to go instead of me? Not that I don't want to go. And then there is Mrs. Fortner that wanted to talk to you about me studying law."

Tom's mother moved to place a hand on his shoulder. "Tom, your brothers are needed here and the trip would do you good. Remember how the heat got to you last summer, and you were sickly some in the winter? You are stronger now … growin' into a young man. Why, you will be eighteen in June. And, if you got your heart set on goin' to study law, the money Art is offerin' would come in handy."

Ma Gentry turned to Art. "You can make a way for Tom to return before winter or fall so he can get more schoolin'? That's the only reservation I have about him goin' off into the mountain."

Art stuffed his hands into his pockets. "I reckon I can. I'm told there is a tinker that travels from Asheville up Cherokee ways once in a while. If we can't get Tom hooked up with him we'll find another way. It wouldn't hurt for him to stay a year with us before goin' home, I expect."

Art turned to the black boy in the wagon. "Ned, you can go on home now. Tell your master, I said thank you for your loan since I had to let the sick boy go home. I'm much obliged to him."

"Mistah, I will if you holds that dog. He might not like Ned."

The group laughed. Sue spoke up to comfort Ned. "Herkimer here won't bother you." She scratched the dog's head and looked up at Ned. "He only gets mean at night."

Art put a few gold coins in Ned's hand and patted him on the back. "Appreciate all your help Ned."

* * *

The next morning Uncle Art was ready to leave. Tom said his goodbyes to the family. Ma was brave and held back her tears as she hugged her youngest boy.

The caravan started out westward over rough roads. The next few weeks turned out to be exciting, tiresome and difficult. In good weather they slept out in the open or under the wagons. When the cold spring rains came at night, the little party of three was forced to huddle in the covered wagon that held their family belongings.

Many days Tom shivered on the wagon seat in the rain behind the mules. In the evenings mud and boredom were often discussed as the daily enemy. When not too tired they enjoyed the sunny days and would pass comments from one wagon to the next.

One afternoon after a hard rain, Tom heard his aunt yelling. He looked back to see her mules had stopped and covered in sweat. Her wheels were too deep in the mud. Tom pulled his team and wagon as far off the road as he could and shouted, "Uncle Art … Hey Unk, I think Aunt Eleanor is stuck."

Art stopped his team and looked back. "Tarnation and bother. What you reckon we ought to do nephew?"

"I think we ought to use my team and even yours to hook up to hers. Sure would hate to unload that wagon."

"Good thinkin', Tom. That's what I'd do; so that's what we'll do. Should have another team for that wagon. After we get her out we can stop for the night … give the animals a rest."

* * *

Several days later when they finally viewed the approaching mountain peaks, it put a spring back in their step. Excitement replaced boredom. The early hardships were soon forgotten.

On one occasion Uncle Art was quick to warn Tom and Aunt Eleanor. "Keep on the lookout fer copper heads and rattlers. They kin be pizen you know."

The young traveler noted the changes in the greenery with interest. It was as if he were experiencing a new spring each day or two. Aunt Eleanor picked wild flowers cautiously for fear of snakes and bears.

Uncle Art kept a couple of sawhorses and tools hanging on the back of the family wagon that were used to hold the wagon while an axle was being greased. They placed a long pole on one sawhorse as a fulcrum before resting the axle on the second sawhorse.

On the first occasion to grease the axle and remove the wheel, Art looked at Tom in amusement. "Tom boy, this here is my own invention. I don't know how others done it, but this is the way we do it. We three puts pressure on the pole and I drag the sawhorse under the axle with a piece of rope tied to my foot. The idea is to be sure the one with the rope ain't goin' to snag up on a root or rock."

A day's journey from Old Fort, a wheel on the lead wagon dropped in a deep rut and broke. Uncle Art mumbled, "Since it's midday, we'll rest the animals while we replace the wheel with a spare." He turned and winked at Tom. "Aunt Eleanor can make us bigger meal than usual to bolster our spirits. Give us a mite more strength too."

After replacing the wheel, Art sat down with his plate next to Tom. He studied his nephew before picking up his fork. "Boy, we got one more spare and it's not too good. The wheel rim on that busted wheel is still good. We can heat it up and hammer out the bent place. I can whittle out a couple of good spokes but we got to get a black smith to sweat that rim back on in Old Fort, if they got a smithy."

The Gentry caravan was a real curiosity when they rolled into Old Fort. Two men stood outside the blacksmith shop watching the three wagons approach. Tom noticed one of the men speak to the smithy, who was putting a shoe on a brown mare. Tom didn't make eye contact with the man.

He was more interested in the few people about the area, particularly the two young people staring at them from across the road.

I wonder what they make of our outfit. Sure look to be mountain folk. Wonder what they think about states' rights or even if they care.

The blacksmith placed the horse's foot on the ground, looked up at the new arrivals, and wiped his hands on his apron before speaking. "What kin I do fer you travelers? Where you headin'?"

Uncle Art stepped down from his wagon and pointed to the busted wheel. "Can you take that dent out and sweat the rim back on this here wheel? I done repaired the wheel the best I could."

"Well, sir. I reckon I kin. They calls me Smith. Don't that take the cake, callin the Smithy Smith? What name do you go by, pilgrim?"

"I'm Art Gentry, that's my wife Eleanor on the back wagon and my nephew Tom on that one. We would be much obliged if you can take care of that wheel. We are on our way to the other side of Asheville. Sure glad to find a smithy here in Old Fort."

The blacksmith motioned for Tom to hand him the wheel and rim. "My old grand-pappy on my ma's side was the first smithy in these parts. He had himself a shop right inside that old fort. This here is more convenient now days."

One of the men that had been watching the shoeing pointed to the cow behind the first wagon. "Want to sell her mister? I'll give you a fair price. Looks like she might be calfin' soon and won't make it past Asheville."

Art turned to Tom. "Tom, you see to the wheel while I talk with this man. I been worried about this cow the last few days."

Tom nodded as Art stepped off a few paces to talk trade. Aunt Eleanor didn't look too pleased about the prospect of losing one of her cows, but said nothing.

The smithy had Tom work the bellows on the coals while he heated the rim to take out the dent. This turned out to be hot work, even from where he worked the bellows. Heating the rest of the rim was more of a chore but after what seemed forever to Tom, the iron rim was soon hammered or "sweated" back on the wheel.

Uncle Art returned from his "cow tradin'" looking grim. "Eleanor, Tom, it pears, from what this feller tells me, we will have to double team the wagons to get them over the steep places and getting' round some of them curves is goin' to be tricky. Lucky we spread the weight between the two freight wagons. Mr. Ferguson here is goin to loan two pairs of oxen in trade, to pull one freight wagon and I'll use the mules on the other. We'll have to park the wagon with our belongings and come back with a team to pull it to the top."

"Tom, I hate to have to ask you to stay with the last wagon but it's got to be done. Don't see no way around it. I hope we won't be gone more than a few days. Aunt Eleanor will stay with a family till we get back. Me and Mr. Ferguson will get back as soon as we can. Do you think you can handle it?"

"Sure, Uncle Art. Just leave me with a musket and the dog. We can manage for a few days. I'll park the wagon near the stream. Might even catch a fish."

Uncle Art looked puzzled, "What dog you talkin' about, Nephew?"

"I thought he was included in the tradin', that wooly half starved dog beside the water trough. I suppose you were saying somethin' else when you're arms were wavin' this way."

Smith laughed. "Mister Tom, you kin have that poorly dog. He done took up here a few days ago. Feed him and he will follow you all the ways to Cherokee country, I reckon. Think he belonged to an old traveler we had to bury last Wednesday."

Uncle Art clapped his hands together. "Well Tom, that settles it. Sorry I'm going to leave you with one team of mules to attend. The curves over the mountain wouldn't allow for more than two teams for one wagon and the borrowed oxen for the other. Hope to see you in a few days."

Tom cooked his evening meal of corn fritters and pork. After cleaning his pan in the creek gravel it was time to put up the mules. *I'm right proud of this stick corral uncle and I built. It's close enough to the stream I don't have to carry water far.*

The first evening after Uncle Art and Mr. Ferguson left with the wagons, Tom decided to do some fishing. He had not had time to think on anything other than driving, tending the team and gathering firewood since they left. *Now I have time to fish and rest for a spell. I put a line and pin hook in the bottom of my travel bag. Got to be careful I don't stick myself with the pin. What's this wrapped up in a cloth?*

Tom removed the cloth revealing a small pistol. A note stuck out of the barrel. He pulled the note that read: 'Uncle Casper wanted you to have this. We hope you don't have to use it'. Further exploration into the bottom of his bag revealed five more loads and enough powder for the loads in a wooden match holder.

I feel a lot safer … secure with this pocket pistol along with that old musket. I'm suddenly too tired to fish. Tomorrow morning will be soon enough.

He knew that sleep would not come easy this night. The excitement of finding the pistol and being alone, except for the dog, wouldn't lend itself to bringing on a restful sleep. It was easier to sit on a stone, feed wood into the fire and stroke the dog.

At dusk, Tom had just thrown a stick on the fire. The dog stood up, growled and was looking in the corral direction. *I should have the musket with me or at least the pistol in my pocket.*

There was thump and a yell of pain, followed by, "Oh, oh, oh!" The moaning was now accompanied by one of the braying of one of the mules.

Tom jumped up, grabbed the musket and pistol from under the driver's seat. The dog waited for Tom before venturing toward the corral.

"Keep quiet, Junior. You want the whole country down our throats?"

"That aggervatin' mule done busted mah laig. Think he broke hit, Slim!"

Tom crouched down behind a large bolder, rested the musket on the top before cocking the hammer, hoping it made a loud enough sound. "Slim, I strongly suggest you help Junior to a doctor. I have you both in the sights of this ten-gage shotgun. You only get to the count of five. Now get." *I'm glad I haven't had to talk much today, to make my voice sound deeper.*

"We're a goin'." It was Slim's voice. "Take it slow with that shotgun. We was just passin' by."

"No boys. You figured to take my mules. Time is up. I better hear you moving away from here. When my finger gets tired it begins to twitch."

There was the sound of scrambling and deep moans from the brush. Tom could hear their retreat for about a minute. "Dog, stay close to the wagon tonight. I imagine I won't get must rest. And Dog, we shouldn't have to worry about them two and the mules, unless Junior wants revenge."

The remaining days rolled by slowly waiting for Art and Mr. Ferguson to return with the oxen and the two teams of mules. No more was heard from Slim and Junior. Tom had taken precaution by stringing flat creek stones to rope so they would clatter if disturbed at night.

* * *

It was several days later until the three travelers and the wagons were back together, making their way to Asheville. Tom decided the town was busier than Lexington or Salisbury, and had a few more buildings. Their arrival in Asheville attracted more attention than when they first got to Old Fort. Ladies carried shopping baskets and a few had small children tagging along. There were some well-dressed gents that watched from shop doorways. However most of the men in the streets wore their work clothes that included muddy boots.

Tom and Uncle Art noticed three ragged mountain men watching them. They appeared interested in the wagons. This interest disturbed Aunt Eleanor as well as the men.

Art spoke only loud enough for Tom to hear. "Since it's early in the day, it would be better to pass through as quick as possible, cross the French Broad and go as far beyond the river as the day will allow."

Art hailed a passer-by loud enough for the three suspicious men to hear. "Stranger, is there a place on the other side of the river to camp for the night?"

The stranger stopped to look at Art. "Well mister, there sure is, but some fancy folks that live in West Asheville might not take kindly to your teams in their yards.

There's some right nice homes over there, it would be better to go by them a ways, if you know what I mean."

Art touched the brim of his hat and slapped the reins on the mules before replying, "Thank you kindly; we will do just that."

When they were beyond earshot of the three men, Tom decided something needed to be said. "Uncle Art, I know you don't intend to stop, but you reckon we ought to travel as long as we can see? Last night the moon was starting on the decrease but if the clouds don't block out the moon, we might have light enough to travel for a few hours."

Art chewed over the suggestion for a bit. "We'll just have to stop before it gets too dark. The hills and trees might block out too much light from the moon. I don't want to bust another wheel. If the dog lets us know them three is snoopin' around, I'll warn them we got us two or three shot guns. Tom, them fellers sure looked real mean to me... could be trouble."

"Uncle Art, one of them men looked like one I saw at the edge of our farm. He was standing near a murdered man we called Buttons. He or his partner admitted to killing another man before they found Buttons. One of them took a shot at me when I ran for help"

"Your paw told me somethin' bout that. We got to be real careful."

West of the river, Tom looked back to see the three mountain men following at a distance. One was a big lumbering brute, the second was of medium build and the last one was rather thin. One of the men would limp occasionally.

When Tom glanced at Art, he was looking back as well. Art then looked at Tom and pointed ahead to two other travelers seated on a farm wagon. *Uncle Art intends to join those two; it will be safe for all of us if we do.*

The next morning little was said. It was time to hitch up the team after a quick bite of breakfast and be on the trail. Their minds were on the three rough characters that had followed them the evening before. Now that the rogues could not be seen troubled them.

Art looked first at Eleanor and then Tom. "It's probably my imagination, and I'm frettin' over nothing, bout them three tough ones we saw back yonder, but it's best to be cautious."

At the top of a rise, the wagons stopped for a rest and to check on their back-trail.

Art fished in the box under the wagon seat, pulled out a field glass and handed it to Tom. "Tom, take a look-see back the way we come. Never could hold them steady enough for very long."

Aunt Eleanor giggled. "You eye sight is gettin' older, Art."

Tom moved to the wagon and took the glasses. He braced his elbows on the wagon seat, and studied the trail behind them. "Uncle Art, I see four of them now. It's the same three with another added who might be older than the others. The fellow with the limp is still there."

Art took the glasses back. "As long as they stay their distance I'll feel a lot better. The travelers we took up with last night done branched off from us back there. We're on our own now."

* * *

Four mountain men sat around a campfire warming their hands while they waited for their coffee to boil.

"Slim, we waited too late to get us some decent grub from them travelers, and some warmer dudes too. They get too close to Waynesville, might be too many farmers about."

"Junior, I recollect cousin and Paw talkin' about a shipment of goods for the new store near Cherokee. He heard one of them Indians talkin' about it. Let 'em labor them goods all the way to Cherokee. Leave them be until then. What's the big hurry?"

* * *

Several days later the wagons came to a wide river. Art became excited and animated. "Eleanor ... Tom, we're almost there. We just follow this river downstream till we see the roof of the store. I think the river is called the O-con-o-luftie. That's what Will Thomas called it in his letter. He said to look for a trail off to the right, and you will see the roof on the store I told you about."

NEW FRIENDS

Tom gazed over the landscape, took in the smell of the breeze from the river, and observed the mountains about him with wonder. When the wind changed, he still smelled mules and dust again, but now there was a difference. Their journey was almost at an end.

It was late in the day when they found the store. Uncle Art signaled for them to stop. He looked over the store and its surroundings with a smile of approval. He threw the reins over the brake lever with a deep sigh.

"This place appears in better shape than I had figured. That means there's little fixin' up to do. Hop down and take a look inside, Tom."

Weary as he was, the excitement moved Tom to investigate. On opening the heavy door he shouted back. "There's one fair sized room reserved for the store goods and a room in back for a family. I'm goin' on in." He walked through the building and back to the door. "The back room has space for a bed, a dry sink and a cook stove. A ladder in the back of the store goes to an attic. Looks like a low ceiling. That would have to be my space. Come see for yourselves."

The tired travelers decided to sleep in the wagons one more night before attempting to unload.

Tom was awakened by the smell of coffee and bacon once again. Aunt Eleanor called. "Tom, time to get up. Go on down to the river and clean up before we eat."

"I will, Aunt Eleanor. I'll just grab a bar of soap and my towel and be back quick as I can."

Tom ran down the path they had taken the evening before. On reaching the river, he was surprised to find a skinny lad about his age, fishing. The young stranger was so intent on his fish line, he didn't to hear Tom.

Tom decided the neighborly thing to do was make his presence known. "Catchin' anything." The boy jerked in surprise, turned to look at Tom and grinned.

"Nope, been tryin' to catch that big'un. See her there. She done slipped away. You must be one of them what moved into that old store."

"Yep. They call me Tom. What do they call you?"

"I'm Franklin, John Franklin. Live the other side of the river. Fishin' is better here. I got me a canoe under that big tree yonder. I reckon my ma and pa will be right glad to hear the store be open again."

"John. Soon as I wash up a bit, why don't you follow me back to the wagons and have breakfast with us. We got plenty for now. My uncle and aunt would be glad to share with you."

"I would be right proud too, but I been gone long enough. Might be I would later. Say! You want to set up a trap line with me along some of these here creeks flowin' into the river. I seed plenty of tracks. We could get plenty of furs to sell."

"Sounds good to me, John. Just look for me along the river or at the store."

After the new tenants' first night in the store, it was time to replenish the shelves. It was warm work and they kept getting in each other's way. About lunchtime, Aunt Eleanor had had enough of the men. "Tom, why don't you take that fishin' pole I saw leanin' against the building and see if you can catch that big fish you were tellin' me John Franklin was after. We might have her for supper. Art, why don't you split us some wood and kindlin'? I'll take care of the store for now."

Tom had eyed the pole the day they arrived. *Now it was time to give it a test. Come on pole. Let's see if you can catch a fish.* He was about to whistle a tune while walking the path, when he heard fast running feet. The sound came from a path that ran almost parallel to the wagon tracks. Tom stopped, knowing the path merged with the road near the river.

What he saw made his mouth drop open. An Indian girl was running as fast as any one Tom had ever seen. She had pulled her dress up to her knees to allow for faster footwork. The loose fringes on the bottom of her brown dress fluttered in the breeze. The creature was like an apparition … unreal to Tom. What he saw in her face was pure joy. She didn't see Tom when she flashed by, adding to the enchantment of the moment.

Another figure, an Indian boy, ran from up river to cut her off, breaking Tom's spell. The boy grabbed her by the arm spinning her around. The two laughed between gasps for air. It was too much for Tom to watch. He suddenly felt like an intruder.

Not any point in trying to get to the river now. Let those two have it for the time being. Might as well go back to the store and make myself useful. Boy! She is about the prettiest thing I have ever seen. Too bad she has a boy friend.

Tom entered the store feeling downcast. His thoughts were on the pretty girl until the voice of a tall Indian he hadn't noticed brought him back to the present. The fellow wore white men's clothing, which surprised Tom. The blue-striped shirt and black pants fit him well.

"Tom …" Aunt Eleanor motioned to the Indian. "Meet Howard Crow. He will be helping out in the store two days a week. He knows the people here a-bouts. Can be a real help. Why you look so down in the mouth when you came in. You give up fishin, already?"

"I didn't want to disturb two people courtin'. They were runnin' down by the river. I thought I would let them have their time alone."

Howard studied Tom a moment before speaking. "That could be most any couple, but it could be Little Fawn and Running Deer. She likes to tease her brother by beating him in a foot race. You mentioned them runnin' … sounds like them."

Two days later, Tom made another attempt to go fishing. This time when he got close to the river, he heard the voice of two women, and splashing. Wet clothing hung on bushes. It was obvious they were washing their cloths and possibly bathing.

I'll not go any further today. Back to the store again. One of these days I'll catch me a fish.

He turned and took two steps and froze. There sat an Indian boy on a log. It was the same one he had seen chasing the pretty girl. The boy wore deer skin trousers and shirt, trimmed in the fashion he had seen near the O-con-o-luftie River. The expression on his face told little but the flintlock musket across his legs spoke a warning.

"You're smarter than most white boys, Tom. Made the right choice by turning around. Let me give you a bit of advice. Watch your step around the Goins family. They can be right mean."

Tom realized he hadn't moved since he saw the Indian. "How come you know my name? And how come…" *How come he talks such good English?*

"You're wondering how I speak good English? My paw is white and my maw is Indian. He taught us good, my paw. And we got schools around, you know. How do I know your name? My sister and I know such things. We have been watching you. My sister named you Skinny. Skinny, you keep trying for that big red fish, if you want. But I aim to catch him first."

Tom grinned from ear to ear. *She is his sister! I got an idea how to get an introduction.*

"That sounds like a challenge, to see who will catch the big fish. If it is, we can have a friendly wager, if I can come up with something to wager. You must be Running Deer and that must have been your sister Little Fawn?"

"Catching the fish will be reward enough, Skinny. I wager you will lose."

* * *

Tom hadn't been back at the store long when who should walk in but Little Fawn. She tried to shut the door behind her, but a tall slight bent slim man in ragged-acrid smelling clothes pushed his way through the door. It was one of the three men Tom and Art had seen in Asheville.

"Com-ere Injun gal. You ain't too good fer me." The intruder made a grab for the girl. She twisted away and made a dash for the back door of the store.

"Slim! Leave me alone," she yelled as she ran.

Her pursuer almost reached her except for Tom, who grabbed a broom and stuck it in front of the slim man's legs making him stumble.

Slim shoved Tom against the wall, keeping his eyes on Little Fawn, he pointed at Tom while making for the fleeing girl. "Boy, I'm a goin' to get you fer that."

The two burst through the back door making Uncle Art drop his armload of wood. "What in tar-nation? That feller's been drinkin for sure. Look at that pretty gal run. He'll never catch her. I'll bet my boots on that."

Often bad news travels faster than good news. Before the day was over, a group of white and Indian neighbors were searching for Slim Goins. They intended to run him off or hang him. Fortunately for Slim, his brothers and pap took him south.

* * *

The next morning, Tom decided to seek the red fish Running Dear mentioned. He stuffed the last biscuit in his mouth before starting for the door.

Uncle Art held up a hand to stop him. "Before you go too far from the store, stick this under your belt." Art handed Tom a small muzzle-loading double-barreled pistol. "You're a man now, so look out for yourself."

Tom accepted the pistol. "You know I already have a small pocket pistol. One more load in that second barrel is a powerful persuader. I thank you for the loan."

John Franklin was already fishing when Tom reached the river. "John, I been thinkin'. Animal pelts this time of year might not be so good. They will have their summer coats. What else can we trap?"

John pulled his line out of the water and turned to look at Tom. "Muskrat furs will still be good, I think. And beaver should still be good. We can try for them."

"I found some steel traps behind the store, John. We can start today. You know the lay of the land. Or we could ask Running Deer's help. Do you know him?"

"Do I know Running Deer? I hope to tell! Our folks are good friends. His pap helped my pap a heap o' times. We got to include him."

* * *

Tom helped at the store during the busy time of day, and then spent the rest of the time trying to catch the fish or checking the trap line with John. Running Deer helped find locations for the traps but had little time to help Tom or John. Despite the limited time the three had together, they became good friends.

Friday, Tom finished his store responsibilities and picked up his favorite fishing pole. He soon found John trying to catch the big red fish. "Looks like you are about asleep, John. Having any luck with that fish?"

"Na. Did get us some pelts though. Funny thing … some of the traps that is easy to see are sprung and nothin' there. Somebody is a robbin' some of our traps. I'm pert near sure of that."

Suddenly Running Deer sat down beside the two. He had approached without making a sound. "I like to keep in practice. Never know when being quiet like will come in handy, since the Goins have been seen south of here. They could be the ones robbing your traps. You friends better be careful from now on when you check our trap line."

Running Deer turned to see who was approaching. "I see I'm followed by my sister and our cousin Mandy. It's good she's got somebody to come to this part of the river without me. John, Tom, meet our cousin Mandy Adams. Mandy, say hello to my two white friends, John Franklin and Tom Gentry."

Mandy smiled and nodded to the two boys. "Pleased to meet you both. Kathryn has told me much about you. I can tell which is Tom ... or Skinny."

Little Fawn's cheeks flushed red as she whispered, "Sometimes you talk too much Mandy.

"I see Skinny, or Tom looks confused a bit. Tom, didn't I ever tell you our given name or the name our father gave us? I see not. Mother likes our names but prefers to call me Little Fawn and brother here Running deer."

"I'm really Kate Adams and brother is Johnny Adams. You can call me whatever you like. I answer to either and Johnny will answer to anything at mealtime. Now are you properly confused?"

Franklin looked at Mandy approvingly, which didn't escape her notice. He attempted to put on a bold face.

Mandy smiled and remained quiet. Kate is always tellin me I talk too much. If I talk now I might stumble over my words.

Running Deer noticed Tom and his sister seem to be more than a little interested in each other. He studied Tom for a moment and decided to test his skinny friend. It might also serve to test his sister's interest. "Are you going to stay the winter Tom? Or are you going to return home at the end of summer?"

Tom looked down at his feet for a moment. He made a quick glance at Little Fawn. "I'm not too sure about that. I want to stay the winter and my uncle and aunt want me to stay and help. It kind of depends on what my folks back home say. I still want to study law and I don't want to go home."

"It's been a wonderful summer so far." Tom added. "Why don't we forget about what I'm goin' to do. We can enjoy the rest of the warm days and each other's company. Everybody will know by the time fall comes one way or the other."

Mandy couldn't hold back any longer. "What do you think he should do, Little Fawn, uh, Kate?"

"Tom can make up his own mind. I agree with him; don't waste the summer."

TRAGEDY AND TRIALS

Aunt Eleanor picked up three of the breakfast dishes. "I'll put Franklin's breakfast in the oven. He's usually on time when it comes to my cookin. Tom, you did say he would be here after checkin the trap line?"

Tom took a last sip of coffee before wiping his mouth across his sleeve. This brought a frown from his aunt. "Yes mum. He should've been here by now. I'll go see if I can find him. He might need some help, had a big catch or somethin'."

"Take your coat with you. It pears like it's goin to be a colder day … clouds and such."

He stuffed the last biscuit in his mouth, as usual. *I'll take the coat off the peg. Cold or not, it will please my aunt. The path to where we start in the stream isn't far … won't take long.*

Tom hadn't gone far when he discovered an empty trap. A few steps further, another empty trap. He began to talk to himself in a low voice. "Franklin has been through here … except these are the last traps. If he had come through here he would have come to breakfast." He gasped, "That looks like blood in the stream! Oh Lordy …"

The stream flowed clear by the time Tom found the next trap. Why has it been thrown aside like that? Franklin would never do that. His shoes, I see those old patched holes.

"Franklin! What's wrong?"

The scrub trees hid Franklin's torso; his legs stuck out in plain view. Tom parted the brush. His friend's body lay next to the stream, his eyes open. Tom could see his throat had been cut.

Tom knelt down to close Franklin's eyes, and began to weep. "Who could have done a thing like this to you … as if I didn't know. I swear" he choked down a sob, "I swear I'll avenge you. I swear! Now I got to get you home to your folks. Nothing else to do now."

He put his coat on the body before he picked him up. Tom carefully viewed the area. The ground and grass around where the body had lain revealed little. There was one boot imprint that appeared to ride over to the left.

If there was a scuffle, it didn't last long. If this is a nightmare, and I can't wake up, this can't be real? Tom struggled with the body. "I am determined to carry my friend as far as I'm physically able. What will I say to his paw and ma? Arms, I know you are about to break. Don't let me drop him … don't give out on me now."

Where did I see a boot mark like that? Time to think on that later. Got to get you home, Franklin. You were a good friend and partner. This is the least I can do for you, before I get revenge.

Tom could see Uncle Art through the trees splitting wood. "Uncle Art, Uncle Art! Come help, please. My knees and legs are give out, got to sit." He knelt down on the forest leaves still holding John Franklin.

Uncle Art ran to where Tom sat, took one look and pulled John out of his nephew's arms. "I'll just lay him gentle like on the grass. I can see what happened. You all right Tom? You look plumb tuckered. Just set here. I'll go ring the bell that came in for the church. It ought to bring help in a hurry."

* * *

Tom threw a hand full of dirt on the wood casket, and turned to glance at John's folks. Mr. Franklin had tears on his face, and Mrs. Franklin looked years older than the last time he had seen her. *Poor woman. She can't cry any more. I can't either.*

Mrs. Franklin turned to face stones next to the new grave. "My babies, all my babies. Now there are four. What's a body to do, Lord? What's a body to do?" She raised her eyes to heaven and gave a deep sigh.

Preacher Denver patted Mrs. Franklin on the shoulder. "Don't know we will ever know this side the Pearly Gates. Your younguns is in a better place. Keep your eyes on Jesus. Get your strength from him."

"You still got us, mama … me and Nan. We ain't goin to leave you." It was John Franklin's younger brother.

Tom walked away before he started to sob again. I can't take this anymore. Which is worse: caring for a friend or hatred for his killer? Is it the same? Someone fell in beside him and placed an arm around his shoulder. He could tell it was Johnny Running Deer.

"Be careful Tom. Let the law take care of this. Don't do anything foolish you will regret. Were you paying attention, when your aunt said revenge is mine saith the Lord? She is right, you know. We can take comfort in that. Even if the sheriff can't find enough evidence."

"You said it. The sheriff can't find enough evidence. You know what I think? I think he is afraid of the Goins family. Then again, if he had more evidence to show, he could get men to back him up."

"You're probably right Tom. But please listen to me. Another word of advice you might want to consider. I'm told that Slim keeps a big skinning knife in a sheath on his back. If he reaches behind, better back off quick."

The next morning Tom put on his coat and made for the creek. *I'll gather the traps and put them away for good. I would like to walk the trap line one more time. I suppose the sheriff and the rest have trampled down any more signs.*

He reached down to pick up another trap. Then a twig snap drew his eyes up the trail. Slim Goins walked toward him but didn't see Tom. Slim stopped when Tom stood up.

"Well, look at Skinny the store-keep. What you expect to find out here Skinny?"

Tom's hurt and pent up anger exploded. "You thieving murderer. You are goin' to get your neck stretched or worse."

Slim's right hand spun to his back. A wicked skinning knife flashed. Tom recalled Running Deer's advice but didn't back off fast enough. Slim made a swipe with the big knife. It cut through the front of Tom's shirt. In dodging the blade, he lost his balance, falling backwards down the bank into the creek. It was time to run.

"Who's goin to make it worst fer me, Skinny? You? A-ha-ha-ha-hee-hee. You be glad I got this bad leg."

Tom threw the remaining traps behind the store. *I wish I had one of the pistols with me. How stupid can I get? Do I tell the folks about it and have to show the shame of running when I wanted revenge?* His head hung low when he entered the back of the store.

Aunt Eleanor had to move or Tom would have bumped her. "Tom, you have to get a hold of ... What happened to your shirt? The seat of your pants is wet. You want to tell me what happened?"

Uncle Art entered the store while Tom explained his encounter with Slim. He gave Eleanor a worried look. "This ain't good. What you figure?"

"Art, we got to get this boy home. It's time for his schoolin' anyhow. That tinker should be gettin' to Asheville about now, don't you reckon? We could ask Running Deer or Howard Crow to take him on one of the mules." Eleanor pushed the door aside and called into the store. "Howard. Come in the kitchen please."

As Tom moved a chair so Howard could sit, he said, "Makes me feel like I'm running away."

Howard looked sheepish on entering. "I couldn't help hearing. My game leg won't let me go and Running Deer is off with his pop on some business. I'll go see if he is back." He turned to leave but stopped to speak. "Mr. Art, you been talkin about gettin' rid of one or two of them mules. Tom is a man. Let him have one to ride home."

"That's good if you can spare it, Unk."

* * *

Tom pulled on the last rope to secure his things to the mule. Howard hadn't returned and his uncle and aunt were fretting about the delay. *I feel lower than a black snake's belly. The only reason to rush me off is fear for my life.*

Tom was startled by Kathryn Little Fawn's voice. He turned his head to look into her dark eyes. "Were you going to leave without saying good bye?" She didn't wait for an answer but continued. "Howard told Ma and me what happened and why you have to leave. It was a good summer. It was a very good summer … the best I can remember."

"We will miss you. Brother Johnny Running Deer will be sorry you had to leave. I know he would like to say so himself." Kate stepped up to Tom and patted him on the arm. "Don't forget us."

Tom's face felt warm. *I thought she was going to kiss me at first. Sure wanted to kiss her ... too many folks around. It's too bad I won't have a chance now. There will be a chance someday.*

"How could I ever forget you ... your brother ... the times we've had. I will be back. This place is in my blood now. I'll miss these mountains. I've got to come back. Don't you forget me either."

Aunt Eleanor embraced Tom, pushed him to arms length and smiled. There were tears in her eyes. "You be careful a goin' home. Write us soon as you get home so we'll know how you're doin'. It's been a pleasure havin' you help out and stayin' the summer. Uncle Art and I will miss you like ... I don't know what all, especially your great help around here. Remember, your money is sewed in your blanket."

Uncle Art took hold of Tom's hand and pumped it several times. "Tom, I do hope you can come back. Things might be more settled by then. You picked a good mule. Nancy is the most dependable."

Tom felt a lump in his throat. "Thank you kindly. I better see if I can fit on this old saddle." Climbing aboard he nudged Nancy ahead with his heels. After a few steps, he turned to view the little group. It was a scene to remember, especially Kate 'Little Fawn' Adams smile.

He winked at her as he rode off down the road.

The journey back from Cherokee homeward was uneventful. His great concerns for getting lost or being waylaid proved to be unfounded. After a week he began seeing familiar territory.

"Won't be long now!"

HOME AND PHILADELPHIA

Tom gave the mule the final push up the lane to the house. He is quickly greeted by Herkimer's familiar bark. "Hello, Herkimer. It's good to see you too, and it's even better to be home."

Paw Gentry came out of the barn to check on the new-comer. "Well, well, the Prodigal returns. Welcome home, Tom. It's good to have you back. Figured it was about time you returned."

Sue and Ma Gentry rushed out of the house.

Sue was the first to reach Tom and threw her arms around his neck. "You were gone too long, brother, and now you'll have to soon pack up for school."

Ma scolded Sue, "Don't be in such a big hurry to send your brother away again. Welcome home, son. You're just in time for supper. Sue made another apple pie ... your favorite."

Mom embraced Tom and at the same time Paw pumped his hand.

Paw slapped Tom on the shoulder. "Well, let's get to the meal so we can stay ahead of the mosquitoes."

The next morning at breakfast Tom complained, "I just get home and have to pack again for a place I know nothing about. I hope it will be worth all the trouble," Tom moaned.

Ma chided him. "You want to be a lawyer, don't you? We don't want to see you leave so soon either, but the time is right. Take advantage of the opportunity. Your aunt and uncle in Philadelphia are looking for you. Just think. You will be able to stay with them while you study at the University. Your aunt, my youngest sister you know, can cook almost as good as me."

The train gave a warning blast on the whistle. Tom put a foot on the first step, turned to look at his family one last time. "Willie, Homer, look after our sister so she won't break too many hearts. Pa, Ma, I'll write or telegram as soon as I get there."

Willie had to have the last word. "Don't you up and marry one of them Northern gals, you hear."

* * *

The conductor tapped Tom on the shoulder. "Wake up son. You're here. Better untangle yourself from that seat, stretch to get the kinks out. You were beginning to look like a rag doll. Never could see how a body could sleep in one of them seats. Must have been all that distance. Don't forget your carpet bag."

Tom tried to stand. One of his legs had gone numb, there was a crick in his neck and his shoulder hurt. I wonder why I always wanted to ride a train, must have been out of my head. My first time and it was enough. Don't care if I never have to ride one of these things again. The ride was too rough, and I have feared for my own safety.

Tom stepped off the train, spotted a woman that looked a lot like his mother and two others. That must be Aunt Janie. The man beside her has to be Uncle Saul. But who is the boy with them?

Aunt Janie smiled, approached Tom and extended her hand. "You look just like your father. It is Tom, isn't it?"

"Yes, it sure is. I'm happy to finally be here and meet you folks."

A man in a worn business suit was the next to offer his hand. "I'm your Uncle Saul … Saul Wilburn. This is your cousin Ronald. Welcome to Philadelphia. We have a rather long walk so we better get started. Ronald, help Tom with his bag. He looks all in. Don't know if you heard all the details concerning your stay. You are to help in our store with Ronald when you are not in school or studying. We live over the store and don't live too far from the university. It can be very convenient for all of us."

Aunt Janie stumbled on one of the cobblestones. "Goodness me!" she exclaims as she grabs Uncle Saul's arm, "I'm still learning to walk."

Uncle Saul said, "We better hold on to each other. You have been losing your balance too frequently lately."

"We'll have stew beef when we get home, Tom. You must be half starved."

"This is true enough. I've had very little to eat since leavin'."

Ronald laughed. "Our classmates will love your accent. Don't lose it too soon."

"Cousin Tom, here are a few facts that might interest you about our school. Old Ben Franklin, himself, started it as an academy back in 1751. The law school was added in '90 after Justice James Wilson lectured at the academy. The academy is now a full-fledged University.

"Professor George Sharswood, one of my professors, was elected Professor of Law in 1850. You could say he rescued the Law School. The Law School hadn't been of any account for years. The rest of the University history timeline, you will have to dig for yourself.

"Professor Sharswood is teaching Constitutional Law at present and perhaps it's not too late to be included in the class. I'll see what I can do for you."

Ronald pointed out various streets and businesses as they journeyed through town. "This is the street we normally take to the university, Tom. You'll get used to every brick and stone. It will be hard to pass that bakery, The Fresh Loaf, without going in."

The little party hadn't walked long before they reached the store. "Your room is on the third floor, the warmest in the house ... or store for that matter."

* * *

Tom's excitement and nervous energy was difficult to contain those first few days. To be a part of this great university was like a dream. He accepted the good-natured teasing over his accent with a laugh and smile. This enabled him to make friends quickly.

Tom's previous education in Latin and law made a favorable impression on his professors. William Coleman turned out to be one of his favorites. Tom's interest in history endeared him to the middle-aged professor. They both shared a common interest in English history.

At the end of one of Professor Coleman's lecture, Tom was about to leave with Ralph Campbell, a new friend. The professor called to Tom. "Mr. Gentry, may I have a word with you?"

"Yes sir. I will be right there."

Ralph smiled and patted Tom on the shoulder. "Why don't you stop by my father's store on the way home?

There is a sign in front with a piano painted on it and the name Campbell's Music."

The professor began, "Tom, concerning our discussion after class Wednesday about the English Long Bow, would you care to shoot one? Friday afternoon does not look busy at my law office and I should have some free time. Too much law talk will dull the senses without some distraction. Will you be working at that time?"

"I'm usually working then but should be able to make up the time. I'll explain that my professor wants to introduce something new, which is the truth."

"Very well. Shall we say about two o clock?"

Work in the store went fast for Tom. His mind was kept busy with thoughts of shooting arrows and the lectures. One afternoon he approached a regular customer that usually went to his Aunt Janie. "Where is your Aunt Janie, Tom? She's usually here this time of day?"

"Come to think on it, my aunt hasn't been in the store for the last two days. I think she's taking advantage of my help to do things on her own."

"Tom, perhaps your young eyes can't see that she's right peaked. She doesn't look well to me. Do you see any change in her?"

He thought for a moment. "Hm … you may be right. She does seem slower lately."

* * *

Tom was about to walk up the steps to Professor Coleman's law office. He stopped short when the professor rushed out the door. The professor held a quiver with several arrows and a long cloth covered object that stood strangely above his head. "Well, Mr. Gentry, are we ready to try our hand at English archery? I see you are on time as usual."

"Yes sir. I have been looking forward to this ever since …"

"Let's hurry along then. I suppose you have heard the other students joke about how I always rush and hurry about. There is so much of this life we need to live and so little time in which to do the things we like."

For some reason Tom glanced back. *A lanky figure turned quick to dodge between two buildings. That's curious. Twice this week that's happened. What would he want with me? Perhaps he thinks I have money.*

Professor Coleman stopped to pull the cloth covering off the bow. "This is as close to a copy of the Long Bow as I could make. I laminated and bound the grip with leather. After I string it, take a shot at the target. If you like the bow, I'll show you how to make one. I have material to make them."

It soon became routine to meet on Friday afternoons. They would talk points of law, discuss history, shoot the bow, and work on Tom's new Long Bow. It appeared that the professor had adopted Tom as his young protégé.

A cold Friday in February, Tom stopped by Professor Coleman's law office. "Sir, we have another cold day. It's enough to hasten the arrows back in the quiver on their own accord. I surely hope we don't have to wait until spring for target practice."

"I will say amen to that, Tom. Have a seat. We can chat until my next appointment, if he shows up. As you know I usually don't schedule anything on Friday afternoons. I made an adjustment since winter is determined to make herself known."

"There is something I have been meaning to discuss with you, Tom. It appears that by spring I will have taken you as far as my talents justify. We are not talking about law of course. If you agree, I will approach Professor Sharswood and see if he will take you into his good council, not just in the courses you take, but as an understudy assistant in his office."

Tom blinked in astonishment. "Sir, I would be honored, pleased beyond words. Certainly I agree to such a proposal. I know it is usually reserved for the ones that have completed two years."

"Some second year students find themselves in law offices, Tom. Then, I will see what I can do for you. Our little faculty has been watching you. It shouldn't be too difficult."

The excited student could hardly contain himself on reaching home. "Aunt Janie, Cousin Ronald, I have exiting news."

When Tom related the conversation with Professor Coleman, Aunt Janie was thrilled but Ronald was obviously jealous.

Oh ... oh. I can see by Cousin's expression he is not happy about this. Is this the beginning of family troubles? I surely hope not. Did it sound like boasting? It was not my intention?

Aunt Janie looks pale and normally she would have gotten out of her chair, left the table and given me a big hug. "Aunt Janie, is something wrong. You look tired. Is there anything I can do?"

Ronald grasped the back of another chair. "Tom, you have been so busy with work and the university, not to mention your association with Professor William Coleman, you have neglected the family. Mom has cancer. The doctor confirmed the fact yesterday. Mom has been sickly for the last month."

Aunt Janie cleared her throat to get Ronald's attention. "Don't be unkind son. You have been busy with studies and work as well. Neither of you have neglected me, or the rest of the family. Don't feel guilty on my account. Your schedules have not allowed for time other than work and study."

"That's not true, Mother. Tom has spent far …"

"Shush, I will hear no more talk of what should have been done or what will be done. Let's make the use of our remaining days productively, for however long they may be. I think I hear Saul coming. Will you two set the table please?"

* * *

Tom sat in a chair to remove his shoes. *And I can't believe dear Aunt Janie has this dreaded sickness. She did her best to liven up the spirits during the evening meal, and so did I. Uncle Saul could tell Ronald was upset. What else is Cousin hurt about? Now that I think back, Ronald has been sullen and short with me since the professor took an interest in me. Figured then it was a mood habit. I can't help the circumstances.*

His thoughts were interrupted by a loud discussion down stairs. It appeared to be between Uncle Saul and Ronald. Ronald's voice sounded agitated and sometimes angry. Footsteps were soon heard on the stairs to their room.

It was a stern face that entered the room. Ronald picked up a blanket off his bed. "I'm sleeping down stairs on the couch tonight. You can have this confounded room all to yourself. Good night."

Tom sat stunned. Ronald's footsteps disappeared. The room suddenly felt empty and confining. *I'm the one that should be taking the couch. One of us will have to leave and I know which one it will be.*

A subdued knock on the door didn't comfort his frame of mind. Uncle Saul's cough only added to his misery. "Tom, I would like a word with you please."

"Yes sir, come in."

Uncle Saul stood and looked at Tom for a moment. It appeared he was trying to decide what to say. "Tom, in view of your aunt's sickness, I think it would be better for you to find other lodging. It would solve many of the present problems. You can find sufficient employment at the docks. I can give you a letter of recommendation. Please be ready to leave here in the morning." With that pronouncement, he spun on his heels to leave.

* * *

"So, friend Ralph, you now have the story as to how I came to find a room in Mrs. Thompson' rooming house. She likes to mother me, more than my aunt. The exciting prospect in all this is the lack of help on the docks. I make more money and enjoy using my muscles for a change. It can be dangerous work. Some of the danger comes from the outlaw type that frequent the docks. Don't look so concerned. I'm doing rather well."

Ralph put an arm around Tom's shoulder. "Please be very careful down there. Keep your wits about you. When it comes to the rough and ready crowd, mind your own business. I think this is enough excuse to celebrate. What do you say we plan something that includes some of our classmates?"

"I have been advised to mind my own business once before. My landlady knows much about the docks. It was she who suggested the person I needed to ask for work."

"Tom, you have almost lost your entire southern accent. Not only mind your own business, but don't draw too much attention to yourself when you talk. This is especially true after you get paid."

"You can rest assured I will do that, Ralph. When I was being stalked on one or two occasions after class or after shooting the bow, I became leery. When and where are we going to celebrate?"

"Leave that up to me. It's time for me to help at my father's piano store. I'm required to replace leather on an old piano's hammers with felt. This will be interesting since I have never done it before."

* * *

On a Saturday morning, Tom decided to pass through the market on the way to work. He intended to get a couple potatoes and an apple if he could find any. Uncle Saul and Ronald entered from the other end of the street. *They don't see me, and this would be a good chance to visit Aunt Janie. I must hurry.*

Tom wheeled around and raced through the streets to the store. Even though it was too early for the store to open, a customer approached the store. *The customer, however, didn't appear to want the use of the steps. Why is he more interested in the alley? I better make myself unseen.*

The customer looked about nervously. He approached the side window and pulled out a fair sized knife. The stranger slid the blade under the sill just before Tom spoke.

"This little pistol is faster than your knife. Don't turn around. Remove the knife and walk on. This is my job. Now move."

Tom pulled back the hammer to make it click. The thief did as Tom commanded. The man's knife was replaced in its sheath and he calmly walked down the alley.

Tom let himself in at the door since he still kept a key.

A lady Tom recognized as the customer that always asked for his aunt met him at the foot of the steps. "Oh, Tom. She will be so happy to see you but don't stay too long. It tires her so to talk." He smiled and nodded before entering his aunt's room.

He stopped in the doorway to observe her, not knowing what to expect. Aunt Janie was propped up on pillows. Her eyes were closed and she looked so pale and waxy. It pained Tom's heart to see her.

Janie opened one eye to look at Tom. The other eye quickly opened with the accompanying smile. "Tom, it is so good to see you. I knew you would come somehow. Don't be too hard on my other men folk. They mean well. You can forgive them can't you? Ronald is young and has much to learn about this old world. I think he has changed since you left. Come embrace your tired old aunt one more time."

Tom was in tears when he went to the bed to embrace his aunt, his mother's sister. He sat by her bedside and held her hand.

"Aunt Janie, let me read this latest letter from Ma."

"Thank you, dear. You are a good boy, Tom."

After he had read the letter he stood and said, "I will always remember you and your kindness, Aunt Janie. Now

I fear I must run so there will not be another, uh, problem. And I don't want to tire you more."

Janie started to say make another comment, but started to cough. She patted him on the arm instead.

Before Tom got to the door of the store, his uncle was unlocking. *Uh oh, this is not to my best interest I think.* Tom kept his slow pace to the door. His uncle stopped in the doorway when he saw Tom, who handed his uncle the key as he passed.

Ronald grabbed Tom by the arm when he started down the steps. *Not now Ronald, please.* He stopped to face Ronald who had tears in his eyes.

"Tom, Mother wanted me to ask you to be one of the pall bearers. I've never been able to find you. No, that's not true. I've been avoiding the issue." Ronald's eyes revealed real pain. "I know you will."

Tom nodded consent and choked down his tears. He patted Ronald's hand before he pulled away to run down the steps.

* * *

Sam, one of only three black men that worked the docks, shouted at Tom. "Mistah Tom, I's glad to see you this mornin'. And glad you don' have classes on Satahday. We gots lots 'o hunnert pound bags o' grain or rice to unload. Boss put us together cuz we works good as a team. He was watchin us last week. Didn't think he would allow me to come back but he was short o' help that day."

"You're strong and steady Sam. He has to put you on steady work. And you're always happy ... full of good-natured talk. But Sam, I haven't handled bags that heavy for very long at a time."

"I knows. But the boys and the boss say you much stronger now ... not like when you first come. I grabs my end of the bag by the ears at each end like this. You do the same on your end and jerk it on the sled in one quick motion. Now jerk." The motion was smooth and almost effortless. "See how easy we done that? Why we can work like this all day. We just got to find the right rhythm."

"Sam, I'm glad they put us together. Some of the others made me find how to work on my own. You've taught me a lot in a very short time. The first time they put us together was suppose to be a joke ... me the Southern boy and ..."

"I knows, I knows. Tom, sometimes I was treated better in ole Virginnie than here. My boss let me buys my freedom. Not many blacks where I come from had it so good. You notice how happy I is today? Do you?"

Sam can talk without losing his breath. Me, I have to catch a little breath after each bag. "Yes, I suppose I do notice. But you've been happy or cheerful most all week. Did you get a good letter from your wife or something?"

"Yes I did. I surely did. I prays the good Lord will make it happen. She says she hopes to get a ride on de railroad. That means she and my little boy, Elmer ... ceptin he's not so little no more ... will travel the railroad away from her boss man. Be free to jine me here off dat railroad. You prays, don' you Tom? If'n you do, prays fo us to be together again."

"Haven't been much for praying lately Sam but I'll sure do it for you and your wife. You make it sound as if this is a special train, or railroad. Did you buy their freedom and train fare?"

Sam glanced around to see who might hear. "Her boss man's wife wouldn't sell her fer nothin'."

"Sam's talking about the Underground Railroad." Tom turned to see Lester, one of the older white workers. "You never hear of the Underground Railroad? I see not. Well, that's where sympathetic whites helps runaway slaves slip to the North. These conductors, we'll call them, work together from the South and North to help the slaves. Most have to go on into Canada. For fear some will think I have a part in this, I will leave you two with your thoughts."

CALLED HOME

M rs. Thompson, his landlady, was holding a piece of paper when Tom entered.

"Tom, you got a telegram from home. Have a seat at the table and I'll make you a cup of tea while you study the telegram."

It's the first time I have ever gotten a telegram. Is it good or bad news? Tom took a seat before he unfolded the sheet of paper. What met his eyes came as a shock.

'Tom Gentry stop come home stop Paw hurt we need you stop Sue.'

What could have happened? Sue was too brief … typical. "Mrs. Thompson, did you read the note?"

"It wasn't folded when the boy brought it. Didn't mean to be nosy but couldn't help notice you were called home. I sure have enjoyed having you here and hate to see you leave. When do you plan to go?"

No sooner had Tom finished reading the telegram than there was a knock at the door. He turned to see the young boy from the store standing in the threshold. The boy was out of breath and the look on his face told the story

"Tom, the family wanted me to tell you your aunt died. The funeral will be day after tomorrow at one … you know the place."

"Thank you, Jason. Tell them I'll be there as promised."

The day of the funeral Ralph approached Tom and insisted, "Tom, wear my black suit. It might be tight and you know your jacket will not be suitable."

"Thanks, Ralph. You are a true friend. This morning I remembered my angry encounter with Uncle Saul, but I pushed the occasion from my mind to dwell on the wonderful times with my loving aunt. She will have many friends to tell her farewell … or to say, 'until we meet again.'"

When Tom walked aisle with the rest of the pallbearers, he noticed many of her friends, and especially the lady that had asked for her the last day at the store. What a wonderful tribute to a wonderful person.

At the graveside Tom observed his uncle and cousin. Uncle Saul was stoic, but Ronald was obviously in pain. It touched Tom to see his cousin in such distress.

Tom ignored Uncle Saul and stepped over beside Ronald and placed his arm over his shoulder. Ronald leaned against Tom and they both wept. Manly or not, it was healing for the two.

"Ronald, I must return home now. Pa is injured and they've called me to come home."

* * *

"Tom, we decided to await your return to our little circle before eating. I overheard Professors Sharswood and Coleman discussing your problem. So I shared the news with the others. Have you gotten any further word from home?"

"Yes I did. I still don't know the extent of the injury. The last telegram read not serious, can't work on the farm. I know Lem, a Negro I grew up with, will help until I get there."

They are thinking we own slaves and I lied about owning any slaves.

"We borrow Lem from one of our neighbors rather often. He has become almost like one of the family. When I get home, I'm going to ask a Quaker family if they will buy his freedom.

"Ralph, and fellers, I'm puzzled why my brothers are not able to help. You will have to excuse me until later this evening. I need to turn in my resignation to my boss at the docks. Since I can't afford to travel by rail, I'm going to try for work passage on a steamer. We should all meet for a meal later." Tom waved and trotted off.

Once Tom was out of ear shot, Ralph stood up and held out his arms as if to make a speech. "Daniel, and the rest, don't you think we can do something grand for Tom before he leaves?"

"Sure we can," Daniel answered. "Ralph, why don't you make arrangements at the Frenchman's Wharf? Henry and Joseph can help. Aaron, Mark, and I will do what we can. Don't concern yourself about cost. Nothing is too good for our friend Tom. We want to surprise him but how do we get him to the party?"

"On the second thought," Daniel continued, "Ralph is the logical one to persuade Tom to go and eat. I will arrange the party if the rest will help with the plan."

* * *

Activity on the docks had not diminished since Tom left the evening before. He was still due a week's pay they held back because of his starting date. Now there was a line at the pay window. This would mean a delay and a late meal. His boss, Wade Smith, stood at the office shack door. Tom decided to see if he would help speed things along.

Wade saw Tom and motioned to him. Two men got in Tom's way and began to struggle. One pulled a knife and made a swipe at the other. Tom backed away just in time or he would have been cut. Wade hit the man on the wrist with a stick. The knife flew out of his hand.

Wade yelled at the man. "Get your pay and get off the docks." Boss man Smith followed the man with his eyes and twirled his stick.

If looks could hurt, the man would have forgotten to hold his sore wrist. "This is one good reason I always carry this little club of mine."

A sheet of paper stuck out of Wade's shirt pocket. "I think this is what you came for. Take it to the paymaster. Just wave it over your head if there's a line. He is expecting you. We will miss you. You're a good worker, improved as the weeks went by. If you want to come back you've got a job."

"Thanks boss. I hope to be back in a year. We will just have to wait and see what happens. If I do, I hope there won't be any big knives around. This is the second time in my life I've had to dodge one of those things. Hope it's not going to be a habit."

Tom had just finished stuffing his money belt when someone shouted his name. He looked up to see Ralph wave. *He doesn't want to come on the dock this time of evening and I don't blame him. Stand in the road long enough, friend, and I'll join you. It's funny. I just realized I'm shaking a bit from that fight. No wonder I had trouble stuffing that last bill. Makes me remember the first time too well.*

"Hurry, Tom. All the good food will be gone by the time we get there.

"I'm hurryin' as fast as I can. It's been a long and tiring day. Where are we going? I could eat a horse."

* * *

The Frenchman's Wharf was busier than usual. Ralph signaled to the Frenchman who had his ear to a discussion between three lawyers. The proprietor answered Ralph's signal with a toothy smile and pointed to the stairs. Tom felt uncomfortable and confused. Nevertheless, he followed Ralph up the steps.

At the head of the steps, Ralph stepped aside and ushered Tom through the door. A choir of voices shouted. "Hail the departing hero. Huzzah! Huzzah!

And then they began singing:

For he's a jolly good fellow.

For he's a jolly good fellow.

For he's a jolly go felloooow ... which no one can deny."

There was much slapping Tom on the back and good-natured ribbing. Camaraderie was obvious to the young boy delivering food to the table. Since they all wore triangle shaped paper captain hats, Ralph placed one on Tom's head. Someone had made good use of scrap notepaper. Tom was ceremoniously ushered to a spot at the table that held a fair sized board. Each person had written a message on the board followed by their signature.

Tom made a slow scan of the room. He made an attempt to memorize the faces of his classmates. "Thank you one and all. I will remember you with much affection. How could I forget such a charming bunch of practical jokers? Here is Henry Stovall, the only law student that wants to be a doctor." The comment was answered by laughter. "Then there is David Goldman, who on the first day asked synagogue directions ... on a Sunday."

"Was it Asa or Mark that came up with the prank: disassemble a buggy and put it back together in the building on the administration level?"

Mark pointed at Tom. "I think it was your idea, and David had to help you replace the wheel. You were going to put it on backwards, even after your mountain trip tale."

Tom held up his hands in mock surrender. "I helped but the thing originated with Ralph and Henry. I'm still glad we decided not to tie a goat to the buggy tongue."

In an attempt to prolong the joviality, Ralph teased Tom about girls. It was an attempt to keep Tom's mind off his father's injury. "There must be a girl back home? A handsome lad like you must have broken a heart or two. You once mentioned a pretty blond headed girl from church. Tell us about her."

They all shouted, "Here, Here."

"There is little to tell I'm sorry to say. The pretty girl from church I mentioned once before is more interested in the upper crust fellows, and not me. There are no others to consider. I will have to spoil your fun."

It would not be fair to mention Little Fawn. These fellows might not appreciate her. And why have I not tried to write her?

Mark couldn't resist chiding Tom a bit more. "Tell me, our Southern friend, why is the South so upset with the

North? We are all one country. I understand feelings have festered since the fifties and earlier. At one point I hear taxes are an issue and another is slavery "

Ralph was chewing or he would have interrupted.

Tom's demeanor didn't change. He took a swallow of his tea and looked at Mark. "You are right on both issues. This is the way I understand the problem: taxes are unfair … taxes the past administrations leveled on everything shipped from southern ports. As to slavery, I know the complaints, our economy in the south is based on slave labor, and slavery is inhuman. I think I've mentioned somewhere before that our family doesn't hold to slavery. My uncle freed the few he had and I practically grew up with a black boy. We still remain friends. I'll answer the unasked question. South Carolina is the state that rattles swords, not my state."

Mark started to say something else but Ralph interrupted. "This is supposed to be a party, a going away party for a dear friend. Let's not forget that."

"Fellows, it has been great fun and I enjoyed every minute. The entire evening was engineered to perfection. You boys need to study and I need to finish making arrangements to travel. Tomorrow will be another busy day."

Mark turned to look at Ralph. "Why don't you escort our guest home? The rest of us committed ourselves to clean up. Remember, the Frenchman said we need to clean up after ourselves."

On reaching the bottom floor, Tom could smell wet coats and bodies. "Ralph, it's been raining. Tobacco smoke can't hide the smell. Too bad I didn't remember that dark cloud we observed earlier. Should have brought my slicker."

"Take mine. I'll borrow one hanging on the hook. I should come back and help clean up."

"Ralph, I'm old enough to walk by myself. Stay and help the others. I will borrow your slicker. Will I see you before I leave?"

"Rest assured you will. I will drop by your rooming house first thing in the morning."

Tom tried to put on Ralph's slicker. It turned out to be tight across the shoulders. If I take off the wool jacket and wear only the slicker, it will be too cold. In the process of putting on his coat and slicker, he hesitated by the lawyer's table. Their conversation there was of a serious nature. One man was trying to emphasize the importance of news he had received.

The speaker bent over the table to place himself in easy earshot of the others. "Nelson, I tell you this is scandalous. My brother in New York says the Governor of South Carolina commissioned an army officer and an agent of that state to purchase arms. Governor Brown wants twelve cannon, shells and a great amount of lead. The merchants in New York have no conscience and they will sell. I don't know what steps are taken to prevent this."

Tom decided he had heard enough. It was time to face the weather outside. The storm at the table gave reason for thought but not to his tired mind this night. His thoughts were of travel and home.

Wind tried to tear the door from his grip. He had to release his hold on his collar in order to secure the door. Rain mixed with sleet made its way down his neck. Sheets of rain sometimes blocked the lamplight and buildings. Most windows were already dark which contributed to his depressed mood. Tom pulled the coat tighter around his neck. The merriment of the evening no longer made him forget what might lay ahead. There was light enough to avoid stumbling on the cobblestones.

He muttered to himself, "Tom, get a grip on yourself."

It will be good to get home after all and get away from this miserable Philadelphia weather. I dread that side street that leads to the rooming house. No light, mud and too close to the docks. But who else would be out on a night like this. No cause to be scared of shadows. Ma would have a fit if she could see me now.

He made a right turn into the muddy side street and stepped in a puddle. *My feet are wet so what difference does it make. I need to walk closer to the buildings.*

What's that?

Someone stuck his head out from between two buildings. Tom thought his hair stood on end and held his hat above his head. The figure moved from between the buildings. Tom had not been seen. Two others soon followed. A door to Tom's left opened and a lady threw out a basin of water. Light from the door revealed the four in the middle of the street. Tom recognized the one in the middle ... a slave from back home in North Carolina.

Tom decided to speak to relieve the tension. "Aren't you Jethro Wiggins' man, Daniel?" This is a strange situation.

"I ain't no mo, mistah Tom. I's a free man now."

"Is Lem still there?"

"Yes Suh, he is. Master Wiggins treats Lem good cuz Lem is always happy. He don' treat me good. Now I's free."

"Well, good for you. I never much cared for Jethro myself."

The first man started walking past Tom. "Don't mean to be impolite but we got to be moving, you understand."

Tom noticed the man that spoke had a long beard but could see little else. Poor light from the windows didn't help. He only nodded as the three disappeared in the dark.

Now this is unusual. I have heard much of slaves escaping from southern states and making their way to this city. This must be part of the Underground Railroad. Never thought I would experience any part of it. When I think of the way many are hounded by cruel masters and bounty hunters with their chains and dogs ... makes me feel horrible ... could never do that to any human being ... would trouble my conscience.

I don't hold to abusive treatment and most decent folks shouldn't either. I'm glad I practically grew up with Lem. I watch him develop into a strong, honest worker. It left a good impression on me almost from the beginning ... and he is smart. I wonder if he knew I covered for him when rain blew in between the chinks and damaged one of Uncle Casper's books. Wouldn't Unk be surprised to know Lem could read.

Tom could see the boarding house, but something wasn't right.

A movement to his right caught his attention. Someone was standing in the shadows. *Not another one? There is something familiar about this fellow. I don't like this. I've seen that coat and hat at the docks. His back is the same. That is most of what I've seen of him. I can tell he is the one that follows me.*

Tom continued his pace but kept watch out of the corner of his eye. *I am ready to take hold of a big rock. Wish I had carried my little pistol. He has to be one of the "head knockers", those thieves and murderers from the docks. I was warned about. A glance back revealed the man had vanished. He must not be after me, or is biding his time. Wonder why he is skulking around here?*

It's time to find my key, now which pocket? Tom stopped in the shadows of his rooming house. Two houses up the path, a door opened. Light revealed a shadow of the head knocker. Perhaps the man can't sleep or is a sleepwalker. Ha, ha.

Tom avoided the squeaky step on the stairs and remembered to lift on the door handle. This would avoid another squeak, otherwise it would rub against the floor. He kicked his wet shoes under the only chair. Coat and slicker were thrown carelessly on the chair. *I'll be a sleep before my head hits the pillow.*

But sleep came slowly. It had been a busy and exciting evening. Tom was about to fall into dream world but there was a noise. It sounded like someone kicked a stone against a bottle. He pulled himself out of bed to look out of his window. It's the man I saw in the shadows and that must be the glint of a pistol. He is going to ambush that man coming down the street. Yes, the new policeman that Mrs. Thompson said moved in next door. What can I do? How can I warn him?

NEW ENEMY REVEALED

"Get in them boots, toes. We've got important work this night." With difficulty Tom slipped his feet in his boots. Haste made him more nervous. A final glance out the window revealed the policeman was within fifty yards of the killer.

The squeaky door to his room was forgotten. Tom grabbed his coat out of habit and bound down the stairs four steps at a time. He peeked through the kitchen window before touching the doorknob to confirm his suspicion. *That's a reflection from the hammer on a pistol ... same coat and hat ... same skulking no good. Slow to open the back door for fear of alerting the assassin, he hesitated at the door stoop. The murderer is taking aim. There is no time. I pray this bluff works.*

He judged a good jump would allow him to hit the slanted basement door with at least one foot to make a loud noise. When he jumped he shouted as loud as he could. "There he is men, don't let ..." A shot fired in Tom's direction interrupted his shout. Another shot was fired at the policeman as the assassin ran from his hiding place. Two more shots were fired at the policeman from the running figure.

When the shooter cleared the end of the house, the policeman took aim and fired his weapon. There was a yell from the would-be assassin who kept running. He was soon lost in the shadows. His footfalls could be heard for several seconds.

In the excitement Tom hadn't realized he had fallen against the house. He was shaking so much his teeth had started to chatter. It's a good thing the house is here to hold me up.

The policeman approached the house with his pistol pointed to the ground. "Come out whoever you are. I want to meet the army that came to my rescue."

The front door of the little house opened and a young woman wearing a night coat stepped onto the porch. "Are you all right, Cliff?"

"I'm all right, thanks to this young man. Go on back in the house Nellie. I'll be in shortly. What's your name sir?"

"I was about to laugh at myself for shaking so. I'm Tom, Tom Gentry. I recognized the man from down at the docks. Saw that fellow skulking around and knew he was up to mischief. There was not enough time to give a warning." He went on to explain how he discovered the man earlier.

"That was the reason for my so-called army, sir. I think I have seen him with three others on the docks." Tom stopped to reach for his bandana. "My boss warned me to avoid that bunch. They are always after easy money."

"You are right about him and the docks, and account of him being up to mischief. I must be bothering him and his friends more than I thought. Look here. It looks like he dropped his pistol. Sounded like I might have hit him, too. My weapon isn't good at that range. It was a lucky shot.

"Tom, you live in Mrs. Thompson's house, don't you?"

"Just until morning. I'm going to have to return home. My father has been injured."

"I think I recall my Nellie mentioning that fact. She and your landlady Mrs. Thompson exchange talk frequently. I hope and pray your father is not hurt seriously. If it were not so late, I'd invite you to a cup of coffee. Can you come for breakfast? My wife can make a right good meal. It's the least we can do for the army commander that saved my life."

"If you're sure it won't put too much on your wife. I wouldn't want to impose, but the invitation appeals to my stomach. Also, I'm afraid I don't know who it is I might have saved this night."

"Tom, I apologize. In the excitement I overlooked introductions. I'm Cliff McFarland, new to the police force here, late from New York. Let me shake the hand of an angel in disguise." Cliff took Tom's hand in both of his and shook mightily. "Now let's get some sleep. Nellie and I will look for you around eight. Does that sound good for your?"

"Yes Sir, I will be there."

Each said goodnight and started for their beds. Tom entered the kitchen by the same back door and realized the lamp had been turned down. A shotgun stood next to the landlady's door that had not been there before. This time before ascending the steps, he blew out the lamp. Without light it was difficult to avoid the squeaky stair step. That step doesn't make any difference now. Mrs. Thomson must be awake after all the commotion.

* * *

Tom awoke to the smell of fresh brewed coffee and frying bacon. Sleep had not come easy after the evening's excitement. He wanted to just lie in bed without moving for a spell. *Get yourself moving, Tom ole boy. You have to get your things together for the trip home. And don't forget the breakfast invitation. .*

"I'm rather pleased with myself. Amazing, I slept well after I finally got to sleep." *I better keep quiet. Don't want to disturb the river pilot, the other boarder.* He washed and shaved as best he could and put on his last clean blue shirt and black pants. Last night's damp pants still hung on the back of the chair. The damp pants hurriedly joined the rest of his belongings in the canvas bag. It made the room look almost deserted.

The weeks have been good. I miss Aunt Janie, but I was glad to get away from her husband. Some uncle he turned out to be.

When he reached the bottom step he realized the shotgun was gone. Mrs. Thompson rose from the breakfast table and handed him a cup of coffee. "I've been expecting you. I know you don't usually drink coffee, but try this. We Swedes know how to make good coffee. That's what my own Tom use to say."

Before Tom could object, she held up her other hand. "I know, I know. Nellie came over and told me about the invitation. She also gave me a report on what I missed last night. If she hadn't, I would be out of this ragged night coat in two shakes to find out. Oh, go ahead and take a sip."

Tom took the cup and after taking a sip decided it was indeed good coffee. His father always made his too strong. "Can I take this cup with me? If that clock is right and I know it is, I need to get started ... already late."

"You didn't say yonder. Are you losing your southern accent Tom?"

Already late, he moved toward the door and said, "Not entirely. Can't help adapting to the talk around me. I'll be over to get my things a bit later. Will you please figure my bill?" He was out the door before she could start another conversation.

Mrs. Thompson is like another aunt. She does like to talk. Must miss her husband considerably, especially with so few people around. Now that Nellie moved in the next house, it should help.

Cliff opened the door before Tom had time to knock. "Come into our humble home, my friend in time of need. It's a grateful couple you will find this morning. Nellie fixed a big meal for us. We have biscuits and butter ... honey, ham, and some apples from our cellar. Have a seat." He pointed to a chair before moving to the opposite side of the table. The chair next to his was obviously for his wife.

Tom couldn't help admiring the feast before him. It looked grand, especially when he considered the food he had had to endure lately. "This is wonderful. I appreciate the chance for a good meal more than I can say."

Nellie handed Tom an empty plate. "Help yourself Tom. Really, we should be thanking you. You saved my husband's life. You have brightened this dreary day and we will always be grateful for your quick thinking. This meal is a small way of saying thank you."

Tom's face felt hot. He was embarrassed by the comments and didn't know how to react. It was a relief when the attention was focused on Cliff when he reached for Tom and Nellie's hand.

"Tom and Nellie, let's give thanks for last night's experience and the bounty that is set before us." Cliff said a brief prayer of thanksgiving for their new friend and the Lord's provision. Cliff hesitated for a moment and then gave thanks for His deliverance by the hand of his new friend.

It was a short prayer compared to Tom's mother, but he could tell it was from the heart.

After he filled his plate, Tom glanced around the room between forks of food. Earlier he had noticed Nellie wore a simple light blue calico dress. Her hair was pulled back into a bun like his mother's. Cliff wore a pair of dark stripped trousers held up by what appeared to be new suspenders worn over a faded blue shirt.

The table and chairs must have been in the family for years. Ornate scroll-work on the back of the chairs must have been added in recent years. An old chest backed against the wall under a recent picture of the couple. It was a stern but strong looking couple that looked back at Tom from the picture. A sink could be seen under a back window. The pump on a short pipe stood above a cabinet next to the sink. Pump handles, Tom had observed since he arrived in Philadelphia, were as well worn as those at home. Limited space was used well.

He took only small portions for his second helping, though encouraged to take more. He suspected they had dug deep into their larder to feed him. More of the dried apples appealed to him. *What is the polite thing to do? I don't want to appear ungrateful by offending the cook.*

Tom was uncomfortable, but Nell dispelled his discomfort by saying, "Tom, you might have noticed some cloth and thread on the little table under the front window. I do some sewing, and we do well selling blankets I piece together. We have help from our parents north of New York where we're from. Cliff gets more money since we left the big city. They were glad to have an honest policeman here." Nellie looked Tom in the eye. "Do you have anything that needs mending?"

"No thank you. I thank you for the offer. I doubt there would be time anyway."

Cliff emptied his cup and wiped his mouth with the back of his hand. "In the City, New York, a policeman was expected to get what he could from the merchants to get by. Some got more than their share. You had to buy your next promotion from your captain. That was the way it was in the station where I worked, and much of the rest of the city, I've been told. I'm sure there is some of that here but I have not seen any evidence."

"Cliff, do you go down to the wharfs, docks?" Tom wondered. *Why was the shooter from the docks interested in Cliff?*

"I have been trying to discover what is going on down there, spying you might say. Everyone knows there are outlaw gangs about. There has been too much thievery, smuggling of goods from the south to avoid tariffs, a few stabbings, and occasional shooting problems. I'm beginning to identify several gangs and their interests."

Cliff looked out the window and took in a deep breath. "I've been thinking of getting a big dog. Nellie doesn't like guns. Last night convinced me for the need to take steps to protect my wife."

"Now Cliff, how are we going to take care of a big dog? Remember, you taught me to shoot and I can if I have to." Nellie gave him a stern look to emphasize her remark.

"That reminds me." Cliff got out of his chair and walked toward another room. "Keep your seat. I'll be right back. Shortly he was back with a pistol in his hand.

"Tom, try this on and see how it fits your hand. It's a 36 caliber New Navy Colt our friend dropped last night. Just the size you need. You undoubtedly made an enemy last night. But can't help wonder how he got this new make pistol I just heard about."

Tom accepted the pistol and began to look it over. "I have a small single shot pocket pistol my uncle gave me. With six shots I would feel safer. But don't you need it for evidence?" When he continued to examine the weapon, he discovered there was something scratched on the handle.

Cliff pointed to the scratches. "The initials JT, I already know his name or at least his last name. I'm sure it's your landlady's no-good brother in law. He's a man to watch. They call him Dipper because he is quick to dip his hand in the till. Too many on the docks are afraid of him. Then, there are a few he would be afraid to bother, I venture."

"Surely the pistol is a loan and not a gift?" It was beyond Tom's imagination, more than any one in his family could afford. I wonder if Paw would think this pretentious.

"It's yours to keep. You need to get some different grips. There is a black man that works on one of the ships, if he is in harbor. He could carve out new ones in short a time."

They were interrupted by a knock on the door. Cliff reached to his back pocket for his weapon and stepped to the window. "It's the same young man I saw earlier coming down the street. Could it be a friend of yours Tom?"

The new visitor now stood at the open door. The meal had improved Tom's humor, revealed by his shout. "Is that you Ralph?"

"In the flesh. Mrs. Thompson said you would be here. She also said a bit more, or I would have been here sooner. I apologize for interrupting the visit, particularly in regard to your experience last night. It sounded rather exciting."

Tom stepped forward to make introductions.

"Ralph, this is Cliff and Nellie McFarland. Obviously you know how we became friends from my landlady. Ralph is a good friend. We shared some of the same classes at the university."

Ralph's hand disappeared in Cliff's. "When you are a friend of Tom's you are a friend of ours. Welcome."

Ralph grinned through the pain of Cliff's grip. He was relieved when his hand was released.

"Thank you. I appreciate the friendship more than I can say. The other boys and I didn't appreciate Tom until he had to leave. I came to tell Tom I couldn't get the wagon until after lunch. A piano has to be delivered. I know you said you could carry your things by yourself but the ride would give us a last chance to visit."

Ralph raised an eyebrow. It was meant to indicate he had an important announcement to make. "Father thinks he has a working passage on a boat for Tom. It's the The *Pretty Alice.*"

"You better call her a ship in front of the Captain, Ralph," cautioned Cliff. "For the short time I have been here I have come to know the captain of *The Pretty Alice* and his ship. You will work hard but will be treated well." Cliff's face revealed a thoughtful expression. "Captain Farmer … yes. A fair man I believe."

Ralph pulled out his watch and motioned toward the door. "Friend, we need to meet the wagon at the end of the street. The time has come. If he is not there I'll help carry your belongings myself."

Cliff walked toward the door. "I can help you get started. I don't have to work for several hours but there is someone I need to find before then. Nellie, I'll be home at the usual hour."

Tom expressed his thanks once more and dashed off to pick up his things. He turned to shout back. "I'll be back shortly with my bag. If we all go it will take longer. I hope it won't take long to settle my bill ... be quick as I can."

"Go ahead. Ralph and I will get better acquainted."

Tom made his way up the stairs to his room. He placed the cloth-covered bow under his left arm before stooping to pick us the two bags. Mrs. Thompson waited at the bottom of the steps.

"Tom, here is your bill, paid in full as a going away gift. Don't look like you are going to argue about it. You've done me many favors and I will miss you. I know you will have expenses getting home. Now, get yourself out of here. Your friends await you. Don't want you to miss your ride or a chance to board the ship. Ralph told me all about the ship."

Tom's belongings were distributed between himself, Ralph and Cliff. Their friendly chatter had to end on reaching the wagon.

Cliff grabbed Tom's hand with both of his. "You must find a way to visit, write or something. We haven't had a chance to get acquainted." Cliff turned on his heels and stepped off at a good pace before anyone could say more.

There were two large draft horses hitched to the wagon. Why all this to take my two light bags? That must have been a heavy piano. "I only have these two bags. I could have carried them myself but it's good to have your company."

"Don't forget your bow and arrows. Professor Coleman wouldn't forgive you if you lost his gift. By your taking an interest in archery you made a lifelong friend."

"Ralph, I didn't have very good opportunity to talk to my uncle or my cousin after the funeral. Would you take this note that will explain why I had to hurry and why I'm on the way home? Actually I had difficulty making an effort. Would you take this note for me?"

"You know I will Tom."

DANGER ON THE PRETTY ALICE

Cliff had beaten them to the docks. "Would you look at that, Tom? He knows the short cuts. That policeman has someone cornered already. That sure is a big fellow he's talking to."

Tom could see the stranger was a tall well-built sandy haired man. His clothing revealed him to be a working-man by his worn red shirt and stripped blue trousers. The wide belt and black suspenders made him look powerful. When they got closer Tom noted the big man was grinning. It was a very animated conversation. Cliff still had his back to the two friends. The tall man had a bag beside him that suggest that he would be sailing, too.

Cliff turned, waved when he saw Tom and Ralph and moved off in the opposite direction. The big man in the red shirt now held his bag and began to look over one of the ships.

"That's *The Pretty Alice*, Tom. She doesn't look like much now, but she must have been pretty at one time, but they say she is sea worthy. You wouldn't want to ride the train I know. It would be faster and like I said last night I would loan you the money. You wouldn't have to work out your passage on the ship."

"I know you would and for that I thank you. If my sister did not tend to exaggerate and my two brothers were not at home I would take the train. But after the news of that last wreck I'm almost afraid to ever get on a train again."

The two friends approached the gangplank of *The Pretty Alice.* Tom noticed with amusement that someone had attempted to mark out "Pretty", but another attempt had been made to clean off the smudge. *The Pretty Alice* was a side-wheeler with two small smokestacks. She also carried two masts that held rolled sails. She looked to be in need of new paint but appeared in good repair. Some of the crew unloaded large boxes and bundles while others loaded more cargo.

A man with a loud voice shouted. "Come aboard, gents. I'm Captain Farmer. You must be Tom Gentry. Wiley, show your new ship mate where to store his gear; take him in tow, will you?"

Tom turned to smile at Ralph and extend his hand. "I suppose this is good-bye for now. That captain is all business. Wish me luck. Better yet, pray for me."

A big black man with a wide grin grabbed one of Tom's bags. "Follow big Wiley, young sir. We'll find a space to stow your gear. We sleeps next to de boiler room where it's warm."

Tom followed Wiley, too caught up in his surroundings to say anything. Steep steps took them down into a dark room. It took them a moment for their eyes to adjust. Wiley pointed to some shelves and shoved Tom's bag on one. Tom placed his other bag next to the one Wiley had shoved in place. The bow was too long for the shelf.

Wiley pointed out a hammock. "You can hang dat long thing on de bunk ropes. What is dat thing any ways?"

"Dat's, uh, that's my English bow. A good friend gave it to me. I like to shoot it and it might come in handy someday."

"I knows about de English Long Bow. Read up on it sometime back. We works and we have time to read. You'll like it here. Now you can follow me to de boiler room. You can help me be de oiler and coaler."

Tom decided he liked this giant of a man. "Thank you Wiley. I know I'll need a lot of guidance … help, you know."

Wiley wore a perpetual grin and walked with an easy gait. He began to show Tom around by pointing out various grease fitting and places to be oiled. Tom was relieved to see the boiler room was much cleaner than expected. He also realized it must be a fairly recent new boiler or Wiley and the other man kept it spotless.

They soon got the signal to start the engine. Wiley handed Tom a rag and oilcan.

"We wipes up the drips and such to keep down grime so's it won't clog up de workin' parts."

Wiley pulled a lever and the machine began to move with a hiss. It was a fascinating experience for the young sailor. The trip home was going to be enjoyable.

"Wiley, I appreciate all your help. My brother would be jealous. He has always wanted to go to sea … always wanted to be a sailor every since my uncle started telling his stories about his sea-faring life." They had gone down the river but a short distance when they were signaled to stop the engine. "Are we making a stop to take on more cargo and passengers?"

"We can go see for our own selves."

Tom, Wiley and another crewmember climbed the steps to the deck. Wiley motioned to the crewmember that followed them up the steps.

"Dats de other coaler, Tom. Jus' call him Jones or J.J."

J.J. only grinned in response.

Two new passengers came aboard. Tom sensed someone looking at him. When he glanced at the people on the dock he saw a familiar figure, one with a bandaged hand staring at him. The hair on the back of his neck stood up. *It's the assassin. I better start carrying my small pistol in my pocket. I'll back off the rail and pretend to be busy.*

One of the new passengers was a very pretty lady dressed in black. Her hair was unusually curly and well kept. She carried one valise and a parasol. She had pulled her veil to the side so she could see her way up the gangplank. The closer she got Tom could see she held a hat with the parasol. *That lady sure is well composed. And she is unaffected by the ship's activities. From the looks of her dress, she must be a recent widow lady.*

Another lady stood on the docks and waved at the pretty lady who had just stepped aboard. She also was dressed in black. The one on the docks removed her veil to dab at her eyes. The same hanky was used to wave.

This beautiful new arrival caused some distraction among passengers and crew. It seemed all eyes were on her. Work slowed for a short time until the captain shouted. Little notice was given the tall man that followed her. Tom decided he would study the man that followed for fear of being caught staring at the pretty lady. The man carried a carpetbag of considerable size in one hand. He held his hat in the other hand obviously out of respect for the ladies in black. His black coat was worn over a vest that revealed a gold chain.

Tom noticed the moustache was trimmed shorter than usual for the times. He must be in his early forties. That could be one of the gamblers who travel the river, Tom concluded.

Tom glanced back at the lady who was now closer. She appeared to be much younger than when he first saw her. Their eyes met briefly. Aware of Tom's notice, she smiled briefly.

Is she friendly or amused at my coal stained face and clothing?

"Tom boy," whispered Wiley. "Dat feller totin' de blue carpet bag is a gambler, and keeps a sleeve gun. Some say he done kilt a passel of folks but I doubts it. He always be a gentleman on dis ship."

The gambler went one way while a member of the crew showed the lady to her room. It appeared to Tom she was to share a room with another woman that was already aboard.

"Tom, judging from de first lady's face paint, I doubts the purty lady and she will get along. They sho ain't alike."

Captain Farmer barked orders. "Cast off all lines. Wiley, get ready to start the engine." Wiley jumped for the ladder leading to the engine room with Tom close behind. Tom was already into the routine. It was a comfort to be able to adapt so quickly. He believed he could now make an honest contribution as a member of the crew. Keeping up with J. J., the other coaler would not a problem since he was smaller than Tom.

Glancing at Wiley, Tom thought, *I wouldn't try to keep up with big Wiley. While working he continually shouts instructions above the noise with a smile ... as if he enjoys showing off his strength to us younger fellows. Now that's a man.*

Tom's physique had expanded since he first arrived in Philadelphia. He was no longer the skinny boy from home.

His work on the docks had helped build his strength and stamina. To his credit he had avoided fights by attending to his own business. Hard work had also gained the respect of his fellow workers. After the money from home became scarce and his uncle Saul turned him out, he was determined more than ever to continue his studies.

Two meals a day aboard were sufficient, but he longed for his mother's cooking. After J.J. relieved him, Tom cleaned up to go on deck. He placed the small pistol Uncle Casper had given him in his pocket. After the man with the bandaged hand made his presence known, Tom felt it would be prudent to keep it close. The Dipper might have friends aboard. I will take Cliff's warning serious.

Wiley had suggested Tom should go on deck to cool off. Except for an occasional smell from the river, the breeze was refreshing. He heard laughter coming from the main cabin and decided to peek inside. His thumb played with the grooves his uncle had filed on the pistol hammer. Boxes stacked on deck made it difficult to reach main cabin.

He had just stepped out between two large boxes when someone put a vice grip on his arm.

"Think you're smart don't you? We'll just see how smart you are in the river mud," growled a voice.

In the lamplight Tom could see a bandaged hand. He was shoved roughly toward the railing.

Dipper hissed in Tom's ear. "I'll jerk your arm off before …"

Tom's thumb slipped off the hammer before he could remove the pistol. The gun's flash lit up the surprised assailants face.

"You pup of a … you done busted my arm again!" The Dipper released his hold, stepped backwards, and pulled a long knife from his boot. "I'll cut out your gizzard and feed it to the fish." He started toward Tom with the knife.

"I see you lookin' for somethin' to defend yourself. Backin' toward the coal hatch ain't goin' to do you no good."

"Oh! Who the devil?" Dipper yelled. Tom was surprised to see his assailant rise in the air. A big man had him by the nap of the neck and the seat of the pants. At first Tom thought his rescuer was Wiley.

"Let's see how well you can swim with a gimpy arm? If not, you can feed the fish your own gizzard," bellowed the big man. With a mighty heave the Dipper was thrown over the railing. Dipper's yell was interrupted by a splash.

Others had come on deck by this time but all eyes were on Tom and his rescuer. It was the man Tom had seen talking to Cliff.

Lamplight revealed the big fellow's broad grin. He extended his hand to Tom who stood speechless.

"Tom Gentry, my brother Cliff said you might need help before you left the river and he was right. They call me Adam … Adam McFarland at your service sir. That river rat won't be of concern to good folk for a time. I suppose we should have held him for attempted murder but his kind is like those chiggers you have in the South. They get under my skin. I didn't give him another chance to bite."

"Tom! You're on fire!" Adam pointed at Tom's leg. "The leg of your trousers is on fire."

Tom quickly beat out the little blaze with his hands. "The powder charge must have set my leg to smoldering and the coal dust didn't help. Reckon I have some sewing to do. I decided to carry the little pistol when I saw The Dipper at the last stop. That's who you threw over the side."

"Tom, did you burn your hands or leg?"

"No, but I was a bit warm there for a minute."

Tom gripped Adam's hand with both of his. "I didn't expect Cliff to pay me back and certainly not this soon. With only one load in that pistol and it used, I was in serious need of finding another weapon. You showed up at the right time. Many thanks to you and your brother."

Captain Farmer bent over the pilothouse railing. "I heard the shot and saw the man with the knife. Tom, you didn't have much choice. It wouldn't have been wise to face that rat head on, him holding a big skinning knife. You people that aren't working better get to your cabins. We got one more stop before Wilmington, Delaware. We will want to know everybody that comes on board from now on, so stay close to your cabins the next time we make land."

Tom looked puzzled? "Adam, when did you come onboard? I don't remember seeing you?"

"I followed the tall fellow with the large bag. All the eyes were on the widow. There was a job waiting for me on the docks. Cliff talked me into following you to the end of the river. I wonder how Dipper got here. He's a mighty slick one."

Tom was embarrassed to see the pretty widow with the bystanders. "I better go down and change into trousers without a hole. I'm starting to feel a breeze on my leg. I'll be right back"

Tom tore down the steps two at a time. He could hear Adam explaining to the remaining folk what had led up to the confrontation.

On Tom's return, he found Adam standing under the deck lamp with his arms folded. The pleased expression on Adam's face revealed his satisfaction with the evening's work.

Adam could see from the question on Tom's face that further explanation was needed.

"I was between jobs and had come for a short visit with my brother and his wife. Cliff had suggested the day before that I might find some work for a few days at the docks. He explained what happened last night and you might be in danger and I agreed to watch for trouble. You know the rest of the story."

Tom felt he was indebted to Cliff, and especially Adam. The gunshot to Dipper's arm wouldn't have prevented him from trying to cut him up and feeding him to the fish. He told himself, *its food to meet new friends and it appears I was in need of a friend.* The poor light made it almost impossible to find something to defend myself with.

The gambler had remained on deck and had watched the exchange between Tom and Adam. When he realized his presence was known, he started for the main cabin. On passing, he gave Adam a pat on the shoulder. Since Adam and Tom were discussing plans for breakfast in the morning, it appeared that all parties were intent on getting rest, except the gamblers.

The hammock Tom lay on made him think of the bed at home. It would be more comfortable. The thought of home reminded him of the letter his landlady had given him. He pulled it from his pocket but hesitated to open it, and scolded himself. *I should accepted the loan from Ralph and taken the train. It would have been faster, even if not safer. The history of frequent train wrecks should not have prevented me.*

Tom opened the letter and tried to hold back the fear of what it might reveal. If things were serious I would have gotten another telegram rather than this letter. Unfolding the letter he began to read.

Dear Tom.

Your father is improving and able to walk with a crutch. It's been a painful experience for him, especially not being able to get out and work. I'm sure you want to know what happened after getting Sue's message. Your father was cutting down a tree when the wind shifted. He tried to keep it from falling on one of the out buildings, tripped and the tree fell on him. Lem, Sue and I were able to pull him out after digging around his leg. It was a good thing Paw had hired Lem from Mr. Wiggins for the day. He had been plowing a few yards away.

Homer and Willie don't know about it since we can't reach them at sea. They should be back before you reach home. Their time at sea is about over. If we overlooked telling you they are at sea, it was due to all the sickness around us. Paw and me have had to help some of the neighbors. Things are better now. Whooping cough and diphtheria took the life of Mr. Wiggins' father and a new neighbor to the community, Mr. Frazier. We hope this reaches you before you start home. It probably wouldn't be necessary for you to come now that Mr. Wiggins lets Lem help. He is a hard worker but turned moody since Wiggins got him. We miss you and wish you were here but we will let you make the decision about coming or staying.

Love Ma.

RIVER PIRATES

Tom stuffed the letter in the travel bag, gave a great sigh before placing his hands behind his head. He was still wide-awake after the evening's excitement.

So that is the reason my brothers were not around to help. Sue probably didn't know how serious Paw was hurt and wanted me home. I now realize how close Sue and I have become. Paw is a tough man. Hope they can keep him still long enough for him to heal.

* * *

While Tom was reading his letter, two men in a skiff paddled to intercept *The Pretty Alice.* They cautiously approached from the dark side of the river where there were no lights. There were too many houses on the opposite shore. As soon as the two saw the ships' light they had moved from their hiding place. Timing had to be perfect or the ship would pass them and the paddle wheel would grind them to a pulp.

The one in back spoke in a low voice. "Watch out for that side wheel, Rock Head. We don't want to get chewed up by that thing." The one called Rock Head pulled up behind the paddle wheel. He paddled feverously to hold a position so Josh could throw a hook fastened to a knotted rope on the railing. Soon as the skiff was secured, Josh climbed the rope.

Josh looked around the deck before signaling his partner to come aboard. Rock Head was heavier and slower getting over the railing. He panted while bending over with both hands on his knees. "I'm worried about them horses, Josh."

"Stop fretting about them horses. They can find their way back to the farmer's. We got to find this Tom fellow. Got to knock him on the head before we throw him over. You don't want Dipper to get mad at us again. He said this Tom was a sly one."

Two passengers strolled insight. Josh ducked and pushed his partner behind a box.

"You have a light? I'm out," spoke one of the new arrivals on deck.

"You can have the rest of mine. I have more with my bag. That gambler is a real slick fellow. Makes you think you could be winning and bang. He throws down a better hand. Wonder how much he won tonight? I didn't have much to lose so I pulled out. Want you to know, I don't gamble enough to be any good."

"Look at those lights ashore. Wonder what those people do to get by?"

The two passengers continued forward. The rest of the conversation was lost by the sound of the side wheels churning up the river.

"You hear what they said, Rock Head?"

"Sure, I heard. Wish you would stop callin' me Rock Head. I can be smart too, at times. You think what I'm thinkin'? We could take some of the winnings of that gambler. He could always get more."

Josh whispered. "Let me think. We gotta stay hid till we find which one is the gambler. But first we got to get rid of that Tom. Dipper was awful mad and half drowned. If we don't get him we better not go back. You know what I mean?"

Josh slid over toward the Great Room window. "Uh … I got an idea Rock. You watch out here since you know Tom from the docks, and I'll look for the gambler through the cabin window. Umm … this should be the right window here. I've been on this ship before. Then we do what we got to do."

Josh rose from a crouch to see through the window and peeked in. He began to snigger. "I've seen him before. Now I know which one he is. Gambler is dressed up right nice like and has a pile of money."

Unable to sleep, Tom walked up the steps. He wasn't concerned about disturbing any one. The night was still young and there was plenty of noise coming from the Saloon. The noise of the big wheels hid his footsteps as well. *It's getting stuffy in the hold. Some fresh air will do me good. My turn to shovel coal half the night will come soon enough.*

Tom soon found a resting place between some big crates. *It is good to escape the oppressive heat below. I'm not use to sleeping near so much heat. My old room back at the boarding house could be like an iceberg. Like to see an iceberg some day. This will be my favorite place to rest.*

There were other voices on deck that interrupted Tom's thoughts. They were not going to help him relax. He strained to hear what they said. Two men passed his resting place. Their conversation could now be distinguished at first.

"Well Rock, we know which one is the gambler. If he comes out by himself to smoke, we can knock him over the head. I don't think he will smoke around that lady and he will have to come out soon. We know where this Tom man is, too. We don't have to tell Dipper about the gambler. Two birds with one stone, I say."

To have his name included in the head bashing made Tom's hair stand on end. He eased from crate to box so he could listen and observe. One of the voices sounded vaguely familiar. It belonged to an occasional dockworker.

"Alright Rock, you get his attention when he comes out. Ask for a light. Hold your pipe so he can see and I'll knock him on the head like usual. But we better lower him into the water soft like so as not to make a big splash. We don't want them yellin' man over board or somethin' like that."

Tom got the picture and figured that he was in trouble once again, and now the trouble included the gambler. *Those two don't know I'm here but I can't pretend to be an army this time. What do they want of me? Did I hear Dipper's name mentioned? How did Dipper have time to round up these two? I'm counting on the coal dust to hide my face and clothes. Just might be able to slip by those two and warn the gambler or the captain.*

He considered a rapid crawl on all fours to the dining room door, but decided against that move. *If I crawl I'll be exposed too long before reaching the door. It's too bad, since the gambler is in there.* Tom slid backwards between boxes for more cover. His hand came to rest on the coal chute cover.

Tom mumbled to himself. "This is it, Tom my boy. Just what you needed." He moved the cover with some difficulty, but made enough room to drop into the coal bin.

B. Neil Wilson

His Colt pistol Cliff had given him was under clothes in the carpetbag. Digging through his belongings to locate the pistol slowed progress enough to make him nervous. *I sure hope the gambler is not in a hurry to smoke.*

Arriving back on deck, he was momentarily blinded by the ship lantern. He noticed two men had started for the rail. One reached for a pipe and the other drew a cigar out of his vest pocket. The one with the cigar had to be the gambler but Tom didn't recognize the second man. At first he didn't see the thieves. A movement to his right revealed the two behind some crates. Their slow progress from behind some boxes appeared to be the start of an attack. It couldn't be worse; the smokers were in Tom's line of fire.

AMBUSH OR RESCUE

One of the thieves carried a black jack and the other a club. They moved quickly toward their intended victims. Tom was about to jump to the side with his pistol and shout. Everything stopped when a door slammed and two ladies came on deck. The thieves froze about the same time Tom pulled back the pistol hammer.

One of the ladies spied the gambler when he drew on his cigar. The glow revealed his face. "Evening, gents. Care if we join you to take the air?" It was the painted lady that shared a room with the widow.

Before the men could reply, the other lady spoke. "You go ahead Beth. I've had enough of this day. I'm going back in."

"Well," returned Beth, "I might as well too. It's awful damp out here and it's getting chilly." In the dim lamp light Tom could see the two men by the rail give knowing looks to each other.

The two head knockers didn't wait for the door to slam before they started to creep again. Now they each raised their weapons.

Tom cocked his pistol again and removed one of the deck lamps from its hook. He purposely stepped toward the thieves. The intended victims were absorbed in the lights ashore and the ship's approach to a well lit dock. It was another small town along the river. Tom put the light on a box that made shadows move around the men. This movement of the shadows didn't alert either the thieves or the men by the railing.

It's time to announce my presence. Tom jumped to the side to keep the smokers out of his line of fire. He shouted, "Stop right there. Drop the clubs. What do you think you are doing?"

All four men wheeled around to face Tom. The one with the blackjack threw his weapon at Tom and reached for a knife. Tom fired his pistol over their heads. At the same time he fired, the blackjack bounced off his shoulder.

"The next shot will be in your gut. This is a revolver, not the little pistol I used to shoot Dipper."

A deep smooth voice behind the assassins spoke. "You two can also count on my sleeve gun that's pointed at your back. You do as Tom says: drop those weapons! Just what was your intent? To do us harm? To relieve me of my winnings?" The gambler took a step forward and pushed his pistol into Josh's back.

"Drop your club, Rock Head. It won't do you no good now," complained Josh morosely. Josh removed his knife and Rock dropped his club.

The two ladies returned followed by several others, most likely out of curiosity. Adam McFarland burst through the group and stopped when he observed the scene before him. A second later Wiley appeared at the top of the steps.

Adam asked, "Are we having more trouble? It seems to follow this ship. I see Tom is in the middle of this. What happened?"

Josh spread his hands in disbelief. "Me and my partner here were about to arrest this gambler and his friend when that boy shot at us and interrupted our arrest. That Tom needs to locked up too."

Captain Farmer stepped forward to look Josh and Rock in the face. "It's going to be you two that gets locked up. I know you two River Pirates. You are wanted for suspected crimes and possible murder. Wiley and Tom, chain these two until morning. When we get to Wilmington, Delaware they can be removed like all these crates on deck. Can't have trash aboard when we get to sea, can we? The rest of you that are not involved better get to bed. It's getting late."

Adam looked closely at the would-be assassins. "Folks, these two are part of a no-good bunch that hangs around the docks in Philadelphia. Their specialty is to cut gentle ladies purse strings, and they would pick your watch in a flicker of a bird's wing. Tom, you have done enough for one day. Wiley and I will take these two in tow. When we reach Wilmington they can enjoy many days behind bars. This next little town might not have a jail, so we'll keep them chained below."

Josh spread his hands again and put on his false grin. "Jail looks better right now than them two pistols and you two giants. We're your prisoners. Rock Head, might as well throw down your knife too. It shows above your belt like that lantern."

Wiley grabbed one river pirate and Adam the other.

Adam cracked, "Off to the hold for you two tonight." Before they reached the steps Adam turned to the gambler and his friend. "How does that suite you gentlemen?"

"Quite well, my good man," replied the gambler. "Don Blocker is the name. Just call me Don, and this is my friend Mr. Ted Frye."

Don Blocker returned his pistol to his sleeve and moved to shake Tom's hand. "Young man, you just saved me from more than a bump on the head. If you had not intervened by the time I saw the approach of their shadows it would have been too late to save my skin. Mr. Frye and I are indebted to you. Would you join us for breakfast in the morning? We will be at the corner table in the dining room. It would be small payment for your part in this evening's excitement. We can do that much for you at least for now. I'm sure the captain would allow such, after I speak to him shortly."

The gambler could see by the expression on Tom's face that he was mulling over the invitation. Don hesitated a moment and then asked. "When must you go back to work in the hold?"

Tom started to answer but Don Blocker continued. "In fact, you can be my guest until we reach Charleston. Can we assume you will accept our invitation?"

Tom felt the Mr. Blocker's strong hand shake and liked the appearance of the man. "Thank you for the offer, sir. The breakfast sounds most inviting. The crew's food is fine but I would like to see the inside of that dining room. Sir, I'm only taking the ship as far as Wilmington, North Carolina. Then figure how to get from there to my home near Salisbury. And again, thank you for the invitation. My name is Tom Gentry, ah ... and you are Mr. Blocker?"

"Yes I am, but you can all me Don. You know my trade, at least most of the time. After a moment's hesitation Blocker went on. "Did you see the two ladies who were on deck after the hullabaloo was over?" Tom nodded. The gambler continued. "The lady in black is a young widow and is also getting off at Wilmington. If I were a young man and ... uh ... perhaps, if I were in another line of work, I would go ashore in Wilmington too. But she is a real lady. The reason I mention this is that she is alone and could use someone like you to watch out for her until she reaches her family. I overheard her relating her story to Beth, her roommate."

Don cleared his throat indicating there was more. "I usually don't get this long winded, but this has been a rather eventful evening. And you will join us at breakfast?"

His raised eyebrows revealed the question was meant for further confirmation.

"With pleasure, Sir. I can get relief for a short time, and I'm looking forward to a meal in good company, and conversation."

"Well, good evening to you Tom," and added with a smile, "and bring a good appetite."

The ship eased toward a dock. There were two lanterns each side of the dock to aid the pilot. Side paddle wheels stopped shortly but back-paddled for a short distance. This movement eased the ship to the dock. The first mate shouted a few orders. All the crew knew what they had to do.

The captain stepped out of the saloon to address the passengers. "We will proceed no further this night. If anyone wishes to go ashore, be back by twelve o'clock and go with someone that has a time peace. After the commotion this evening we will post a guard and allow no visitors for the remainder of the trip."

"Wiley and Adam, there is a sheriff or deputy in the village. Don't bother to leave the prisoners in the hold. Take them toward the lamplight? You'll find what you're to look for."

* * *

On his return to the ship Adam had no difficulty finding Tom. He could see Tom as he leaned over the ship rail. Adam yelled. "You are not trying to get sick are you?"

"Nope, just contemplating. You and Wiley got those two locked up, Adam? Don't I have to sign an agreement to be a witness or something of that nature?"

"They were wanted for other crimes as well and I figured you needed to get home. Besides, I told them I saw it all." Adam ran up gangplank "I also promised to be a witness if necessary. The first mate, Mr. Frye and Don will have to sign an affidavit. I believe that's what the deputy said. It can be dropped off in Wilmington, Delaware. I left your name out of it."

Adam joined Tom at the rail. The excitement of the evening made them both restless and energetic. Adam gave an audible puff. "Whew. We took care of that little matter, right Tom?"

"I'm beholdin' to you and Cliff, and that is not easy for a fellow raised on the farm and spent time in the mountains. We don't like to be beholdin' to anybody or owe a thing, even if it's kin if we can help it."

"You surprise me. I've been to Salisbury. You call those rolling hills around Lexington or Salisbury mountains? That's where you told your landlady you were from. Don't take me too serious. I like to joke with friends a lot."

"Didn't know you'd been in North Carolina. By the way, Adam, you're a lot like my brother Willie so I'm accustomed to joke around. I spent part of a year with my uncle and aunt west of Asheville. Friends I met there joked and pulled pranks on each other. Those were good days."

"Tom, you were invited to take breakfast with those two gents. I might have to leave before then. Wilmington, Delaware will be my last stop along the river. You are the kind of friend people like to have, and especially myself. Our friendship doesn't have to end here does it?"

"Not at all. I tried to think of a way to say the same thing. If you can come to North Carolina, and soon I hope, I would like to introduce you to my family. I have a pretty sister you know. How is that for an inducement?"

Adam wiggled his eyebrows up and down. "Now that sounds interesting. I would like to visit your part of the state again and meet your family. You could lose your sister, you know."

Tom ignored the remark about his sister.

Adam continued, "I've worked on the railroad a time or two as a fireman and brakeman. We came through that area several times. The fireman's job is much safer. My boss was going to make me an engineer but I decided more education was needed. I really have not decided what I need to do."

"You must have given it some thought. What else are you interested in?"

Adam was about to answer after a yawn but Tom quickly added. "I need to know before I introduce you to my sister." Tom looked out of the corner of his eye and suppressed a grin. He was curious to Adam's reaction.

Adam drew back a step, sucked in his breath and bowed his head pretending to be hurt. He looked down at his feet before giving a great sigh. "Suppose I will have to give up the idea of being a gambler. As you might say, reckon I better give this some thought. I could shovel coal on a ship if you would teach me?"

The good nature ribbing bonded the two even more. This type of humor was a characteristic trait of both men.

Adam continued, "Well sir, I intend to make something of myself before I become an honorable brother-in-law. I might even become a lawyer like Cliff said you intend. And I assure you dear sir, I intend for my intentions to always be honorable among the young ladies."

Tom laughed and slapped Adam on the shoulder. "That was a pretty fair speech. With that bunch of superfluous verbiage you could make a good lawyer. You might even succeed in politics. Watch out Mr. Lincoln."

They could still see each other's features by the dim lamplight. River fog began to drift around them, which created two ghost-like figures in the misty light.

Adam added, "I have given it much thought lately. Money is always a problem. I would like to become a doctor, but could you imagine these big hands trying to save some poor soul?"

Adam cleared his throat, glanced at the pilothouse. "Law does interest me. It would be easy for me to start police work with my brother. That's almost too easy. I would like to do something on my own. Following the steam coach, as I do now, will not satisfy me forever."

Tom didn't hesitate to make a suggestion. "I could give you the name of the lawyer I was to study under. That might be a start."

"Hmmm, that's a good idea. It would be a great help. All I needed was to get an introduction, and you have just added the last nail in the horseshoe. After one more trip on that hot steam coach that keeps on the two rails, I'll accept your offer. I had promised to make this trip. You can be assured I will examine the work and studies possibilities. Thank you for the offer and encouragement. Like you, I like to keep my promises."

"Adam, I'll write my name and address for you in the morning. If I miss you I'll sent it to Cliff."

Grasping each other's hands, they held on for a few seconds. Adam had to make the next statement. "If I don't find you in the morning, you can be confident I will make an effort to find you in Lexington."

"We are well known around home, Adam. We're not hard to find."

"Good evening to you, and don't wear out that coal shovel."

* * *

Waking up was a difficult the next morning. They had not yet left the dock and Wiley was just beginning to stoke the boiler. Yawing, Tom reached for his pants.

"Wiley, do you think you could carve me some new grips for my pistol? This is it. I kept it in my travel bag until last night. It still has one load so be careful."

Wiley grinned and reached for the weapon. "I c'n fotch yo' handle 'fo' we reach Wi'min'ton. But Tom Boy! Th'ain't no mo' loads in dis thing. Yo must ah use de las' one on dat feller's hat. 'Yo got de makin's fo' mo'? Yo gotta be mo' keerful."

"No I don't have any more loads. Could we come by some at the next stop? There is still three left for my little pocket pistol. Now I need to help you run this ship and forget about the loads for now."

With some difficulty Wiley talked Tom into going to breakfast with Mr. Blocker.

"You go on up to dat dinin' room and enjoy yo self. J.J. don' mind fillin' in fer you, do you J.J.?" J.J. grinned and nodded.

"I will but it makes me feel guilty. I wanted to do his share before I clean up."

Tom cleaned up as best he could and put on his good coat and trousers. His shirt needed ironing and he couldn't find his tie. None of that mattered when he stepped into the dining room and smelled the coffee and food. The wonderful odors reminded him that he was hungry. The anticipation of a good meal with the passengers increased his excitement.

Half the tables were already occupied with travelers. Tables were covered with white tablecloths and silverware. That was only a momentarily distraction for Tom. He was immediately drawn to a corner table by a wave from Don Blocker. Mr. Frye, the widow lady and her cabin mate were also seated at the table. All four smiled at him as he approached. Tom was excited to see the two ladies and the gents from last night's excitement. The widow wore a different black outfit, but her traveling companion's blue dress was low cut and revealing, a dress one would wear at a ball.

The widow's lady companion isn't made up like last night I'm sure that's Wiley's painted lady. Must be too early to add the paint. Tom felt his face getting warm when the lady in black smiled up at him. The other smiles were lost on him.

Every one appeared to be in fine spirits. Don and Mr. Frye stood when Tom reached the table. Blocker held out his hand to Tom before commenting.

"Good morning Tom. I hope you rested well? Have a seat. The porter will bring our breakfast shortly. Take this seat here so we can get better acquainted."

"Thank you. It did take longer to get to sleep than normal. It must have been the excitement last evening. I haven't had the pleasure of meeting the rest of your fine company. I'm Tom Gentry bound for North Carolina."

Mr. Blocker turned to the widow. "Pardon my manners this early in the morning ladies and gents. I don't believe you have met Mrs. Talent and this is Miss Elmore."

Before Tom sat, he bowed respectfully to the ladies and smiled broadly. "I am honored to find myself in the company of these young ladies and gentlemen."

The two ladies, in turn, smiled and nodded politely to Tom.

Mr. Blocker adjusted himself in his chair. "I don't believe you were properly introduced to this gentleman last night. Meet Mr. Ted Frye. He and Mrs. Talent will be going to Wilmington. I believe that where you plan to exit this fine ship Tom."

Mr. Frye nodded and smiled. "We are in your debt, Mr. Gentry. I will go on to Charleston after a brief stop in Wilmington to deliver a letter. If you are ever in Charleston I would be happy to show you the town."

Tom was about to respond, but was interrupted by the cabin boy with a large platter of food.

I'm hungrier than I thought. Tom, ole boy, you be on your best behavior!

While the food was passed around they made polite conversation about the food. They compared it to other fine breakfast meals they had enjoyed. Even though Tom favored the food, he paid little attention to what he ate. His interests were drawn to his surroundings, especially Mr. Blocker and Mrs. Talent. Don Blocker dressed like a well-traveled businessman. His shirt and tie were the only difference from last night's apparel. There was his usual stripped trousers and coat.

Tom noticed a watch chain and cigar in Don's vest pocket, and there was no sign of the sleeve weapon the gambler showed the night before.

As for Mrs. Talent, she remained neat and modest in her widow's weeds.

Pleasant conversation revealed much about these traveling companions. It appeared Mrs. Talent was a recent widow on her way home to be with her parents in Wilmington for the immediate future. Miss Elmore was traveling to Charleston to care for her aging parents.

The agreeable conversation took a different path when Mr. Blocker suggested Mrs. Talent tell why she was going home. She put her coffee cup on the table and took on a serious and thoughtful look. The mourning veil she wore had been pulled back so it would not interfere with eating. As she began to speak Tom noted her beautiful eyes and dark curly hair that escaped from her veil.

"You gentlemen have become very close due to last night's confrontation. I, however, feel very much alone at the present. I don't mean to seek sympathy but only to help you understand part of my predicament. My husband was killed when he fell from his horse. Now I am not only alone, but also have very little resources.

"You see, our marriage had been arranged, but I won't bore you with the details. Now I am returning home to my parents; I would feel more comfortable…more secure with them. At least my husband's sister was kind and helpful. I don't know what I would have done without her.

"I'm glad you are to pass through Wilmington on your way home, Mr. Gentry."

"It would be my pleasure to be at your service."

Toward the close of the meal when the conversation began to lag, Don leaned toward Tom and peered at him earnestly. "Tom, as I mentioned last evening, since you will travel through Wilmington, perhaps you would be willing to escort Mrs. Talent. You could see her to her door since she has no gentleman escort. Ted will not have time since he must attend to business and his stay will be short."

"By the way, we also need to exchange addresses. I would like very much to stay connected. Mr. Frye and I owe our lives to you, and there must be something we can do for you. But back to the question of escorting Mrs. Talent, what do you say?"

Tom put his hands on his knees, sat up straight and mustered a serious facial expression. "It would be an honor, Sir. It would be no trouble at all."

He turned to the lady in question and added. "Mrs. Talent, when we arrive in Wilmington I will be at your service. I'm pleased to be able to assist you with whatever I'm able to do."

"Your gallantry is comforting, Mr. Gentry," the lady replied in her gentle southern way. "Thank you. There really is no need, but it comforts me to know you will be available to escort me when we dock in Wilmington. My family will not know the time of my arrival."

Tom pushed back from the table, stood and bowed slightly to his breakfast companions. "If you will excuse me, I must see to my duties. I fear I may have imposed on my fellow workers long enough."

Don and Ted Frye stood and each in turn extended their hands. "Once again, Ted and I are indebted to you. I for one will be eternally grateful. You can be assured we will see more of you before the end of this journey. I meant what I said last night about no need to work in that hold. I will gladly pay the rest of your passage."

"Thank you most kindly Sir; however, I promised to help as far as Wilmington and if I accepted your offer Wiley would be short one hand. I have enjoyed the breakfast and conversation. I regret I must depart this fine company. I do pray there will be other opportunities for us to talk. And Mrs. Talent, once again I look forward to be of assistance when we arrive at our destination."

The two men stood as Tom left the room. *These gentlemen honor me in a way I have never experienced before. However, Ma would remind me to keep a level head.*

Tom suddenly remembered Adam and stopped in his tracks. He looked back at Don Blocker and asked, "Has any one seen Adam this morning?"

Don reached in his vest pocket to retrieve his watch. "Tom, Adam got off the ship at the last stop to get a small package for you. He had to send the package back by Wiley. Adam expected to return but when he found immediate transportation back to Philadelphia there was little time to come back. He felt you were safe from any more River Pirate trouble and therefore sent his highest regards. He said he promised to visit you soon. He also said to encourage you to be kind to your shovel."

Don watched Tom walk toward the door and commented, "There is a true young gentleman of the South, Mrs. Talent; you will be in good hands until you reach home."

"I agree whole heartedly," the lady murmured graciously.

* * *

After many days on the sea, one late afternoon *The Pretty Alice* entered the Cape Fear River on the way to Wilmington. They had not gone far when the captain shouted. "You down there, stand on the bow and watch for logs or somethin' we might hit with the wheels. Will be more likely the further we go in. We're slowin' her down some."

The seaman turned to a shipmate. "We don't know if storms up river pushed some big trees down river. The cap'n is smart like that. So's you watch that side for me, Wes."

There was much excitement on board. Most of the passengers were visible as they watched their approach to land. Their journey up the river seemed slow. Most of the sailors were idle. By the time they reached the dock everyone would be busy. By now passengers knew to stay out of the way of the crew when they docked.

All passengers got off the ship to test their legs on land again. This would also allow the cargo to be unloaded without interference.

Tom, Don, Mr. Frye and the widow made up one little group of travelers off to one side. Don patted Tom on the shoulder. "Here's another small package for you from Mr. Frye and myself. Please don't open it until after the ship goes back down river. Try to stay in touch."

Mrs. Talent touched Tom's arm. "Oh, Tom, I thought a sailor would get my big bag. I'm sorry. Would you retrieve it for me? It's beside my cabin door."

Tom smiled, nodded and ran back on board the ship.

DANGER ASHORE

Tom placed Don's gift in his pocket, hefted the widow's bag and hurried down the gangplank. There were at least three more ships in the harbor, with their sailors milling about the dock.

Tom spotted a shiny cab with two black brown horses in front.

"Mrs. Talent, follow me to that cab. Doesn't look like he has a fare."

The driver turned on his seat to view the two approaching travelers. Tom asked, "Are you available for two passengers and their baggage?"

"Sho nuff, suh. Let me help you wif them things."

"Good. I'll be right back soon as I get my bags."

Wiley had placed Tom's things at the end of the gangplank. There were his carpetbag, his small clothe covered suitcase, and the covered English bow. When he bent over to pick up his bag, a shadow fell across him and his belongings. An arm of the shadow raised and Tom tried to duck. Something struck him on the side of the head and he was knocked unconscious.

A seaman observed the action. The thief ran with Tom's bag. Tom's body was sprawled on the dock. The seaman didn't hesitate to look for an object to throw at the thief, found a board, and threw it at the runner with the bag. The board bounced off the dock and went between the thief's legs. Board, legs and thief hit the ground; the man slid a bit and lost his prize.

"Hey mate! Stop that man. He knocked down a man and tried to run off with his bag."

Another sailor tried to intercept the thief but the crook was too fleet of foot.

The first sailor went to Tom's aid, picked him up, and examined him. The seaman felt the side of Tom's head. There was a sizable bump starting to rise.

"Charlie, go fetch some water to douse on this fellow. He is breathin'. He's not hurt much, I hope. Stop lookin' around for a bucket. Use your cap."

Charlie took off running.

"Now you're cookin'. I see them eyes startin' to move."

Charlie was soon back … emptied his cap over Tom's head. Tom opened his eyes and looked up at his rescuer.

The seaman spoke with caution in his voice. "Take it easy young feller. You got a thump on the side of our head. Wait until you feel up to sittin' before you move much. We got your bag over here. Some no good knocked you on the head and tried to rob you. What's your name, young fellow?"

Tom thought for a minute. "Don't know right off. Strange, I don't know who I am. My head hurts a little but that's all. Think I'm fine."

"You don't look worried about not knowin' who you are. You could be at a tea party and not carin', what's goin on. Sure you don't know who you are? Charlie, look in his bag and see if you can find somethin' that will help here, with your permission of course young feller."

Tom sat up and nodded his consent. "Can't hurt to look."

Charlie opened the carpetbag and found a letter on top of the clothing. "Here is a letter to a Tom Gentry. That be you?"

"It has to be. Yes, I'm on my way home, wherever that is. Might come back to me."

Charlie pointed at the letter and looked at the first seaman. "George, that there letter can tell this feller, Tom here, more about himself. And it don't look like he lost his memory for good. You know, I saw him escortin' a lady in black to a fancy coach. He put her things in the coach. She could help him. But the coach is gone now."

Tom started reading the letter from home. He began to remember a few things. Someone was supposed to be waiting for him on the docks. Who was it?

"Thank you, Charlie and George, for your help. I think I'm on my way to Lexington. If you will point out the way, I'll see what I can do."

The coach appeared to be returning. It soon came to a stop beside the two seamen. A lady in black stuck her head out the window. Her face expressed irritation and concern. It was Mrs. Talent.

"See driver. I told you he is not the kind to shirk his duty. You were too anxious to get another fare."

Mrs. Talent looked at the men. "Is something wrong?"

"Miss, Tom here was knocked on the head by a thief and lost some of his memory. I saw him with a lady. That must be you."

Mrs. Talent motioned to the men. "Please, help him into the coach?"

"I can still walk and I can climb in on my own." To prove his claim, he stepped into the coach. "But you can hand me my bag of stuff." Charlie handed Tom his carpetbag.

"Again, thank you two for all your help."

Mrs. Talent smiled at the two men, motioned for the driver to proceed. A snap of the reins and they were off.

Charlie turned around and called his friend. "Hey mate. This smaller suitcase and this long thing must belong to Tom. I bet he didn't know he left some of his things. I'll look see if his names in them. Couldn't be anybody's but his."

When he started examining the small suitcase, he found Tom's name. He was about to tell George when he noticed the second mate walk by.

"Say, Gentry. Y'all have a younger brother?"

"Reckon I got two younger brothers. Why do you ask Charlie?"

"Hit's a bit of a story. This young feller got hit upside the head and lost his senses for a spell. He was nearly robbed but I stopped the thief. This here bag ... or suitcase and long thing belongs to Tom Gentry. That be your brother?"

"The little suitcase looks familiar. He is supposed to be in Philadelphia gettin' more learnin'. This long thing has a bow and arrows in it. He was always interested in ... Let me look in the case."

Homer Gentry began pulling some of the things out of the suitcase.

"Not necessarily Tom's. Could belong to anybody. Here's a Navy Colt pistol? He never had ... What's this? The small pistol Uncle Casper gave him before he left home. Charlie ... George, I'm much obliged. Which way did he go?"

"He got in a carriage with a woman dressed in black. You saw that fine coach when it left, didn't you?"

"I didn't notice a coach. Charlie, did you happen to hear her tell the driver where to go?"

Homer's perplexity is interrupted by a new voice. "Mistah, dat coach be back directly. Dat driver be my daddy. He don' miss much chance to get payin' fares."

The three seamen turned around to see a boy they judged to be about twelve. He wore no shoes; his clothes were worn and too small for his frame, but he was dressed cleaner and better the other boys that were around the docks. His smile was bright and cheerful.

"Sometimes I holds the hosses fer rich white folks." The youngster made his chest puff out as he grinned and looked proud.

"Well, thank you for that information. What do they call you?"

"Most times they calls me boy around here. At home they calls me Abner." He turned and pointed. "See what I tells you. Dat be my pap a comin' now. You can axe him now."

The coach pulled up to a hitching rail under a shade tree.

Homer smiled and gave a short wave to his shipmates. "I thank you for your help. Now let's see what that driver knows."

Homer approached the driver who wore a perpetual grin. "Driver, will you take me to the place you delivered the young man and the lady in black? You picked them up less than an hour ago."

"Dat be twenty-five cents, mistah. Just you climbs aboard."

Homer shook his head at the fare but took a seat anyway. "You're kind of steep, ain't you? You already know the way."

"Yep boss, but this hoss don't. And I might forget. I is gettin' old and wore out traipsin' back and forth."

Homer began looking for some change in his pocket while they bounced along. He handed the driver an additional twenty cents and looked sideways to get the drivers reaction.

The driver glanced at him and grinned. "Thank you kindly. You look up ole John if you needs anything. There she is. Dat be the place boss."

They had pulled up before a three story brick house with long steps that led up to the front door. Homer picked up the suitcase and the bow case and jumped down. He noted that the house was not much different than the other homes in Wilmington; however, there were brick paths that let around each side of the steps that led to the front door. Two doors appeared to lead into the lower part of the home. Two windows on each side of the doors were barely visible behind rhododendron bushes and suggested servant's quarters.

Homer leaned the covered bow against the wall before using the doorknocker.

The door opened shortly by an elderly black maid in a neat white apron that hid most of her blue dress. "Can I help you sir?"

"I'm Homer Gentry, and I'm looking for my brother Tom. I understand he was brought here."

A glance behind the maid made him uncomfortable. The grand surroundings made him feel out of place.

"Yes sir, come in. He is in the parlor being treated by the ladies of the house. Just follow me please."

Homer lugged the rest of Tom's things along. If a mere glance into the setting made him uncomfortable, following the maid through such a grand place intimidated him. The fact that the maid sounded educated didn't help his self image at the moment.

"Mr. and Mrs. Cook, Mrs. Talent: May I present Mr. Homer Gentry, Tom's brother." After the announcement, the maid stood aside to allow the new guest to enter.

Two ladies rose and a man's voice spoke from the right near a fireplace. "Thank you, Ann. Come in sir and see how we treated your brother. The damp cloth he's holdin' should take care of the swellin'. Join me in observin' the ladies do their doctorin'."

Homer went over to the couch beside Tom and grasped his hand, saying, "What kind of mess have you got into now, Little Brother?"

Have a seat, and would you have some refreshments. We have cold water and cold cider."

"I'm Mrs. Cook and this is my daughter Mrs. Joan Talent. Excuse me, but she will always be Joan to us. We are most pleased to make the acquaintance of our young friend Tom. He escorted our daughter from the docks. We feel relieved to have his assistance. Young ladies should not have to travel without a trusted escort."

"Thank you sir … ma'am. I would like a taste of cider if you please."

The ladies smiled and made a short curtsy. Not knowing what etiquette required, Homer made a short bow to each of the ladies. Homer stared at the beautiful widow like a hungry puppy and gingerly sat down in an overstuffed chair.

"How are you Tom? Looks like you're in very good hands."

Tom grinned back at him. Homer could tell Tom was enjoying himself.

"I got myself a healthy lump to trouble me for a spell and lost a little hair and skin but nothing hurts anymore. Strange … when I regained conscience I didn't know who I was, where I was and didn't care. Real relaxed is the word. I forgot some of my luggage. Memory has started coming back gradually like.

"I brought the rest of your things you left on the docks. But what in the world are you doing with those bow and arrows?"

"Bow and arrows? Oh that's right. It's a long bow, made in the fashion of the old English bow used in ancient times, though not quite as long as the originals. It was given to me by one of my professors. He made me love history."

"Homer, are you heading home too?"

"I sure wish I were able. Soon as our cargo of cotton and tobacco is loaded we will be shippin' out. I'm curious why you decided to come home. Did you decide you didn't need more schoolin'?"

The maid appeared at the door, and Mrs. Cook held up five fingers without saying a word. The maid made a short curtsy and left.

"We will all gather at our dinner table shortly. We insist that you be our guests for dinner. We don't have opportunity to entertain guests as we once did. Business is fairly good but the tariffs are cuttin' too much into our profits."

Mr. Cook rose from his chair. "Now, Mrs. Cook, that is supposed to be men talk. And it must be about time to settle in for a good meal. Just follow us, or your nose if you so desire."

The party followed Mr. Cook as if on signal. Tom looked at Homer with a pained expression. "Have you been home lately? Is Paw hurt much?"

Homer stopped in his tracks. Tom could tell by Homer's expression that he knew nothing about the accident.

"Don't worry. Just before I left Philadelphia I got a letter from Ma, and she said he was hobbling about on a crutch and figured he was better. A tree had fallen on him."

The Cook family heard the discussion. They moved ahead to the dining room to give the brothers a little privacy.

Homer and Tom silently followed the family in the dining room. Mr. Cook motioned to the chairs around the table.

"You boys sit here next to each other so you can catch up." Mr. Cook took his seat at the end of the table and the ladies sat opposite the brothers.

The maid was quick to enter followed by another servant. The ladies smiled pleasantly while the food was placed on the table. Before the servants could retire, Mr. Cook launched into prayer giving thanks for the provisions set before them. He was quick to add his thankful heart for their daughter and guest's safe arrival.

While passing the platters of food, Mr. Cook asked Tom to tell about his father's accident. Tom told what little he knew. "Somehow a tree didn't fall like it should. I suspect the wind changed when the tree began to fall."

Homer put down his fork and looked at his brother. "Tom, I promise to make it home the next time I'm in port. I'll leave a note for Willie so he will know. If I didn't have this important shipment, I would go home with you. And Paw doesn't seem to be all that bad from what you say was in Ma's letter. Hate that I can't go with you, but you will explain won't you? It would mean more money for the things Ma needs."

When it seemed that they had caught up, and the conversation lagged, Mrs. Talent asked. "What of your brother Willie? Was he not with you Homer?"

Homer face flushed at the widow's attention. "Uh … well, when I made second mate Willie couldn't stand the competition and decided to ship out on a different vessel. He figured to make second or even first easier away from big brother. Then my orders wouldn't mean anything to him."

Tom couldn't help chuckle. It was difficult not to laugh out loud. "Willie never liked taking orders from our older brother. That is the way it has always been."

"I know another brother that didn't always like taking orders from his older brother, or Ma and Paw for that matter."

Tom noticed that Homer would steal a glance at Joan Talent every chance he could without her notice. One time too many and he was caught. The widow began to blush.

That was the first time Tom had seen her blush. I wonder if she blushed because of Homer's attention. Big brother is a handsome brute and has turned the eye of many young ladies. His ability to turn on the charm and switch from the local home dialect to polite conversation is a mystery. We all have the same gift of gab. Must have gotten that from Ma.

Mr. Cook rose and placed his hands on the back of his chair. "Let's retire to the parlor while we still can. I hope everyone has had sufficient this evening?"

Each in turn politely said how much they enjoyed the meal and the company.

"Miss Ann, could we have coffee in the parlor or drawing room?" The maid mumbled a word or two that must have been an inside family joke. The family laughed as they proceeded down the hall.

Mrs. Talent smiled at Homer. "Ann always says, you don't have to tell me. I always bring the coffee or tea after a meal. It's traditional in this house."

Mr. Cook turned to face the brothers. "Young sirs, do you have a place to stay the night? I think we can make provisions on that account."

Homer cleared his throat before replying … a family trait. "I thank you for your hospitality, Mr. and Mrs. Cook. I will not impose on you any longer. There is the need to leave a note for our brother Willie, pack a few things and be ready to sail on the next tide or when given the word. Tom, you are welcome to stay with me and sleep in Willie's bunk."

"I better come with you. It might be a long time before we see each other again. You need to tell me about your ship and such."

Mrs. Talent wanted to be the good hostess spoke excitedly. "You don't have to depart so quickly. Ann can bring us more coffee and perhaps something sweet. Do relax for a bit longer. I have gotten to know Tom quite well on the voyage and have heard a lot about his family. I would like to hear some of Homer's sea stories, too, Tom. Mother, Dad, you would too wouldn't you?"

Mr. Cook acknowledged his daughter's plea. "Why, most certainly, Joan."

Homer was in his element talking about the sea and his ship. "I think it's exciting to sail with steam and sail. My crew works well together and respects one another. I think they respect me, too. There is boredom as well.

There are times when the crew gets in each other's way. Days of tight quarters cause problems, but that was the way of the sea for centuries."

Mr. Cook seemed especially interested in cargo handling. But while they talked and questions were answered, they were distracted more and more by a commotion out in the street.

Homer took little notice of the increased noise outside, because he was more interested in impressing Joan Talent. Mr. Cook got up to investigate and drew Homer's attention away from his sea-faring tales.

"I'm goin' to go find out what all that shoutin' is about."

The brothers followed Mr. Cook.

Mr. Cook cautiously opened the door. Not seeing any danger, he stepped onto the porch.

Someone shouted at him. "Sir! South Carolina has fired on Fort Sumter. South Carolina has got herself a war. It's time we joined the secession."

Mr. Cook stepped back in the house and slammed the door. His face was pale.

"Those fools … too many hotheads. Couldn't wait to work it out. When my brother wired me that the government had sent in supplies to the fort, we figured there would be trouble."

Mr. Cook regained his composure and looked at the gathering. "Wonder what this will do with shippin' and sellin' now?"

He then explained to Homer and Tom. "My brother in Charleston and I are in business together. I handle the business here and, well, you can see this could affect the security of our family. And I don't want to profit off a war either."

HOME ... COMFORT AND TRIALS

Homer held out his hand to Mr. Cook. "Again thank you for your hospitality. Should I find interesting cargo, might I call on you sir?" He stole a quick glance at Joan Talent at the end of his question. Tom knew that was not the reason that Homer wanted to call on the family again, without a glance at his brother or the widow.

"Please do. And you too Tom." Joan and the Cooks smiled politely. Tom tried to detect another blush but could not. She was a lady that could be a lady at all times. And Homer ... he was more experienced in the ways of the world.

* * *

Homer carried Tom's bag while Tom carried the rest. Homer jauntily skirted one puddle and jumped another.

"Tom, I'm going to marry that widow lady some day. Just you wait and see." He looped the handle of the bag on his shoulder and rammed his hands in his pockets ... as if the matter were already settled.

"Good luck big brother. I saw her first you know." Tom grinned as he turned his head to observe Homer's reaction.

The challenge didn't seem to make any change in his countenance.

"That you did. But I thought you were courting that pretty blond girl that the fellers like to crowd around at church? Their family has influence because of their land. And then there's the slaves they bought from down east. She could be a good catch, you know." Homer began to slip back into his 'home language'.

"Her parents, the land and servants make her too good for the likes of me. She likes to make the other boys jealous and I'm of interest only when none of the others are at hand."

"I know she needs to grow up … might take too long for you. Well, may the best man win.

"Here we are. Willie and I have a room in back."

They had arrived at what appeared to be a rooming house, with a well-beaten path between two closely built houses.

Tom was more than a little pleased that Homer now regarded him as possible competition. *This means that my older brother finally considers me as a grown man and not simply a little brother. The younger brother could compete for the widow … but I won't.*

Homer found the familiar key and unlocked the door. He turned to look at Tom to make another appraisal.

"Homer, I'm just foolin'. I'm not a competitor for Mrs. Talent. I like her very much, and there is a lot I can tell you about her. We are close to the same age but she is more a lady than I'm a gentleman … and more mature. I was not serious when I made myself out to be your rival. At present I don't think you have a rival. She would be in mourning for at least a year before you could begin to court her anyway."

Homer sighed, "That is a big relief. We need peace in the family, especially now with all the talk of joinin' South Carolina. This part of the state is for separatin' but the folks at home and the west will want to support the federal government, I think."

They stepped into the semi-dark room, and Homer threw his seaman's jacket on a chair. "Speaking of being a gentleman: that is something I must work on. I do a lot of reading in my off hours and listen to passengers. When I consider Joan's own circumstances, I don't measure up either. But as Uncle Casper might tell me, I'm smitten."

A bed squeaked. "What you smitten over, Homer? And where did you find little brother there?"

The next sound startled them as shoes hit the floor. In the dim light they could barely make out Willie sitting on the bed.

"Light that coal oil lamp so I can see if it's really our little brother?"

"It's me, Willie. I'm not a ghost yet."

As their eyes adjusted to the sparse light, Willie grew impatient. He felt for the lamp at the table. The globe was quickly lifted with one hand, and the other hand felt over the table.

"Anybody got a Lucifer stick? Can't find mine."

Homer lit one with his thumbnail and lit the wick. The room came alive shortly with the added light.

"Oh my! Look at our little brother. He ain't so little no more. Bet he could take on me, or you, Homer. Yank land must agree with you."

Hand shaking followed with a good bit of backslapping.

"Sit a spell and give an account of yourself Tom. How come you're home from Philadelphia?"

"I got a telegram from Sue that Paw had been hurt, and they need me at home."

Tom tried to bring them up to date. He didn't see the necessity of mentioning the conflict on the ship. He quickly explained why he was on the way home. Homer told Willie about meeting the Cook family and meal. He intended to only causally mention the widow but found it difficult not to say more.

Tom had started to tell of his attack on the Wilmington docks, but Homer couldn't hold himself back any longer. He suddenly interrupted Tom.

"You should see her Willie … Mrs. Joan Talent, the widow lady I mentioned. She is a real lady, beautiful but not highfalutin' … real friendly. Her dad was not too happy when someone from the street yelled that South Carolina had started her own war by firing on Fort Sumter. That really poured cold water on the beautiful afternoon."

Willie jumped up suddenly. "What's that you say? They fired on Ft. Sumter? Don't they know there are federal troops there?" He pounded his fists on the table. "I suppose you said it right though. They've started their own war." He scratched the stubble on his face in deep thought. "That must account for the excitement on the docks when I left."

"I'm not surprised," Homer added. "Tempers on both sides of the argument were running high when I left Charleston last week. The merchants we ship for were most upset over tariffs. One gentleman was fightin' mad … invited an official of the government to a duel, right in front of me. The official wisely ignored the man and left. I'm glad the merchant didn't call him a coward. I suppose he was too angry."

"Was he then a coward, scared or just smart?"

"I don't know, boys. The official had a Boston accent, I think, and didn't appear to be troubled by all that anger. I figure he played it smart or he didn't think the merchant who challenged him was serious. Sorry I can't entertain you with a story about a duel."

Willie looked curiously at Homer then Tom. "I bout forgot to ask what the competition was about? Don't have to ask what Homer's smitten over, but what about you Tom? You not interested in the Widow lady? You just teasin' cuz you're interested in the Green girl back home."

"Well, if you must know, Mary Ellen is more interested in Walter Buchanan. His people have more land and a few slaves. Seems like several summers ago I met a prettier girl."

"Tell us more!" his brothers chorused.

"No way," Tom laughed.

When it looked like Tom didn't want to tell more, Homer interjected something that he had been toying with since leaving the Cooks. "What kind of cargo do you have Willie, or know about? Anything a lady or gentleman would be interested in?"

"We got French and English cloth but I think it's already sold. I know I don't have to ask why. Ha, ha!"

Tom chuckled, "Homer is looking for an excuse to go back to the Cook's home and see the widow lady. Is that not correct?"

"Never truer words were spoken little brother."

"We got to stop callin' him little brother, Homer. He's fillin' out like a man ... well, almost."

Willie's stomach growled, interrupting the conversation. "My belly is remindin' me I've forgotten it ... or thinks my throat's been cut. Since you boys et at the Cooks, you want to come watch me eat? I'm starved.

Haven't eaten since breakfast. Besides, wouldn't that be an excuse to walk by her house?"

"It would indeed, Willie. Come on Tom. Let's take Willie and get his belly filled. Otherwise his growling stomach will keep us awake all night."

The three brothers were on their way. Tom and Homer continued to rib Willie about his appetite. When they reached the street Tom situated himself between his brothers. They marched to the cadence of their own contented hearts. At one point, someone said "now", and Tom stiffened is arms with his hands in front, which allowed the brothers to lift him by his elbows. They didn't carry him far but soon let him down with a grunt. He was heavier than when they had last carried him. Occasionally a few people or a horse and buggy required them to go single file.

The three soon found themselves in a neighborhood of two and three story homes. Most of them had iron fences and gates and were made of brick. These were obviously very large homes and had lots with more shrubbery than others. The street where they now found themselves had homes with large oaks in the yards.

The Gentry boys were the only ones on the street now. This was the time of day when most folks had settled down in their homes for the evening.

"That's the home of Miss Joan Cook, or I should say, 'The Widow Talent. Mr. Cook must have a business somewhere near. He received some of our last shipment. I remember seeing Cook and Cook on a manifest. His brother in Charleston must be the other Cook. There are bigger homes further on. Perhaps they are not as prosperous as some of their neighbors."

A door slammed but no one wanted to appear interested. Someone shouted at them. "Tom! Tom Gentry, wait."

All three turned to see who would be calling.

"Adam! Where did you come from?"

"I arrived this morning by train. It was rather difficult to find a Mrs. Joan Talent or her home. No one knew her by her married name. I was sure I could find you here in Wilmington, or before you got too far, if I could find that house."

"Adam, these are my two brothers. This big one is Homer and this is Willie. Brothers, Adam came to my assistance on the ship. That's a long story. How did you get here so fast? Oh yes, the train."

"Before I answer your questions, it's a great honor to meet you Willie and Homer."

After the normal greetings between the men, Adam resumed. "Tom saved the life of my brother, Cliff; therefore, my brother and I made up a way to protect Tom against a reprisal from the thugs."

Footsteps behind them came to a stop. "Well, Tom and Homer, it looks like you young gentlemen have come upon some friends."

They all turned to see Mr. Cook as he surveyed them. "I just returned from my warehouse office. It is good to see you two again."

"Sir." Homer wanted to be the first to speak. "This is our other brother, Willie. Mr. Cook. Have you met Adam?"

"I have not had the pleasure. It is good to meet you both. Please come in and have some refreshments before you journey further."

Willie's stomach growled again. "Please excuse me. I haven't had my supper yet. We really need to find a place to eat, but thanks for the invite, sir." Willie patted his stomach to make a point.

"You must call on us again soon. And Homer, let me know if you can ship tobacco and how much cotton you can take. I would like to ship some barrels of molasses I've had since last fall. Is your ship already full?"

Homer stroked his chin, giving the question some thought. "How many barrels are you considering, sir? We had planned to pull in the lines first thing in the morning. But a delay for more freight could be profitable for us both."

Mr. Cook's face exhibited a broad smile. "Our maid can find something left over for Willie while we talk business. Come in and we can talk business while Willie satisfies his cravings."

Tom commented, "But sir, you don't need all of us. Let Homer and you talk business. Just point the way to a fair eating establishment."

Tom could see that Willie was not comfortable entering the big house. More than anything he wanted to fill his stomach.

"Gentleman, continue up this street to the next crossing. Then turn left and you will find what you are looking for at the end of the street. It's a good plate they will sit before you. Come Homer, my young friend. We have a need to discuss tobacco and cotton."

The remaining three started for the crossing Mr. Cook had mentioned. With food on their minds and freedom from the confines of proper etiquette, it was a relief to be moving. Willie slapped Tom on the back. "Little ... uh, Tom. Can you imagine all the good luck? Homer's about to bust a gut to see that gal, and her father throws an invitation at him he can't turn loose. But, if they talk business in his office or someplace he might not get to see her."

"Willie, even if he doesn't get to see her now, he'll soon be in good with the father. That's the next best thing. Might be even better at this stage of a courtship." Tom paused for a moment. "When do you have to go to sea again?"

"I would like to see the folks first. You sure Paw is better? I haven't picked up my mail since I got back. We changed boardin' places. So, if there's a letter from home I haven't seen it. I got to go to the old place where they charge too much to reserve a room, which we don't need to do any more. One of our crew told us about his mom and pop's place. Now we got a place to stay when we are ashore. They were glad to do it for their son's shipmates ... for a fair price."

"Are you going to let me answer your question? Ma said so in her last letter. If you can't come home, when will you get to go, Willie?" Tom's voice revealed impatience.

"Not sure, Tom. We are still trying to add more cargo. A couple days at most. I'm lookin' for a promotion and really need to make this trip, don't you see".

"I smell food and cheap whiskey. This must be the place."

With Willie in the lead, the three men entered the establishment. A few patrons looked up to observe the new arrivals. One man in particular looked on with a great deal of interest. He elbowed his drinking partner.

"I want a piece of that'n's ear, Freddie. He thinks he's so smart getting on the good side of the cap'n, in all. Hey, Willie, you too good to drink with the likes of us?"

Willie paid little attention and pulled out a chair. He motioned for the others to have a seat. The talkative man moved in front of Willie and almost walked into Adam. Freddie started to move around the table and bumped into Adam.

"Get out of my way before …" Freddie looked up at the great size of Adam and began to sober up.

Adam crossed his arms across his chest. "Before what? Man, your breath would take the finish off the furniture. Don't believe I would light a cigar any time soon. You might go off like a British rocket at the battle of New Orleans." Willie stepped aside and Loud Mouth stumbled over a chair and fell on his elbows across the table. The big mouth raised his right arm expecting a blow that didn't come. He then glanced up into Willie's grinning face. Freddie stood with his mouth open. On gaining his balance, the first antagonist felt for his big knife.

"Don't he talk good. That there feller is a yank, Freddie. Where we come from …"

UNEXPECTED DEVELOPMENT

Willie calmly addressed the two drunks. "I would offer you gents a seat and buy you a drink but you have had enough. Why don't I get you something to eat instead?"

Loud Mouth ignored Willie and stared at Adam.

A heavy-set short man approached the table. He held the thongs of a two-foot club.

"You two are always makin' trouble."

The room had gotten quiet before, but now you could only hear heavy breathing. All eyes were now on the big man with the dirty cook's apron.

"Last warnin' to you two. You quiet down yourselves or out you go. No more whiskey for you tonight. I could most likely chase all you boys in this here dispute, so let this be a caution to you-all."

The sullen Loud Mouth and Freddie returned to the bar and their drink. The new arrivals took their seats and grinned at each other. Tom gave a sigh of relief and Adam smiled from ear to ear. Willie, unperturbed, sat down as if to a fine banquet. Then a young lad quickly placed a large wood tray with water on the table.

A tall thin man that sat at the next table leaned over and spoke quietly to Willie. "Those two could cause you a great deal of trouble not too far down the road. It might be possible to make friends by invitin' them to join your meal, unless they are too far into their cups and still want a fight. A kind word or two can soothe ruffled feathers."

The tall stranger straightened up in his chair. Willie and the others looked at the stranger. He appeared to be in his late thirties. His was a kindly face, one that drew people's trust. His features were that of an honest man suggesting that of a preacher ... a godly man.

Willie glanced at Loud Mouth and Freddie trying to decide. "What do I have to lose?" he muttered to Tom, seated beside him.

He spoke in as friendly a manner as possible and addressed the two at the bar. "Jonah, Freddie ... I'll drink with you anther time ... on my money. Come have a meal on me. After all we're ship mates and have to share much of the same space, and that space gets powerful small on *The Caroline.*"

Freddie had drunk more than Jonah, the loudmouth, so Freddie looked at his friend to see what he would do. Jonah turned to view the three at the table and saw three smiling friendly faces.

Willie motioned with his arm. "Aw, come on over and eat with us. Think on the times your money runs out and your ole friend Willie will have money left. When will you ever get to eat with the new first mate again?"

Jonah thought it over for a moment and grinned, "When you talk like that, I got to say yeah. Make room for two more, I reckon."

The tall stranger at the next table rose and motioned to his seat. "You've only room for one more. Please take my table and join with yours. I have almost finished and can move to the bar or another table."

"That shouldn't be necessary," Adam quickly added. "We can join the two tables and you can finish with us. Your company is welcome, sir. They call me Adam and these are my two friends Tom and Willie. You know Jonah and Freddie. And you, kind sir are?"

"B.T. White at your service. Most folks call me Preacher White. In an hour or so, I have to catch a train to Salisbury. I usually do circuit ridin' in the mountains but have friends in Salisbury that ask me to preach since I'm down this way. Suppose you gents will be departin' shortly?"

While the minister talked, Tom and Willey exchanged glances before deciding to further examine the man's features.

Tom knew before he asked, "Do you have a brother that's a preacher … covered three churches south of Lexington? He meant a lot to me when I was growin' up."

"That has to be my brother, Charles. You need to get your supper, and I need to do a few things before I catch a train. We might meet and talk another time. Gentlemen if you will excuse me? It has been a pleasure."

"We will probably find you soon. Adam and I will be going as far as Lexington ourselves tomorrow. That was the original plan. Willie, you don't have room for two more tonight, do you?"

"To give you an honest answer, Tom, if you don't mind to sleep on the floor with the bugs and such? And some of those big bad bugs can carry you off. Adam could sleep on my cot but his feet would be against the wall, or out the door."

Tom gave Adam a questioning look. "I had not considered the size of the bugs I've seen around here. Do you think you could sleep on a train?"

"I thought you didn't like to ride trains? What made you change your mind?"

"It's ride a train, walk, or ride a slew of farm wagons for days on end. We don't have much choice as I see it. Willie, I hope you won't be too disappointed if we don't stay."

Both Adam and Willie tried to speak at the same time but Willie interrupted, "I hate to see you leave so soon after we've separated for so long. And I would like to chew the fat with you two for a spell longer, but I know you're ready to get home. I also know you want to see that pretty little blond gal you eat with at church socials."

Tom playfully punched Willie in the arm. "Forget Mary Ellen. I'm not in her plans. As soon as we eat we'll join the preacher. What do you say, Adam?"

"Just say when and where, Tom," added Adam. "I'm your guest for a few days."

At that point the cook brought a large wood platter that held bowls of thick stew and cornbread. A rather fat woman followed with another tray of cups and a pot of hot coffee. Conversation was forgotten for the next few minutes. Their attention was now on the food. Freddie and Jonah ate quietly.

Tom was the first to rise after his fill. "Can't hold any more. Two suppers in one afternoon is too much for me. Willie, gents ... it's time we start for home. Willie, I hope you can be home for Christmas. It won't be the same Christmas without the family together. Look after your-self Willie."

Homer grabbed his two brothers in a big bear hug before they parted.

Jonah and Freddie had become more mellow and sober with time, the meal and coffee. Jonah stood and extended a hand to Willie. He lacked the social graces of the others but it didn't stop him from grasping Willie's hand. He stood first on one foot then the other, his discomfort obvious.

"Freddie and me are beholdin to you for this fine supper ... you bein' the first mate and all, we kin be of help any time you need us. Ain't that right Freddie?"

Freddie nodded his head in agreement and continued to chew on the last piece of cornbread.

Willie smiled and added, "I thank you, and I'll remember to yell for help when I need you. It's time to see these two on their way."

After shaking hands all around, Tom and Adam grabbed their travel bags.

The two travelers walked to the train tracks. They soon found the preacher who napped against a shed wall. Neither wanted to disturb him, so they quietly sat down to wait for the train. It wasn't long before the engine noise and the hiss of steam had them fully awake. When they boarded, the new passengers tried to get comfortable. Tom and Adam attempted to sleep on the coach seats but the sway of the train made it almost impossible.

To get off at various stops to take on water and coal could be a humorous experience. The need for food let to such an occasion. At one stop they were challenged with a pitchfork because they stared at a well-built hen house. Then when they turned around, they faced an enterprising young lady that sold them ham biscuits. They figured out later the pitchfork was part of the sales effort, though not needed for hungry folk.

As a boy, especially while he traveled by horse and bumpy wagon, Tom dreamed of train travel. He credited his desire for a train because the trip to the mountains seemed to last forever. A train at that time could have been better, except there were no train tracks where they traveled. Now he tried to forget the stories he heard about train wrecks. His uncle and father were always saying, "For a boy your age you worry too much, it'll make you old before your time."

Day travel presented different problems. There were heated arguments and discussions between passengers regarding North Carolina's stand on Unionism and succession. Tom tried not to be drawn into the discussions. Adam didn't speak at all unless he was sure the other person wouldn't a secessionist. His accent would identify him as a meddlin' Yankee to the other side of the argument.

That night the two managed to rest well. When the train stopped at the next station, Tom and Adam got off.

"If you get tired enough you can sleep most any where Adam. I suppose we will walk most of the way from here. I have cousins, the Yarboroughs, not far from here. I can leave my big bag with them and carry the rest home with us. Do you want to stay here at the station until I get back?"

"I'll come with you. I want to see some of the sights. It's been a while since I made it this far south. And now that I'm fully awake ... Why didn't we get off in Lexington?"

"This is the way the roads and carriages go, it's easier to get home from here. When we have to go shopping, we go to Salisbury."

While they walked along, Tom watched for a wagon that would go toward his cousin's home. They soon spied a farm wagon drawn by two mules and then waited for it to catch up to them. The travelers admired the animals as the wagon pulled up next to them.

"Hop in back boys, if you're a mind to." The farmer removed his hat and wiped his forehead probably out of habit since the day was cool. His face had started to tan and his forehead revealed a steak of white where his hat protected. The fact that the farmer was clean-shaven and wore clean work clothes, told Tom the man had cleaned up to go to town.

"Boys, I just sold some corn from last year's crop. This year promises to be a good year. I'll take you as far as I'm a goin."

"We thank you for the lift, neighbor. Come on Adam. We still have a lot of walkin' to do later."

The new passengers made themselves comfortable. Tom looked down at the road before and glanced back at Adam and the farmer.

"We appreciate this road. Although it had been well traveled, it was not too bumpy. After some of the tracks we went over, this is a welcome change."

The view was new to Adam but not to Tom. "Tom, what is that tall building with a fence around it?"

All three riders' eyes were drawn to a figure with a musket standing by the fence.

The farmer spat a stream of tobacco juice in the direction of the tall building. "I reckon that's a prison for no account law breakers and such. It used to be an old cotton mill."

"Well sir," added Adam, "I would sure hate to be locked up in there."

Tom looked at Adam and a feeling of ice came over him.

HOME COMING

A short distance from town, the farmer pointed to a different track. "I turn left down there and head home. Where you-all headin'?"

Tom jumped off the end of the wagon.

"We plan to stop by my cousin, Clarence Yarborough's place. Then start for home. We thank you kindly for the lift."

"You fellers will want to follow this road a piece till you get to a cross road. Go right a spell and you will see your cousin's place. Good luck to you."

A white house soon came in view. They had gone only a short distance when a black and white dog faced them and barked, and then it turned and looked back toward the house.

Tom spoke. "Hello dog. We are friendly. Hope you are?"

The dog continued to bark but wagged its tail.

A woman sitting on the wide front porch yelled at the dog, "Hush up! That's cousin Tom Gentry."

"Uh oh! Adam, that's my second cousin May Bell. She likes to talk and it's been a while since we visited. We'll have to let her know we need to be home before dark.

I'll be firm and determined." Tom and Adam approached the house in a hurry.

"La, is that you Tom?"

"Hey Cousin May Bell, good to see you again. This is my friend, Adam. How's everybody."

"Oh, 'bout the same I reckon."

"May Bell, I can't stay … on my way back home from up North. May we leave my carpetbag here for a few days? We need to get on home and see how Paw is doin'. It might be dark when we get there. You probably heard about his accident?"

"Yeah, sorry to hear that. You can leave it here as long as you want. Put the bag here on the porch. I'll take care of it. Wish you could stay longer but I know how I'd feel if it was my pop. Get yourself a drink at the well before you go."

Back on the main road that led north, they spotted a coach. Tom decided they has walked enough and flagged it down. It came to a stop in a cloud of dust.

The driver shouted down, "Get in. We are runnin' late. Me and these folks is hungry and thirsty. Need to get to the next stop."

No one seemed interested in talk. Tom and Adam were tired, so that suited them. The other travelers had almost gone to sleep again when Tom signaled the driver to let them off.

"It's not a long walk from here, Adam. It only takes a few more paces from this old store before we come to the lane that leads to our family homestead."

It was now dusk. Most of the farmers and their families were sitting down to the evening meal. They discussed this as Tom led the way up the lane.

"Just remembered, Tom, we haven't eaten since those ham biscuits last evening."

Tom slowed to smell the new plowed ground and view the new growth on the trees in the moonlight. The smell of animals made it obvious they were on the farm.

"This is home. Didn't think I would miss it when I left. Adam, I hope you don't have to sleep in the barn. I see Uncle Casper and Aunt Jane's rig in front of the smoke-house."

"I've slept in lot worse places, believe me."

"I joke, foolin', as they say around here. Mom would give you my old room and I would be the one in the barn."

Tom stepped on the porch, hesitated for a moment to look at the familiar rocking chairs.

"Not much has changed much that I can tell. It's going to be good to see the new growth. Corn has probably popped up."

The door opened unexpectedly, and Tom's sister, Sue, stood there. She grinned from ear to ear.

"Well! Are you goin' to stand there like a schoolboy? Give your sister a big hug."

Tom picked her up off her feet and gave her a swing around the porch.

She squealed, "You're goin' to knock me and the chairs off the porch."

Sue pulled Tom through the doorway. "Get in here before the mosquitoes find us." She playfully pushed him toward a chair.

Tom had to take a step back and then pushed Sue, who stumbled against a table. To keep from losing her balance, she sat down in a chair.

Their mother appeared at the dining room door and gave a little squeal. "It's my boy come home! Be careful you two. Good furniture is hard to come by. Welcome home son. Who is your friend?"

Tom gave Sue a hand to help her stand.

She peeped around her bother to get a good look at Adam.

Adam ducked his head when he entered the room out of habit more than need.

Sue's mouth dropped open when she looked up at him. Although she was tall as many boys her own age, it was the first time she ever had to look up at a boy.

Since Adam was such a handsome fellow, Sue made a point to not be her typical tomboy self. She smoothed her hair and brushed flour from her dress as she shot covert glances in his direction.

Adam couldn't take his eyes off Sue. His face flushed, and the sheepish grin on his face proved that he was well aware Tom's pretty sister.

"Ma, Sue, Aunt Jane, this is Adam McFarland from around Philadelphia. There is quite a story how we happened to be together. I'll save that tale for later. Should be a good one to tell at supper. Where is Paw?"

"He's milkin' ... should be comin' in about now. Come on in the dining room. It's almost time for supper.

"Adam, if you need to wash up, go out to the back porch. Tom, get him a clean towel. You know where they are. There's some lye soap and the pump still sounds like a banshee.

"We do most of our cookin' in the next little room. Before Tom left, we had a room for cookin' just off the porch, but it caught fire one Sunday before the boys left. The boys and Paw got it out but not before it ruined. We tore what was left down and plan to build it back soon."

Ma looked at Tom with a shrewd side-glance. "That's right, is it not son?"

"We will Ma. If Paw is milkin', he must be getting around better than when I got the wire from Sis."

"He is, Tom. Just in the last week, he has gotten well enough to do the milking. I was mighty concerned about him."

"I'll grab a towel. We better clean up, especially if we want to taste some of the best food in North Carolina. Adam, you haven't eaten biscuits or corn fritters until you've taste Ma's."

Sue couldn't help blurt out. "I made the biscuits and friend chicken." Her face turned red.

Tom observed his sister. *She said this to impress Adam ... first time I've ever seen this tomboy blush. Could it be that little sister has grown into a lady?*

Tom motioned for Adam to follow. On the back porch Tom poured water into a shallow washbasin before he handed Adam the soap. After his turn in the basin, he toweled off. Suddenly, a gruff voice got his attention. It made him wonder how long they had been watched.

"You are right, Casper. It does look like my youngest son. The prodigal has returned. Welcome home son."

His father dropped his cane and handed the milk bucket to Casper. He then grabbed his son's right hand in both of his.

"It sure is good to see you Paw. I see you exchanged a walkin' stick for the cane. Adam, you probably figured out that this is my father and that is my Uncle Casper. Unk ... Paw, this is my friend Adam. We've traveled a lot together lately. Will have to tell you all about it at the table."

Mr. Gentry held out a hand to Adam. "Welcome to our home. I'm pleased to meet you, young man."

Ma called from the house. "Time to eat. You can come in and have a seat."

When they entered she pointed to the chairs. "This one is for our guest." Paw went to the head of the table, his usual seat, but it was obvious to everyone that Ma was the boss of the dining room and kitchen.

Sue found herself a seat across from Adam. She kept her eyes on her plate and stole looks at Adam now and again. When Tom related some of his ship experiences and told of Adam's help, the conversation became more comfortable and lively. He noticed that while Adam's and Sue's attention was on the conversation, they were more relaxed.

Before Tom could delve very far into their experiences, the men moved to the sitting room. Uncle Casper and Paw took seats near the window to light their pipes. The women could he heard while they cleared the table in the next room.

Pa looked over the two boys. "Nothin' like facin' troubles together to bond a friendship. It sounds like you fellers had yourselves quite a time. Adam, I hope you can stay with us a spell."

"I would like that sir. In a week or two I have to take over for another fireman or engineer. Most likely it will be a fireman."

"What do you two think about the Lincoln election? What's the feeling in the North, Adam?"

"Sir, I suppose I should have watched politics closer. There's been little talk about possible trouble and none that got my attention. It's probably different since South Carolina started the fireworks. What about you, Tom?"

"When I left the Frenchman's place after a party, I overheard some lawyers talk about the governor of South Carolina. They said he ordered and bought cannon and powder. That was in New York. Don't think he had trouble with the purchase either by the sounds of the conversation. What about here Paw?"

"Most of this part of North Carolina is Unionist. Now east of here some are agitatin' for separatin'. We don't hold to slavery, so our family is strong Unionists. I hear tell the merchants in the east are hollerin' about unfair tariffs the government placed on us."

Uncle Casper had nodded off, but he suddenly jerked awake.

"Don't hold to the tariffs the government put on us down Wilmington way. Some in the North condemn us for slavery but I reckon the slaves I had, all two of them would say they was treated right. One is now a good neighbor and helps me at times. The other one I allowed him to buy his freedom. Now take our neighbor Jethro. He treats them worse than animals."

He interrupted himself long enough to relight his pipe and paused as if to listen.

"Hear them dogs? I'll bet you a good tobacco plug they are after one of his people now."

The men could hear the hounds fade in the distance. Tom stretched as if to listen.

"Unk, I would say they lost the scent. Who would be the bounty hunter, Paw?"

"Don't know the sound of them dogs. Could be the Warfield's from down east I've heard tell of. I hope they just keep on movin on out of the country."

The three women passed the men on their way to the front porch, still chatting among themselves. Tom observed Adam and Sue with interest. He saw Adam's eyes follow his sister.

Soon he could hear the sounds of the rocking chairs go bump, bump on the uneven porch floor. The ladies had settled to rock and talk. Aunt Jane could be heard to dominate the conversation, now that there was no food to stuff in her mouth. The men continued to puff on their pipes and listen for the dogs. Adam's ear was cocked toward the women on the porch. Tom smiled, assuming that he was listening for Sue's voice.

Everyone's attention was drawn to a new voice. Someone talked loudly from in front of the house. When the voice was closer, it sounded agitated and obviously excited. Paw and Uncle Casper hurried to the porch followed by Tom and Adam.

The visitor was no stranger.

Paw commented, "You look like you lost the store, Virgil Mason. Why are you so upset?"

"As I said to these ladies. I'm mad as a wet settin' hen and ready to go to war, me and my boys." Virgil stopped to take a breath and stomped his foot.

"Why? Is Mrs. Mason ridin' you again about the way you give away shoes and such? I think you're askin' a fair price. No reason to go to war. Or is she still wantin' you to move close to Lexington?"

"This ain't none of that, Gentry. This here is serious. Mr. Lincoln is callin for 75,000 troops to invade the South. He even wants boys from North Carolina. You should be mad too, Will, you and your boy, Tom here."

Casper took a step closer in disbelief. "Is this true Virgil?"

"It's not only true but it's in the Raleigh paper. Virginia is talkin' succession. That would be the first place the North would invade' I reckon. We need to organize quick and teach them government people a lesson and get it over with. North Carolina ain't goin' to take invasion sittin' down."

Adam looked from Sue to Tom and back. "Mr. Gentry, do you think North Carolina will stay in the Union?"

Tom tried to see the expression on his father's and uncle's faces in the fading light.

Paw sighed audibly, "How can we eventually stand as a nation divided? If we start breakin' up into separate states countries ... I don't know. This is what I fear most for the outcome. But, if we consider the South joins and stands firm ..."

After a pause with every one expecting Paw to continue, he went on, "Together we might force Lincoln to change his mind; however, I doubt he would, considerin' his speeches. What do you think Casper?"

"I'm sure you think the same as me. I'm afraid there will be war. Askin for troops to invade South Carolina, our sister state, will change a lot of minds to separate. It should be short, if we show we are bound to be our own state."

Ma put her hands on her hips and spoke forcefully. "War or not. Don't let this talk spoil the evening. Forget politics. We have company and you know we made ice cream that needs to be eaten now. It won't last long, you know."

"Ice cream?" spoke the men in unison. The response, in part, was to placate the lady of the house and to lighten the mood.

"Sue and I cranked it up on the ice cream maker this afternoon. The ice was shipped all the way from Wilmington in sawdust, came from some place up north. Will you join us Mr. Mason?"

"Thank you kindly, Miz Gentry. I better be movin on afore the Missus comes a-lookin' for me."

Uncle Casper and Paw didn't try to muffle a chuckle.

WINDS OF WAR ... COURTSHIP AND MARRIAGE, THE SAME?

Ice cream did change everyone's disposition. The atmosphere was now more festive; however, Adam took his bowl and looked for a secluded place to sit and think. The most likely spot turned out to be a bench under a tree. He had noticed it when he first arrived on the farm.

Since Ma filled everyone's ice cream bowl, Sue was free to find Adam. She had seen him start for the seat under the tree. When she approached the seat he scooted over to make room. With one hand she held her bowl and smoothed out her dress with the other before she sat.

"I can't let our guest be ignored, can I?"

Adam turned to look at Sue. "I'm glad you're here. This is a very kind gesture for our host, especially in view of the political differences between our states. I intended to join you if you decided to sit down. You have been very busy. And, I might add, I would dearly like to become better acquainted with my hostess' daughter. Is she really all 'tomboy' as her brother would picture? Or is she really the pretty young lady she appears to be now? There's this speech, manner of talk that has been a puzzle to me. Sometimes you talk back woods and other times educated. Tom does the same thing. How do you ...?"

"We do have schools here you know." Sue finished a bite of ice cream and moved her head to one side to study what she saw as a strong and kind face.

"You like to tease. Well, for your information I'm growed, uh, grown up and grew up with teasers. To answer the important question, I reckon I'm both: tomboy and lady."

After a brief pause she added, "I can be both when I want. How many girls are you engaged in teasing, Adam?"

"Well now ... only one at a time. I'm trying to narrow it down to just one. I do not think it will be difficult just now."

Adam had never been comfortable around girls before; however, Sue made it easy.

"I'll bet you have lots of boyfriends. Any one in particular?"

"Probably not as many as you have girl friends, and I have no one in particular. There are two friends at church that pay attention to me."

"If they, the two friends at church, don't realize that you have grown into a pretty young lady, it's time they grew up. As pretty as you are, I'm surprised you aren't spoken for. And you joined me here on the bench? I feel honored. I've wanted to ... uh, talk to you all evening. Do you mind?"

Sue looked surprised at the attention. She sat silently for a moment before answering, "No, not really. Remember I came and sat beside you. I know you said you were goin' to join me if I finally sat down, or so you implied. I'll bet you talk to a lot of girls. Do you have a special gal?"

"Never seemed to have enough time to hold on to, what you say, 'a gal' ... always worked on the railroads. Do you think you could ever be interested in a, uh, 'feller' like me?"

Sue had to stifle a giggle. "You don't waste time, do you? How many times have you said that to a gal?" She decided to remain quiet for a bit longer to tease.

"Sue, I apologize for the great hurry. Don't want to wear out my welcome here and don't know how long I should stay now. You are beautiful, smart, and I can't help it. I think on my chances. There's my work, for now, that calls me back shortly and I don't want to leave but will have to. I will need to work and study steam engines, and I talk too much some times."

After a painful pause, he added. "May I have your permission to court you and then ask your father?"

The thrill of the romance glowed on Sue's face. She grinned and held her peace for a bit. Then turning her head to respond, she answered, "Well, if you really want to, I suppose it would be fine."

As she looked at Adam, she could see his expression in the dim light from the house. Was that pain on his face, or was it her imagination? She forgot she was a tomboy who liked to torture both herself and her suitors.

"Adam, I am flattered. To tell me I'm beautiful makes me blush. Nobody has ever said that to me, not since I was a baby anyway, so I'm told. How could I not want the attention of a handsome feller like you … especially you? I hope you don't have another girl and it doesn't sound like you do. You don't have to leave too soon do you? Might you stay and help on the farm for a spell? Can't believe I'm saying all this."

"Sue, then I have you're permission to court. I would like to ask your father's permission to court you seriously.

It would have to be long distance for a time. What do you say?"

"Adam, I can't believe it. Yes, if you like. Paw will likely say, 'She'll have the last word anyway.' I don't give a hoot how long distant it will be."

It would have been normal if he jumped up and shouted, but gentleman that he was, he merely said, "Now to get the courage for the next step … talk to your father."

Ma Gentry pushed open the door from the sitting room and stood on the porch. She then spoke loud enough for everyone to hear, "Tomorrow is to be a busy day. Tom, you've slept in the barn before on warm nights, but take a blanket. Adam, once again you can take Tom's old room tonight. When you smell bacon it will be time to rise. Paw, Uncle Casper, Aunt Jane, and I will be up to start the day well before we eat. Good night to all."

Tom carried a blanket and a lantern to the barn. The barn doors were not secured by the board that slides between two uprights.

"That's strange. Neither Paw nor Uncle Casper would leave it unsecured." Tired as he was, the door was quickly forgotten. It was time to fasten the lantern by the old rope and use the pulley, pull it to the top of the ladder above the loft, and climb to bed. Before the usual climb, a knot in the worn rope was slipped over a stout peg. Now there was less danger of a lantern to fall and burn down the barn. It now hung above the barn loft.

At the top of the ladder where the slats ended, the posts continued for hand-holds. Tom gave the lantern a quick glance of assurance before he finished his climb. When his head came above the loft floor, he was startled to hear a pistol hammer click. Though temporarily blinded by the lantern, he could still make out the business end of a pistol. His hands froze on the ladder.

"I ain't a-goin back, mistah."

After the pistol hammer shock, it was a relief to recognize the voice. Tom blew out a stream of air. "You are not going back?"

"Hee hee, still the teacher ain't cha? You always done right by me and my folks, Mistah Tom. I will always remember you tryin to teach us, and slippin' books for us to read. If I had knowed it was you I wouldn't a-pointed this here pistol at you. It ain't loaded nohow. But you still tryin' to be the teacher."

"I tried Lemuel. I tried. What are you doing here Lem?"

"When Widder Jones died, her worthless son sold me to Master Wiggins. Most of his darkies done run off. He ain't ... uh ... don't have money to buy more. That makes him meaner. Now he is goin' to be powerful mad, if he's not already. And Mistah Tom, I'm sure sorry I pointed this pistol at you. Like I said, it don't be loaded. Couldn't find any way to load it before I left. You ain't goin' to turn in Lem is you?"

Tom pulled himself up beside Lem and stroked the stubble on his chin. "No Lem, you know I couldn't do that. Besides, I don't have any more respect for Wiggins than you, and my folks don't either."

"I remember you trying to teach me and Brother. You saved my hide when one of them books got wet and the rain came in through the chinks. That was before your uncle sold me to Widder Jones. She promised to take good care of us. Brother ... that was all we called him ... done run off from his master. The Widder and Master Wiggins never found out we could read and write. Figurin' numbers helped me keep the Widder Jones from bein' cheated a time or two. You sure took a chance on Brother and me, teachin' and all."

"What are you going to do? How are you going to get away, Lem?"

"Oh, I got to meet up with some folks a ways from here. It be better you don't know. I put turpentine on my feet to fool them dogs. Still got some. I fooled them dogs, I reckon."

"Lem, we better get some sleep. I'll try to get you some food to eat before you slip away." Tom started to roll over on his side but stopped to speak again. "Is it not better to travel at night around here so close to home?"

"Not the first night, Tom. And thank you kindly for offerin' to get me somethin' to eat."

* * *

Breakfast would have been uneventful except for Adam and Sue grinning at each other from across the table. Paw and Ma Gentry gave each other a knowing glance. Uncle Casper observed the quiet demeanor of the couple and began to realize what must have taken place in the family. Aunt Jane had been informed while the women prepared breakfast. Normally Tom would have noticed a change in everyone's behavior. He was too concerned about Lem's troubles.

Tom rose from the table. "Please excuse me. I'll finish in the barn. I've got to think about this Lincoln and troops development."

Ma studied Tom for a moment. "You've been quiet this morning, son. Don't study too much on last night's news." She pointed at the plate of ham biscuits and added. "Take some extra ham biscuits. I noticed you eat better these days."

The steady look on Ma's face told him she suspected he wouldn't eat them all. The hounds last night told part of the story.

When Tom stepped onto the back porch, he was startled to find himself face to face with a young boy in worn trousers, no shirt and barefoot. Tom's nerves on edge, since the events of the night before, jumped and then giggled at the absurdity of his fear in front of a mere boy.

"What can I do for you?"

"I'm real sorry to trouble you sir. Widder Jones daughter sent me over to tell folks from church that Mr. Wiggins done died from *apopoplex*. He got too excited, upset … plumb mad."

"Step on in and tell my folks. I need to get to the barn. You must be Joe Hardy's son?"

"Yes sir, thank you."

Tom stood on the steps a moment to listen to the word exchange. The new information he gathered indicated that Mr. Wiggins had become uncontrollable and gone into a rage. The last slave was gone when he went to give him a whipping. The man collapsed and could not be revived.

On the way to the barn, Tom said to the tabby cat that was licking his paw, "This could bode good or bad for Lem."

OVERCOMING OBSTINATE OBSTACLES

"Have some breakfast Lem. It's too light to run now, not that I thought you would. And I have some news for you. But first, how do you and Mrs. Wiggins get along. Is she good to you?"

"Most times. She don't have no chance to say nothin'. Master always a yellin' at us. You know I plans to stay hid today befo' runnin and give them bounty hunters chances to move on. What news you got?"

"And Lem, I meant to mention last night, you don't have to slave talk around me, you know what I mean. The news: you don't have to worry about Mr. Wiggins any more. He fell over dead from pure anger. You can get the rest of the story later." Tom rubbed his chin and thought for a minute. "I have an idea. Food will be more plentiful in a month or two, and there will be more bushes and leaves on all the trees and greenery to hide you."

"I can't hide that long Mr. Tom. You can't hide me if that is what you're thinkin'. You would get yourself locked up in that old cotton mill they call a prison at Salisbury for sho'."

"What I'm thinking … you know of any bee trees about? You could return with some honey and say you got lost yesterday. Take the widow Wiggins honey. You would be shocked at the master's death."

"I been gone since sun up yesterday. Well, since before noon mostly. Mrs. Wiggins be upset about her man might take the tale about honey for the truth." Lem, with a curious expression, studied Tom' face. "You suggestion that this good Christian lie about bein' gone?"

Tom smiled at Lem. "No, just don't tell everything. Leave out the things that would get you in more trouble. I suppose that would be a lie too. If you have to, tell her that you had a change of heart. If she is upset and blames you, then you might have to run. Then again she could sure use your help right now."

"What if she has me put in irons and wants to sell me? I might get a whippin' just to prove who is the new boss. I can't take no whippins. I would run firs' if I could."

"Are they that bad off that they would have to sell?"

"Yes sir. I knows for a fact. Ole man Wiggins done put too much into slaves and they run off cuz he so mean."

"Ma once wrote to told me that Quakers around here bought slaves. So if it comes to that we could get that done for you. Who would know which Quaker is your owner? You could work for wages … might even buy that pretty maid of the Greens. Go see what happens. Ma says all things work for our good, right from the good book."

Tom slowly walked back to the house. He thought on the rapid political and volatile changes that had taken place. *It sure is a confusing time. Our family doesn't want to see the Union divided and yet we don't want to experience the invasion of our sister states or possibly our own.*

Tom began speaking his thoughts. "We are caught between South Carolina who will surely succeed if they have not already. And Virginia won't stand for northerners runnin' over their state. I fear North Carolina will be drawn into this trouble."

He stopped at the porch steps, looked down at the sleepy cat. "Fuzzy, my friends and cousins are about to form companies. They are all fired up to get into a fight. I'm reluctant to jump into the fray. I'm still torn between the two sides ... got friends on both sides of this issue."

Fuzzy looked up at Tom and yawned.

"You've got a full stomach so why do you care. But you know I always listen to Paw and the uncles when it comes to major life decisions. I respect my family. The cousins can declare their independence from family, and I could too. When I remember the stories Uncle Casper tells of the Mexican war, 'it ain't no berry pickin' affair.'

"Not that I'm not confident to make a decision, or join up with cousins because I'm angry as hops with Lincoln. And supply troops to invade South Carolina? I'm so upset at our sister state for starting this mess."

* * *

Adam was a great help on the farm and enjoyed the hard work. Sue, always the independent one, didn't need Pop's permission to be courted. The family became quite fond of the giant of a man. That made it easy for Sue and Adam to get better acquainted. However, Adam's loyalties belonged to the North. It was past time to depart.

Tom's concern for Lem and the new widow Wiggins distracted Tom. He explained to Adam before his departure, "I should have been a better host these last few days. Not that it mattered. Sue seemed to keep you preoccupied, when you were not in the woods or fields with Paw. With you help, Paw didn't have to be concerned with his leg. And it gave me time to help Uncle Casper on his place."

Adam gulped as though he had a big lump in his throat. "I'll miss you all. I thank you for the immeasurable hospitality I've enjoyed." He hesitated but afraid his emotions would overflow quickly added. "I'll follow Paw's advice and flag down the train at the lumber yard."

Paw Gentry, in a rare show of affection, grabbed Adam's hand in both of his. "I'll expect to see you back down here soon. You take care of yourself, you hear."

Uncle Casper piped in. "Was goin' to say the same thing. Hurry back."

* * *

The evening after Adam left, Pop called Tom aside. He had just come in from the field and was washing up on the back porch. At first Tom thought his father wanted to talk about Sue and Adam.

"Tom, I heard one of the Hardy boys talkin' about buyin' Lem from the new widow. I know you put a lot of store in that boy and his Paw, Uncle Billy. That Widow Wiggins' nephew had him plopped in irons as soon as they decided to sell. And right after he came back to help the widder out. Lem worked hard on her place. Helped her like he promised and nobody bothered him until that nephew showed up. So if you got any idea of talkin' to the Quakers, now would be a good time." Paw grunted angrily as he tossed a pan of wash water into the drainage ditch.

"I thank you Paw. I'm glad you told me. I'll get a bite to eat and then see what I can do. This might take all night. Please ask Ma to save breakfast for me."

Tom's first stop was Mason's Country Store. When he walked up to the front, two farmers standing outside the store were discussing what to plant next and when. On the inside, the loud talk centered about what local companies were to be formed. There was a lot of excitement among the three younger men. They made it sound like it was going to be a lark. Two old Mexican war veterans tried to get their attention.

One veteran yelled at the young men. "I warn you. It ain't goin' to be no 'dinner on the grounds' picnic. It will stink, and most likely last longer than you want."

Tom was amused at the reaction of the younger men.

Tom approached the store-owner with the thought he would leave a note for Mr. Quimby, the Quaker but thought better of the idea. If the note falls into the wrong hands it will look bad for Lem and me. Mason could read it.

"Mr. Mason, have you seen Mr. Quimby?"

"He was by here earlier. Don't come here much. Think he said he was goin' over to that new German farmer's place down the road a ways. He's done talked that feller into becomin' one of his friends or some such. Baumgartner was the name."

It was dark by the time he got to the Baumgartner place. The sudden deep bark of the Quaker's dog made Tom's hair stand on end. His thoughts were too consumed by his task to be aware of his surroundings. The dog startled him.

"I'm friendly, dog. I hope you are. Didn't know you lived here."

The dog rose from the porch and growled a warning as it watched Tom approach.

The door of the house swung open and a man stood in the entrance holding a lantern. "What you barkin' at Dandy? We got visitors?"

"It's me, Tom Gentry, Mr. Baumgartner. I came to talk to you about Widow Wiggins man Lem."

"I know why you're here. Me and Quimby was talkin' about it earlier, so I know. Come on in and we can talk. But you got to know, our farm's just gettin' started and it ain't been too good a year. Not much we can do."

Tom followed Mr. Baumgartner inside. Three boys carved on sticks of wood. There was a pile of shavings at their feet.

Baumgartner noticed Tom's interest in his sons' activity. "We can use them shavin's to start fires when they get finished with them table legs. What you got on your mind, Tom. How you want to fix this? I'm out of ideas."

"I don't have any money myself. I was in hopes you could at least make a deposit before you talked to the other Quakers."

"Pop." One of the boys spoke up. "You can sell my hog and use it for a deposit."

"You sure, John? You want to do that?"

"Sure do Pop. Lem fetched me out of the pond when the ice broke last winter."

"Well, its settled Tom. I'll see what I can do with the other farmers. Quimby was by earlier and would be in favor. I'll see him on the morrow. Me and him will talk to the others. What's your interest in Lem?"

"Other than his good appearance and always being friendly, everybody likes him, he has a real concern for others, like his dad Uncle Billy. He is intelligent, a hard worker, and taught me a few things about survival in the woods. My Paw used to rent him from his owner once in a while. And then there was the time I nearly got snake bit. He chopped its head off with a hoe just in time.

"Mr. Baumgartner, I do sincerely appreciate your takin' on this responsibility. My folks might be concerned so I reckon I better be on my way."

When Tom reached home he would smell dust in the air. He could see a horse in front of the house. Can't be bad news again so soon. Before he opened the door he could hear excited talk between Sue and Mom.

Sue heard Tom walk on the porch and opened the door. "Tom. We have been invited to a ball ... a real ball. Us! I can't believe it! And ... your little Indian friend from the mountains will be there."

"How can that be, Sis?"

"She studies in Asheville to be a teacher. I had written her a few times and had copied her address when we forwarded her letter to you. Kate came home with her friend Jessie. Jessie has been sick for a while and needed to come home for a week. So Kate came home with her. I'm going to write Adam and see if he can be here."

"This is too much. My head is about to explode with questions. Are they still in school? Are they released for the summer? Is she on a work-school set up or something?"

"You will have to ask her, Tom. All I could get from the Hardy boy is what I've told you. What I've figured out is Jessie wanted to study with Mrs. Ferguson. You remember our special class with her don't you? Mrs. Ferguson had moved to Asheville to be with her sick sister. Jessie's folks sent her and her brother Davy to stay with them and study. I had mentioned that to Kate in a letter."

"When is this to be and where?"

"At the Green's fancy place. Mary Ellen's folks are giving it. You remember the pretty blond headed girl you use to be stuck on? When? I almost forgot. It will be a week from tonight."

THE BALL

Mr. and Mrs. Gentry took Tom and Sue to the Green's home in the Sunday buggy.

Ma Gentry turned to look at her two children. "I know you will behave well. Enjoy yourselves and don't stay there too late. This ride should keep the dust off your shoes, skirt and trousers. The walk home should be nice, since it's cool.

"Can't think why they would want us old folks to come. I have no wish to go in that house myself. From the looks of all those buggies, it's going to be a big affair. Scoot along now and mind what we told you."

Young trees lined the buggy track to the house. The four white columns stood out in the last rays of sunlight. The brick two-story house was not more than three years old. Lamps lit the steps that led to the open doors. Fiddle music and jumbled voices could be heard. Tom glanced back to observe fashionable late arrivals.

"Tom, why would they invite us to this fine shindig? We're not in their class."

"I was thinking the same thing. Well, you are pretty and fit well in that new blue dress. Now, my suit ... well look at how my arms stick out of these sleeves. And I can't button my coat. Should have bought a new one but didn't have time. Didn't worry about it that much until now. If it were not for Kate I would turn around and go home."

"You are not about to leave brother. Just follow me."

Sue pulled up the front of her dress so she wouldn't step on the hem. The seven steps were too wide for the size of the house. At the top she turned and smiled at Tom. "Come on, you know you want to see that pretty girl from Cherokee."

No one was at the door to greet or announce arrivals. Inside, Sue stopped suddenly. Tom almost bumped into her.

She turned and spoke just loud enough for Tom to hear. "Would you look at the fancy patterns on the red walls? Must be wallpaper. And long green curtains with green rope to hold them back? I never ... must be because this is the Green family."

"They did well by the two chandeliers too. Let's head for the punch bowl. I'll taste it first just in case."

Mrs. Green spotted them and rushed to greet the pair. "Oh, I'm so glad you could come. Enjoy yourselves. Have some punch and meet some of the young folks. Of course you know most all of them already. Toodle-de-do ... must see to the rest of our guests."

The hostess was gone almost as quickly as she had arrived.

On the way to the punch bowl, they looked over the crowd.

"Sue, there are more young folk than people our parents age." Tom stopped and took hold of Sue's arm. "Oh, I get it. See those two over there in uniform. Must be the Confederate Uniform. Mr. Green is about to raise a company of boys. This is an attempt to recruit. What you want to bet?"

"No bets, brother. Go test the punch. I see a cousin that I haven't seen at church for too long. I'll find you later."

Tom approached the punch bowl but didn't quite make it. A maid handed him a small cup of cider. She figures I'm too young to try the punch. Have to tell Sue. Tom picked up a cookie and was about to take a bite when a gray uniform filled his vision. To the uniform's right a beautiful blond girl hung on his arm. Her hair was different but Mary Ellen was the same. She wore a tight-waisted white dress cut low that revealed ample bosom. Long blond curls fell on her bare shoulders. Tom refused to dwell on her beauty. The blue eyes could captivate and capture most young men in an instant.

"Tom, I would like you to meet Captain Robert Armstrong, my fiancé. He is a cousin to the Yarboroughs in Salisbury you know, so you two must be related."

Mary Ellen turned her head to the side to smile at Tom. She looked very pleased with herself. "Robert, this is Tom Gentry, an old friend of mine."

"Mr. Gentry, it is a pleasure."

"And it a pleasure to meet you, Sir"

"I noticed you are not yet in uniform. Is it your Yankee friends? Mary Ellen mentioned that's what probably is holding you back, or do your loyalties not belong to the Confederacy?"

Tom was determined he would not to be drawn into an argument. He grinned and stroked is chin. "If the Yanks try to invade our state, I'll fight. By all accounts it will be over before you experience a fight. I do have friends on both sides of the argument, to answer your question. As to my loyalty, I belong to North Carolina; I am loyal to my state."

"We still have room for boys in my company. I'll make a soldier of you in the 57^(th) North Carolina. Think it over. You will excuse us." The captain turned abruptly to Mary Ellen. "Come, my pet. It's time to get some cider."

In disgust, Tom turned to the punch bowl. "I'll never serve under that man. Who made him king of the hill?"

A girl Tom didn't know slid up to his side and spoke in a voice meant for him. "I heard tell the men in his company wanted to elect their own captain but his father wouldn't stand for it. His old man has political pull."

"I didn't know soldiers could elect their own leaders?" Tom didn't feel sociable at the moment but felt that out of courtesy he turned to face her, but he didn't recognize the girl.

"My sister-in-law wrote from Texas sayin' that a company they formed down there tried to elect their leader, but didn't happen, much the same. So I suppose it is possible. It's political anyway."

She obviously knew Tom, and continued, "Tom, we have a mutual friend. There is an old friend of yours that stands behind you a ways next to the back stairs. Do you see who I mean?"

When Tom turned toward the stairs to look, he didn't recognize her at first. She was taller than most of the girls and some of boys near her. He had always remembered that she had straight hair. Now it was wavy and as shiny as he last remembered. Her white full dress made her brown skin more obvious, especially among the other ladies. Then he noticed two boys from church talked with her. She smiled at them politely.

"I wonder if they know she is sometimes called 'Little Fawn' and is sister to Running Deer? Kate has those boys wrapped around her little finger. And she is much prettier than I remember … so beautiful and grown up, this Kathryn Little Fawn Adams."

Tom was embarrassed. He turned to see if the girl beside him had heard, but she was gone. He was startled when she looked across the room at him. Caught, it was considered impolite to stare. She raised a white-gloved hand and waved. Tom walked in her direction not conscious he had moved. Kate made a remark to the boys as they parted to allow her to proceed in his direction. Several feet from Tom people gathered to visit that blocked their way. Kate stopped, raised her arm and pointed to an open door.

They stepped through the doorway at almost the same time. There they found themselves on a side porch occupied with three other couples. Tom took hold of her two hands in his. When he looked into her dark eyes, it made him feel an excitement that he had not known. It was almost uncontrollable.

"You are even prettier than I remember. You've grown into a lovely young lady. No wonder those boys had cornered you."

"And you have grown into a handsome young man. You filled out considerably I might add, to judge from your sleeves."

They studied his jacket sleeves and laughed.

"Oh, I shouldn't poke fun. You are obviously not the skinny boy I used to know."

"I don't wear a suit enough to take notice. And hard work added some weight. Noticed you didn't lack for attention when you were standing by the stairs."

"They were just curious, I think. Some of the girls think of me as a well-to-do farm girl because my skin is darker than theirs. They are appalled that I spend so much time in the sun. They had rather hide under bonnets and parasols."

"I was about to say the same thing, about girls who stay out in the sun. You will notice a few farm girls and boys about this evening, and I find this unusual. Aren't balls usually for the upper class? I'm almost certain this party is meant to recruiting and politics ... and so the farm girls might look for healthy husbands."

"They will have to hurry. From all the talk, most of the boys are determined to join a company and fight for glory and honor."

Kate looked at Tom more intently in the weak lamplight. "I hope they find what they want. Tom, do you intend to join too?"

"Am I to understand from your tone you that you do not approve?"

"When pressed for a decision, where will your loyalties lie and what will you do?" She didn't want to be perceived as being intrusive, Kate added, "Just a matter of interest. Tom, I think my family is staunch Unionist, but the Cherokees I know are not."

"If North Carolina is threatened I will be bound to bear arms against the North. I don't see any other choice."

Tom became conscious he still held her hands. He didn't want to release them for fear of breaking the spell that came over him when he looked in her eyes.

I need to keep talking. "I don't really want to fight because I have too many friends on both sides, and relatives in the North. I don't feel as passionate about the political argument as most of my friends, or that captain I just met. But to protect our state I think we will have to stop the North in Virginia. They will have to come through us to get to South Carolina. Lincoln called for 75,000 troops to invade the South. When I think about it, that's a slap in the face. How can we reconcile our differences now? Kate, let's not concern ourselves with talk of war and politics."

Tom took a deep breath and pulled her closer. "And you asked what I would do if pressed. At present I feel pressed to kiss you, if there are no objections? I know I'm being too bold, so please forgive me."

"You're certainly bolder than when you were in the mountains. A handsome young man has never kissed me or a homely one either. Since it is you, I see no harm."

His lips on hers interrupted her. Oh how wonderful and exciting. Tom wanted to hold her but felt restrained. The touch of her lips would have to suffice for now. This tender moment would be remembered forever.

"Kate, I'm not really this forward. I suppose I've wanted to kiss you since ..." Tom tried to think of something clever but couldn't. "... since I saw you by the stairs."

"Were you about to say something about some previous meeting like down by the river? You were not so inclined when you stayed with your Uncle. It wouldn't have been because of my big brother, would it?"

"It probably would. Besides, I couldn't have caught you back then. I don't think you could outrun me in this pretty dress. I'll bet you could still outrun me or your brother dressed like you used to, when you ran to the river."

"It doesn't bother you that some of the girls and gents shun this part Cherokee? What of the other girls? Didn't my friend from school tell me there was a blond you were interested in? Could that be the one that hangs on that captain?"

"That's the one and that was months before I went to study law when I was interested. It was just a temporary flirtation on her part when none of the other boys were handy … the ones with property. It didn't take long for this old farm boy to realize I was a temporary convenience. As to what others might think, well, to look down their long noses irritates me. Unfortunately they don't know you. I know you Kate, and there is no pretense about you. You're too good for those that look down their noses and judge."

Kate put her hand on his chest. "You've grownup a heap, my father would say. I hope you don't find yourself in the fix he's in, but then I think you have. He's caught between neighbors that might persuade him to join with the secessionists. Our Chief, Will Thomas, has talked about the formation of a Cherokee Company. That will include many of our white neighbors I'm sure. This was mentioned in mother's last letter. When Lincoln asked for troops to put down the rebellion it angered everybody."

"Yes, I'm in the same predicament. I will have to join the troops soon."

"Tom, my maw persuaded Paw to let me go to Asheville to study with Mrs. Ferguson. That's the reason, in part, why I was able to be here tonight. The real reason I think, was to get me away from the Goins boys. Most of our men folk are preparing for war, and when they go, there will be no protection from them for me."

"I heard the rest of the story about Jessie from Sue. Kate, listen to that. The fiddles now play a waltz. At least I can dance to that; can you? If so we can talk war later, much later."

Kate smiled and nodded in response. Tom gently took her arm as if it might break. They were soon on the dance floor with the others.

Tom should not have been surprised how well she followed. She's good at everything she tries.

"Did they teach you how to dance at school?"

"No, but one of the girls taught some of us. For a farm boy, you step out very well. Oh! I don't want to make fun of farm boys. As I said before, you've grown into a handsome man and I'm trying to get acquainted with the fact. I remember ..."

"You don't have to mention that awkward boy store helper. I did manage to trip one of the Goins boys with my broom. He almost had you."

"I always knew that was the cause for that red and blue spot on your face, and for days. I never got around to thanking you properly for your assistance. That was a dangerous chance on your part with those mountain boys. You know how the three of them fight for each other, and for little reason."

I won't tell her that Slim nearly cut me with his big knife when he caught me on the trail later. He could still carve me up if he had a chance.

"You did thank me in one of your letters. We both found ourselves too busy in school to write much. Let's get some cool cider, if there's any left."

"You were bold to kiss me. You know, my paw didn't kiss Maw until after they were married?" Tom looked surprised and couldn't think of anything to say.

"Don't look so pained. I'm glad you did. It means it was special. Let's promise to write more faithfully. Perhaps this will be a short war like they say.

"Tom, I see by my friend Jessie's manner she is tired and ready to go home. You know she was ill for a time and tires easily. It is time to say our goodbyes. This has been an evening to always remember. Will you walk with me and meet her before we leave?"

* * *

On the way home, Tom ran the conversations with Kate over and over in his head. He started to mumble to himself. "Tom old boy, what chance do you have when she goes home for the summer? Long distance courtships do happen. Seems to work for Sue. Too bad Adam couldn't be here. Then there's this war a brewin'. I have to decide if I am to join a company and which one? What does my conscience tell be about this?"

He kicked a stone in disgust. *I need to have more confidence in myself. Ma would say, "It's not in yourself you need to place your faith. Place your faith where it belongs."*

"I will not join Captain Armstrong's company, distant cousin or not. If my cousin, Joe Boy up in Wilkes joins, I'll go with him. And if Kate is as interested in me as I am in her, she will wait. I will not give up easily."

Tom stopped in his tracks. "I forgot Sue!"

He wheeled around to retrace his steps. He jumped, startled that she was only several paces behind. He could see the grin on her face in the moonlight.

"Oops! I'm shamefully sorry Sis. I guess I was too pre-occupied."

"I wondered if you would ever remember your little sister. That pretty girl sure got your head mixed up. She's got a spell on you for sure. I assume that was Kate ... Was that Kathryn ... Little Fawn?"

"It was. I will begin to court her seriously now, mostly by mail."

"It looks like you have started, to court I mean. She is what you would call a beauty. No wonder she's got your head turned. Mary Ellen can't hold a candle to her."

"I'm glad you think so. She is more sensible than Mary Ellen will ever be. Everyone that knows Kate would say not false or pretentious. What more could I ask for in a girl? I would shout hallelujah, but it would wake up the neighbor's mules, chickens and such. If the roosters started crowin', and the mules carryin' on, everybody would think it's time to get up and start the day. Might mess up their head clocks for a week."

THE INEVITABLE ... WAR

Most of North Carolina wanted to stay in the Union and most didn't see Lincoln's election as a threat to the state. Governor Ellis was condemned because he advocated seceding from the Union. Take a "Watch and See" attitude was the argument those used against leaving the Union. When Zeb Vance became governor, he was a vigorous advocate for staying in the Union and was a voice of compromise; however, the Washington Peace Conference of March 1861 resulted in failure. The Watch and See advocates could not match the emotions of the secessionist movement and the die was cast. Lincoln asked for troops to invade the South. And the April 15th attack on Ft. Sumter didn't help the cause of the pro-unionists. This added fuel to the fire to those that wanted out.

Officially, North Carolina left the Union slowly and with sorrow. She was the last Southern State to do so. North Carolina felt, as did Gov. Vance, that the United States Government didn't have the right to coerce a state. To add to the dilemma, North Carolina didn't want to fight against their Southern neighbors.

Tom contemplated the State's impending problem. The unsealed letter before him he that had written to Kate revealed his state of mind.

Kate, the Gentry family has come to accept the inevitable, as do most of our neighbors. My decision to stay home for the present doesn't sit well with some of our neighbors. Most of them are becoming more hostile day by day. It bothers me that Ma no longer wants to go with Paw to the store. Church is no longer pleasant for her and she's always been religious about her Sundays. The polite South, at least in my world, is no longer polite, gentle and friendly.

After Tom fed the stock, he washed up on the back porch. While he washed, his parents talked about a letter from their Western relations. It was apparent Cousin Joe Boy had joined the 26th North Carolina under Col Zeb Vance. If he heard correctly, some of the mountain boys around Wilkesboro and especially Ashe County would be part of this outfit.

By the time Tom entered the house, he had made up his mind. "Folks, I have an announcement to make. I had told Captain Armstrong that when North Carolina was threatened I would join to protect my state. As you know I want no part of that Captain. I think I'll become a part of the 26th with Joe Boy. If I don't become a tanner or another trade the Confederacy considers essential to the war effort, I will be conscripted anyway. The North has too many boys to choose from. Conscription is inevitable. Paw, you and Uncle Casper can handle the farm without me. You did it while I was away at school."

Tom wanted to honor his father and felt he had somehow stepped out of bounds, added. "I realize I don't need your permission to join the army, but I would like your blessing." Tom stood politely and patiently and awaited his father's response. He knew what it would be.

"You're of age and a man now. If you are lookin' for my blessing, you have it. I'm not in favor of this war. We didn't ask for it but we got it. Just remember your upbringing and remain faithful to your convictions. Listen to your conscience. It is almost always right."

Paw rose from his chair and held out his hand. "We will miss you. It's not like when you went to be with your kin in Philadelphia. You just take care of yourself."

Ma pushed herself up from her chair where she sewed. She quickly embraced him, then pushed away to look in his eyes. "We will always pray for you. When will you be leavin?"

"Soon as I can pack a few things."

Sue entered the room and folded her hands in front. "You might be fightin' against Adam and some of your Yankee friends … even Cousin Ronald you know?"

"Can't be helped, Sue. I smell some of your cooking. Think I'll wait until morning."

* * *

The house was awakened by Paw's angry voice. Tom opened his eyes. It was still dark except for light that flickered on the bedroom wall.

"It's light from a fire outside." He jumped out of bed in a hurry. Tom could hear his father run to the back door. By the time Tom got there, Paw had the back door open. He was surprised to see Pop with a shotgun in his hands.

There were three figures around the fire. They were about to run after they set the chicken house on fire.

"You put out that fire and skedaddle, unless you want some shot in your mangy trousers," Paw called out.

Tom didn't have a weapon but knew the three arson-ists didn't know it. "Make that two shotguns aimed at your trousers. I recognize you Gimpy. You got no call to do this."

"Next time we'll have guns, Yankee lover. I'll bet my last gold piece you will be in jail or marchin' to a Confed-erate drum in a day or two."

"What you call me? I'm practically in Col. Vance's regi-ment now. What do you think of that? You better kick that hay away from the hen house now, or I'll let fly with a charge of shot. The law won't look kindly on you settin' fire to a Confederate Soldier's property."

Two of the figures kicked burnt straw away from the hen house. One turned to pick up a bucket of water out of the chicken yard. He threw it against the wood and straw that smoldered. Gimp just stood where he was and stared back at Tom. Paw cocked the shotgun. Gimp turn to find his two friends gone. His sullen face couldn't be seen in the dark as he stuffed his hands deep in his pock-ets and stomped off.

"You better check the shed, Tom. We don't want it blazin' up durin' the night." Tom obediently stepped off the porch to check the shed. He placed his hand against the damp wall, satisfied that all was well. When he stepped back in the house, Tom couldn't help chuckling. Paw waited for him, slapped him on the back and laughed. Father and son returned to their beds, chuckled as they went.

* * *

Young men, such as Tom, can be adventurous and bold; however, it was not enough to soften the goodbyes to his parents, Uncle and Aunt ... and Sue. That was only the second time Tom could recall that Sue threw her arms around his neck. Tom noted that both of them had tears in their eyes. To even the most casual observer it would appear that this was a close family, and indeed it was.

Once again his father grabbed Tom's hand and held it in a firm grip. "Take care of yourself, son. Remember your mother's charge last night. Let your conscience be your guide but governed by your faith. Don't take on the bad habits that some soldiers do. We believe you will make good judgments about what is right and wrong."

Ma looked stern. She was determined to avoid tears. "Here's the burlap bag with your next meal. You'll find some clean clothes in the bottom. They should hold you till you get a uniform." With the last remark she pushed him toward the door. "Now, be off with you and don't forget to write."

"If I'm as home sick as I was when I went off to school you will get a bunch of mail."

* * *

The Raleigh train station was busy the afternoon Tom arrived. He felt alone and wished he were some home. There was no one from home that he cared to join with. Most of them had already joined. *Cousin Joe Boy said in his note he would join one of the mountain companies, but which one? He had a friend in the Wilkes Volunteers. That could be the one. That would be the place to start. Like me, he didn't want to be under a captain from home.* When he examined his cousin's note again, it described Crab Tree as the place where they were to train.

He spotted a young girl that sold what looked like ham biscuits. His attempt to reach her through a crowd of people became impossible. A wagon drawn by two dark brown mules stopped in front to him. The black driver on the rig looked around, as if he expected somebody.

When he made eye contact with Tom, he smiled. "You be lookin' for the Crab Tree Camp? If you is, throw your bag in back and hop in. Soon as Corporal Sims gets here we'll will be a-goin'?"

"I must look like a lost recruit. Thanks for the information and the offer of a ride. Would that be Corporal Sims coming there?"

"That be him ... his own self."

The man that approached them wore a new uniform with corporal stripes on the sleeve. When he spotted Tom, the Corporal broke into a broad grin. "We got ourselves a new recruit Sam?"

"Yes suh. I believes we does."

"They call me Corporal Sims. Larry Sims to be exact. Just call me Larry. By what handle do you go by?"

"Tom Gentry from near Lexington. Suppose I'm just plain Tom."

"Well, let's just climb on this here chariot and sashay on down to the camp, plain Tom. You didn't come with the outfit from up your way? Must be a reason."

"Think I can explain between bumps and wheel ruts if they don't give me the hiccups. I had rather be with my cousin from Wilkesboro. That was mostly because I didn't want to serve under a certain Captain from up home. Have you run across a boy by the name of Joe Boy Gentry?"

"Nope, not yet. Well we got us a good Captain I reckon. Only met him once. The men say he is a good leader, this Captain Carmichael. You sound educated, Tom. You had much schoolin'?"

"I did go to school and started to study law. That was for about a year before they called me home when my Paw was hurt. You must've had some schoolin' … made corporal."

Larry interrupted with a chuckle. "My Maw taught me much. She was educated and wanted me to be too. I spent more time in the one room schoolhouse than I really wanted to at the time. In fact, my Maw taught me most of what I know about history and literature. If I sound too educated around the boys from home, they think I'm puttin' on airs. You know what I mean?"

"I know what you mean, from personal experience mostly. Larry, do you do much target practice, drill and such? How long will it be before I get a uniform?"

"Sam, he is real anxious, ain't he? As to target practice, we don't have that much powder or loads right now. Most of us mountain boys know how to shoot already. I was raised near Asheville before my Pap moved us near Wilkesboro so I reckon I shoot pretty fair. Afraid we only got a few muskets, rifled muskets and shotguns we brought from home. You might have to drill with a stick. And we will do a lot of drillin'. Uniforms? They are right scarce now. I'll see what I can dig up."

"Well, here we are. Give Sam a hand there and I'll fetch us more help. Here comes help now. Tom, you make a right smart impression on folks. I'll bet you would make a good officer what with your education and such. Would you like to be an officer? I think the boys would take to you."

"Yes, I think I would like that. I'm not sure I would want the responsibility right away. I had hoped my education would make a difference. There is so much to learn and information I still need. Can you teach me some about army life to get me started, Larry? You're not fun-nin' me are you?"

"Well, might be just a little, but for truth I think you will make a good leader. Me and the boys will teach you all we know. The rest will be up to the officers. Are you willin' to lead men and take orders yourself?"

"I'm more than willing to learn."

"I reckon most of us won't know everything until we smell gun smoke, Tom. My Pap fought the Mexicans and Grand-Paw fought in the war of independence. They all allowed you don't know your own grit until the men around you start to fall. That will be true of us I reckon."

"Now's the time for you to report to that tall Lieuten-ant ... the one that came out of that building. I'll see to your other needs. See that tent with the pot steamin' in front? You can share the tent with Charlie and me. He cooks real good."

* * *

Tom took to drill like he was made for army life. In a couple days he caught up with the others. He did his best to be a good soldier, first to form in line, obeyed commands, and stayed with the formation. The company of mountain boys was easy to get along with. Everyone seemed to fit, especially those that shared the same cook fire. It helped a great deal to have a friend like Larry.

Larry, Charlie and Tom were eating their supper when Tom started to ask Larry a question.

You ever run into the Goins gang up in your neck of the woods?

"Goins? Does he have two or three brothers and an old man meaner than a cornered he-coon?"

"Must be. Their reputation west of Asheville is well known, and it's not good."

"I know about them boys, Tom. My Pap warned me to stay clear. From now on boys, call me anything except Larry. Better call me Corporal around the officers and sergeants."

The second Sunday, Tom sat in front of the tent and attempted to write a letter home. He had just completed a letter to Kate that he intended to send with the letter home. Her letter to him had taken a week to reach him. Now they would know each other's address, at least for the present.

While he continued to compose the letter, he suddenly realized that footsteps of two individuals had paused in front of him. Glancing up he realized that Captain Carmichael and a young Lieutenant were looking at him. Embarrassed, Tom quickly laid aside the letter and started to stand.

"Sit easy soldier. You earned a day of rest, or at least a half a day before we drill again this afternoon. Since a couple of the boys mentioned that you were educated and wanted to become an officer, me and the Lieutenant here, we've watched you. We agree with the boys. Unfortunately the Officers Corps for this company is full. There's a need for another sergeant. You could make a good one. It's up to you. What do you think, Gentry?"

Tom rose to his feet when the Captain spoke. He didn't think it was appropriate to sit, while his superiors were speaking to him. After the little talk, Tom cleared his throat to help gain his composure. "Sir, I consider it an honor and will do my best to do my duty."

"This is no more than we could expect. Consider yourself a sergeant. You may well earn those stripes before it's over. I suspect this war will last longer than most people expect."

Tom saluted the two officers. They returned the salute, and then continued their walk through the tent area.

"Tom, ole son, here is somethin' else to write home about. I had come to learn sergeants had to have more experience … what a surprise."

He immediately felt conspicuous, like someone watched. It was a sense that comes when someone knows he's observed, and would serve him well. Tom jerked his head to see who was behind. There was someone. Sims and Charlie grinned from ear to ear.

"Charlie, I was a-feared we had lost our tent mate there for a spell. Reckon we're good enough to share a tent and victuals with a new sergeant?"

"I reckon we can at that, Corporal. It might put us in good with the rest of the boys to have a real sergeant sleepin' in our tent and eatin' out of our cookin' pot. We can still make room for you Tom, if you're a mind?"

"You have my gratitude. And I thank you for the offer." Tom thought for a moment, still taken aback by recent developments. "Don't I have a bunk in this tent already?"

Corporal Sims cut his eyes at Charlie and stroked his chin. "Well, I was thinkin' like Charlie. It would be to our benefit to have a sergeant close by to look after our interests. We can't push you out now, so we wouldn't consider losin' this advantage. Besides, Charlie and me just like to have a little funnin' at the expense of sergeants and officers. But you don't have to worry cause we will adopt you as our favorite sergeant."

Corporal Sims suddenly rose to sit on his haunches and looked at Tom questionably. "What about that cousin of yours that's in our outfit? Did you want to share a tent with him?"

"Been so busy trying to be a soldier, I almost forgot Joe Boy. Only got a glimpse of him a few times. I will need to explain the situation with him. Not even sure he knows I'm here."

"You might spot him when we form up this afternoon. I couldn't begin to tell where he might be in this gatherin' of boys. Why don't you finish your letter to your sweetheart? Plenty of time to find your cousin later."

Tom felt his face grow hot at the mention of his letter to Kate. He realized how very much he wanted to tell her of his promotion. It thrilled him she had included her school address in her letter. It must have been written the day he left.

The letter to Kate was carefully reopened. Much of what he had written was the same things he told his parents. He spoke of the drills, food and fitted with a uniform shirt and cap. The trousers he wore from home would have to suffice. There were not enough uniforms to go around. Tom didn't mention the kind of food they subsisted on, even though they fared better than most. Charlie was indeed a good cook, the envy of the other tents.

When they formed for drill, Tom looked for Cousin Joe Boy. After a bit he spotted him. Tom waved but his cousin didn't seem to notice.

To stand at attention with a stick galled Tom. Order arms seemed almost pointless. All the men with sticks were just as displeased with their weapons. There were a few men with muskets and shotguns from home. *Wouldn't be surprised to see a flintlock. Someday I'll have a real weapon.*

After the evening meal Tom attempted to finish his letter to his folks. Sims and Charlie were soon asleep but

Tom was too tired to try. He needed a distraction for a while.

Dear Mom and Dad,

We drilled to day as usual. Must have marched enough to make it home and back. I figured that if I got here in August it would be cooler than July. Except for rain it has been terribly hot. A new boy from Union County, named Lonzo something, came by. He is friendly and likes to joke around like Larry. The new boy and his friends were encouraged to pitch a tent next to us and share our cooking pot. Some argumentative fellows complained about Charlie's cooking and had been threatened with his big spoon. When they moved on the Union Co. boys took their spot.

I'm glad you for forwarded Kate's letter. Thank you. It is good to have her address. Yes, I like her very much. You were right about Mary Ellen, Ma. She thinks her family is too good for the likes of us. She got herself a Captain and wouldn't settle for anything less.

There are rumors that Gen. Burnside has plans to invade North Carolina. That bit of gossip trickled down from a runner Sims knows. The runner just came in from the telegraph office. It appears our spies in Washington are doing a fine job.

I have seen Joe Boy, but I haven't had a chance to talk to him. I thought about recommending him for corporal in the sharp shooters, but another man from Union County got the position.

I'm finally sleepy so will finish this and write another later.

Your son, Tom

* * *

Several times since news of the battle on the Outer Banks, the 26th had been marched to the trains but called back. The Confederate forts had fallen. Eastern North Carolina was threatened. Some men had already been loaded on trains for the east. News of a Union fleet seen off the coast put Tom's company on the move. The men were ready for battle. All of them were anxious to protect their State. Tom and the rest of his company were moved toward the coast. They had to move and put up tents again near Goldsboro. From there they expected to move to the coast.

On the second day a shipment of new Enfields arrived. They were distributed among the men until the shipment was exhausted. Tom took his and then saw the new man from Union County didn't have one.

"What's your name, private? Sorry we been so busy ... oh, you're Lonzo from Union County. I apologize again. These are exciting times, Lonzo."

"Yep, Sergeant. That's me and it's gettin' excitin'. Looks like they ran out of muskets before they got to me. Think you could round me up a weapon of some kind, Sergeant. I noticed two boys in one company was totin' pikes. Can you believe that? Could come in handy if they face cavalry."

"You know your history, Lonzo." Tom studied the situation and looked around for someone that might help.

"Corporal Sims, can you spare a minute?"

"Sure Tom. What you need from this old thief? Lonzo here in need of a musket?"

"Yes and I'm tempted to give him mine if I had my pistol. Left it home for my brother when he comes home. Be too late to write and send for it, if they would let me have one."

"Well, ole son. I believe sergeants are permitted to carry pistols. And here is a bit of news you could use. Captain Carmichael posted a notice that he has two pistols and would sell one. You figure givin' your musket to Lonzo? The Captain's extra pistol is the answer. What do you think?"

"The musket is heavier than that stick I got used to. Pistols are lighter then muskets when it comes to marches. Sounds real appealing, Sims."

"You better work on it the first chance you get. The Captain let it be known he would sell it to the first person to show a real interest."

Tom approached the Captain's tent. It was the first time he had been in the officer's area and it made him uncomfortable. But he was resolved to buy the weapon if it were still available. Captain Carmichael sat in a camp chair in front of his tent. The Lieutenant Tom had seen with the Captain sat on his right and another officer he didn't know sat on his left. At first it appeared the three were smoking. But only the two Lieutenants held pipes. Tom came to attention as soon as the officers noticed him.

"What do you have on your mind, Sergeant?"

"Captain Carmichael Sir, do you still have that pistol for sale?"

"Yes I do, and you're the first to come askin'. It's almost new and shoots better than most. You take it and try it for a spell and then we can settle on a price ... a fair price for truth. This one I'm sellin' is one I bought; the other one was a gift from my folks. They didn't know I already had one. Just don't shoot yourself in the leg with it."

THE PRICE OF WAR

It was time for Tom to post new guards around the officer's area. Charlie and Lonzo's turn had come up so Tom walked with them. He was about to post them when the Captain's aggravated voice startled them. The conversation was one sided and it was not apparent who else was involved. The guards being relieved walked away, and the relief fell to without a word. Tom hesitated long enough to listen.

"Gentleman, after Union General Butler captured the forts on the Outer Banks, we can expect the rest of the 26th will be on the move. The forts were under Henry Wise, if you didn't know. We lost 2,500 men, wounded, dead or captured. Our boys were overrun by Federals. Fellers, you know what to expect. It's well known that the Union wants to control Hatteras inlet. The word is General Burnside will follow up, venture on into our fair state. Don't know why Butler can't do it. So, we'll soon see battles near Roanoke Island, if they're not fightin' there already."

"I'm only a Captain, but as I see it, we can't lose control of shippin' in and out of Albemarle, Pamlico or Currituck sounds. If we don't stop him, Burnside will capture

New Bern, follow the railroad to Goldsboro and cut the railroad lifeline to Wilmington."

* * *

Tom sat between Lonzo and Jason, another friend from Union County. "Can you give me a little room for my writing hand fellers?"

The men shifted to give Tom more room. Lonzo grumbled, "You goin' to write your sweetheart or folks on this contrary movin' rickety ole train, Sarge? Good luck is all I got to say."

"Thank you for your sacrifice. I'll remember you in my will. Would an extra canteen be sufficient? Or the first one to my body gets my pistol?"

He got no further response from the men. Tom started to write.

Dear Mom and Dad.

At present we are on our way to New Bern, down on the coast. Our company is to join the rest of Col. Vance's 26th and help defend the town from Blue Coats. We got another name for them but I won't mention it here since I've already got all the lectures from Mom and Sis stored up about how not to absorb army language.

This train rumbles and shakes something awful. I hope and pray it stays on the tracks. We got on in Raleigh with Joe Boy. He is still sore at me because I made sergeant. I thought I would at least make Lieutenant, because of my education. I do hope to finish my law studies but with all the marching here and back, not to mention drills (and new responsibilities) there is little opportunity. So, I sent the rest of my books home before we left Raleigh.

We feel more than prepared to meet the enemy, and we will push them into the sea. When we got the report that Gen. Butler's troops invaded Roanoke Island, we were ready to fight. Some of us were held back in reserve until the Union fleet was spotted. Col. Vance sent word to the Captain that we were to join them as quickly as possible. These mountain boys that came with Joe Boy are anxious to prove that they know how to shoot. Looks like they're going to get the chance very soon, to judge from Burnside's activities off the coast.

We are about to stop. I do hope to get off. My backside is sore. There are no seats in this freight car. And the Lieutenant just called me to have the men unload and form up … must run.

March 13th.

I will start this again. We marched to the Croatan Breastworks. That is what the Captain called it. Just heard an officer yell. A dispatcher is leaving so I will give him this letter. We will soon be very busy. Pray for us.

Your Obedient Son, Tom

Before Tom and his company could get settled into their defensive position, shells started to fall. The explosions made a terrible racket … a terrifying experience for the new men. He wanted to duck when he heard shells come overhead but wanted to show bravery before the men. Only an officer or two and the Sergeant Major had experienced battle in the Mexican War. They were probably the only ones.

Heavy rain began to fall. Tom heard the Captain yell at the Lieutenants. "I'm afraid we will be cut off. We needed to make a concerted effort for a stiffer defense somewhere else."

It was soon apparent the Captain had received orders from Col. Vance: "Abandon this defense and follow me. We'll move to a position on the right flank to support the 33rd North Carolina."

"You sergeants have our boys form up quick and in good order." The Captain added under his breath, "if that's possible to do under the circumstance?"

Soldiers responded to commands and grabbed their equipment. They all scurried to avoid the shells. Soon they were formed into orderly lines. The drills had produced good results, despite the limited time they had to train.

Tom noted a gap in the line where the new defense made a bend. When he looked around for a way to fill the gap, he spotted a brick kiln. *I hope the officers noticed that break in the defense. It's a weak defense spot but might work.*

A strange clamor made him turn. He was startled to see a ragged bunch of men on his left armed with shotguns, clubs, and shovels. One man carried an ax, no, several carried axes. "What is that group of men, Lieutenant?"

"Sergeant, I do believe they are called militia. They don't have much trainin'. Don't know what to expect from them poor devils. General Branch was only able to muster about four thousand men, and I'm told the Federals have twice that many. We got our work cut out for us, Sergeant."

In short order, more shells and shot whistled over their heads. Most of the militia panicked and fled. Some of the regulars started to flee, but the Lieutenant stood in their way.

Tom followed his example. "You're not goin' to leave the good Lieutenant and me to carry the battle by ourselves. What will the folks back home say about you?"

The few scared soldiers stopped and waited for someone to tell them what to do next. The Lieutenant waved his sword for Tom's company to join the rest of the 26th. Tom again followed the Lieutenant's lead, but since he had no sword, he waved his pistol.

There was so much noise and smoke it was almost impossible to communicate. Mud had become another enemy. He was tempted to find shelter in a small depression for no more than three boys. A man in front stumbled that reminded him of his responsibility. Tom caught him by the arm and pushed him forward. A shell burst over their heads. It sent a piece of hot metal through his shirt, across his chest, and the outside of his left arm. At first he didn't feel pain. There was too much excitement in the heat of battle.

Tom waved his pistol and shouted, charged ahead to move and encourage the men He did this as much to keep up his own courage. Someone fell against his legs. The badly wounded man pinned him to the ground. When he pulled himself free, pain shot through his left arm. It was then he noticed the blood on his chest and arm. Tom looked to his right in time to see a Bluecoat charge Sims with a bayonet. Sims struggled with another big Bluecoat and didn't see the danger. Tom raised his pistol and pulled the trigger, but it didn't fire.

Tom yelled a warning loud as he could, charged the last few feet to intercept the Bluecoat. The enemy heard the yell and the bayonet turned on him. Tom used his pistol to parry the bayonet and grabbed the soldier's musket. The injured left arm was of little help. The Bluecoat easily wrestled the musket free and raised it to use on Tom's head. To compensate for his weakened condition, he charged into the Bluecoat and knocked him on the head with the barrel of his pistol. Both combatants forward movement carried them to the ground.

The pain in his arm made him dizzy. He rose to his knees anyway, shouting, "I have me a prisoner. Someone take him off my hands for I'm wounded."

Before he reached his feet, Tom was struck on the side of the head by a spent minié ball.

When Tom regained conscious, he realized his two friends Sims and Charlie held him up. They dragged him to the end of a train trestle.

"How long I've been like this?"

"Not long. Maybe thirty minutes or longer. We thought you was dead for a bit. Reckon you saved ole Corporal Sims bacon. I should thank you. We got to look after our favorite sergeant don't we Charlie?"

"Fellers, sure is smoky. Smells like burning tar or ..."

"We just crossed a burnin' trestle. Not goin' to leave it for the Yanks."

"No wonder my feet felt so hot. My trouser legs look a bit scorched too. Turn me loose. Let's see if I can walk on my own."

He felt weak and tired but still tried to walk. With some difficulty he was able to put one foot in front of the other. "I don't have my musket. What happened boys? Where is my weapon?"

"You gave it away, remember? I've got your pistol. You lost a lot of blood, Sergeant Tom, ole friend. You are goin' to be out of it for a few days. Don't you agree Charlie?"

Tom lapsed into unconsciousness again. When finally awake, he experienced a wonderful and comfortable peace. He started to daydream about home, until jarred to reality.

I'm on a miserable train again. I started a wonderful dream. Thank goodness it wasn't the nightmares I used to have about that mountain man Slim. Maybe I'll have to face that another night, but it's good I haven't had that nightmare lately.

The train swayed and someone groaned. *To think I use to want a ride on these things.*

"Take it slow young feller. You must've taken quite a lump on your head? You been drillin' and marchin' men the last hour, orders and such."

"Where am I going and who put me here?"

"A couple friends of yours put you in here with the rest of us wounded. We're headin' to Raleigh. Goin' to put you in a hospital there. All the bad wounded we had to drop off at Goldsboro. They had about all they could take. They said some had to be taken to tents this side the river."

Tom looked around to see who else he might know. Light filtered through the cracks but didn't reveal anyone he knew at first. But then he spotted Captain Robert Armstrong, Mary Ellen's new husband. The man recognized him but he couldn't talk. It looked to Tom like the man was dying.

The man who had been talking to Tom continued. "There are two from the 33rd North Carolina. Never knew their names. Could be there are others from my company in the other cars, or worse. They might be back in Goldsboro where the more seriously wounded are treated. Poor fellers might not survive this train ride. Not sure I'm will?"

He looked around to see if any one heard him. The train made so much noise it didn't matter.

"Oh boy!" Tom felt sick. "I'm suffering shock? The smells and this rockin' ship of a train. Fellers, I'm about to give in to be sick." He avoided feet and legs of the wounded as he made his made a dash for the door.

One man with a leg wound stood to open the railroad car door. This permitted Tom to stick his head out the door. The look on Tom's face and his hand over his mouth told the story. The fresh air that blew on his face helped considerably.

I remember Willie got sick when hit on the head by a flying pulley. The rope that broke was older than we thought. We thought he was a goner.

The wounded man that opened the door held Tom's arm. "You feelin' better, Sergeant?"

"Think I am. You know, I wonder if I was really unconscious, or so tired I could just have gone to sleep on my feet, with all the marchin' and heat of battle? I'll let my head hang our here a little longer."

Cold rain started to beat on his face. It made him feel better. He pulled himself back in the car. "No need to get too wet."

Tom tried to sleep, but just about the time he dozed off, the train stopped and someone shouted, "Get off if you want to relieve yourself."

He followed a man on a crude crutch. When the man dropped to the ground, he rolled over with a groan. Tom sat on the edge of the doorway before he dropped to the ground. It was a useless attempt to favor the throb in his arm.

Tom intended to help the soldier with the crutch, but the pain in his arm made him stagger against the train.

A soldier with a bandage around his hand came to the crippled man's aid.

"Hello, Cousin Tom. Looks like you got yourself wounded too."

Tom turned to see Joe Boy approach from another car. Joe Boy held his bloody bandaged left arm.

"Should've had my wing put in a sling. There was too many wounded for them to doctor. We might be the lucky ones, Cousin."

"Well, I'm glad you're not any worse off. Do you know how we made out in the battle? I was unconscious or asleep through a good part of it."

"Me and a bunch of the company, along with Col. Vance himself, nearly got trapped and cut off. We ran through some swamp and came to this here river, the Trent I believe. Most of us swam across but two couldn't make it ... must of drowned. Col. Vance was able to swim his horse across, after some coaxing and persuasion. My shoes got wet, but didn't take time to take them off. I slipped and fell on somebody's bayonet. That was after most of the boys dropped theirs before they crossed. Don't that take the cake? I dodge a passel of minié balls and fell on a bayonet and sliced my arm. How the battle went? I think we lost this one Cousin. Your head and arm don't look too good. Hope you get good treatment."

Tom was about the thank Joe Boy for his concern when the train whistle blew. A lieutenant shouted it was time to get back on board. Tom, with the help of another soldier and his good arm, they hoisted the man with the crutch into the car.

Before he climbed up himself, Tom held out his hand to Joe Boy. "You take good care of yourself and don't let them spoil you in the hospital. If you get a chance, tell your folks we're determined we'll be all right."

"I'll do that Cousin Sergeant Tom. You do the same about me when you write your folks. We better be a gettin' so they can patch us up to go back to fightin'."

It is more difficult to get back in the railroad car than getting out. *I'm weaker than I thought. It's goin' to take more than a few days before I'm fit.*

The soldier with the wounded leg and another with a bandage around his head reached to pull Tom back in the car.

A private was about to close the door but Tom motioned for him to stop.

"Would you leave it open half way? It would do all of us some good and pull some of the bad smells out of here." The private that held the door stopped and left the door half open. When the private turned to find a seat, Tom could see that the soldier's trousers were split and he had a bandaged thigh.

Since Tom's train stopped in a curve, it was easy to see that another train approached from the rear before they began to move again. After a few minutes they could hear the other train stop. Tom and the wounded private observed the other train. Soon armed soldiers disembarked and were followed by men in blue.

"Sergeant, it looks like they are transferring prisoners to our train." A few of the walking wounded, overcome by curiosity, joined Tom. They watched the handful of prisoners walk past. The wounded in the car greeted them with a mixture of angry comments.

Tom thought one of the prisoners looked familiar. "Could that be the Yankee I clobbered over the head with my pistol?"

The Bluecoat looked up at Tom. There was a brief moment of recognition. Before Tom could nod at the man he looked away.

The evening of the third day Tom and the others arrived. The walking wounded followed ambulances and moved to a makeshift hospital that smelled like a tobacco warehouse.

Lucky I wasn't put in a tent, but I must have been checked over in one, but I just can't remember. He fell asleep soon after they placed him in a bed … the first bed in months.

The next morning he awoke to see an elderly gentleman standing over him holding a stack of bandages. The man didn't try to talk, which suited Tom at the moment. The gentleman proceeded to remove Tom's bandage, and then poured rum over his wound. Tom thought it smelled like the rum that had been passed around some of the men one evening.

Tom had to turn his head away from the smell or get sick.

"Sir, the stitches look good to me, and does that bowl of food on the stand look even better?"

The gentleman smiled and held out a large spoon of thick broth.

Tom didn't realize how hungry he was until that moment. When he tried sit up it occurred to him that he no longer wore his filthy uniform, and felt clean. Before a question could be formed about his dress, there was another spoon full of broth in his mouth. He decided there was little need to know.

Tom heard a doctor say, "This man's in shock." He started to turn his head to see who the doctor was referring to, but the prospect of broth in his ear overcame his curiosity. A wave of pain shot through his head and reminded him that he had been wounded.

As the gentleman that fed him rose to attend another patient, Tom said, "Thank you, sir."

The man only smiled in reply.

After the food, it was a delightful sensation to sleep most of the morning. A sweet female voice brought him to full awake.

"How is the arm and head today?"

Tom turned his head to see a beautiful young girl. Her black hair was done up in a bun and tied with a white ribbon. The light blue dress with white collar made her even more stunning. She also wore a small white apron, smaller than the attendants he had seen.

"You're lookin' healthier than when you first came in here."

At first Tom could only stare. "Here, let me feed you. If you're goin' to get better you have to build up your strength."

"Since it's a pretty girl, how can I refuse?"

She smiled and fed him from a bowl. His comment about her beauty didn't seem to affect her.

She knows she's pretty and has probably been told many times before. Her presence lights up the day.'

The food in the bowl was more substantial than what he had first received. This bowl contained chunks of meat, carrots, potatoes and some kind of beans.

"All I've done since I arrived here is sleep and eat."

He wanted to ask who cleaned him up but thought it better not to ask this young lady. It hurt his head to chew some pieces but not enough to stop.

"What's..." (More food in the mouth prevented talk for a bit.) "... your name, pretty little miss?"

"Constance. What's yours, soldier?"

SICKNESS AND BEST LAID PLANS

"Constance … that's a pretty name." Tom hesitated for a moment. "This time I remember my name after a head bashing. They call me Tom, Tom Gentry."

The question on her face required an explanation. "Once before I got a good lick on the head and didn't know who I was for several hours. It's a story I would like to share some time, if you come by here again. I was knocked on the head by a no good thief and, well, it's a long story. I don't think you have time for it."

The expression on her face said there was something she wanted to say. "Your last name is Gentry?"

Tom nodded while he chewed.

"I met two Gentry brothers who said they were sailors when I waited for a train. They said they were on their way to Wilmington. Could they be related to you?

"Had to be my brothers, Homer and Willie. They must have been home to visit our parents. I hope they are careful when they travel, considering the conscription law.

"That must have been them. One was named Willie. He was so handsome and had such a pleasant smile."

The conversation was interrupted by the familiar voice of the doctor.

"Daughter, there are others that could use your attention if you can extract yourself from this young man. Soldier, how are you feelin' this evening?"

Tom was fairly sure it was the doctor that had examined him. "With all the fine attention I get, I'm much better thank you Sir. My head hurts off and on though, and the arm is fine if I don't try to move it."

While Tom talked, Constance picked up the empty bowl and gave him a smile and moved down the aisle between the sick and injured.

It appears Willie could have a new girl friend. Homer has someone to court and my girl is miles away.

An attendant down the line of beds called to the doctor. So he made a slight bow to Tom and moved in the direction of the voice.

Tom's attention was drawn to a sudden movement across the aisle. A soldier with a bandaged head began to thrash and toss about. This brought running feet in their direction. It was a large male nurse followed by two women.

One of the women yelled, "He's havin' another fit. Hold him, Clarence."

The other woman pulled down his jaw with a lot of effort and placed a wooden spoon handle in his mouth. Tom was fascinated and horrified at the same time.

The nurse held the soldier down with difficulty, even though he was strong.

After they worked with him for a time, the soldier began to relax and breathe evenly.

The attendant relaxed his grip and stared at the soldier. "Poor boy. One of these times he might not come out of it."

Constance startled him out of his concern for the soldier. "Here, Tom. It looks like a letter from your home. You can read it yourself. I would help but have to deliver the rest of the mail, so I will look to your care later."

Tom was going to say thank you before she hurried off. He was still too startled by the struggle across the aisle and mail from home so soon. The opened letter revealed his mother's writing, but it was an old letter, as expected. Someone from my company must have sent it on to me.

Dear Son.

I hope you are well and taking good care of yourself. We would be doing better if the deserters would leave our garden alone. It hasn't been too bad but Uncle Casper said it could get much worse if the war continues. Next year we will plant one on his place where it's not so easy to find. We hear from your brothers often. If it were not for them sending money, it would get difficult this winter. Sue keeps turning down proposals or chances to court other fellers. You father is still improving but keeps saying he's lost his boys. If you could get some leave it might snap him out of these bad moods.

I worry about him. Paw is losing interest about the farm and everything. If he could only see you or your brothers it would do him a world of good. Take care of yourself and come when you can. I should mention Doctor Young here said he could use his influence to get you transferred as a prison guard to Salisbury. He remembers how sick you were one winter. This would get you closer to home and your father. You could visit each other. I know you don't want to leave your friends for your home. But you could still serve as a guard. I tried to crowd too much on this little sheet of paper. We love you and pray for you.

Ma.

My left arm's unable to hold a musket for a while, but then there is my pistol. They might send me to guard prisoners if I show this letter to the doctor here. As a prison guard, I will still be supporting friends and regiment. I'll leave this stinkin' place as soon as they will let me, pretty girls or not. I'll just get sick leave and go see my folks before I have to fight.

Tom sat up. He felt better about his decision.

Tom looked for the surgeon that appeared to be in charge. At the same time he realized that he had slept for most of three days. He also knew that he had received good attention and much for which he was not aware.

"Tom, ole boy, you need to get the attention of an orderly and get the wheels rollin' on this sick leave. Wonder how long it will take?"

Tom tried to get an orderly's attention but they were too busy.

A shadow fell across his bed. The elderly gentleman that had fed him when he first arrived stood by his bed.

"You look deep in thought. Did the head wound do that to you? On the other hand you do look much better."

"Yes Sir, I do feel better, thank you. I was figurin' on asking the surgeon if I could have a bit of sick leave to go home before joining my company. Although I figure I'm needed at both places, I need to get back to my soldiers soon as possible,"

"Don't be too anxious there, young feller. I suspect the war will be around longer than people realize. Besides, you need to gain back more of your strength."

"By the time the train gets me back, I should be strong enough. You know how slow they can be, and with all the stops. I know you have attended me for some days back, and I don't even know your name so I can thank you properly."

"Joseph Wheeler of *Jones and Wheeler Law Firm* at your service. I do what I can here at the hospital. If it will make you feel any better I'll ask the physician in charge to see what he says about your discharge from the hospital."

"For that I would be in your debt again, sir. And thank you for all your help. I'm glad to have help from men folk. The ladies seem to be constantly busy."

"They do indeed. Well, I must be movin' along. I will probably see you Saturday.

* * *

It was the following Monday before Tom was released. He felt disappointed to find that he would go straight to Goldsboro with no sick leave. The doctor and staff were sympathetic but the war in the east had put demands on his regiment. All able body men were to report. Home would have to wait for the present.

The confusion of recent events, not able to get sick leave, and the order to Goldsboro left him dazed. Tom trudged along in the hot sun and began to perspire. It was then that he realized his uniform was clean. His socks and shoes were new.

Strange I didn't notice before. I'm still not well. Got to find some shade and rest.

His weakness and the heat made him dizzy, which made him ignore his surroundings. However, several other travelers, mostly soldiers, were about with their travel bags. He spotted a shed that ran the length of the depot; it would be a relief from the heat.

Tom sat on his small travel bag just as three soldiers approached. One was an officer accompanied by a corporal and a sergeant. He thought of reaching for his hospital discharge paper but just didn't have the energy.

"Where you goin' soldier?" The three studied Tom suspiciously and waited for a reply.

"Going back to my regiment ... just got out of the hospital."

Tom pulled out the paper signed by the doctor and handed it to the sergeant, who in turn handed to the officer. The officer only glanced at the paper and handed it back to Tom.

The officer gave a little sigh. "They must need you real bad. You don't look too good ... ought to be back in the hospital. Now I see your stripes, Sergeant. What outfit you belong to?"

"The 26th North Carolina. I had hoped for a medical leave to take me home to see my paw who is feeling poorly. Could use the rest but glad to be getting back to my company. Are you headin' east too?"

The other sergeant nodded. "Aha-yep, I reckon we are. And by the looks of the black smoke a headin' this-a way, we'll be on a train directly."

Tom and a few late arrivals, mostly soldiers, waited to the last minute to climb aboard. After a couple false starts the train finally picked up speed. This time there was enough room to lie down. They had not traveled far before he fell asleep. It was a fitful sleep. He dreamed of the battle and wounded men. It seemed he was always running.

After a bit the train stopped for wood and water. The Sergeant that had questioned Tom earlier shouted. "You men got time to get off and cook some bacon and fritters. Get yourself a cup of coffee. Might not get a chance later on."

Tom stepped down from the car and moved toward a fire. A corporal handed him a cup of coffee.

"Thank you Corporal. Never drank it much before I got in the army. My folks never encouraged me to drink it when I was a youngster so never learned to like it much, but this is good."

The bacon was too salty but he was hungry and wolfed it down. *The hospital food was good compared to this fare. Wish I could have gotten home and into some of Ma's cooking.*

When the train started to move again, Tom began to feel sick. It must be that salty meat. By the time they reached the next stop, he couldn't get off soon enough … and just made it.

He heard someone say, "He'll get the scours next, any bets?"

Before he could get back on the train dysentery hit him.

"I'll get over it. Seen enough of it in camp."

Tom was wrong on how long it would take to get well. He was so weak by the time they stopped for water again, that the corporal had to help him off the train.

The officer that had checked his papers walked to where Tom sat. "Sergeant, we're not far from Goldsboro, but there's a new field hospital at Kinston. Been a little fightin' there. I'm callin' for an ambulance to take you there.

"Corporal, go tell Sergeant Boyd to get me an ambulance. This soldier should still be in the hospital."

Tom lay on the ground near the tracks. "Almost wish that minié ball had finished the job."

He turned his head slightly when a team and wagon pulled up. The Captain's remark to the driver didn't reach him but the answer did.

"I is sorry, cap'n, ah gots to take this here wagon back yonder and fetch mo' wood so de next train can get on down de track ... dey done tol' me fo sho'."

Tom heard another voice. "I'm a doctor. Let me look at this soldier, Captain."

After the doctor examined Tom and asked a few questions, he pronounced with a loud voice, "This man will lay right here until the next train goes to Raleigh ... and to the hospital where he came from."

The doctor gave him something that made him feel better, but he just wanted to lie on the ground and rest. Just as he was drifting off, he felt someone cover him with a blanket. He was soon asleep.

Around midnight, Tom was moved to a train bound for Raleigh. He didn't care how or where, as long as his condition would improve. His dreams were torment again, but this time they were interspersed with Mary Ellen's smile to tease him unmercifully. Then there was the confused face of the young Indian girl, Little Fawn. When jolted awake at one rough track section, he purposely concentrated on the Indian girl. It delighted him to still see her race with her brother. The expressions on their faces were real, and so happy. A picture of the laughter on her pretty face would stay with him forever.

"Strange, I never ran a race with my sister that I can remember. That must be an exceptional family."

Soon the train stopped again. The car door opened and more injured were placed on the floor around him.

An angry voice said, "Get to movin' soldier. We got to get back to Kinston."

Tom couldn't make out the rest of the conversation, not that he cared.

Movement outside the door made him rise on his elbows. Blue-coated Yankees were marched by the open door. The prisoners stumbled and walked gingerly, since they wore no shoes or boots. Their shoes had been 'donated' to their captors.

A soldier beside him asked, "They goin' to put them blue bellies on the same train?"

The train jolted and squeaked at that point and the noise swallowed any reply.

There were other stops along the way. The wounded were allowed to get off the train to get coffee and a meal, if they were able. Tom was only interested in water and no food was forced on him. The other soldiers were only too glad to eat Tom's portion.

On the last stop, the wounded soldier beside him offered a corn fritter and a potato. "Here, you got to eat somthin' Sergeant. Hit don't hardly have no grease. I got a tater besides … cooked in real butter. Done it myself."

Tom sat up gingerly, and backed against the coach wall.

"Thank you. I'll try it. See what happens. My name's Tom." He didn't wait for a reply but began to nibble on the food, while he eyed his benefactor to determine his wound.

"You're most welcome, Sergeant Tom. They call me Jake. Don't know what else to answer to been so long since I heard my real name. I got me a laig wound. The saw-bones took one look after he done lay out his saws and such, and says, the ball done gone through the calf. Just causin' a lot of blood but missed the bone. I'll be off my laig for a while. You might notice I limp more in front officers and such. It do need to heal before I go back. You need a lot of healin' too. You're not only sickly but your arm is bleedin'. I've done a spell of healin' animals. Let me take a look. Might be I can stop any infection."

Tom was drawn to Jake. The private probably would give his shirt off his back to help or his last biscuit to another. "I'm beholding to you, Jake. It's been troubling me some but I didn't pay much attention. I sure would appreciate you looking at it for me. Sure don't want it to get infected."

Tom unbuttoned his shirt. The bandage had slipped to his elbow and the wound looked red and angry.

Jake looked around and shouted, "Anybody got any whiskey ... liquor of any kind?"

A captain stepped up and handed a flask to Jake. "Thank you kindly, sir. I'll only use what's necessary."

"Don't matter, soldier. I can get more but he can't get another arm. Pour it on."

The alcohol burned like fire, but Tom refused let them see his pain.

"Here come some ambulances. Looks like you're goin' to get a ride."

"Tom, we can get off this here cattle car and find a wagon or amber ... what you call it."

"Sounds good. I'm ready for a more comfortable ride."

Tom had noticed the coaches held a few men dressed in business suits, ladies and officers, while the common soldier rode in boxcars. "Times have changed. First time I rode to Raleigh, it was in a coach."

Tom joined Jake and some other wounded in a walk from the depot. They were soon exhausted and sat down where they were. An ambulance soon came by and the black driver got down to help the men.

"You all climb aboard my chariot. It ain't goin' to heaven yet but I reckon it's sent by my Lord fo' your journey to the healin' place."

Tom was slid beside another man on the upper level. There were two lying on the bottom level in stretchers under Tom. Jake got on the seat beside the driver.

Sam glanced at the driver. "Who you workin' for, chariot driver?"

"I works fo' myself and the hospital. I done bought my freedom a while back. My master, he was a good man. Him better than most, I reckon."

When they began to move, the ambulance noise covered any attempt at conversation. The man next to him moaned at every bump. Tom was still able to sleep in spite of the jostle of boards beneath him and the squeak of the horse's harness. A strong attendant and a guard help unload the wounded.

When Tom was able to look about, he was surprised to find this was not the hospital he left. The brick building stood four stories high. The windows appeared to be boarded "What is this place? Where am I?"

"Sergeant, this here is now a hospital. Was supposed to be a girl's school called Peace Academy, College or somethin'. We're takin' you to the bottom floor first for the doctor to see. You don't want that top floor. That's where they take the dead. If you're not too bad off, I'll take care of you. Like to take care of sergeants and officers, hee, hee."

HOME OR PRISON

Tom was placed across the aisle from Jake. He didn't recognize anyone else, but it mattered little. The bed was comfortable, his arm had been treated, and he had been fed. The stomach sickness seemed to have passed. Tom was almost asleep again until he recognized a familiar voice.

It was the lawyer Mr. Wheeler. The lawyer talked to the doctor as they walked between the two rows of beds. When they recognized Tom they stopped.

Mr. Wheeler was the first to speak. "Well, soldier, it's Tom, isn't it? From the looks of you, you're going to be with us a while longer. I'll visit later and let the good Surgeon here do his work."

"Dr. Logan at your service, sir. What seems to be the trouble? What can we do for our fine soldier?"

Tom explained his problems and decided not to leave out a thing. He simply wanted relief. In the back of his mind, he hoped for sick leave that would allow him to go home. Mention of the winter when sickness made him so weak might help.

"If I could just get some of Ma's cooking and her remedies I should get well quicker."

It was difficult to concentrate on the other questions for the thought of home. The arm examination satisfied the doctor, who then motioned for a male nurse. "George, bathe and dress the wound please."

The doctor was about to move to another patient when he must have thought of something.

"Tom, who is your doctor back home? You're from near Salisbury, aren't you?"

"Yes, near Salisbury, sir. We usually call on Doctor Young if things get real bad, but my mother does most of the doctoring."

"Would that be Tom or John Young?"

"I think it is Tom Young. I'm supposed to be named after him since he helped bring me into this confusing world."

"I know Tom Young. We were in school together, and he has a brother here in Raleigh. I think the brother is a lawyer and dabbles in politics."

The doctor stood for a moment and rubbed the stubble on his chin as in thought.

"I would like to get a message to him ... I'm speaking of the doctor of course. You wouldn't object to sick leave would you? We could use the good doctor right now. His brother has influence with the governor which might be useful in the days to come."

It was difficult for Tom to keep excitement from showing. *I will have to tell friends this is the moment when I started feeling better.*

"Sir, do suggest that my ma should do some of the healing?"

Doctor Logan stroked his chin again and gave Tom a calculated look, but his expression changed to one of concern. "I suppose I did have that in mind; however, and I do not want to offend a brave young man like yourself, but I'm afraid if we send you back to this war too soon, you might not last long enough to help our cause. From what I hear of problems near your home, deserters and occasional need for guards at the Salisbury Prison, we need good men there."

"I might, with the help of Mr. Wheeler and my recommendation, get you appointed as a guard. We might persuade the prison commander to give you and a friend or two some latitude, which should permit you to help the Home Guard. I wouldn't be surprised to discover some of the Home Guard sympathetic with deserters. The way I see it, we could use an agent to look after our interests in that area. I would appreciate it if you would consider what I've said, but don't mention the agent part to anyone please."

Tom had not heard of problems with marauders or deserters. The thought of that possibility troubled him. Tom decided to respond as if he knew something of the matter.

"Sir, that could be part of the problem. With the increasing number of deserters, some criminal element in the Home Guard are taking advantage of the situation and holding deserters hostage for their criminal dealings."

"Very likely. Well Sergeant, I must be about the care of other patients. After a few days I should have leave for you, and a talk with Mr. Wheeler regarding the lawyer Mr. Young and a secret agent."

Dr. Logan moved quickly down the row of beds at the beckoning of a nurse. The men on either side of Tom were asleep and didn't seem bothered by the doctor's skipping them. One had a head bandage, and the other had lost a leg below the knee.

Tom looked down the row of beds. He hoped to see the doctor's pretty daughter. Her face would add even more happiness to his day. What he saw was his friend Corporal Sims on one crutch. From a distance of nearly fifty feet he could see Sims grin.

My friend's clothes are much cleaner that when I saw him last... must have had a bath, too. I figure neither of us smelled too good when we arrived at the hospital.

"Tom boy, how you feelin' now you got cleaned up, fed, and bedded down? You lookin' a sight better, I think. Could be my sight is a failin' me too."

"It's good to see you too, you old scoundrel. You're lookin' fit and ready to knock some heads with that dangerous looking club you're leaning on. Have a sit down, on the bed."

Tom observed Sims as his friend gingerly sat on the edge of the bed, still with a grin on his face.

"You might say I'm too poorly to be sent back any time soon. I've got responsibilities back home and I want to go back to my company. I'm torn between duty to my state and duty to my family. Not that I have a choice. The doctor and a lawyer I met have worked on a plan to send this worn out body to Salisbury Prison as a guard. It might be soon.

"Sims, how bad is you leg. Will you be fit to march when it heals? If not, you could ask for a transfer to the prison like me."

"I don't rightly know ... not for sure. That ball took out a chunk of my upper leg but didn't touch the bone. It gives me so much pain that the laudanum don't help much."

The male nurse was about to pass them but stopped when he saw Sims. "Soldier! You get back to your bed. You want to finish bleedin' to death? You stubborn soldiers is the reason they hired the likes of me. Lean on me and we'll get you back to bed so that laig will heal."

Sims grinned at Tom as he was led away. "Tom, I'll bear in mind what you told me about that prison. Would be this leg won't allow me to do much marchin'."

* * *

Dr. Logan stopped his lawyer friend at the door. "Mr. Wheeler, are we sending this boy on a fool's errand or can he actually help our state? Never-the-less, it puts him where he should be healthier."

"You speak of Tom, the Sergeant. He seems intelligent and resourceful. Just might help solve one of our problems." The lawyer thought for a moment, then turned to study his friend. "Doctor, what is your interest in this young man?"

"He's resembles my own son so much it haunts me."

* * *

The thoughts of home cooked meals, the family greeting and his own bed helped make the train trip home pleasurable and exciting ... things he dreamed of when in the hospital. Tom was determined the frequent stops and delays would not dampen his spirits. He had looked forward to homecoming for days. Once again he patted his shirt pocket that held the transfer to the prison.

When the train slowed for the Lexington stop Tom gazed out the window. He turned to the conductor in surprise and exclaimed. "My folk's wagon!" And I would recognize that horse anywhere. Excuse me, I'm getting off."

Tom hurried down the steps and ran into his mother's arms.

"Ma, it's good to be home."

She held him at arm's length, smiled and exclaimed, "Welcome home son. You don't look too worn for wear but you could use some fattening up. What do you think Paw?"

Sue wormed her way around her mother, squeezed Tom about the middle and gave a little squeal.

Mr. Gentry grinned and took hold of Tom's hand and began to pump vigorously. "You had us worried there for a spell son. Climb aboard the family chariot everybody. Supper is loudly callin' our names. Take the reins, Tom. See if you can still handle old Nan. Your letter said somethin' about reportin' to the prison. What do you do next?"

Tom gently flipped the reins on Nan's back. "Paw, my sick leave is almost for a month. But I need to report sooner to avoid questions from the folks around here. I'll be visiting from the prison regularly so I should go there first thing in the morning. Can I borrow the mule? That will give me an excuse to return sooner. I won't go before breakfast. I've looked forward to Sue's biscuits and gravy a long time."

After breakfast Tom jumped aboard mule, the same he had ridden from Cherokee. All were present. Even Uncle Casper had ridden over to join the rest of the family to see Tom off. He turned to face the family. "I'll be back in a few days. Take care of yourselves." Every one yelled and waved at the same time.

PRISON GUARD DAYS

Tom approached the front gate of the prison for the first time. He wondered: *I hope that this is not a mistake. Mr. Wheeler and Dr. Logan's casual mention of spy activity in the Home Guard assignment could be a ruse ... a way to get me out of the hospital and make a prison guard out of me. Then again, there's some truth to the deserter story. So once again I follow my conscience.*

"I grow stronger every day. Sick leave came at the right time. Mom's cooking and attention made a difference. The walks around the farm felt good. Could I have returned to my company? Naw ... I need to be closer to home, what with Pop's bad leg. No need to risk the sickness again. Don't want my nightmares to keep the men awake. It's a good thing I slept in the barn, poor animals. Deserter problem could get worse as this war continues, and then there is this spy assignment. I will miss the walks around the farm with Paw and Uncle Casper."

Tom decided he wouldn't be concerned about his appointment with the Noncom in charge. *Not after what I've been through. I've gotten tougher and it's just another new job.*

The letter from the Commander of the prison made it clear he was needed and would be a welcome addition to

233

his command. He was to report to the Sergeant in charge who assigned guard duty. Tom could just make out the sergeant's name, Mason, on the paper.

A private leaned against the gatepost, obviously not on duty. "Where do I find Sergeant, Mason?" The private spat a stream of tobacco juice and pointed to an open door. Tom was about to ask about the sergeant again when he entered the room.

Someone yelled "Over here, sergeant. You're goin' to be my second in command. My other second got sick on me. Welcome to this hell-hole. I'm Sergeant Mason."

Mason held out his left hand. In spite of his right arm missing from below the elbow, he was a big man and truly intimidating.

"I can still load and fire my musket but this stump still bothers me some. I lost part of my arm on the farm. Worst part is I can still feel the dirt under my fingernails on my missin' hand.

"Pardon my manners. You'd be Tom Gentry?"

"That I am, Sergeant Mason. I'm glad to part of your ..."

Mason interrupted. "You won't be so glad when you find what we got to put up with. We got mostly ole men and wounded like us to guard these blue bellies. We got young boys still wet behind the ears and not too healthy. Might as well be Home Guard. The healthy ones are already in the fight."

"Cam, make room for the new sergeant over there. He can bunk in Smith's place. Store your gear under the bunk. I'll try to fetch you a musket, or you kin borrow one from another guard when he comes off duty, till we get some more. Get yourself acquainted."

Mason pointed about the room. "That there is Josh Yarborough. Corporal Josh there says he is a cousin of your'n. Don't wake him up. He's a real grouch after comin' of duty. That there is Ted Thompson we think. He got a lick on the head same as you."

Mason studied Tom's head for a moment.

"Heard all about you. You should a-got an award or somethin' for puttin' up with that hospital. One word of advice: you don't want to work the east wall. I'll help you get most of your guard duty on the south-west wall or west wall, dependin' on how the wind blows. The smell's gettin' too ripe down there. And it's goin' to get more crowded, I'm told."

"How's the food, Sergeant Mason?"

"Tolerable, just tolerable. Call me Mason, unless the camp commander or his second is around. You report to him yet?"

* * *

Early days at the prison were not too difficult. One day was pretty much like the next. Tom only had to mention the nearness of his family's farm to interest Sergeant Mason to the idea of foraging. Tom was immediately assigned to gather food stuff for the prison.

On returning from one foraging expedition, Tom was amused to discover some prisoners were in Salisbury. One cheerful fellow he recognized. When he saw Tom, he pulled out a piece of paper to wave. "Sergeant, some of us can get passes to go into town. We promised to be good prisoners and return before dark, hee, hee."

Tom smiled, waved and proceeded to the prison. *Some of the clothes those boys have won't be enough this winter, and that's around the corner. The last prisoners weren't so bad off, except shoes and boots. Too bad our boys relieve them of their footwear. They swap a lot until there's nothing to swap. My clothes and that of the rest of the guards are getting worn. I hope we get new ones soon but doubt it.*

The guard at the gate was a friendly sort. He would always touch his cap when Tom entered. Tom pitched him an apple.

While Tom was still outside the gate, he heard a guard gripe about his trips to town and home. Sergeant Mason yelled at the man. "Don't he always bring some fresh stuff from his Mom's garden? He might bring a ham some time. Cam, you like to eat. Make friends like with the feller. It would be to your benefit. If we ever run short in our larder, he and some of the folks around here will come in handy."

Another guard piped up, "Don't know how he does it, more privileges than most. But them fresh eggs were enough to stop my complainin'."

When the subject changed, Tom decided to enter. *Their comments remind me of the reason for my freedom to come and go. I need to writer Mr. Wheeler and let him know there is nothing to report. In fact, I've seen very little of the Home Guard. There have been no recent signs of deserters around the farm.*

Tom sat on his bunk. It was time to write a short note to Kate. He couldn't think of what to say, so he put his pen and paper away in frustration.

When Tom returned on one of his jaunts, it was the 4th of July. It appeared Salisbury was in a festive mood. People in the streets were laughing and visiting as if there were no worries.

A boy shouted across the street to another youth, "Hey Joseph, my Maw said when I turn eighteen next week, I can join up. Might fight alongside my Paw."

A lady Tom had spoken to before smiled at him. "That's a good boy. Promised his Paw he would stay home until he was eighteen."

When he approached the prison, Tom found himself in a small crowd of town's people. *The rumor when I left must be true. It's the 4th of July 1862 and we're to have a baseball game' a game between our guards and some of the prisoners. I'll be satisfied to watch and guard. No need for me to get hot and sick again. That's as good an excuse as any since I don't know the game that well. Let the ones that know how play.*

Cam yelled from the doorway. "Just in time, Tom. Would you take my place on guard duty so's I kin play ball? I'll owe you big, if'n you would, Sergeant."

"Sorry, Cam. I'm already schedule to guard. You'll have to find …"

"I'll do it. Let me borrow your musket." Tom turned to see a new guard. The man looked friendly. His dark complexion spoke of Indian blood to Tom. He was of medium build and his clothes were not as worn compared to the other guards.

Cam beamed and stuck out his hand. "Why, I'm much obliged. That was right friendly like. What name they call you by, stranger?"

"My name's Don Lambert. Enjoy the game."

Tom thought: *It's strange how people enter your life and you seem to know they are going to somehow play an important part of that life. Or perhaps it's because in the back of your head you want them to be a part. A real trusted friend is hard to come by. I'll bet this new guard is a man of few words.'*

"Lambert, that was right friendly of you. I'm Sergeant Gentry. Just call me Tom. Are you the one I heard tell was part of the Home Guard for a spell?"

"That's right, Sergeant, uh … Tom. Not much call for another injured lumberman around here and the guard don't pay nothing. Take a spell for my shoulder to limber up. I better get to the wall."

"I'll walk out with you. Did you hear or see anything of deserters when you were in the Home Guard? I heard tell of a few hiding along the river."

"There was some talk but not more then what I heard while lumbering. People complained of missin' chickens and one farmer lost a hog … another said he lost a cow. Since food is scarcer, it could be anybody stealin', not just a body dodgin' the war … or a deserter."

"Tom." Sergeant Mason stopped them before they ascended the wall. "I told Lambert here you might be interested in the Home Guard bunch. You be careful, Tom. You're makin' a few enemies in that bunch … nosin' about. That be the reason for letters to that Wheeler feller? I know he's a good man and his brother too. I might be figurin' wrong but the connection is just too convenient. Don't take me wrong, I like you and want to keep you around. Other than that, it's no skin off my nose."

"I appreciate the warning, Mason. You probably figured right. I'll back off."

If Mason were connected to the Home Guard in any way, the bunch should relax if I back off.

Tom listened as two of the guards talked about the baseball game.

"Think they will be playin' by what they call the Connecticut Rules, one of them New England states. Most likely I'll get it wrong. One of them rules says when you hit the ball, the player that gets the ball can throw it at the runner to get him out. The ball bein' hard like a rock wrapped in cloth or somethin' could hurt somebody. This I got to see."

Tom attention was drawn away from the game. Some new arrivals had come, and a group of prisoners who were better dressed that the general population of the prison, gathered around them.

One of the new ones immediately caught Tom's eye. He looked like Cousin Ronald from Philadelphia. Have to check into this.

What happened next disturbed him. The three new prisoners were quickly relieved of what valuables they had. Their pockets were emptied. Then one lost a blanket, another lost a cap.

This confirms what Mason and I have suspected. There's too much thievery among the prisoners. It could be bad this winter for them if they're still here. Some might be exchanged which will help, but how can we stop this?

* * *

Long gone were the days when town-people tossed food over the fence to the prisoners, except for a few ladies with compassionate hearts. Some of these ladies found ways to slip a bit of food to the prisoners. Other guards were soon permitted to forage for food with greater frequency. At first the guards could return with eggs, bacon, potatoes and corn. In season there would be pumpkin, squash and tomatoes.

In the beginning, the progress of the war had little affect the local citizens. The prisoners had been permitted to visit Salisbury and, with few exceptions, were treated well. The gentle South with their polite friendly manner tolerated their unwanted guests. But as word of dying and wounded reached their families, many began to voice their bitterness and hostility toward the prisoners.

The war no longer appeared to be a short lark. Lincoln and the Yankees were not going to give them their freedom, even after Bull Run and other Confederate victories.

There were rumors of deserters and a few conscription dodgers that hid in the forests and along the riverbank. He had heard of caves and bluffs where one could hide, but didn't know their location. Tom's father cautioned him when he used the team and wagon. The chance they might lose the animals would require Tom to pack in the food on foot. This would leave more for the family, and he wouldn't have to ask fussy neighbors for help.

This led to a conflict with deserters on one of Tom's first trips near home. Five men stood in the road. He knew they intended to relieve him of his wagon-load.

"I'm called Big Horace, and me and these others need what you got, neighbor. In fact, we will take it. It depends on you."

"It would be to your advantage to let me pass for several reasons, Big Horse (emphasis on Horse). I come this way right regularly. I'll give you some of what I got. If I don't show up in a few hours, guards from the prison along with the Home Guard will come lookin'. Those hungry guards put a right smart value on me and what I bring back."

"The name's Horace, not Horse. Give us half. That will last a day or two. We don't worry much about the Home Guard outfit. Ain't catched us yet. They play hob trying to catch us. It's been good doin' business with you, Sergeant."

"Big H., only take two days worth, if you want me to come this way again."

With the prospect of food to follow, Tom was allowed to pass. After that Tom used several different routes and was able to avoid Big Horace. It could be that Big H. had to find another hiding place.

The Home Guard was another matter. After he showed the captain of the Home Guard his papers and threatened to bring some of the prison guards, he was allowed to keep his load. Tom couldn't tell if his bluff worked or the captain was an honest man. Honesty would have been unusual since the reputation of most such units was not much more than a lawless mob. Tom had heard of one group west of Lexington and Salisbury he hoped to avoid.

One memorable day Tom started back with a good load. He picked up supplies at home and at some of the other farmers that considered it their Christian duty. These farms were well known to him. The use of Uncle's wagon and mules was a great help. And Uncle Casper had a lot of influence in the community. His load consisted of corn, potatoes, onions, two-dozen eggs and a slab of bacon. This load would be a cause for a celebration.

These supplies might get me that other stripe that has been mentioned.

Round a bend of trees and brush, Tom came upon six men. He recognized three of them and one that had been a constant thorn in his side ... Mick. "Now what's to happen? It's the Home Guard without their captain to control them."

Tom had to pull on the reins to stop.

Mick strutted up to the wagon, stuck out his chest and yelled, "Where you goin', boy. What you got there? You're a mighty brave deserter."

"I'm on my way back ..."

"We've a need for that there wagon and animals." Mick and two of his cronies moved to see what was in the wagon.

241

"As I tried to say, I'm on my way back to the prison, as usual. Those two know me and where I've been and where I'm going. Ask them."

"We got us a new captain, at least until Cap gets over the vapors or somethin'. Them two got no say and I don't believe you."

As Mick came closer Tom said, "I remember you from school, Mick. You know me as an honest boy who always told the truth. Now why are you trying to give me trouble like you used to? We are both grown men now. This is not the school yard."

"Mostly cuz I don't like you and I'm better than you, smarter than you ever was. Now climb off that wagon, I ain't askin'."

That runt is not going to get this without a fight. If I can reach my colt fast enough?

Tom heard the sound of a musket being cocked. It was somewhere behind him. It made Tom's hairs of his neck stand up. A commanding voice got everyone's attention.

"I reckon you won't be takin' anybody's animals or wagon today. You and your 'girlfriends' just mosey on back to where you came from."

That voice is familiar. No matter, it couldn't sound better … or at a better time.

One of Mick's cronies whispered to Mick. "There's only one back there in the weeds. We kin rush 'm from around the wagon."

Mick spoke out of the side of his mouth. "Whatcha been drinkin' Charlie? You go and do it. See if the rest follow."

Yet another voice spoke from another direction. "Don't make another mistake. We got you in our sights.

This here musket don't care who it's pointed at or who you are. You heard my friend. Now head for town!"

"Mick," one of the other men said nervously, "Buck and me done stopped Tom onst before, besides. He ain't done nothin' wrong. We don't want to make that prison commander mad at us. And Tom's got friends in the army … and them men in the bushes … we better do as he says."

"All right, we'll go. But you and your friends back there better stay within the law, military or not. Wouldn't be surprised if them in the weeds be dodgin' the conscription. Next time there'll be more of us." Mick growled at the others and motioned for them to follow.

Tom watched the six men retreat around the next turn before looking for the familiar voice. A thin figure emerged from the weeds with a wide smile on his face.

"Where in tar-nation did you come from, Larry Sims? I thought you were back with the 26th, or what's left of it? And who is your friend?"

Larry stopped, bent over, slapped his leg and laughed. "I am. I'm me and my friend, too. I talked lower the last time. You remember you tellin' me about a one-man army back in Philadelphia? I fooled them gents, anyhow. Why am I here? Let me climb on up with you and I'll tell you all about it."

Larry slung his gear in the wagon and took a seat. He turned to Tom and started his animated conversation, and grinned the entire time.

"When you left the hospital to join up with the prison guards I got to thinkin'. When I get back to our old company, I would join you at that prison if I got wounded enough and not get killed. Well, sure enough, I got this here leg wound. Wouldn't let the surgeon cut it off, you know. Lost part of my ear too, but it don't bother my hearin' none. And since I look a heap older than I am and exaggeratin' my limp considerably, I talked them into a transfer. This leg pains me too much to march, you know." He glanced at a grinning Tom and added. "Well it does."

"Then why are you walking now? You intend to march all the way to the prison from the hospital?"

"You're funnin' me again. I already reported in and Mason let me come meet you since I knowed you and you might need help with supper fixin's."

"You show up in the nick of time again, Larry. There's the time at the burning bridge, and now this. I'm pleased to see you again. We better get to moving or we won't get there before dark."

"Before I left to meet you they was bringin' in more Yankee prisoners. One of them was a feller we met when there's a kind of truce, you might say. He was right friendly for a Yank. We swapped newspapers, and I gave him some tobacco for real coffee. Poor feller didn't look good a-tall this time."

"Larry, I hate to hear about more prisoners. We don't have room for the ones we got, and how are we going to feed them? Sergeant Mason told me Major Gee, the camp commander, made more than one appeal for food, clothing and blankets. Food is getting scarce in the towns too."

"I hate to tell you Tom, but the army has trouble gettin' food too. It's harder and harder all the time. There was this hurt feller from our outfit came to the hospital the day I was released said they was about to march north. He overheard some officers talkin' about Pennsylvania. My laig wouldn't make it half way."

It was almost dark by the time they approached the gate. Tom noticed the same lady he had seen before throw something over the fence. "It's probably potatoes and onions again." The gate soon opened, a man stepped out, waved, and turned to walk down the railroad tracks.

"Larry, I'll have to introduce you to that man one of these days, if he will stay still long enough. We call him Preacher. He ministers to the prisoners and the guards."

SWIFT JUSTICE

Tom approached Mason. "Sarge, if we are to believe the new prisoners, we're not exactly winning. I'm not sure we get all the news from Raleigh. They can't cover all fronts, war in the west, on the Mississippi or New Orleans. The shortage of food and clothes for our troops means less for the prisoners too. Since these prisoners have to fend for themselves, there are more holes in the ground and probably more side rooms that branch out from those holes. It's a poor attempt to stay out of the elements."

"Tom, I reckon you notice how we're getting' over crowded. That means them side rooms can turn into tunnels. They will be hard to watch. Those poor devils in the holes will escape most of the bad weather. Not much we can do for them or us. I hope you can still smuggle in food from your farm."

"I'll do my best. You notice that lady from town who throws food over the fence to the prisoners? They don't fight over the food in front of her, but as soon as she's gone, the fight begins. It's not the first time."

With a twinkle in Mason's eye, he said, "Nope, didn't hardly notice the white hat she wore Sunday or the pink parasol. Eyesight ain't what it use ta be. Must be a right carin' lady ... Christian like."

Tom had to chuckle at Mason's response.

Sims joined Tom and Sergeant Mason. Tom shared his observations with the two men.

"These crowded conditions and lack of privacy only lead to violence. They fight with each other for food and clothes. You know that group of eleven troublemakers on the top floor of the old cotton mill part of the prison ... I've seen when new prisoners arrived, these bullies surround them, and then beat the new arrivals for their few belongings if they try to resist."

Sims commented, "Yeah, and they don't stick to theivin' just the new prisoners. If any of the prisoners try to oppose them, the bullies protect each other till they're back in the cotton mill."

Mason added, "Oh, yeah ... 'The Cotton Mill Gang'."

Tom told about one particular incident. "Yesterday I saw one prisoner who always tries to keep himself clean. This fellow walks about, tries to discourage misconduct and keeps up the morale of the prisoners. There was nothing unusual this day except he kept watching the Cotton Mill door. He stood off to himself with his thumbs hooked in his galluses. And then I saw several of the others that shared two or three hovels watched the 'clean' prisoner from both sides the door."

"Men, you notice that neat prisoner this side that ragged tent. He looks to be at attention? This is the second day I've seen him stare at that door."

Larry studied the prison yard for a time. "No Tom, there are several ragged tents. You mean the one with no beard? What about him?"

"That's the one, and several men on one side the door and another number on the other side the door watch the 'Neat Prisoner' from time to time. I have an idea that if we get some new prisoners, we'll know why they act this way. This should be interesting."

The gate soon opened and four new prisoners were ushered into the hospital. Tom glanced at the Neat Prisoner who had just changed his observation of the upper floor windows.

"Mr. Neat has his eye on the hospital door. I think I'm right, but we're about to see some sort of retribution or protection for the new arrivals. I truly hope so. I hate thieves and no good cowards. They have troubled us for too long, haven't they, Sarge."

Mason agreed, "That's right, Tom. I need to go. We can discuss this later."

Noise wouldn't distract Tom and Larry's concentration on what was about to happen. Soon as the shoeless prisoners exited the hospital, someone near the gate waved his cap. Several men bullied their way out the Cotton Mill door. The Neat Prisoner's arms rose to remove his cap and smooth his hair, then walked toward the gate. A group that had lounged on both sides of the door followed the Cotton Mill Gang. Uncertainty on the part of the new people, led them into the mill gang circle.

Tom watched in fascination as the biggest of the loungers moved to block any attempt to retreat. For a change, the thieves now found themselves victims. A free-for-all followed but the Cotton Mill Gang was outnumbered. Two of them managed to beat their way past the big fellow at the door and one managed to escape in the crowd. One prisoner was taken by the arms and led toward the prison wall. He started to scream when he realized they were going to push him across the dead line. That would mean his execution. A mighty shove placed him across the dead line where a guard fired a shot at his feet. The man jumped back to safety only to faint dead away.

"Lambert fired that shot, Tom. Must have figured killin' him would be too easy. Look at that crowd headin' to the oak trees."

The alarm was sounded but before the outnumbered guards could respond, three of the Cotton Mill Gang had been hanged by counter attackers. There was little the guards could do.

Tom's attention was centered on the events in the prison yard, but he hardly noticed that his relief was late. I suppose they got what they deserved and I doubt there will be any more trouble from that gang anymore.

Tom stared into the crowd and contemplated what had just happened. He was feeling sick. But then he felt someone's eyes were on him. It was Cousin Ronald. Ronald stared directly at him, and if looks could kill, Tom would be hauled to the dead house behind the dead prisoners. There was no love lost between them when he left Philadelphia and there was none now.

Tom spoke low. "It's a pity. We could have been good friends."

What is he doing here in this part of the yard? He isn't supposed to be here. Ma said he was a First Lt. Yep, some officers from the 71st Pennsylvania tore off their applets for fear of snipers.

After his relief, Tom decided to look up Preacher White. He had been seen among the prisoners lately. Tom walked into the hospital.

"Anybody know where Preacher White is right now?"

No one answered and shook their heads.

I heard he stays with a friend near the depot. Perhaps the preacher could help Ronald with a bit of food and comfort. After all, he is kin. Can't turn my back on him. To do that wouldn't be Christian.

Tom made tracks to find the preacher. *This will be a welcome change. I don't mind guard duty. It breaks up the monotony. If we weren't short on guards, I wouldn't have to guard since I'm the second sergeant in command. Lucky I know where this preacher stays. He is not the only minister to visit the prisoners. Like Mason said, "We got Baptist, Methodist, Presbyterian and Episcopalian that are right faithful." And yes, I've seen them among the prisoners each week.*

When Tom left the prison gate, he didn't have to walk far. He spotted Preacher in a conversation with neighbors that lived close to the prison. Tom stopped a few yards from the neighbors. The preacher glanced in his direction and Tom nodded. That was all the encouragement the preacher needed.

"Preacher White, I met you in Wilmington. I'm Tom Gentry, one of the guards."

"Yes, Tom, I know who you are. What can I do for you?"

"Preacher, my cousin Ronald just arrived as a prisoner, and I can't turn my back on him. Is there any way you can help him?"

The preacher thought for a moment and looked Tom in the eye without changing his expression. "Tom, I can't show favoritism but I will tell you what I can do. There is this lady in town that takes pity on prisoners and likes to help. I will tell her. She might slip a bit of extra food and a shirt to your cousin. This lady would be glad to employ her talents in this manner. Don't ask how. I will tell your cousin what to expect. It's Ronald isn't it?"

"Yes, and thank you, sir."

Tom turned to make his way back to his bed. *I suspect this could be one of the women that help escaped sick and wounded prisoners. I wouldn't want to dig too deep into that matter. Some of the other guards feel as I do. Those poor fellers, enemy or not, deserve to be treated with more dignity.*

* * *

The fall of 1864 brought more prisoners that resulted in more disease and starvation. Families at home had to guard their provisions more carefully. Tom found his trips home for supplies had become less effective. These trips home bore on his conscience. Neighbors that were willing to help in the past were now sullen and resentful. They blamed their hardships on the enemy and the prisoners were still the enemy. On occasion Tom had been accused of an attempt to feed the prisoners before he fed the guards.

One neighbor shouted at him on the last trip. "Let the Confederate Government feed them fools. That's their responsibility. We don't got enough fer our own boys. That's what my son done writ."

One afternoon, as Tom was passing by his cousin, Ronald looked up and saw him, and when he did, Tom thought he saw him hide an object in his arms. *Hiding food from the others, I'll bet.*

Ronald nodded at Tom as if to acknowledge his help.

Tom mumbled to himself, "The lady from town must have found a way."

A large group of new comers drew his attention away from cousin. One looked familiar.

"Good Lord," Tom exclaimed rather loudly. "It's Adam ... Adam McFarland. I hope he doesn't see me. If

I move he might see. Then, what does it matter? Neither of us wanted this stinkin' war. What will Sis say now? How will this effect Sis and Mom?"

When Adam extracted himself from the others, Tom could see a filthy bandage around his neck and left arm. Otherwise he appeared to be in good shape. Adam didn't notice Tom but continued to study the walls.

Larry noticed the look on Tom's face. He drew up closer on the wall walk. "You see a body you know Tom?"

"I see an old friend, someone who saved my life once, and now I can't help him. He is a good friend and my sister's fiancé. Larry, this is terrible."

Tom continued to walk his post as had become his habit. The more he thought on it the more morose he became.

"Will this war and all its hateful influences ever end?"

The next day was wet and unseasonably cool. The cold rain came in waves, torrential at times. It would slack off for a bit and then pour. The worn spots in Tom's slicker made it almost useless. All the guards suffered from the cold; it cut through their clothes to the skin.

I'm cold and the boys down there must be freezing.

The prison yard was a mess and the Death Gate was open. Tom looked through sheet of rain to see a wagon loaded with bodies pulled to the gate.

Why don't they wait until after this storm? The reason must be the stench. Some prisoners were marched with the wagon to bury the dead. He turned and spoke to Larry. "The Death House can expect more after this weather."

When the gate closed, a hat blew off one of the guards once again and usually an occasion for laughter. "Why isn't this funny anymore?"

Larry moved closer to Tom. "Sergeant, I don't like this …watchin' men die like this. Battle is one thing, but this is like murder. I'm thinkin' of askin' to be transferred back to my old company, what's left of it. My injuries don't bother me like this does. Why don't you come along? We aren't doin' anybody any good up here on this here wall."

"I'm inclined to agree Larry. Let's wait until the weather lets up. Tomorrow the weather might be better, but. I'll give it some thought."

After his relief came, Tom returned to his cot to change clothes. He had only one more patched pair of trousers and shirt. The room smelled of wet clothes that hung by the stove. There was little room for him to join the others by the fire. The room was unusually crowded for this time of day. It appeared that a gust of wind had blown the door open. Wind behind the preacher helped him into the doorway. Preacher entered, stomped his feet and removed his slicker so he wouldn't get anybody wet. Someone slammed the door shut.

"Tom, your cousin Ronald is in the sick house. I think he is very sick, what with the cough and fever. When I left I promised to write his father if he got worse. He told me his mom, your aunt, died. Did you know that? I think he meant for you to know."

"Yes, I was at the funeral, Preacher. He must not be thinking straight."

The preacher hung his wet things on the end of the cot that faced the fire and said, "Fellers, if my shoes didn't have so many holes, they would hold more water, and warm water by the fire would warm my feet. My slicker's got so many holes, fleas left for a warmer and a drier place, Texas maybe. There's just no place for vermin or varmint in there."

Someone added, "Get any closer and water in them shoes might set to bilin'"

Tom turned to the preacher. "Preacher, I haven't seen that big feller Adam in a day or two. Don't suppose you saw him in the sick room? He would be hard to miss."

"I know who you mean. No, I haven't seen him today that I can recall." After a pause, the preacher added. "You know there have been several escapes over the months."

Preacher White looked Tom in the eye, and Tom wondered, *has the word gotten around that Adam saved my life and is courting my sister?*

The next day was still cold and intermittent drizzle continued to fall. It was supposed to be Tom's day off but he agreed to fill in for one of the sick guards. It gave him a chance to look for Adam. Preacher White had advised him not to go by the sick room to see his cousin. There was enough sickness and permission might be awkward. He searched the place for his big friend but he was nowhere to be seen. The next day there was still no sign of Adam or the days that followed.

"Tom," Larry interrupted his vigil. "You still lookin' for your old friend? I hear there's been some escapes. It's hard to keep track of how many we still got. Could be he made his escape. Sergeant Mason signed a pass paper for you. He can sign like Major Gee you know. Wants me to tell you to fetch us some eggs and bacon if you can."

Mason found Tom placing his musket in the rack. Before Mason spoke, he removed his old tobacco pouch. The Sergeant looked at Tom as if to speak and began to pack his old pipe.

"It's hard to realize them prisoners used to get passes to Salisbury. We was pretty much friendly back then. Now's the war's gotten worse, longer than anybody thought, and we're gettin' more prisoners, we can't think of doin' that now. You ready to get us some food?"

"I'll leave for home right after I talk to Preacher White."

Information from the preacher revealed no change in his cousin and still no sign of Adam. A neighbor near the prison supplied Tom with a mule.

Tom had not ridden a mule for some time and the mule seemed to know it. It took some persuasion to keep it from returning home. The mule must have smelled feed and water at the end of the road. He didn't need to be encouraged to pick up its pace. The old home place looked good to them both. Tom turned the mule into the corral and sprinted for the back door.

Sun peeped out of the clouds for the occasion as if on command. It sure brightens up the place, outbuildings and all. The warm sun put a spring in his step. One jump placed him on the porch.

Tom opened the door, ran through to the living room, and came to a sudden stop. Sue stood in the middle of the room and gasped when she saw him. Her hand went to her mouth. Fear was written over her face.

SURPRISE GUEST, OR WHAT TO DO ABOUT THE VISITOR

"What's the matter little sister? What's wrong? You look like you suspect I'm a ghost."

Their mother entered the room from the kitchen. She held a basin of water and there was a towel across her shoulder. Tom also noted there were strips of cloth across her arm. Sue had not attempted to answer his question and it began to alarm him.

"Who's hurt Ma?"

Ma ignored the question and said, "Oh, here's a letter from your brother Homer."

Tom stuck the letter in his pocket and demanded again, "Who is hurt, you two?"

Both Sis and Ma looked at him not wanting to say anything. Sue still looked scared and Ma appeared stern.

"Well, someone tell me what's happened. Is it Paw again?"

From the look on Sue's face, I hope in my heart that I know the answer: It's Adam.

"Tom ..." Ma spoke in her gentle but commanding voice she used when there was an unpleasant task. "We have a very sick guest. He is in your bed and needs our Christian charity, I suppose you could say. You come and see, but don't disturb him. You remember your upbringing."

The two women entered the bedroom ahead of Tom. Sue stood beside the bed as if to protect Adam. The guest was sleeping soundly, despite the floorboard squeaks. Adam looked pale and his cheeks were sunk a bit. He was clean-shaven and his hair had been recently washed and combed. Sue took her eyes off Adam to look at Tom. It was a pleading on her face that touched his heart. He could see tears in her eyes.

This was too much for Tom. He smiled at Sue, put his arm around her shoulder and kissed her on the head.

"What do you know? My good friend came to visit. I'm a guard at the prison Sue. I'm not the guard here. How did he get here, and how are you to hide him? You know you put yourselves at great risk. To hide a prisoner, the enemy, is against the law. Does the rest of the family know?"

Sue answered, "They know, but pretend they don't. We'll find a way."

Ma cleared her throat to signal she had something profound to announce. "Adam stumbled on the back porch after dark the day before yesterday, dog tired and starved. We had to burn his clothes, delouse him, clean his wounds and replace bandages. I think we stopped any chance of infections. Trousers and a shirt to fit this big boy is another problem. How he got here he will have to tell himself when he is able. All he wants to do now is sleep and eat, and I do mean eat. That boy must have a hollow leg. Then he was almost starved when he got here. Adam hasn't said much more than thank you."

"Ma, he really hasn't eaten that much." Sue wiped her eyes and smile weakly.

Adam stirred and looked around the room and quickly spotted Tom and groaned, "Am I captured again?"

Tom grinned. "No, you got me surrounded. I surrender."

"You mean you're surrounded by the women?" Adam tried to smile but it hurt his neck.

"Now that I've had a chance to think about it, that is precisely what I mean. How did you get away, Adam? Do you feel like talking? Don't be concerned. You are in friendly hands."

"That's real hospitable. I think it's time to talk." Adam glanced at Sue and Mom as if to assure them he was well enough. "I feel almost human again and would like to tell what I can remember. I've lain here long enough and I know you're all curious about my escape and trip here."

Sue placed another pillow under his head before he prepared to give an account.

"I was part of a burial detail when a guard's hat blew off. I grabbed the hat. It rained so hard they couldn't tell guard from captive. I put on the floppy hat, picked up a blanket and pulled it close, mostly to get warm. I assumed that they confused me for one of the guards later. When it came time to dig I hid behind a tree. A guard saw me behind the tree, but I guess he thought I was one of them and told me to fall in. I did, but I carried a shovel under the blanket like they did with their muskets, with the handle pointed to the ground. It helped, too, that it was getting too dark to see my face. The Lord must have sent a good puff of wind and rain just as we got to the gate. While they struggled with the gate, I moved to the outside wall and hugged it until they closed the gate."

"That's some tale and believable. I saw the burial detail and the guard's hat blow off. I didn't know you were in that detail."

"One of the letters Sue smuggled to me mentioned that you were a guard. It didn't occur to me until now that you are one of the guards at the prison."

Ma looked thoughtful. "With the Lord's help we will manage. We'll find a way to hide Adam. From what information we can glean, we think this war will come to a sad end. It can't go on like this much longer. People will starve, most everybody is hungry. We can't continue to feed ourselves and the army without men folk to plow."

Adam decided to add his thoughts on the matter. "I don't know how long it will take to mend the nation if we become one again. Lincoln sounds consolatory and wants to heal old wounds. I hope ... for this country's sake and the South it's true. Now if I had some clothes I could get out of this bed."

"You just rest a spell longer, young man. One of Uncle's trousers should be made to fit, except for being short and baggy around the middle. A shirt will be the big problem." Ma felt his forehead.

"Fever is gone. He was right feverish when he got here. With the sword wound on this neck and shoulder, and fever, it's a miracle he found us."

Adam turned his head to better take them all in. "Ma, I remember now. A big black man helped me get here. He called me by name. 'You're goin' ta make it' he kept saying."

"Was he young?" Sue asked.

"I think he would be considered young. He found me exhausted when I tried to find the farm in the dark. That wasn't easy, didn't want to be spotted."

"It must have been Lem. He was probably over at the Green Plantation courtin' their pretty maid. He is quite taken by her. Tom's been encouragin' Lem not to give up on her because she's a house maid," Sue said.

Ma looked pensive. "You know, Lem could help hide Adam. He knows the river and the woods around here better than most."

Adam raised himself on an elbow. "I'm putting you good people in danger by my presence. The first day I was away from the prison I saw several old men and boys search houses. They knocked on doors of several cabins and entered one that looked deserted. What's to prevent them from coming here?"

Ma patted Adam on his good shoulder. "We have ways. Our kin told tales passed down from our War of Independence. They knew how to hide from the British. Just leave it to Sue and me."

"If I can get to east Tennessee we would all be safer. Please get me some clothes. I can hide in the barn. Then if I'm caught you good people wouldn't have to know about it, except for food missing."

Tom rubbed the stubble on his chin. "I despair over what happens at the prison. There is little we can do about sickness and starvation. And I'm not determined to return to my old company, if it still exists. The news of the 26th after Gettysburg wasn't to anybody's liking … destroyed. Cousin Joe Boy isn't accounted for and probably the rest of my friends. Major Gee wouldn't release me now since we're short of guards anyway."

Tom took a deep breath. "I have a plan. We need to hide Adam until there's another escape. Then we might have a chance to put the plan into action."

Adam interrupted, "How can another escape help me? Most likely I will get caught whatever I do. This must be a whopper of a plan."

"We could get caught you mean. I know the traveled routes and trails from here to east Tennessee. Avoid the well-traveled routes. There's a need for a well-constructed story to keep us out of trouble when we get further from the prison. For now the old tack room in the barn can hide you. Just keep hay in front of the door."

Adam moved to prop up his head. It made his elbow dig into the soft featherbed. "Are you determined to try this plan? How can you know there will be an escape, and that it will succeed?"

"I saw one of our guards, Lambert, appear to be suspicious of spots on the prison ground. he's part Indian so I trust his instincts. When I tried to see what interested him, fresh dirt was in evidence in spots … and it wasn't wet. A tunnel is under construction somewhere. I would bet my last pair of socks, if it were my habit to bet. Will an escape succeed? We better pray that it does long enough to put the plan in action."

The wounded guest plopped back on his pillows. "I'll ask again, are you sure you want to do this?"

"For my peace of mind and Sue's, yes. I can't watch men die from disease and starvation and not be able to help, enemy or not. It's a terrible time to have a conscience. We can't give them warm clothes, and food has become almost impossible to find. With winter almost here it will be bad, very bad. Medicine is another problem. It's rumored that one of the nurses found a way to smuggle food and medicine into the prison. But that nurse could run out of medicine, or it would be of little use when it gets cold."

"We know our boys in northern Prisons aren't treated any better, but that's no excuse. The Good Book says feed your enemy."

Adam finally nodded in agreement. "You know, that nurse is an angel. The men think so. If you really want to get this involved we need to set a day, time and place."

"Do you think you will be well enough to travel in a week from today, and possibly in a few days?"

"I could be ready in a day if necessary."

Tom looked Adam in the eye and spoke as if giving a command. "We will execute the trip in a week from today, and ladies, help him to be ready for this.

"The prison doesn't expect to see me until after noon tomorrow. Adam looks like he could use more rest. Give me a blanket and one of Pop's old coats and I will sleep in the barn. It started to rain again so it's not likely we will have visitors."

Tom patted Adam on the good shoulder, hugged his mother and kissed his sister on the forehead before he grabbed a blanket. When he passed through the kitchen he grabbed a big chunk of cornbread and some winter squash that had been left on a plate.

It's a good thing I still have my long underwear, even with holes. It will be a cold night.

The climb to the barn loft gave Tom reason to remember one time before. He had come face to face with Lem's big pistol.

"I ain't a goin' back," he said. I knew he wouldn't shoot me but it startled me. He's probably squirreled away enough to buy his ladylove from her owner. The Quakers will do well by him. I hope these times are good to him. He is an honest, hard worker.

Tom picked a spot above the horses in hopes their heat would reach him. After he ate the cornbread and winter squash, he pulled the blanket up to his chin. Sleep came rather quickly. At one point in the early hours, he thought he heard the barn door open, but dismissed it as the wind. In his sleep he dreamed he heard the door several times.

Straw had gotten thin under his right hip. Tom tried to find a comfortable position. In the process he thought he smelled bodies of people. This brought him full awake. He lay still and listened. Wish I had my Navy Colt. Do I hear a faint voice? Yes I do.

A louder voice spoke. "I tell you he ain't a comin, Lem. We got to skedaddle befo' we all gets catched."

"Just you relax some. Somethin' must have slowed him up. Mr. Fritz wouldn't let us down."

The voices got softer and difficult to distinguish. Tom moved to better hear the conversations and dislodged some hay. All got quiet as though they were holding their breath.

There was the sound of the barn door again.

Can this be more folks or Mr. Fritz they spoke of?

"Are you people ready to travel? Did you have a chance to tell your Quaker Friends Lem?"

"The word will get back to them quick, Mr. Fritz. They will know. I don't like doing this to them."

Tom moved his body until he could look over the barn loft ledge. He had not expected a lamplight to reveal his white face. Not that it mattered since he planned to make his presence known. A child squealed and there were several gasps of surprise.

"Lem, you are in good stead with the community, and there's your sweetheart to consider. Why are you want to leave now?"

"Mr. Tom, you ain't heard? Widder Wiggins' nephew goin' to repossess me. Claims he didn't get all his money from the Quakers. The Quaker, Mr. Masters, trusted too much, didn't ask for a receipt. I figure the Widder's nephew wants to sell me."

Fritz raised the lantern to better see Tom.

"I'm of the opinion that you desire not to reveal this night's venture, Tom? We do need to be on our way."

Tom scooted closer to the edge and hung his legs over. He ignored Mr. Fritz for the moment.

"Lem, I don't have the right to ask, but I have a friend in trouble. He doesn't know his way around here like you, and I hoped you would lead him out of here in a few days."

"Mister Tom, you know I would, but where do I hide until them few days is over? They bound to be lookin' for me come daylight. I would do most anything for you and Mr. Adam. I owe you more than I can pay."

"I thought it must have been you that helped Adam." Tom grinned in the faint light. "I've got a little room up here that's a good place to hide if you are willing? Then you could help lead Adam into east Tennessee. There should be two or three others to join you and Adam. I don't think there wouldn't be any more danger, might be less, than the way you planned to travel. Wouldn't the Quakers demand a hearing in court? That would slow down the Widow's nephew."

"Done been a hearin' and we lost. Mr. Fritz, I reckon I will stay for a spell. There's lots of places to hide after they stop lookin' for Lem."

"Go with God, Lem. The rest of you follow me as rapidly as possible for at least two hours. Remember, if you moved anything, be sure you put it back the same way. It's past time to travel."

"Climb up the ladder Lem. I'll show you the place to hide. You might have to share it with Adam before he is well enough to move. Lem, I will forever be in your debt. You can't know how much it means to me, your willingness to help."

"Mister Tom, your sister's man is my problem too. She helped me get to know my Shirley, and that Adam feller will be part of your family. It's like they is part of my family, too, because you and your people are always good to me and my people."

* * *

On the way back to the prison Tom stopped by Preacher's room but he was not in. To leave a note might be dangerous except to say he would enjoy a pastoral visit. The note would have to suffice for the time being.

Should I reveal my plan to help a sick prisoner? Most of the preachers I've heard about would expose me as a traitor. They preach in support of slavery. No, it's out of the question. As much as I like and trust Preacher White, to mention my plan would be stupid. It would endanger Preacher as well.

Preacher seems to care for the prisoners and guards. He ministers to both, and he has a real distaste for this war. Then there is this conversation I overheard between Major Gee and Preacher. The Major had confided in the Preacher his frustration with the Government over acquiring supplies for his men and prisoners. Preacher was sympathetic with the Major and the plight of the prisoners. Preacher would become a friend to Lem and never talk down to him. If my plan is to succeed, and I have to return to the prison, Preacher would be the best person to lead them to east Tennessee.

There was one bright spot on his return to duty. It was to enjoy the humor of his friend Larry. Another was to talk with Preacher.

I hope Larry hasn't asked for a transfer while I was gone. Don't think he can get it.

There was another letter waiting for him when he arrived. This one was from Willie. He scanned it quickly to get the gist of the message before searching for Larry. Right about that time Larry walked into the room, and Tom shared content of the letters with him.

"Willie had to flee into the interior near Charleston after they had to run aground. It was the only way to avoid capture. Engine trouble had put them at risk but he and the crew had gotten away. Willie didn't indicate what kind of work he was doing. Ma mentioned that he tried to get in the Navy, and if he were not able, he would try for Mexico and join Homer."

That reminded him of Homer's letter in his pocket. He pulled it out and read it.

"Good grief! I didn't know my brother was so long-winded. Larry, Here's the gist of Homer's letter."

"Homer's letter indicates he shipped cotton to Matamoros, Mexico that had been smuggled over the border from Texas. Most of the Southern ports were blockaded and this was the safest way to exchange freight. He said he visited Wilmington and a certain widow lady. It's obvious that he and Widow Talent were now more than friends.

"He refers to her as 'Joan' … that's progress … even admitted to holding her hand and kissing her. Don't blame him.

"Another part of Homer's letter tells of shipping from England to the Bahamas and back … that they landed on the east side of an island off the coast of South Carolina and hid the ship. He told of a previous trip they had to run past the Federal blockade.

"He wrote that while he was on the train returning to Charleston, he was approached by a lieutenant and sergeant who demanded his papers and attempted to get him to join the army, but he convinced them he was more needed as a blockade runner for the Confederacy than as a soldier. Listen to what he said to them, 'From what I've seen, you could use more war supplies than you need me.'

"After the lieutenant left him, the sergeant asked him if he had any extra shoes. Willie felt sorry for the poor fellow when he looked at his feet, but he had no extras."

* * *

One evening shortly after Tom returned to the prison, he stood on the wall and looked pensively over the ragged starved prisoners. He still tried to formulate a workable plan in his head. Of the several that he had toyed with, the one that was the most workable would not allow for a safe return to duty, the original idea.

Adam and Lem are the least of my concerns now. Ma will feed them. I hope my nervousness and preoccupation is not showing. The last guard that tried to desert is now in prison with the Yankees so we are being watched ... and we look on each other with suspicion. Who will have the nerve to try next?'

From his post Tom could see unusual excitement at the entrance gate. A heavyset woman was having an animated conversation with Sergeant Mason and Major Gee. Two other guards listened with interest. He spotted Preacher for the first time in days. Tom looked for an opportunity to give a signal that he wanted to talk. Preacher looked up to search the wall. When Tom caught his eye, he pointed to the sick room.

To judge from the commotion and the guard's activity, there must have been an escape. I can't wait for my relief to find what happened. If there has been an escape why have they not sounded an alarm? If it is an escape it could hinder the completion of my plans. Almost wish there were someone else to smuggle Adam and Lem into east Tennessee.

When his relief finally came, Tom handed the musket to the guard without a word. He hurried to the guard's house. When he arrived, there was a lot of loud talk. Some of the guards were angry and some seemed amused. Larry looked on with a great deal of amusement.

Someone asked, "How could that happen, right under our noses?"

Larry chuckled, "Them boys et so many rats they turned into one. Then it was easy to dig out. Tom, my friend, we have a great escape. That fat old busy body came by to tell Mason and the rest she done found the end of a tunnel, and tracks leadin' to the burial ground."

Tom sat on his bunk to contemplate this development.

Sergeant Mason walked in. "Tom, you see that big woman that just left directly after talkin' to the Major and me?" He went on to repeat what Larry had just told him. "You notice there aren't as many prisoners? Course not. We got so many how could you miss a bunch. Accordin' to the foot prints, the lady says most all our Yankee prisoners done flew the chicken coop."

Tom stroked his chin as he thought on the problems ahead. Sergeant Mason was beginning to study Tom closely. This started to make him nervous.

Surely the Sergeant couldn't have any idea I'm trying to help an escaped prisoner? How could he know when I'm still not finished with my plan? Lem is the only one besides Adam and my folks that have an idea. Am I to get the lecture how Ezekiel Collette deserted, was sent into battle, wounded, and disappointed the family. Even friends and neighbors shunned him, or so the story goes.

It turned out badly for Colette, but I don't lay any blame on him. He was lucky. The last two guards were put in with the prisoners.

The sergeant still studies me. He's about to say something serious. Lord, I've prayed very little before this and for that, I'm sorry. I do need your help now, please.

SHOES FOR RUNNING

Sue appeared unusually restless at the breakfast table and Ma noticed.

"What's on your mind, Sue? We're doing the best we can for Adam."

"I know, Ma, it's just that if Adam has to leave us now, how will he manage? His feet are not completely healed, and he has no shoes. None of Unk's or Paw's will fit his big feet. You suppose we could get some from the store without them getting suspicious?"

"It would be risky, but we better try. I've been givin' that some thought, too. There should be a boot Adam's size that would fit. Not many feet that size around here."

Sue started to get out of her chair.

"Keep your seat. I'll get a couple of sticks and try to get his size. Better yet, you go ahead and finish Uncle's socks you are knitting while I size up Adam's feet, but make the socks longer."

Ma Gentry placed a plate of food in the bottom of a wood bucket used for chicken scraps. A round disk that stuck to the sides above the plate was placed next. Chicken scraps in a dish came next. There was probably no one to observe, but Nell Gentry took no chances. Anyone that helped escaped prisoners was not dealt with kindly. Opening the door that had been cut into the larger barn door, she announced. "It's me. All you critters relax."

Adam answered with, "Nobody here but us mules that work hard all day. I truly am thankful for all the trouble you and the family endure on my account. I hope someday to repay. I don't think there is any way I can repay in full all the attention and care you have given."

"While you eat your breakfast I intend to make a way to measure your feet. We got to get you boots or shoes for those big feet of yours. If you go to traipsin' around here and leave foot prints with those bare feet of yours, folks will start to carry shotguns for fear they might come up on the wild creature that makes those tracks, start a rumor about some hairy monster from the river. Then again, no one near here has feet that size. It might occur to them there's a prisoner loose."

Adam finished his meal and placed his plate in the bucket. Nell Gentry returned with two sticks and a knife.

"Mrs. Gentry, do you plan to cut my feet down to size to fit Tom's boots?"

"Now that is a right smart idea. Which one do we start with? No, I'm going to use one stick to get the length of your foot and the other the width, on the chance the store has a size close enough. Hold up one of your feet but don't block the light from the door with that huge mud masher."

Adam couldn't help chuckle. "Thank you for keeping up my spirits. I see where Sue and Tom get their sense of humor. Who intends to look over the store about the foot gear? I don't have any way to repay right now."

"We haven't decided yet. You just stretch, exercise and rest between exercises, to get stronger. There are hiding places down by the river you might have to use. You might have to run. You're still safe here at present."

* * *

Sue and Uncle Casper entered the country store before they noticed several men around the big stove. One man talked about how they had tracked some escaped prisoners and returned them in chains. Another started to relate how efficient his friend's bloodhounds were. Casper approached the storekeeper who was more interested in the stories than customers. He cleared his throat to get attention.

"You have any flour or bacon left. And I could use a pair of shoes this long and this wide."

Sue and Uncle Casper examined the shelves. Most were empty, except for a few bolts of cloth. Sue eyed a few can goods.

"Haven't had bacon for days and sold the last flour this mornin'. Let ... me ... see. Nope, no shoes this size. Now, I might have a boot that size. Up here ... on this ... shelf, don't get many calls for this size. Ah ... yep. This boot should fit perfect. If you don't got gold or silver it will be twenty-seven script. That's it. Sorry Casper, these are hard times."

Casper reached deep in his pockets and Sue dug into her purse. Between the two they came up with the money.

"I thank you. Wish I had some bacon for you. What are you goin' to do with them big boots, Casper? Give them to Tom so he can step on the toes of them prisoners?"

There were a few chuckles and a belly laugh from the men around the stove.

"That's not a bad idea. I'll see if Tom takes to that idea. We better hurry Sue. See if I can get some corn meal along the way."

"I got a ten pound bag of corn meal for a dollar. I'll let you have it for half price since you bought them boots."

Sue smiled and placed some coins on the counter. Casper hoisted the meal on his shoulder and made for the door.

Virgil Mason, the storekeeper, stroked his beard deep in thought. "Now that is strange? I never sold footwear that size to anybody in that family before. Johnson, what do you think? They must've got them boots for somebody else. Now my boy was interested in that Sue, but she paid him no mind, right after Tom's Yankee friend came to visit. Tom fought, got himself wounded and all before he made guard. But that Sue is a Yankee lover. Sue and Casper might be hidin' a Yankee. You all know Casper wasn't for succession. She threw over my son for a Yankee, and it makes my blood boil, I tell you. I think we ought to close early and pay their place a visit with the Home Guard. What do you think, Johnson?"

"I think the Home Guard is too busy hangin' around the prison hopin' to catch a prisoner and make money. We're good Confederate citizens, we can do it. To make it legal, we better send for the sheriff before we pay them a visit."

He nodded to a bystander and said, "One of you go get the sheriff and we'll meet on the road ta their place."

* * *

Sue felt pleased with herself as she climbed the ladder to the barn loft. "Adam, it's me. I've got you supper and a little surprise. Well, not so little I suppose. Come sit beside me while you eat. I made us a couple fried apple pies. Uncle Casper and I have been busy. See what we got."

Adam smiled broadly as he took the boots from Sue. "This is really something. How will I ever thank you and Unk? Before my mud stomp … what did your ma call them?"

"Mud mashers ."

"Well, anyway, before my feet disappear in the boots I'll eat so we can enjoy those apple pies together."

Adam intended to finish his evening meal before he put on the new boots. Then the young couple ate their pies in silence. After they had finished the pie, Sue placed the empty plate under the wood disk that separated plate from chicken feed. She gave him a quick kiss and started for the door.

"See you at breakfast, Adam."

The sun had started to set when Sue got to the barn door. A commotion in the barnyard made Sue hesitate. She peeked out a crack in the door. Sue mumbled, "What's this?"

Several of armed men are in our yard? Several approached the house. It wasn't difficult to identify the big sheriff by his old horse.

"Adam, there are men spreading out around the place. You better hide in the tack room. I'll push hay around the door … hurry. And don't come out for a thing."

She sped up the ladder as Adam scampered into the little tack room. Just as she threw the last handful of hay against the door someone walked in the barn.

"What you doin' up there, Missy?"

"I was looking for eggs. What are you doing here and why didn't you knock?"

"Well, you might be hidin' a Yankee, Yankee lover. You stay up there until I have a look see."

Sue became weak with fear that the man would discover Adam. She prayed silently, raising her eyes heavenward.

The leer on the man's face now made her fear for her own safety. Sue slowly backed away from the hay that hid Adam to draw the intruder away.

"You stay there, Missy. We're goin' to have a right good look around."

The man reached the top of the ladder to the hayloft so Sue backed away. He kept his eyes on her and looked pleased with himself.

She heard Adam struggle with the tackle door. Sue dragged her foot across the floor to hide Adams efforts with the door. Her foot came in contact with the trap door that leads to the stall below. She quickly reaching down and flipped the trapdoor open.

Sue immediately shouted so Adam could hear. "Mister, I'm going to slide down the ladder in this hole to the stall. I dare you to follow. Bessie the mule doesn't take to strangers in her stall and will kick our head off. Bye now."

Sue slid down the ladder with her feet and hands on the outside of the vertical boards like she had seen her brothers. There was no fear of splinters from the smooth boards. Not that it mattered. She was angry and determined.

On her dash from the barn, she looked back and shouted for Adam's benefit, "You can't catch me now!"

She almost ran into the sheriff's horse.

The horse sidestepped several paces. This got the search party and the sheriff's attention. She checked her balance, put her hands on her hips and focused a displeased eye on the sheriff.

She yelled, "That man tried to waylay me. Is this the kind of company you keep?"

A broad smile spread across the storekeeper's face. Mr. Mason started to clap his hands with glee until he saw the angry look on the sheriff's face.

Sue's would be assailant, exited the barn panting. He came to a sudden stop, all eyes were on him. The sheriff looked on the man in disgust.

"Sue, you want to sign a complaint on that rascal?"

Nell Gentry came out of the house in time to hear the Sheriff's comment.

Sue turned to look at her pursuer. "I ought to sign a warrant against that no good egg-suckin' pole cat. But would that be the Christian thing to do, Ma?"

Her mother looked around the group of men and back at Sue.

"That's up to you daughter. Did he lay a hand on you?"

"No ma'am. I was too quick for him. Why are all these people here, and yellin' 'Yankee lover'? Sure, I had a Yankee friend. Some of you men did too. Is that the reason for this little army? You want to forget you had Yankee friends? Sheriff Hicks, you know my brother served, got himself wounded, and now guards at the prison. If you want to, search the whole place."

Sheriff Hicks looked straight at the store-owner. "Some busybody thought we ought to see if you good people were hidin' an escaped prisoner. And did he find any Yankee in the barn? No. I'm sorry for the intrusion on your property. I truly am, but I was just doin' my duty. We will be leavin' now.

"Good evenin' to you Mrs. Gentry, and you Sue. Come on boys, it's back to mindin' our own business again."

Ma Gentry and Sue noticed the storekeeper and one other whispering. Obviously he was not satisfied or happy with the situation.

Ma whispered to Sue, "It's most likely they will put somebody to watch this place. We got to be more cautious than ever."

The storekeeper assigned Johnson and Peabody to take turns. They were to watch the Gentry place until someone came to relieve them. He reminded them that the boots were too large for anyone of the Gentry family.

To aggravate the family, the store owner assigned Johnson to deliver a message and apologize for the men's actions. The man was not always tactful and spoke without thinking, which might was the reason he was sent.

"Johnson, Tell them we have bacon at the store. Then find a place to hide."

Johnson walked up to the porch where Mr. Gentry was stacking firewood. He couldn't remember what his message was.

"Mr. Gentry, I was wonderin' who those big boots were for. It's got me plumb curious."

Will Gentry Sr. pulled out a large ragged bandana and wiped his brow. He studied Johnson for a moment.

"You know how much Lem's been to all the neighbors, and since my boys are all gone we been using him more than most. So the women must have got them for him."

"Well now, Mr. Gentry. Lem is wanted for runnin' off from the Wiggins. I reckon you wouldn't be the only family about that has been usin' that run away."

"I thought that had all been settled, Johnson. Are you sure? Lem has been fairly foot free and loose around these parts for a long time."

"I'll be movin' on. There was somethin' I was supposed to tell you but I forgot. Give my respect to the missus."

Sue giggled through the window, "Paw, you wouldn't be bending the truth about the boots, would you? What would the preacher say?"

"I'm getting forgetful, daughter. Johnson must be rubbin' off on me."

* * *

Later that night Adam awoke to the sound of pebbles against the side of the barn. He looked through cracks but could see a thing but a star or two.

"You up there, wake up. It's time to leave." The voice strained to be quiet and still be heard.

"Most of the family and Lem know where I hide. It has to be one of them."

Adam grabbed the pistol Lem had left him and decided to investigate. He slipped out the barn door and crouched low as he ran in the direction of the voice.

A voice whispered, "Over here. Preacher sent me instead of Lem. He was afraid Lem might be caught and I wouldn't arouse suspicion. This place is watched and we got a way to get you out here."

"I'll be right back. I have to say goodbye."

Adam knew it was risky but had to at least show some appreciation for their help, and to see Sue. He tapped on Sue's window. The tap-tap noise added to the increased tension. Her face soon appeared in the window.

He caught his breath, torchlight approached then from in front of the house.

"Sue, they must be after me and I must leave, love. Men with torches are in front of the house."

Sue raised the window and kissed him. "Take care of yourself and write when you can." Adam made a dash for the woods. Someone shouted, "There he is. Turn them dogs loose. Lem can't get far with them dogs on his tail. Spread out in case he changes directions."

Someone grabbed Adam by the arm and gave him a momentary scare.

"Follow me close. I know how to lose them. When we get to the creek bed, stay in it for a while. It will be daylight before they discover where we get out. It's funny, they think you're Lem. They were countin' on a reward."

Back at the house, Mr. Gentry stood on the porch in his nightshirt. One of the search party stood facing him with a lantern.

"I've been almost certain escaped runaway or two used my barn for a place to gather more than once. Nothin' was ever taken or disturbed except some barefoot tracks and the way the barn door was not shut like usual. Never gave it much thought until now. I had no way to prove my barn was a place to hide or I would have reported it. There wasn't a thing to arouse my suspicion for over a year."

"Mr. Gentry, some of those runaway fellers can be pretty tricky. The boys'll catch him I suppose. I like Lem and almost hope he gets away. Good night to you sir. I regret the disturbance."

THE SEARCH PARTY

The next morning Sergeant Mason motioned for Tom to enter the Major's office. Both men studied Tom. Neither man had changed their expression.

Here it comes. Tom thought. *Sergeant Mason has something on his mind that involves me and I'm not sure it's to my best interests.*

The Sergeant Mason slapped his leg and finally spoke. "Tom, old boy, how would you like to head up a search party? You know the lay of the land and you are the most able. This time there's too many for the Home Guard. And then, they ain't been able to round up them deserters either. They won't do any better with these escaped prisoners. Why don't you pick two or three of the guards and some of the Home Guard and strike out. Does this sound good to you? I'll make it right with the Major. He's not feelin so good right now and would agree to most anything. His dealin' with the government's made him ill in the head."

Whew, thought I was up for a firing squad for a bit. This could be an answer to prayer ... in fact it is.

"Sure Sergeant, I could do this." Thinking quickly, Tom added. "There is this black fellow back home ... if I can get the word to him ... knows the land better than

I do. The first guard I would pick is my friend Corporal Larry Sims. Also there is this Indian Lambert. He doesn't look too well and this might be good for him to get away from the prison. We could use a good tracker and I hear tell he is."

He remembered the preacher and wondered why he couldn't find him home.

"Sergeant Mason, we could use another civilian or two. I'll ask Preacher if he could help me on that, and I'll get Lambert started on the equipment we'll need. Larry will need to go by mule to my home to fetch the black man I mentioned. I need to take a short walk and clear my head, might get word to the Home Guard while I'm out."

Sergeant Major growled. "Clearin' your nose from the smells, don't you mean? Don't be gone too long. You have to lead the search party and not the Home Guard. You know how the Major and me feel about prisoners fallin' into the hands of some in the guard. They might bring them back and then they might not."

"Mason, would the Masons near Lexington, one a storekeeper, be of kin?"

"Yep. Some of that kin we don't claim and that is one of them. And Tom, don't forget to come back. Remember Ezekiel Collette."

* * *

Tom crossed the train tracks to where Preacher stood. He tried to think of the best way to use the escape for Lem and Adam's benefit. Looking up from the muddy path, he noticed Preacher had a smile on his face.

There's something on his mind he's going to say what it is. It must be good.

"Tom, I've talked with Major Gee and he agrees with me that I know this country better than most."

Tom felt his heart race. *I won't be allowed to lead the search. I'll have to remain as guard. There'll have to be another way to help my two fugitives.*

"But should the escaped bunch get much beyond the next forty miles, you know the country better. I'll be the chief guide until we get beyond this country. If we get that far you take over and become chief. The Major and I are concerned about some hot heads in the Home Guard. That's the reason he is convinced I should go. As a minister I could give you support. He has agreed to let your friend Larry and an Indian guard called Lambert to accompany us. Do you know him?"

Tom took a deep breath. How am I going to work Adam into this? Lem will not be a problem.

"I know the Indian well. And I had asked the Sergeant for those two, this is good. Lambert is the guard that shot to miss when one of the prisoners stumbled across the dead line. When the ball hit the dirt, the boy jumped back a good five feet or more."

"Tom, could you find part of a Confederate uniform to fit Adam?" Preacher couldn't help chuckling when Tom's mouth dropped open a couple inches.

"If I were to bait you, your expression would give you away. I sent a friend to fetch Lem and Adam. I didn't know you had already sent for them. Those two are to meet us at a country church I told the friend about. Conditions are too hot around your place. That nosy store keeper could cause your folks a heap of trouble."

Swallowing, Tom spoke slowly, "I thought you were a strong enemy of the Union, Preacher?"

"As a Confederate I think you feel the way I do, but my conscience won't let me overlook those that suffer so much in that prison. I hate this war. It was supposed to be over in days, but figured differently from the start. If South Carolina had not fired on Fort Sumter, we might have been able to work this out. Lincoln didn't help by baiting them; he put supplies and troops in that fort. I know most preachers support slavery by Scriptures, and I did too. But I was never holdin' to bad treatment of slaves. They are here so make the best of it. The Scriptures speak of slaves and masters. Perhaps they were more like servants back then like me and you."

Preacher was beginning to show anger for the first time Tom had known him. "My main objection to the Union is their attitude, tell us how we should live, pay tariffs on all we sell and buy and invade our homeland." He paused to take a breath and began to grin. "Tom, you got me on my political stump. I figure if the Confederacy survives, and it doesn't look like it right now, there will be other splits and possible wars. Texas might get mad over lack of railroads or somethin' and pull out. It would have been better to stay in the Union.

"Tom, your search party is probably waiting for you. You better see to your business with the guards. I will go ahead and meet Adam and Lem. We will look for you at that little church about a mile west of the county line or just beyond the river."

On his return Tom found the two guards had packs, blankets and muskets. Larry handed Tom his musket. All their weapons appeared to be newly captured.

Sure wish this was one of the Henry repeating rifles I heard about. "I need to go by my cousins and pick up my bow and navy pistol. They might prove to be useful."

Tom looked at Larry who grinned from ear to ear. Lambert's face was as unreadable as ever.

Larry spoke out with friendly gusto. "I got your tack, Sergeant Gentry. You want your old friend at arms to carry our orders from the Major? I've got part of a good slicker to wrap it in."

Tom smiled and nodded.

Sergeant Mason stepped up briskly and clapped his one hand against his stomach. "Well boys, wish I could go with you. Do your duty. You will meet several Home Guard a-waitin' to join you at the edge of town. Don't know how many but I heard one is bad tempered. He's a little feisty short feller I met in town. I believe you met him once before, Tom. Good Huntin'."

The little party stepped off briskly to distance themselves from the prison smells and into freedom for a time. Everyone was in good spirits. Larry caught up with Tom.

"Them boys in the prison yard was fightin' for what they believed in. Preservin' the Union for the most part. I believe slavery is a side issue with most ... could be wrong."

"You're probably right, Larry. From the news I get from Raleigh and the new prisoners, we're not doin' very well. I lost some good friends in the 26th at Gettysburg. Was it worth it? If the lack of food for us, our troops, and the prisoners is any indication of the country's condition, our cause is lost. I know we shouldn't talk like this."

When they reached the last few houses, they figured it to be the edge of town. Preacher had not gotten far. It appeared he was held up by the Home Guard. When Tom's company of three walked up, the guard fell in without a word.

They're a sullen bunch.

Tom stretched his steps to fall I with the Preacher, and asked him, "Do you have a plan on how to return the prisoners? I've got an idea or two but they are not that good."

Preacher knows what I mean ... what to do to avoid suspicion about Adam when we find them.

Preacher answered, "Mine is not so good either."

Preacher then spoke so the others couldn't hear. "You figure we need to make Adam and Lem part of the search party? I see by your expression that you do. That means I've got to escape with those two somewhere along the way. You'll need to take the rest another way to give us a chance. Since before we left, I been thinkin' of joining my sister in east Tennessee and keep on goin'. How good a tracker is that Indian of yours?"

"Don't know, but I don't think he likes his job much. I get the impression he would like to be somewhere other than the prison. He might even decide to go west with you. Now my friend Larry doesn't matter much to him which way the wind blows so long as it's not downwind from the prison. He can be happy anywhere away from this war. He's done his duty ... seen enough of this conflict. You must have had some influence with the Major to get us assigned to this work."

They soon spotted the rest of the Home Guard and concentrated on the eight men ahead. One big fellow held three bloodhounds by short ropes. When they got closer, Tom saw Mick step forward with an air of importance.

"'Bout time you got here. We should have gone without you and caught them by now. We better start movin, right now. If the sheriff hadn't told us to wait, we'd been gone."

Before Mick could say more, the man with the hounds interrupted. "You mean Dick here had to remind you what the Sheriff said."

Mick ignored the comment and said, "Since the old man can't lead no more I'm the leader now even if I'm crippled up a bit. That's what kept me out of the army. Get them dogs to doin' their job, Charlie. I doubt they is any good anyhow."

Tom looked at Larry out of the corner of his eyes and Larry winked.

A girl with blond hair sat in a rocker on the porch of the last house. She yelled at them in an un-lady like manner. "If you're lookin' for your prisoners, they passed hours ago. Nearly scared me half to death. I thought I would be attacked. There must have been twenty or more. You will have to do some marchin' to catch up with those Yankees."

Tom recognized her voice. Mary Ellen had changed since he had last seen her.

"You fellers keep going. I have a message for this lady from her husband if I ever saw her again."

He turned to Mary Ellen and asked, "Did the prisoners try to enter your house? Why aren't you with your folks?"

"No, the prisoners passed by hardly payin' any attention to me. It was right scary. I'm visitin' my dearly departed husband's sister. I was engaged again but got news he's missin' too. You know somethin' about my husband?"

I think she's disgusting, but I'm here for the sole purpose to comfort this young widow.

"The Captain told me to tell you he loved you. He said this to me when he was carried to a hospital."

I lied. How could I tell her his throat wound wouldn't permit him talk. In truth, he only motioned to me, pleaded with his eyes, and growled. I think he kept trying to say, "tell her, tell her."

"Why didn't you tell me this before, Tom?"

"I apologize, I've been too messed up with my own troubles, and my head wound must cause me to forget when I should remember. When they carried me to the hospital I saw your Captain. I must catch up with my men, sorry I have to run."

"I thank you most kindly, Tom. Catch them Yankees for me … and the Captain."

* * *

It took longer to catch up with the search party than anticipated. He had almost forgotten to stop by his cousin's to pick up his bow and arrows. His Navy Colt had been cleaned and placed in a new oiled holster.

It's a good thing they were not at home, or I would have had lost more time. But I left a note. Might have thought my bow and pistol were stolen.

Tom could hear Mick's high-pitched excited voice before he saw him. When he made a turn around a bend, Tom could see the company had stopped.

Mick shouted, "I tell you them dogs aren't no good, or they would have caught the scent by now. All they can smell is food … our food."

"Don't speak bad of my dogs, you'll hurt their feelin's and mess up their confidence. They're right sensitive like."

Preacher raised a hand for silence. "Mick, I remind you one more time that I'm in charge until we cross the river and then Tom will be in charge. This is an army matter and you are to assist us and …"

Mick interrupted, "You're a preacher. What you got to do with the army?"

"I'm still an Army Chaplin and Major Gee put me in charge. If we're going to get this job done we got to cooperate. We stand here wastin' time while our enemy keeps movin'."

Mick sensed his own men wouldn't back him, and the preacher was not about to back down. He grumbled, stared at the ground and marched up the trail. That started the party on the move.

Tom saw a chance to split the guard and deplete their numbers.

"You know, the dogs look healthy. I've heard nothing but good things about them good trackers, you know. They just need a chance, too, and a little help. Doesn't the smell of fear get the dogs excited? Did you give them somethin' to smell? All they smell now is anger."

"I reckon, can't say for sure. You're right, my dogs is good at what they do."

Little Mick growled, "You're just makin' excuses, you two. We ain't gettin' nowhere."

"Mick, you're right about us not getting anywhere. I say we split up, spread out some. We're too bunched up to find a trail. We'll keep Lambert to track and you take the dogs. If we find anything, fire off a shot as a signal."

Mick was getting angry again. "Now hold on. I'm in charge here," glancing at preacher he added, "at least of this guard. Searchin' for them Yankees is my business too. I say we go straight ahead."

Mick leaned his musket against a tree and rubbed his shoulder.

Tom grinned. "No, you're not going further. I remind you this is a military matter and this is the County line. I know this country and we don't need a hot head in our company."

This could be the line and Mick wouldn't know the difference.

Mick angrily grabbed his musket and started to swing it in Tom's direction but quickly stopped. His eyes looked very big.

Until that moment Tom hadn't realized he had drawn his pistol. It was a relief to see preacher had drawn his nine shot.

Mick shouted, "I'll telegraph ahead. You haven't heard the last of me."

"You forget, we have papers ... warrants, if you please," added Tom. "You will make yourself look foolish to telegraph all over the place. You've done your part. It's time for you to go home."

In a conciliatory move toward the Home Guard, Tom suggested, "Some of you in the Guard are welcome to accompany us for a while by splittin' up the search."

"Me and the Guard is goin' home. Follow me," Mick ordered.

The man with the hounds had a different idea. "Me and the dogs is goin to split up like the Sergeant said. Anybody comin' with me?"

Five of the guard went along with the man and his dogs, and three followed Mick. The one they called Dick remained with the prison guards. When Mick passed Dick, he grabbed Dick's shotgun without any resistance from Dick.

Tom handed Dick his musket. "My pistol and bow will be enough for me, I carried too much. I'm glad you decided to come along. Will you have trouble with Mick back in the Guard when you get back?"

"Don't intend on goin back in the Guard. I got folks west of here I ain't seen in a month of Sundays. I might keep a goin."

NEW TRAVELING COMPANIONS

It was dusk by the time they come to the little church, the place where they were to meet Lem and Adam. Lem was the first to be spotted who casually rose from behind a bush. Adam soon appeared.

Tom ran ahead of the search party to speak to Adam. "You need to know that now you're a mute, or can't talk. If you say much around the prison guards they will spot you for a Yank. I hope this act won't have to last long." Adam bobbed his head up and down, getting into the act. So the others could hear, Tom asked Adam, "Have you seen anything of escaped Yankees?"

By now the others had joined Tom. Lem answered, "I ain't seen any prisoners, did you Adam?"

Adam shook his head vigorously. Lem added, "Nope, I guess we ain't."

"Boys, this is Lem. I practically grew up with him, and Adam here is as strong as a mule, even if he is a mute." Tom looked straight at Lem when he said the mute word. "They can be a help if we find the prisoners. This is Dick, Lambert and Larry. You know the preacher."

Lambert pointed to the ground and chuckled. "The Yanks will be easy to follow if they stay together. They've been pretty clever up to now, but too many of them.

Surprised they haven't been seen and caught by now.
Their numbers must have helped them."

"I have an idea why they were not easy to see up to
now," Tom added. "Prisoners that escaped, were captured,
and returned to the prison related their mistakes. One
was the attempt to approach a house with food on their
minds. The homes of black folks within a hundred miles
were watched. That's where most prisoners looked for
help and could find it. So, unless you want to be slowed
down, we need to stay away from most homes."

Tom pointed to the church. "It's too dark to go further. Some of you can sleep in there. I will sleep under the
trees. First daylight we better be up and searching."

Although the first day started well until they tied up
with the Home Guard, now they felt the emotional drain.
They were all tired, unaccustomed to travel.

They ate some food out of their packs and bedded
down.

"I'll take the first watch," Tom announced. "There's
no cause for concern. But we don't need any unpleasant
surprises. Use your pack for a headrest or put it where
critters can't get you food. I learned this by experience."

"I'll take the second watch after midnight." It was
Larry's voice.

It was easy to pick up the prisoner's trail the next
morning. Tom's party hadn't gone far when they found
where the prisoners stopped for the night. It was apparent the fugitives didn't travel fast.

Tom considered, *the Yanks must be weak, scared and hungry. If troops had been available as they had when the big break-
out attempt occurred, the prisoners would have been caught and
on their way back. I'm glad I had scrounged for food that day.
The sound of cannon was the first I knew they stormed the gate.*

Too many people died that day. How can you maintain humor at such times?

He turned to check on the men's progress.

Larry took several big steps to catch Tom. "How're we going to get them back when we catch them? It doesn't look like it's going to take much longer to catch up, but there are so few of us and too many of them."

Lem laughed. "Suppose he lets some of them go on, and we take what we can back."

The three of them saw a movement in the brush. When they came to a sudden stop, Preacher bumped into them.

"Mister Tom, that was a big hog gone wild," Lem whispered. "Can you kill it ... with your bow? Gun might bring the Home Guard down on us."

The little group feared the hog would run off before Tom could string his bow. Fortunately the hog was more interested in acorns than the search party.

The hog's left side was visible through the brush. This gave Tom a clear shot. He eased back on the string until his hand touched his cheek like the professor taught. The string was released and the arrow flew true. The hog gave a squeal, ran for several steps and dropped.

Lem let out a whoop. "Thank you Lord, thank you for guidin' Tom's aim and his arrow. We eat good tonight. How we goin' to cure the rest? It wouldn't be proper to waste any, bein' how hungry we been."

"Dick, you any good at skinning a hog?"

Dick nodded.

"Good, you want to help Lem? It should keep until we get to the old Brown place this evening. Since we got food for tonight, we can eat some out of our tack now ... build up some strength. Anybody got coffee ... real coffee?

Larry, you can start a fire while we rest a bit. They can't be too far ahead. No need to hurry."

Larry pulled out his big knife and started to cut shavings off a dead limb. Lambert gathered small sticks while he kicked larger ones to where Larry worked on his shavings.

Adam had difficulty in removing his too-small pack, and in the process swallowed a flying bug that caused him to have a coughing fit.

When he was able, he tried to clear his throat, and finished with a couple growls.

Larry glanced at Adam and resumed his whittling. Then he stopped in the middle of a cut and studied Adam. He then looked up at Tom and back at Adam who made another sound with his throat. Larry smiled, looked at Adam before he stood.

"Funny, I never knew mutes could clear their throat like that? Tom, he sure looks like one of them big prisoners we had a time back."

He took another slice out of his piece of wood before sheathing his knife, and then started to gather the shavings for the fire.

Everyone quietly waited for the next shoe to fall.

"Would he pass for that Yankee friend of yours you pointed out a while back Tom? I reckon if I had a Yankee friend that saved my life I would want him to look like Adam. How about you Lambert? You got any friends you owe your life too?"

"I make friends kind of slow. Been betrayed too many times. You and Sergeant Gentry are my friends, and I like Dick and Preacher over there. Lem is everybody's friend. Think I know what you're askin', and I say any friend of Sergeant Tom is a friend of mine."

Tom moved around in an attempt to stay awake. Trips home kept him in good shape for the march but his concerns for Adam had not let him sleep well. He paid little attention to the chatter. It startled him when he realized what had been said concerning Adam. He looked at Larry and Lambert to see if they were serious.

If they are serious and accept Adam, this is too easy. They can challenge me on my attempt to escort an escaped prisoner. Now is their chance. Dick doesn't seem to care. Adam and Preacher must have heard the conversation. Lambert and Larry don't know Preacher knows. It's time to test friendships and loyalty.

"We better finish our coffee and get back on the trail. There's not much day light left."

It was a tired group that picked up their equipment and commenced to walk. No one was in good shape to march for long periods, or so they thought. On the other hand, Dick walked like a woodsman and was little affected.

The second day they started out fresh and early. But by noon they felt sore and tired. Tom was glad he had given his musket to Dick. Larry had taken the lead and followed the trail of broken sticks and weeds. There were a few barefoot tracks when they came to damp ground.

Larry turned to look at Adam and asked, "You want to take the lead for a spell. Don't need a tracker for this work. I want to light my pipe."

Adam nodded then stepped forward.

"Adam, that coffee I made was strong enough to cure a mute of laziness. It healed your cough-spell back there, so just sing out if you see anything strange."

Lambert gave a couple chuckles and Dick looked confused. Adam looked back to see a sly grin all over Larry's face.

Dick asked, "Tom, how far is it to the, uh, Brown home you mentioned? I would feel better if we had this meat salted down."

"We'll be there well before dark."

Tom walked close to Dick and realized he didn't know much about the man. He could be a thorn in the blanket.

"Were you not interested in the army, Dick?"

"I'm too old. Could've passed for younger, but the missus got sick and my child died so the Home Guard looked fair. My wife died too, shortly after that. Preacher here helped me a heap, still does. Think I'll go on to east Tennessee with him to find some of my people. Now I figure to help him, Lem, and the mute there."

Dick picked a twig off a limb and stuck it in his mouth. "Except the mute talked in his sleep last night a bit. Talkin' to somebody named Sue."

Tom shifted his eyes to Adam, and shook his head.

Talk stopped for almost an hour, until they came to a grove of trees that led off to their left. There was a narrow road made of two parallel tracks made by wagon wheels. The tracks stretched to a large brick house about three hundred yards ahead. Grass grew between the tracks showed it hadn't been used for months.

"Boys, that's the Brown's place. Looks deserted from here." On closer examination, it did look deserted. One rocker stood by itself and another was turned over on the porch. The front door was half open. Weeds grew in the path to the front steps.

"There is a well in back," Tom told the company, where we can fill or canteens there. Larry, you and Lem go around that side of the house and we'll take this side."

They probably wonder what the purpose of that might be.

"I saw some trampled weeds, and that make me suspicious." The yard and paths that lead to the outbuildings were much the same. There were a few broken barrels and furniture among the weeds but not much else. Larry and Lem made it to the back yard at the same time Tom started for the well house.

Suddenly the situation changed. A man who looked half-starved with an axe handle stood out from behind a corncrib followed by two others. An unexpected voice coming from the back porch spoke, "You got muskets, but we outnumber you considerably. And we can jump you from where we stand before you get off a shot. We already decided we'll all die before we go back to that stinkin' prison and starve, or die of sickness. You can keep a travelin' or we will have a battle right here. Wonder what the history books will say about this one?"

The man with the axe handle moved toward Tom in a threatening manner. Tom moved to expose the pistol on his right hip and held up his left hand. The sight of the pistol made the man hesitate.

Tom responded, "Don't be so ready to fight. There might not be a need for anyone to die this day. Let's relax and parlay a bit."

The man on the porch spoke again but Tom kept his eye on the axe handle. "You will not talk us into a trip back there, Sergeant. I already told you we made up our minds on that account. It's time for you to go. If you're a gambler you know your hand's not that good, so I'm calling you."

Tom spoke louder this time. "Relax a bit longer. Have you asked us if we want to go back? It might be that some of us intend to reach for east Tennessee."

"What kind of trick is that, Rebel? If you don't want to fight, then let us be on our way and you turn around. You can tell the Major you lost us. That would be the best thing for you and your puny guards. You might take five or six of us but you can't kill all of us."

"You on the porch, look at that big fellow with the sandy hair in the shirt that's too small. Take your hat off Adam. Does he look familiar to you? He was a prisoner like you but escaped from a burial detail two weeks ago or more. Lambert over there shot to miss when one of your boys stumbled over the dead line."

Tom thought of another detail to further defuse the standoff. "Surely you recognize Preacher White."

Tom pointed to others. "Preacher, Adam, Lem and Dick are for east Tennessee. I can't speak for Larry or Lambert, and you don't know this country like Preacher, or me."

The porch voice spoke less assuredly this time. "We're going to West Virginia, at least some of us are. There is strength in numbers, as you can see, if we stick together. So the rest of my men need to make up their minds."

Preacher spoke up for the first time since he joined them in the back yard. "You're making a mistake to stay grouped up like this. If the Major knew how many had escaped, he would have sent for a Calvary and still could. A large number like this would alarm citizens to the point they would send for help. It would be better if you divided into three or more groups. It sounds like you haven't decided which way to go and who is to lead."

The axe handle man shouted at the porch, "Swanson, you heard the Preacher. I was trying to tell you. This will not work. We will starve on the trail. There are too many to forage adequately.

STRANGE BED FELLOWS

"I'm ready to follow Mr. White and I do recognize that big fellow called Adam. Frank West was in that burial detail and noticed the big boy was gone when they got ready to hand in the shovels. He laughed about that for days."

Swanson growled, "I guess that settles it then. Nate, why don't you take Elmo with you and go with the preacher. I'm tired of your mouth. Any of the rest of you want to split up? According to the sergeant, all of us are too many to travel without suspicion. How are you going to survive, you and your troops, Preacher?"

Larry answered for him. "We got papers that says we are a search party lookin' for escaped Yankees."

Another Yank spoke up. "Swanson, me and Sam are going to Tennessee but we travel south of Preacher's company." Six or seven followed Sam and three joined Swanson. Four others walked back to the road.

Tom tapped Lem on the shoulder. "Do you think you might find some salt in that old smokehouse?"

Lem mumbled under his breath, "Lem, do this, Lem do that. Makes me feel right at home. Lem must be tired." Speaking louder, he started for the smokehouse. "I sure will Mr. Tom. Now what was that just run into that old smokehouse?"

Lem cautiously crept toward the smokehouse, trembling as he went. His eyes darted intermittently to three fresh graves nearby, with wilted flowers covering the graves.

He stepped into the smokehouse and stopped to give his eyes time to adjust to the dark. "You in here salt. Give up now and save old Lem a bunch of trouble. What's that?"

Scratching sounds above his head made him look up. A boy of about twelve dressed in rags stared back at him. He hung on the rafters and looked scared. The boy reached over to one of the rafters and picked up a pistol, tried to point the thing and nearly lost his balance.

Lem gave him a toothy grin. "Boy, we don't aim to do you harm. Come down from there. What's your name, boy? How old do you be?"

"You might not mean me no harm, but what about them others out there?"

He couldn't hold the pistol and rafters too and started to slip. The pistol dropped so he decided to swing down. "I'm caught anyhow. Might as well come down. That old pistol don't have no loads."

"Boy, we got us a preacher out there, and our leader is a real gentleman. You don't have to be scared. Now, what's your name and where are your folks?"

"I'm not scared, and I'm called Grover ... Grover Brown. And I'm twelve years old. My folks is in those graves you saw and my old nurse maid. I'll trade that pistol for some food. You got any?"

Grover noticed Lem staring at the rafters again. "That's a rifle butt you see stickin' out. My brother told us it is an Austrian Lorenz rifle-musket. He smuggled it back home after a battle. Don't ask me how he done it. I only got six loads for it. There's a shotgun on another rafter. You got anything to trade for it. I don't have any powder or shot."

"I wondered who you were talking to Lem. Sounded like you had a good conversation with yourself for a spell."

Tom put his hands on his hips and smiled at the boy. "I'm Tom. What do they call you at mealtime, young sir?"

Grover started to reply but started to cough.

Lem answered for him, "This here is Grover. That's his folks in them graves yonder. We've been talkin trade. He wants to trade this pistol for food, and he's got a shotgun up there to trade. There's no shot for it and there is a rifle-musket on that rafter. We could use more muskets."

"That musket is an Austrian built Lorenz Rifle-Musket. My brother smuggled it home his last trip. It shoots real good. I shot a squirrel day before yesterday. Only got six loads left. That's goin' to be mine."

Tom turned to shout, "Dick, did Mick leave you any shot and powder in that bag when he grabbed the shotgun?"

The boy with his two new friends stepped out of the smokehouse to watch Dick scratch in his bag.

"Yep, I got plenty. Should have made Mick give the shotgun back. What you got on your mind, Sergeant?"

Tom explained to the others about the conversation in the smokehouse, to trade food for the pistol. Lem and Dick convinced Grover the shotgun would be of better use than the rifle-musket. They would throw in extra hog meat and shotgun shot and powder for the Lorenz. When Grover hesitated, Tom gave up his pocketknife. The trading also included salt Grover had hid overhead in the outhouse. It proved to be enough for their meat and some left over.

"Guess it's time to start to trust folks. You fellers seem to be honest and friendly, but I'm keepin' my eye on y'all. Can't be too careful anymore. Lately I've slept in a friend's barn two miles down the same road you travel. No one else lived there. This gives me a good chance to care for the graves. I want to be around if my sisters come back, you know."

Over a meal of hard tack and fresh meat, Grover told them what happened to his family. "I watched from the woods. They butchered my momma and daddy. Saw it through the window. Daddy tried to protect Momma and was clubbed over the head. They shot my momma when she reached for a musket. The maid ran out the back door. One of them let her get halfway to the shed before he shot her in the back, then laughed like it was the funniest thing ever. One of the men, could be two, worked for my daddy a while back. It was pure jealousy. They wanted what my folks had worked for so hard."

"I gave them a Christian burial and said what words I could see through my tears. The cover of the Bible was burnt but the pages were good. I did it for them because that was what I know they wanted. Don't have much use for the book after what all happened. It was good that my sisters were not here. We were all stayin' with friends. Now we'll be movin' west to be with relatives.

"It was too much for these friends to feed, along with my sisters. So I lived off what I could trap in the woods close to home. Don't know why. Nobody will come home again. Trappin' rabbits and squirrels is my specialty. Sometimes I eat possum, groundhog, or raccoon. Must have trapped-out the woods around here, because it's been days since I caught anything. Didn't want to shoot a thing so I can save my shots for the Bushwhackers that done in my folks. I'll see them again someday.

"For some reason, them murderers had it in for my folks, besides the ones that worked for us. I think it was mostly because my daddy ordered Frank Coggons off the place when my aunt didn't want to court him. He knows I'm around and keep lookin' for me. He don't know where my sisters are, good thing. He's been back here twice and me without the gun. I've seen him on the road lookin' for me. Had a clear shot once, but there were too many of them. One of these days I'll catch him by his lonesome and I'll take revenge."

Preacher White tried to make a point. "'Vengeance is mine; I will repay saith the Lord'. Let the law handle him. You don't have to be burdened with what you've seen or thoughts of revenge. Have you talked to the sheriff, or a preacher?"

"Ain't no preachers around, and the sheriff is an old man too scared of that bunch. He don't do nothin' about them."

Tom slapped Larry on the back. "Gents, we might make it to the boy's barn by dark if we start now. I don't think this is a good place to bed down. What do you think Lem."

I know Lem is bothered by these graves ... don't much like them either.

The little company was soon strung out on the path some called a road. It still looked to be traveled by horse or mule recently. Lambert led, and Tom brought up the rear for a change. It would soon be dark and the company was tired, except for Dick who chose to accompany the boy. Grover seemed happy with his choice of shotgun, knife and a good chunk of hog.

Lambert turned to give a warning. "Pass the word: I hear horses."

As if by plan, common sense made them find cover where convenient. Dick pulled Grover with him behind a large fallen tree. Dick rested the rifle-musket against the tree. Now they had a clear view of a clearing in front of their hiding place. The rock foundation of a burned out cabin stood on the edge of the clearing. Further back stood a well, only evidence that life was once cherished on this piece of ground.

Six men on horseback pulled up to the well. One man dismounted and began to lower a bucket. Grover lay down his shotgun and grabbed Dick's rifle-musket. Before he could stop Grover, he pulled back the hammer. That got everybody's attention.

The boy yelled at one man on horseback, "Frank Coggon, you would be a dead man now if it weren't for the preacher here. We're marchin you to the next county and turn you over to the law for the murderin' trash that you be."

Frank yelled at his nearest companion. "Here catch," and threw a jug to him that he had been sampling.

"You little skinny whelp, I'll whup the hide off'n you."

Frank spurred his horse and charged in Grover's direction pulling a long bullwhip from the saddle horn. "Been waitin' …"

Bam!

There was a long blinding flash of gunpowder in the semi darkness. Grover fired past the horse's head into Frank Coggon's upper chest. Frank reeled to the back of the horse, losing his whip. The startled horse came to a dead stop and made a quick turn that threw Frank out of the saddle. One of Frank's feet caught in the stirrup.

The other riders had trouble with their excited mounts. One the men on horseback drew his pistol, big mistake. Another shot from the weeds blew him off his horse. Frank's horse dragged him into the two closest riders. Two men in back started to ride away but stopped short. Tom's company had them surrounded.

"Drop your weapons," Tom commanded. "Live to rob another day. Do it now."

There were only four left mounted so the number of men around them convinced them to comply. There was a moan from one of the men on the ground. Three of the men rode mules and the fourth rode bareback.

"You two on the mules pick up your friends and take them with you. We were sent to clean out the likes of you, so pass the word. So if you got any idea to cause any more good folks trouble, you better try some place like Mexico."

Grover and Dick exchanged weapons before they came out of hiding. Grover had tears down his cheeks and was glad the others couldn't see him; however, it was too difficult to stifle a sob. Dick patted him on the back. "You didn't have no choice, Grover. If you hadn't shot, I would've. Now you got revenge for your mamma and daddy."

"Ain't sure I wanted revenge. Don't make much sense. Preacher reminded me what my mamma always said about forgiveness and "*Vengeance is mine, I will repay, saith the Lord.*" Still wanted revenge but needed to obey my mamma's wishes too. I intended to turn them over to the law. If she is lookin' down, I hope she isn't disappointed in me."

"Grover, listen to Preacher White. I'm sure what you intended to do with those men instead of revenge pleased you mamma. When you get older it will be easier to forgive and not seek revenge, even for such terrible wrongs you've suffered."

One of the horsed nickered at Grover. "That's old Babe and that's Dandy. They were my daddy's plow horses."

At that point there was only one man on horseback. He intended to ride off with the other two riders on mules but the boy's claim to the horses made a walk back a real possibility. "Give me back my daddy's horses. Where did Frank get his horse?"

"Uh, I think it belongs to Frank. Don't know for sure." The answer came from a bushwhacker bent over a downed man. The man studied Frank's foot, and his boot was still in the stirrup.

"Yep ... boot and foot match. Gonna take three of us to load him on a mule."

Tom walked to where he could speak to Grover. "In the morning why don't you borrow Frank's horse and lead your daddy's horses to where your sisters stay. I don't think Frank will care. Your sisters would be glad to see you and those horses. The way you've learned to trap and shoot, they should be glad to have you near."

He turned to the outlaws. "The rest of you no accounts get. Only reason you're not locked up is so this night's work will get told around. We got more like you to chase."

One of the outlaws grumbled something unintelligible as the mules and their burdens made their way. One of them didn't walk too steady.

"He must have drunk more than the rest."

The remark brought a chuckle from some of the company.

"Preacher, part of what I said to the outlaws is truth. If we run into the likes of those murderers we're obligated to take care of them."

Preacher smiled and nodded in agreement.

"Let's see what kind of weapons we captured? Can someone light a torch or something?" After some scrambling about, Nate came up with a bunch of broom straw. Others helped build a fire.

"I only see three knives. Most of the gang must have kept theirs. It appears we now have as much powder, cap and lead as we need. Larry, would you pick the better muskets and pistols we might need and bury the rest. Larry, choose a man to help you."

Larry motioned for Lambert to help pick up the weapons. They were soon dumped beside the fire that had grown to cooking size.

"Here Nate, catch. You might need this pistol. And what's your name fellow? Coleslaw?"

The boy answered, "It's Holtsclaw."

Larry said, Here's a horse pistol made back in the 40's. You want a musket too? Wouldn't do for a search party to be without weapons. Now everybody has one."

"Call me ..." (Holtsclaw coughs.) "... Matt, short for Matthew. I've been called Coleslaw before. I'll take the pistol and that short carbine musket." (More coughing.) "Can't talk without coughing."

Larry turned to the silent one. "What's you name fellow. I haven't heard a word from you since we started."

Nate answered for the fellow. "Larry, if you could see him he would be grinning like an idiot. He will do what you say but he can't talk. We call him Elmo. Don't know where he picked up that handle but he must have seen some horrible thing in this war. It's messed up his mind. Elmo, you want an old musket?"

The firelight revealed the man shaking his head.

"Then will you carry a pack with powder and ball?" Elmo nodded at that request.

Preacher stood to stretch with his hands on his hips. "It's a shame we wait until dark to get acquainted. Everybody wanted to get as far away from that prison as possible. I won't take a chance to write down names since it might not be safe. I have a good memory."

"Most of you call me Preacher and so I am. Preacher B.T. White at you service. For a time I was a chaplain in the 27th. At first they didn't want me but they were soon won over. After a foot wound I transferred to a Brigade whose commander didn't like preachers. That Brigade will remain nameless. In the early days of this war some Generals didn't see any need for chaplains but most did. Weary of suffering and dying, I figure I can be of better service to this little company and the people of east Tennessee. There are enough preachers at the prison. As you can tell I like to talk. We all know Sergeant Tom Gentry. I know Lem, Adam, and Lambert but the rest might not. So, everyone please tell me your names. If we're to travel together, we don't need to find out who we are by accident."

The only black in the group spoke up first. "Just call me Lem."

"I'm Adam McFarland on my way to East Tennessee."

"Nate Melville, and this is Elmo. We look out for each other.

"I'm Don Lambert, but call me Lambert."

"Matt Holtsclaw is my name," Matt struggled to suppress a cough.

"I'm Richard so most call me plain Dick."

"You can call me James, James Mathews. I thought I needed to change my last name from Goldberg to Mathews. The reason isn't important now."

Tom decided to add his two cents worth. "I am Sergeant Gentry, formerly of the 26th North Carolina and presently on a march to find escaped prisoners."

There were a few chuckles.

"And I'm Larry Sims, sometimes Corporal Sims.

"Tom, you need to know where Lambert and me stand on this trip to Tennessee. Like you, we ain't traitors, but don't want to be part of starvin' and watchin' prisoners die from sickness. Seen enough death for a bunch of lifetimes. We'll see how we feel when reachin' Tennessee. Might not want to go back. The war might be over before we reach where we're a goin'."

Dick put a hand on Grover's shoulder. "How much further to where you sleep in that barn, son?"

The next morning when the men began to stir, Tom heard Dick ask one of the men if he had seen Grover. He had discovered the boy was gone. One could still hear the horses in the barn. That meant the boy hadn't gone far. Three men had slept in the hayloft with Grover. Two had slept under a lean-to attached to the barn. The rest were scattered around in the open. It wasn't long before most of the men were up and had prepared breakfast.

Tom approached Preacher who stretched his long arms as if he were a bird about to take flight.

"Preacher White, I'm wondering if we ought to split up this company. There are twelve of us. I hadn't planned on this many. Remember that Yankee that left us said there was safety in numbers? That's good so long as our papers seemed to be legitimate and that say we're a search party. But like another one said, when we forage for food, could be a problem. This land has been scalped almost clean."

"We will have to trust in the Lord, Tom. I volunteered to lead these boys into east Tennessee so I feel led to do that. Could be there is a reason for this number. While we eat, don't you think it would be a good idea to get acquainted and personal to draw us together? But if you still feel like we should split into two groups, I'll take Matt, he's not well, and Elmo and one other. I know you would want to keep Adam."

Tom studied the ground for a time before he answered. "Preacher, every time I get close to people, I'm afraid I'm goin' to lose them, but maybe you're right."

Before he could continue, they saw Grover approach. The boy held a rabbit by the ears.

"Preacher, I think I would vote that we stay together for now. Hope it won't be necessary to divide the boys down the road ... or up the road as it curves into the mountains."

Lem yelled, "Hey Grover. That all the rabbit you got this trip? That won't hardly feed two of us. That rabbit must have relatives."

"Well Lem, I did leave the fattest and biggest black cat with white stripes in one of my traps. You can have him if you want to."

This brought a laugh and more than a few remarks from the rest.

"Naw, I'll leave it for your next trip. Might be good if you can get beyond the smell."

Larry swallowed his last bit of food. "While we ..." He hesitated to pick up his pack. "... saddle up I'll say a word or two. I met Tom while we were in the 26th and told him if I got wounded enough to be a guard I'd join him. Got no ambition up to now but I'm workin' on it. Hope to settle down in Asheville after this is over. I kind of look after Tom, feel kinda responsible for him since that first battle near Beaufort."

Tom slapped Larry on the back. "I thank you for that and for savin' my bacon on the burning bridge. But we better stay quiet on the trail as much as possible. Too much talk could bring trouble further west, and always use caution. Don't think we have to worry about Home Guard around here. It looks like rain so we better put some miles behind us. Mud will slow us some."

Grover tied the lines of his daddy's horses to the saddle horn of Frank's horse. The lines got in the way when he tried to mount. Dick walked over to assist him.

"Hold on, Grover. Climb aboard that horse and I'll hand you the lines. You've got enough slack they should follow right along. When it's safe, leave a message on the first barn rafter tellin' where I might find you. I'm thinkin' about comin' back this way after the war. You take care of yourself … alright?"

Larry stepped up his pace to walk next to Dick. "Looks like the boy is determined to get out of here in a hurry. Dick, you really took a like to that boy. Must miss his family real bad. Didn't Grover say something about having an aunt? You suppose she is still single … and pretty? You ought to look further into this family of Grover's, since takin' such an interest in the boy."

"Hum. Who can say? Sounds like a good idea though. Might look into that."

"What's to keep you on this trail? You could catch up with the boy and help take the horses to his sisters. We would miss your company but most times opportunity only knocks once. You've heard the sayin'."

"I could do that … catch up. But I might be addin' more worry for Grover and his sisters, and the friends they stay with. They sure don't want to see another mouth comin' their way."

Preacher cleared his throat to get their attention. "You could help deliver the horses and get a better chance to really learn their situation. That would ease your mind. The Lord will provide, remember."

Dick turned with a grin and bounded off in the Grover's direction. "That bein' the case, I'm determined to see that boy gets to his sisters."

OLD FRIENDS REUNITED

Three days after Dick and Grover left for the boy's sisters, the company found another deserted farmhouse. It was too close to the traveled road to escape notice. Windows were broken, the barn doors hung on broken hinges, the hog lot fence was down and the outbuildings had been torched. The men searched the house and buildings for signs of food. Nate was able to scrape up a few kernels of corn from the corn crib. The breakfast that morning had been skimpy even by their standards. One more meal off the hog they had killed and they would be without. Even though hungry, they were reluctant to eat their last scrap of food.

Thanks to Larry and Lem, morale was fair to good. They would pass comments up and down the line to keep up their spirits. Talk was kept to a minimum most of the time. Tom and Preacher realized there was a need to keep up their spirits. At least the former prisoners couldn't be happier, so it appeared.

The noon break was only for a rest stop. No one wanted to talk much except Lem and Larry.

Tom looked over the group. "We are too many, and we wear ourselves out in an attempt to stay off the traveled routes. If we find people about, they're probably just as hungry. Can't avoid the roads all together. We're bound to meet folks sooner or later. We'll just keep walking…"

"… And trusting," the Preacher added. "It's now Tom's turn to lead us. He knows this country best. Time to march, fellers."

They picked up their gear, grumbled and grunted until all had joined on the trail.

The man bringing up the rear gave a poor bird whistle. Tom glanced back and observed the men start to find cover. He stepped behind a big oak tree in time to hear a horseshoe strike rock. The ground, wet from rain, had almost allowed riders to catch them by surprise. There were two riders, the one in front wore a slouch hat, and the other one looked familiar.

Nate, who brought up the rear started to laugh. Several others in the rear soon joined. The rider in front was none other than Grover, who wore a slouch hat too large for him. Dick rode behind on one of the farm horses. The other farm horse was led behind Dick's horse.

"You two decide to join us again?"

Dick grinned from ear to ear. "We got mostly corn, corn meal, a little flour and a side of bacon, and another rabbit Grover caught. Figured you could use some of this by now."

Tom reached out to shake Grover's hand, and then Dick's. "We could use the food right now. I thought the people your sisters were staying with were short on food themselves, Grover?"

"They were," Grover answered. "Nobody there. The place was empty. I knew where they hid this stuff, or we wouldn't have it. They left a note in our secret place sayin' they had taken my sisters to Aunt Frances place. She was supposed to marry some gent west of here, at the foot of the mountains near Yadkinville, I think. That's where we're headin'."

Tom smiled up at Dick and placed his hand on the horse's neck. "It appears that the pretty aunt was supposed to get married. But you're still goin' to take Grover to his sisters, I see. You are a good man, Dick."

"Don't know how good I am? Seems like after I lost my good woman and boys I ain't been good for much. I can be good for this boy that lost his folks. He tells me his Aunt Frances got a half-sister that came to be with her. This aunt is pretty too, and single. They call her Grace. Now that is a right good name, don't you think? I might be of help to the whole family up there. Could sell my property near Salisbury or move them down there."

"It appears you have a plan all worked out."

"Yep. We can travel with you and your company today, but we'll need to branch off some time tomorrow, if that is all right with you. You might be interested to know we ran across the trail of the other escaped Yankees. It's good for them that nobody is trying to catch them night now, judgin' from the tracks they're leavin'. That bunch is bound to run into suspicious folk or Home Guard several times before they reach West Virginia or east Tennessee. You might too, so be on your guard."

The men began to look at Tom anxiously and he took the hint.

"It's time to march again. Grover, you and Dick are too easy to see on top of the horses. You two bring up the rear and let us move forward to spot trouble before you are seen. Why not walk your horses for a spell and rest the horses."

Tom took the lead again and wondered what his brothers would say if they could see him. They would probably disown him for his part in the escape.

PROBLEM RELATIVES

The next day Dick and Grover prepared to find the sisters and aunts. Tom and Preacher insisted they take most of the food with them.

Grover offered, "Mr. Tom, keep more of this food."

Tom refused. "Grover, thank you for your generosity, but we'd be just as guilty as the bushwhackers. You didn't have to share any of this food with us, and we're fine for today. True, our food will soon be gone, but we'll come up with a plan to get some to keep up our strength."

By the time they came to a stream to fill their canteens, Tom thought he had a workable plan. "Whose turn is it to stand guard while I try to develop a plan to find more food?"

Lambert moved ahead. "I'll take the lead if someone will watch the rear.

Matt started to move to the rear but Nate motioned for him to keep his seat. "You might start to cough again and give us away, Matt. I'll do it."

"Before we're out of supplies, we can pick a spot ahead like a tall pine, a hill or so for a place to meet. Fan out and see what we can find, then meet at that spot. Go in pairs or by threes. If you find a home or anything of interest, fire one musket shot, and send a runner to the meeting

Victims of Conscience

spot. Further west we are less likely to find food. Too bad Grover's not with us to trap."

Larry stood up after he filled his water bottle. "I like the idea. There's less chance us to get lost or separated. We better move away from this part of the creek. It makes too much noise. Somebody could slip up on us."

Lambert suddenly signaled that there was trouble ahead. The group quickly found places to hide away from the beaten trail.

Four men on horseback appeared followed by three shoeless men tied together with rope. The sorry appearance of the men revealed much about their treatment. There were two others that followed on mules. They could hear them splash through the stream. The horses were allowed to drink but the prisoners were jerked from the stream when they bent to drink. The captors cursed the prisoners and dragged them away after the horses.

When the horsemen were out of sight, Lem was the first to speak. "We coulda had us five horses, and three more mouths to feed if we had a mind to."

Tom looked at Preacher. "I had the same idea Preacher. I'm sure you did."

"Yep, but those five would have been missed, and their prisoners don't appear to be able to last much longer. I wonder if those prisoners had tried to dodge the conscription."

"If they had, it's been for a long time, and just got caught," Larry grumbled, then yelled. "I hear a horse runnin' this way."

One of the prisoners ran down the trail, with a rope still tied to his arm.

Tom's company hid again.

The man dodged into the short pines that had started to grow on the side of the trail. The man on horseback stopped his horse, took aim with an old musket converted from a flintlock and tried to fire. The powder must have been wet. It took a couple seconds to fire. The poor prisoner yelled and sprawled into the creek, presumably dead.

Horse and man again took up the chase, but the horse stepped in a hole, broke his leg and threw his rider. The rider groaned as he picked himself up.

"Well hoss, you done rode your last. Reckon I got to put you out of your misery."

There was another shot and footsteps with the rider now on foot.

The company was about to rise from their hiding places when there was the sound of water splashes, then a sputter and gasp. The prisoner with rope was soon out of sight.

Preacher looked at Tom and remarked, "Well, I never. This is one day for my diary."

"Looks like the person he chased got away," Larry said.

Matt broke into a coughing spell after the captors were out of hearing distance.

When he was able to speak, he approached Larry. "You ever butcher a horse?"

"Nope. I bet Lem knows how."

Tom, hearing the conversation, motioned to Lem. "We sure could use some meat, Lem. Can you carve up a chunk of meat for each of us? And fellers, we need take no more that we can eat tonight and not pack any further down the trail … might spoil and make us sick."

Lem suggested, "Mister Tom, I saved us some salt that might make us an extra meat. Looks like the Good Lord done provided us a meal tonight. Mister Larry, I need help. I know, you're face says no but your stomach says do it. Cuz down the road you knows it will be hungry again."

Lem shook his head. "Wasn't that runner's time to go was it, Preacher?"

"The Lord is Sovereign and still in control. Who knows His plans for any of us? Be sure you are right with God. One of these days I'll have to take time to preach a sermon to this company."

Larry chuckled, "I know some of these boys could use a sermon."

Preacher grinned. "We could all use several, Larry."

The following day Lambert discovered a mixture of foot and hoof tracks. He put a finger to his lips for silence and motioned for Tom to come forward. "I think some escaped prisoners that left us at the Brown place play cat and mouse with the men on horseback."

Lambert pointed to tracks around the stream. "There must be six or eight men on horses. The prison must have telegraphed ahead about the escape, and maybe about us too."

"I'm sure they have, Lambert, the same day of the escape. That would be the Major Gee's responsibility to see it done. We will have to be more cautious from now on."

Larry had to ask, "How can you tell so much from all those mixed tracks?"

"I'm part Indian you know." Lambert muttered, "so I'm suppose to act like an Indian part of the time, whether I believe in what I see or not."

* * *

The next afternoon the little company moved along the fringes of fields to avoid detection. Larry was in the lead again when he motioned for them to hide.

Tom moved in a crouch to join Larry. "What did you see Larry?"

"I heard horses, and not too far away, but they stopped."

"Well, we can't stay here all day. I'll take Lambert and creep ahead, see what we can find."

Tom motioned for Lambert to follow. They had not moved very far before they heard a horse stomp impatiently. Tom glanced behind and noticed the rest followed at a short distance. Larry and Tom took another step that caused a horse to neigh, and then followed by a whisper by one of the riders.

A shot from less than a half-mile interrupted the standoff. "Let's go!" shouted an unseen rider.

The sound of horse hoofs and the creak of leather were followed by another shot.

Nate asked Tom, "Can Lambert and me investigate the shots?"

"Yes but be careful. You should be safe if all the interest is in what they are shooting at." His comment was interrupted by a volley of musket fire.

"Sounds like a war. How many shots did you make out, Preacher?"

"There were four or five ... too close together to really tell."

During the lull that followed, they decided it's over or they were reloading. A very excited Lem ran back in a hurry.

"I followed them ... Lambert and Nate. What we see is three horses tied in the woods and about five men hidin' behind a stone fence. They're aimin' their muskets at an old house. You think like me, we better not stick our noses in this fight?"

Before Tom could reply, Lambert ran back to where they sat on their haunches. He confirmed what Lem said, but added, "A sixth man creeps along the woods toward a blind side of the house."

"Lem told me about the five, what …?"

Lambert started to move back the way he had come, turned and added. "Thought you ought to know. I saw two of Grover's plow horses in back under a big oak. I didn't see the horse Grover rides."

"This changes the situation considerably," Tom thought out loud. "If we start to leave bodies about somebody will call out the army. Let's see if we can bluff our friends free from this little war. We got to get close without getting shot."

The little company crept as close as they dared.

"Uh oh … That feller at the end of the fence is about to go for the cabin's blind side. Lambert, can you bounce a lead ball off a rock close to that boy and get his attention?"

Just as the man was about to jump the fence, Lambert fired off a shot. The man jumped back behind the fence.

Tom stood up and walked out of the thicket. "Hold on there. Them folks in the house are my prisoners. You leave them be before somebody gets hurt. Hey, you in the house. We want them horses you stole, and we want you back at the prison. Dick, you bring your rascal of a son on out soon as we talk these gents into declarin' a truce. You and Grover set easy. You at the stone fence, relax. Anyhow, we got you cornered."

"Says who!" One of them at the stone fence shouted. "We saw them first. They be our prisoners, dead or alive."

"That's alright with me but we got you outnumbered."

Tom whispered to Preacher, "How much Confederate money do we have? Think we have enough to split the reward with this gang?"

Their leader hesitated and asked in a voice that lacked confidence, "You could fight over them horse thieves, or whatever they be, and get yourself shot up?"

Tom replied, "You see we are here. We'll split the reward. I'll leave ten dollars tied to the saddle of your horse and you ride off. They won't be any good to you dead."

"How do we know you will put the money where you say? And we want ten a piece."

"Send one of your men and I'll give him the money. Then it will be up to us to get those two out of the house. Times a-wasting."

The leader tapped the closest man and said something to him. The man then stood, but he remembered the guns in the house and ducked to crawl away. When he felt safe he ran to where he could see Tom and the others. Preacher handed him two Confederate ten bills to ransom Dick and Grover.

"Ain't you got gold? Harry ain't goin' to like this."

Preacher laughed. "Do we look like we would carry gold? Here's another ten, the last we have. Consider yourselves lucky, or blessed. We don't have to do this."

The man jumped on one of the horses, grabbed the reins of the other two, and rode toward the fence waving the bills. This time he forgot the musket and shotgun in the house. The other men at the fence crouched, ran for the woods, and motioned for the rider to follow.

Tom kept his eyes on the retreating men. "Boys, we better keep our eyes on those people. I hope they keep on the move somewhere."

Tom cupped his hands to his mouth and shouted. "Dick … Grover, come on out with your hands up and live to fight another day."

The bunch from the fence stopped to see what would happen. Tom turned to his men. "Company-A, don't let those people get trigger happy."

Dick and Grover stepped out the door holding their weapons over their heads.

Tom turned to the leader, "You got your money and nobody got hurt. We thank you for your help."

The leader growled, "You done spoilt our fun, soldier. We could have had two more horses too."

The man with the money poked the leader in the ribs. "We got the money without havin' to smoke them out Harry. We got things to do."

Money-man turned to one of the others. "Jump on back little brother."

Little brother was quick jump behind. "Wish you wouldn't call me little brother. I'm almost big as you."

It was comical to watch the six try to get on the horses so they could ride double. Lem couldn't resist a giggle.

Larry slapped Tom on the back. "Now, we're 'Company-A'. Why didn't you think up our name before this?"

"Probably should have but there wasn't a real need until now."

When their attackers were out of sight, Dick and Grover shouldered their weapons. Tom and Company-A walked to meet their new prisoners who wore big smiles.

Dick shouted to the onlookers. "I never thought I'd be glad to be taken prisoner. Me and the boy are beholdin' to you boys."

Dick stopped to turn around and yelled louder. "Hello girls. You can come out now."

Dick explained, "When we heard the horses, I told the girls to slip out back and hide down near the creek, and if trouble started, to walk up the creek till they found a trail. I figure they didn't go far. The young one is curious, and would most likely want to watch and see what happens. But it's startin' to look like they done what I told them."

Tom motioned for the company to move up the trail. "Don't think I realized that you two left our company. Dick, why don't you and Grover get the horses and catch up with us. Then we can find the girls. Would they be Grover's sisters?"

"Yep, and right feisty. One sister is called Flo. She's the oldest. The least one Grover calls Jo. They're not more than fifteen minutes ahead of you. Grover, we better get them nags."

The company hadn't gone far when a covey of quail exploded from a thicket. Tom thought: *Too bad Grover's not here with his shotgun. Those outlaws should be out of earshot by now. I'll try my luck.*

"They are out of sight. Maybe I'll forget them."

"If that is Flo and Jo that stirred up those birds, you can come out. We're friends of Dick and Grover. They will join us shortly."

"That be us, I reckon. They know where we are. Hurry Jo. My feet are wet and cold. Don't want to wade that creek no more. You sound like a Yankee, mister. Why you shoot at my brother and his friend if you know them?" Flo's face took on a sudden worried expression, one of distrust.

"Girls, I lived among the Yankees for a spell so I'll sound like them sometimes. It wasn't us that fired on the house. It was a bunch of no-goods.

"The bottom of your dress is wet. You can return to the house now and change."

Flo looked down at her faded blue dress that was a bit too large. It had probably belonged to her mother.

"You better change. We need to be on our way."

"The house looks empty, so I guess there would be room for us. Aunt Grace left to find the girls. We was only goin' to spend the night before we went on to our other aunt, Aunt Frances."

When she observed the confused and tired face of Tom's, she added. "Aunt Frances lives just west of Yadkin-ville. Can you take us that far?"

At that point, Grover and Dick rode up.

Grover yelled at the girls, "What are you girls doin' here? We better stay here until Aunt Grace comes back. She finds us gone, she wouldn't know what to do."

Jo put her hands on her hips and stared at Grover. "We was a waitin' for you, smarty. No, we just got here today. Aunt Grace came back to fetch us to Aunt Frances'."

Dick looked horrified. "Your aunt been traipsin' around this country lookin' for you girls. That's not safe, for her or you girls."

"Mister, you don't see no men folks around to go lookin', do you? Here she comes now."

With strain written on his face, Tom turned to the preacher. "Preacher, this trip has turned into a travelin' band of gypsies. You can keep track of names and rela-tions. Got too complicated for me. I surrender. I'll con-centrate on getting us somewhere."

"Have patience Tom. It won't be for long. They won't travel with us far, I think. If you're writin' a journal, you can say, 'They will enter the story of our lives but for a short time as many bodies do.' Then one day disappear, and we will continue on our trail through life. And they will all be almost forgotten. Good opportunity to develop patience and character."

A lady in a brown homespun dress stepped out of the woods to face Company-A and the girls. She appeared to be confused. It had to be Grace.

Adam touched Tom on the shoulder. "I think we better tell Aunt Grace we are not a threat. She looks like she might be worried about what she sees here." Grover spurred his horse to meet his Aunt Grace.

Flo turned to look at Adam sharply. "Here's somebody that talks like a Yankee. How many Yankees we got in this bunch?"

She began to notice Elmo's and Matt's faded blue trousers. She blurted out, "You're all a bunch of escaped Yanks! You aren't gonna get far if I have anything to do with it."

Grace looked from Grover to the girls and back to Grover, ignoring Company-A.

"Where did you girls find Grover?"

Flo rolled her eyes and pointed at Grover and Dick. "They found us while we were bidin' our time till you got back. Did you find them folks that would put us up for the night?"

"No, I found their path and saw smoke. Figured it would be dark by the time we got there. So we bed down in that old house where I left you. These gents can be on their way."

Grace glanced at Dick who moved to take the path. She intended to reach the house. Then she looked back at Dick who began to smile. Grace stopped and looked at him more carefully.

"Aren't you ... you're Dick Roundtree. It's good to see you. I heard about your family. I'm so very sorry. And my Howard won't return. We were goin' to get married when he got back. He and most of the men of the 26th North Carolina were killed or missing at Gettysburg. We are both unlucky that way. I don't usually talk this much. It's so good to see a familiar face from near home, I couldn't help it."

Dick started to say something but Grover beat him. "Aunt Grace, it might not be safe back at that house. Did you hear shots early on?"

"I thought I did but couldn't be sure the way the creek rumbles where I walked. That house is good and solid. There is not another one for miles. We better get on before it gets dark. What did you mean about the shots?"

Dick rushed to answer. "Grover is right. I'll explain the shots later. There's a bunch of bad boys that might come back and decide to fire their muskets at the house again. We can camp out next to those woods about half a mile ahead. Looks like from the reeds on the edge of the field, there would be enough water and a place to hide if them bad boys come our way."

Dick got off his horse to walk beside Grace. He assumed they would take his advice to heart. He then began to explain what had transpired at the deserted house and repeated why it would be safer to stay in the open. Dick continued to explain what had happened.

"Grace, me and Grover felt trapped when the girls left. We wanted to escape out the back after firin' a few shots. That might've brought them fellers down on the girls and us. We had to stay long enough for the girls to get away, don't you see."

"Dick, that was a brave thing to do."

Dick just shrugged his shoulders in response.

The sisters fell in behind when the company started for their new camp sight. "Jo, you see two of them boys is wearin' blue trousers ... and how many of them talk like Yankees? Those are escaped prisoners I hear tell of. I'm goin' to tack a note to a tree when we leave in the mornin'. We got to leave signs and such so they get caught."

"Flo, you be careful. If they find out what we're about we might get killed or worse."

The next morning, Company-A and the addition of five more, moved cautiously through a weed filled field. The frozen ground made travel difficult and progress slower. They hadn't moved far before they spotted several horseman followed by a small group on foot.

Immediately Jo jumped up on a stump and started to wave and shout. "Over here, Hey!

Lambert jumped and grabbed her off the stump, covered her mouth and pinned her to the ground. "What do you think you're about, girl?"

Adam pinned Flo with a look that dared her to try anything. The damage was done. Two men that marched at the rear of their column stopped to stare in Tom's direction.

DEPARTING COMPANY

Two boys who spotted the girl argued. The older boy pleaded with a man on horseback. "I tell you Marty, I seen this girl atop a rise wavin' at us, wantin' us to come that a way."

The man on horseback looked disgusted. "A fifteen year old boy. You're lettin' your young mind play tricks on you. All you got on your mind is girls. I suppose you figure she is goin' down to that big creek, break the ice and bathe. Did you see anything Zack?"

Feeling embarrassed after Marty dressed down his friend, Zack hesitated. "I think I saw what he saw. Yes sir, I did see what looked like a girl with long hair wavin' and just disappear."

Marty studied the two boys for a moment, glanced around to see how far the others were ahead. "Junior's not old enough to be a soldier, and Zack is too young to think about girls. They might have seen something."

Someone in front of the column shouted for them to catch up.

"I'm goin' to have me a look see," spoke the older boy. "Are you comin'?"

"Just hold back. You see any girls since we stopped? No. Neither has anybody else. If it's excitement you want, come on. We got word them convicts or escaped Yankees is headin' this way." The two boys fell in behind the older men. They continued to give curious glances in the girls' direction.

Adam and Preacher watched the searchers from behind stunted oak and pine trees that had begun to reclaim the field. Adam stood up as the last of the search party disappeared behind some trees.

"It's safe now. We can proceed. Fortunately for us the ground is frozen, and we don't leave tracks, except for these broken weeds. If that party finds our trail they might catch up with us."

He noticed Dick and Grover still held the horses by the nose so they would not give away their location. Grace did the same.

Grace had an idea. "Lambert?" She looked around to see which man that would be. Adam motioned with his head to indicate Lambert.

"You seem to be the scout. See that hill. You will find a large creek that is full to overflow after the rain. The girls and I could cross on horseback in a place or two. There is too much water on most days if we go straight ahead to the creek. It would be better to cross the bridge where those searchers crossed. I can tell by your faces you don't trust me and for good reason. Let Lambert find it for himself."

Lambert was already out of sight. Lem followed at a short distance and Adam was behind Lem as if to relay what they found. In a matter of minutes Adam stood on his toes and waved them forward. They had not gone far before they could hear the stream flow over a deadfall.

Larry moved from the bank to a small sandbar and turned to Tom. "It's real sandy here and the ground is thawing. We can lose our tracks but that bank is too steep on the other side of the sand over there. To climb that would leave tracks."

Dick interjected his opinion. "Larry, I trust Grace, I say we take a look at that bridge."

Grace was pleased to hear Dick say so. "I'll ride on down the stream."

Grace was quick to add. "I don't think it wise to get too separated. We stay together and you girls behave. Jo, just remember you don't like the sight of blood. You almost caused some to get spilt."

"I don't care if it's Yankee blood. I'd like to see some Yankee blood."

Preacher looked down at the girl. "No you wouldn't, Jo. Not all this company of men is Yankees. Most just want to get away from the stink of death at the prison, and away from war. Make your anger against the war and what it's doin' to our country and its folks. Anger and revenge can destroy you from the inside out. How many old folks have you seen that are bitter and hateful because life gave them too much to complain about. Compare them to folks that didn't let problems of life bother them. They placed their faith where it belonged and didn't wallow in resentment over their problems, or hate anybody and are most always content. Which of these old folks you want to grow up like?"

Jo made a face without answering, turned and walked toward the bridge.

Dick had just climbed on his plow horse, looked down on Grace and felt embarrassed. To cover his embarrassment, he motioned to Grace.

"You want to ride on back ... double?"

Grace tried to suppress a grin. "It won't be lady like ... you gents look the other way."

Grover moved his horse toward Flo and indicated he expected her to get on behind, which she did reluctantly.

Tom walked up the stones that made up the base of the bridge.

"The road is muddy and so it the bridge. I suggest we walk backwards across the bridge. I'll bet Grover can make his horse walk backwards across the bridge. It would be better to ford the stream with the horses. The girls might get their feet wet if they stay on board … can't be helped. We can build a small fire and warm them on the other side."

They topped a ridge soon after they left the stream. They could see wood smoke and the top of a barn half mile away.

Grace turned to look at Tom. "You will start to see more houses the closer we get to that town. I think we should head north-west and avoid those houses and the town. We got some food we can share at my sister Frances' place. We could get there by dark. One big problem: I don't know the land in that direction. We always come through the edge of town."

"Looks hilly to me." Lem was getting foot sore, as were the rest of Company-A. Lem prodded Lambert. "Lambert, you think you can make us a trail?"

Lem looked back at Tom and smiled. "Mister Tom. Appears that Flo is interested in our tracker."

After about five minutes, Lambert called back. "Don't think I can make a trail that can't be followed after our company leaves the road. It might be better to stay on the road and wait until dark to pass those houses and the little town. Miss Grace, any chance us slippin' by in the dark?"

"I'm not sure. Hadn't thought about leavin' a trail for the searchers if we went that way. Then what do we do if we get caught tryin' to slip by town?"

Noting the disgusted look on Jo's face, Grace added. "We need to avoid bloodshed, girls. There could be some of your friends that got killed too."

"I ..." (cough) "... vote to stay on the road, if I have a vote." Matt struggled to suppress more coughing. He couldn't control a spell of hacking and strangling. Without a word Tom motioned to a spot partially covered by leaves beside the road under a big oak. The company moved slowly to the spot by the road.

Larry moved over to where Tom sat and squatted down on his haunches. He reached into his pack to pull out the last of his cheese he had been hoarding.

"Tom, if somebody spots us near that town, we can be the searchers. In the dark, who can tell?"

He offered Tom some of his cheese. All was silent as they ate the last of the cheese. Larry decided to sit ... more restful.

Larry fell back on his behind and growled, "That would be good work until the real searchers got back to town with those old men and young boys. But we'll have a head start and more chance to hide."

"That's a fine idea, Larry. I don't have anything better to offer. It can't be too far from this Aunt Frances' place. I'm tired of wet-nursing those girls, especially that Jo ... almost caused another battle. Dick and Grover sure have a way of coming in and out of our lives."

Larry couldn't keep from laughing.

"Get them moving, Larry. It will be dark enough by the time we get by that first house. Then we can cover some ground."

By the time Company-A passed through the south part of the village, it was well past midnight. Everyone was tired and on edge. The women slept or dozed on the horses.

About a mile past the village, Flo woke to look around. The half-moon still revealed objects.

"Aunt Grace, that house near that big barn belongs to Cousin Frank and Jodie, don't it? Couldn't we stop there for a while, get some water and somethin' to eat?"

Tom overheard the conversation, mulled it over. *This might be a chance to get rid of responsibility for the girls, rest a spell and renew our strength.*

"Grace, you think they might have enough food feed this little army? A bite or two? What kind of folks are these cousins?"

"They are fine God-fearin' folks who wouldn't turn away a hungry body. Don't know how much food they got left but we could rest for a spell."

The women led the way on horse toward the dark outline of a house and barn. Company-A followed close behind. All was quiet except for the footfalls of the tired travelers, and the sound of horse hoofs. It was as if the marchers were sleepwalking. When the moon peeped out of the clouds, it revealed wagon tracks and a ground fog that lay heavy in patches. If they strayed off the wagon tracks, their feet got wet.

The bark of a dog interrupted the quiet. At first it didn't sounded like a challenge, but as they got closer the dog began to bark furiously. The first bark had awakened the travelers to a present danger. Now they felt threatened.

Grace rode ahead and started to call the dog by name. A door of the darkened house opened and a figure could be seen in the doorway.

"Cousin Frank, it's me and the girls, Flo and Jo ... and Grover. We got company with us. Sorry to wake you so early."

"Well gal, it's good you found them. Bring them on in to the light. Hush dog. You done your duty."

Frank held the door open then hesitated.

"How much company you got there, Grace? Looks like a passel of folks."

"There's ten or more, Frank. Thank you, and do you think you could spare a bite to eat for this company?"

"We can come up with corn bread or corn fritters. Might get a strip of bacon for each of us, I reckon. Don't got any coffee anymore. Ain't room in the house for all of them, so some can go to the barn, if it's rest they need. They look plumb tuckered. What's the reason for all these travelers?"

Tom nudged Larry, who took the hint. "We're a company that's assigned to look for escaped prisoners. You might have heard of them?"

"Nope, can't say I have. Water your horses and then take your rest. Jodie will have us some food shortly. Might even come up with a biscuit or two. We're at the last of our flour."

The majority of the company was too tired to think of food except Lem. Those who weren't too tired to eat thankfully accepted food. The rest found a place to sit or lay down.

* * *

Jo moved cautiously from under the cover and tried not to wake Flo. She stood in her bare feet but hesitated to make a move for the back door. She had lain awake to figure each step she would have to take … past the table and chair in the next room. Her first objective was to get by her Aunt Grace and another body. She figured Flo was too tired to be awakened but was not so sure of the others. It was beginning to get light outside.

"I must hurry," she said to herself.

On the third step the floorboard creaked, she stopped momentarily, and listened for any sight of discovery. When the heavy breathing continued, Jo moved once more for the back door. She remembered to pick up on the door handle so it wouldn't drag, though it didn't help much. Someone moved around on their mat and smacked their lips. She started down the stone steps and was startled by a rough wet tongue on her hand.

"Good dog. Stay quiet. We don't want to wake the Yankees."

A movement to her right caught her eye.

"That must be Matt. He volunteered to keep watch on into the day. Don't think he can see me against these bushes."

Matt stood to stretch. He had to grab his mouth to stifle a coughing fit. While Matt tried to catch his breath, Jo ran for the barn.

"I hope all the men are in the hayloft. I want that horse Grover rode. The plow horses are too slow. Which is which? It's got to be the first one. Her head is too small to be a plow horse."

She led the reluctant horse out of the stall, pushed her against the barn wall so she could climb the stall boards and mount without a saddle. From the darkness of the barn, the outside world was had begun to be much lighter. She ducked her head and charged out of the barn at a gallop.

Matt Challenged her. "Where are you going, girl?"

"You'll soon find out!"

Her heels dug in the horse to increased speed.

"What happened down there," a voice yelled from the barn loft.

After a cough, Matt yelled back. "That youngest gal rode off with one of the horses. It has to be that Jo girl. I'll bet she's gone off after the guard or troops. We better tell the others."

Jo slowed the horse to a walk when she neared the bridge they passed the day before.

When she topped the opposite hill, a rough voice yelled, "Halt! It's a gal. Where you goin' this time of mornin', gal?"

The horse stopped to nibble on grass. Jo turned to look around. It appeared as though she had ridden into the camp of several old men and some boys. Some stood around as others were still asleep. They had two men bound to a tree.

Jo quickly told them why she looked for them. She rattled on as fast as she could to hurry them on their way to capture the Yankees.

The man in charge made her impatient. He interrupted her, asked too many questions. "You sure how many? How did they get by us, and where are they going? Where can we catch them if they run?"

"I will take you to them if you'll hurry. Follow me for ..."

The older man spoke with authority. "Two of you young boys follow this gal to where they slept. On some consideration here, one of you with a horse go with her and spy on the place. The rest of us will cut across them hills to cut them off goin' west. If they're still at the house, come fetch us or join us where we are. Get movin' before they get far. Two of you bring them prisoners. J.T., when we pass a home, go see if you can get extra help. Stop at every one you pass. Them Yankees outnumber us, and bein' armed as they are we need all the help we can get. One of you needs to go by horseback to homes too far off the pike. Now get."

By the time they were satisfied with numbers, they were near Frank and Jodie's place. Three elderly grandfather types, three women and five more boys were added. Each one carried either a shotgun or a musket that had been converted from flintlocks, except one old gentleman with a pitchfork.

Jo spoke to the rider beside her, "What's you name boy?"

"They call me Junior."

She would occasionally cut her eyes at Junior but was too tired to flirt. She mumbled low enough that he couldn't hear her. "He ain't much. Sure is skinny, like me. I hope we catch them Yankees and see them hang on account of what they're doin' to our people and land."

* * *

Tom, Larry, and Preacher stood together. They moved their arms and legs to warm them up in the morning chill.

Adam stomped his feet trying to get the circulation back in them, and then he trotted in place and then stopped to comment. "Matt is right. That girl with her dislike for Yankees and riding off like that can only bring trouble. We better start marching again and be prepared to fight."

He looked to Tom for approval and got it in the form of a nod.

"Well gents, we're off again."

Cousin Frank was replacing a long fence post between two upright posts when Junior and Jo came into view. He stopped to wipe his forehead with his sleeve despite the chill, and watched as the two approached.

"Enjoy your mornin' ride Jo?" Frank grinned up at them. "Mornin' Junior. I bet you are lookin' for a bunch of men that were by here earlier. They done marched off. Wanted to get ahead of the weather."

Seeing the doubt in Junior's eyes, Frank added, "You're free to look around. You can see their tracks."

Jo spoke angrily, "Frank, you bedded them Yankees down and fed them. That's bein' a traitor, cousin or not."

"You know what the Good Book says about feedin' your enemy. Can I do less? Besides, I'm not sure they are all Yankees, just because they talk funny and some had on faded blue trousers. That don't make them all Yankees. That last letter from our boy he told about strippin' off boots and stuff from the dead Yankees to replace shoes and their worn out trousers."

"Why were they dodgin' them Home Guard then?"

Junior pointed his horse toward the house. "Come on Jo, no use arguin'." We can pick up their trail in the yard. Got to catch up with the rest of our folks.

* * *

Company-A moved at a good pace. It had been a short rest for them. The rest, food, and the thought of the Home Guard catching them was enough to rejuvenate them.

Dick watched as Grace rode ahead of him. The pleased expression on their faces told the story of a budding romance. Some in the group exchanged knowing glances. Larry looked back at Tom and grinned when he saw Tom study Dick and Grace.

Tom rolled his eyes toward the two. "Larry, I think Dick Roundtree has found a readymade family. And that leg wound of his doesn't seem to bother him near as much."

To catch up with Dick and Grace, Tom had to run a few paces. "How much further to your sisters' place?"

"If we keep movin' it will be less than an hour, not much more than a half hour."

"We will keep moving. I want to see you and the girls safe to your sister's place."

And we keep adding to our group ... hope to dodge troops or the guard ... got to get rid of some of these good people. I don't want to be responsible for women'

* * *

Two men on horseback in the Home Guard wanted to run ahead but knew they needed the young boys and their weapons.

Marty looked back at Howard, the impatient one and spoke, "These women and old men we picked up are fresher, and do a better job of keeping up then our tired boys."

Howard pointed to the struggling boys. "That cannon's too much for Zack to tote. J.T., you and Zack swap shotguns for a spell. That barrel is long enough to tickle a squirrel's nest."

"Unh uh. My brother brought it home after the fight near New Bern. He said for me to keep for him. I promised."

"Hit's about to tucker you plumb out. Let me carry it on this horse and you can have it when we get to where you need it. Come on, I won't hurt it."

Zack lifted the heavy shotgun up to Marty, who placed it across his lap. "No wonder you're winded. What gage is this cannon?"

"My brother John said it was a duck gun from down off the coast. It's a ten gage I think"

Marty eyed the shotgun from one end to the other. "You ever fire this thing Zack?"

"Nope. If'n I do, I want to be squattin' or sittin' down so I won't have so far to fall."

"That double barrel you're a totin' don't look light either, J.T. Can you fire it?"

"Yes sir. And I think I just saw a man bobbin' along about a half-mile away like he's on horseback. There, see … somebody is a followin' on horseback. You should have seed them before me Howard, you bein' on that horse."

Marty galloped ahead to the next rise. He took out his field glass and tried to get a better look.

"That's Junior and that gal, Jo!" yelled Marty. "They must be trackin' them Yankees. There's smoke comin' from beyond that hill to the west. Might be where that gal's aunt is. We better scout ahead."

* * *

Tom and Company-A reached the wagon tracks that led from the trail they traveled. Wood smoke from behind some trees encouraged their pace. Each of them lost in their own thoughts. Flo looked at the others to see if they could see her. It seemed she was alone for the moment. Pretending to extract a bur from her dress she tore off another piece off her petticoat and dropped it on the ground. Grover led one of the plow horses with Grace on its back. Dick walked to get the stiffness out of his bad leg.

Lambert walked up behind Flo and startled her. He smiled at her and handed the girl a hand full of petticoat pieces.

"Miss Flo, we are leavin' a trail that anybody can follow, even from horseback. You should save what's left. It will take a spell to sew them pieces back on."

Flo felt foolish. Lambert presented a non-threatening countenance, and his eyes spoke of kindness. She couldn't help grinning back at Lambert's smiling face. He had not made a show of his discovery to the rest, and Flo realized her actions could have been revealed to the leader. Embarrassed as she was, Flo didn't watch her step ... slipped on a stone and turned her ankle.

"Oh, I hurt my foot. And it hurts to step on it."

"Get back on the horse, Miss Flo."

Lambert helped her mount. "You can get your aunt to look at the foot when we get to the house."

Tom spoke loud enough for all to hear. "When we get to the house you know what to do. Matt, you and Nate take the first watch. Hide the horses soon as possible."

Around a new growth of pine, stood Aunt Frances' house. A woman shouted from the doorway, stepped out and raised her arms, and ran for the girls.

Before Flo and Grace could dismount there was a loud report of a shotgun followed by another shot. It knocked the two women from their mounts, and one of the horses started to buck. The men immediately took up defensive positions.

Larry and Lambert in one voice yelled. "Who is hurt ... how bad?"

Grover yelled in panic, "It's Aunt Grace and Flo. I got a shot in the leg and arm too."

* * *

Marty yelled at the two boys. "Why in thunder did you do that? We weren't in any kind of position yet. Don't nobody else fire. You done hit women."

"My shotgun just went off. I barely touched the trigger. Didn't mean to fire, Marty."

The younger boy then yelled. "I figured it was time to shoot when Zack shot."

Grover yelled again. "Aunt Grace ain't movin' and Flo is bleedin' bad. Mr. Tom is down."

Jo spurred her horse forward from behind the trees with tears running down her cheeks. Shouts from both sides yelled "don't shoot".

DEPARTING FRIENDS

Tom rolled over and raised his head to get a better view. He couldn't see anything except the dissipating gun smoke. Then glanced back at Larry who was crouched behind a stone fence. Tom would have laughed if the situation were not so serious. Larry's face told of his concern for his friend.

"I'm not touched Larry. Somebody taking care of the girls and Grover?"

Jo rode into the yard, jerked the horse to a stop and slid off the back. Jo's tear and dust stained face revealed a pale and frightened girl. She ran to Grace and her sister … found Dick holding Grace's head in his lap. Jo began to weep in gasps.

Marty shouted to Tom's men. "You-all put the wounded in the house and the rest come out peaceful like. We've got you surrounded and outnumbered. We'll give you five minutes … no more."

"Don't shoot."

Tom decided to say no more. His accent might be mistaken for a Yankee. In a hushed voice, he spoke to Larry. "Tell them we're going to take care of the wounded. After that we'll discuss their demands and how many people they have. You might mention something about our papers … orders to catch prisoners."

Larry considered he would stand in full view, but then thought on the shotgun blasts. "Tom, I'll shout from behind this stone fence. One of those guns sounded like a small cannon. You and Preacher say a prayer while I do my best persuasion yell."

Tom nodded to Larry with a smile.

Larry yelled loud enough for all to hear. "We're goin' to take care of the wounded and we know you're bluffin'. Our Indian guide done told us how many you are. Why did you shoot at us without findin' out who we are, and who am I talkin' to? I like to know who I'm talkin to."

"I'm Mar … it don't matter who you're talkin' to. You got four minutes now. You're wastin' time."

"We got you figured out. You're worried town folk or Home Guard. Well, here are the facts, mister Mar. Jo girl here is a true Southern girl that thinks we're all Yankees because some are wearin' faded blue trousers and some talk with a different talk than where she come from. She might even question why we dodge most folks. We don't have time to talk to every curious folk that we come across. We are on a mission and the only reason we stop to talk is to see if they've seen any sign of escaped prisoners we search for. We got papers chargin' us to do just that. A passel of them escaped. Why don't you send a runner with a white flag and let him read it to you? But be sure you send somebody that can read. No use somebody else getting' shot over a misunderstandin'."

Larry turned to look at Tom, and they both grinned. They could hear some argument in the trees. By now all of Company-A had found better defensive positions in the event Larry's speech failed.

Dick slipped out of the house to give a report on the wounded. "Fellers, Grace got a ball across the side of her head and her wrist. She's goin' to be all right. Grover got a shot in his left arm, went clean through. He lost part of his ear. Flo got one in the leg, right arm and one went across her shoulder … just missed the collarbone. She lost some blood and is goin' to be weak for a spell. Just hope we don't have to kill that horse. Grover puts a lot of stock in those horses you know."

Marty stepped out of the timber to yell. "We're sendin' over somebody with a white flag. You honor that flag and we might avoid more bloodshed. Go ahead Howard."

Howard held a crooked stick with a faded yellow cloth tied on top. He stepped out briskly then yelled, "I'm a comin'. This here ladies scarf is the closest to white we got."

Larry rose to meet him half way. He was relieved to see Howard didn't carry a weapon. Then he realized that he still carried a pistol in his belt. Larry pulled out the pistol and dropped it on the ground.

"Here's the papers that authorize us to go after escaped prisoners. Read them out loud if you want."

"I read too slow for that. I'll read it and then tell them if it looks right."

Howard read over the papers carefully for what seemed like forever to both sides. "Marty, Home Guard and all, it looks official and it's signed by this Major Gee, prison commander or somethin'. And this bunch is well armed and all. They could cost us a lot of blood. I say they are what they say they are."

Marty shouted. "We're comin' out. We got two prisoners already. Not sure what to do with them. Our jail will hold them with a guard watchin'. Now, all you folks that came to help us can go on home. We appreciate yer help. Sorry you had to traipse all this way fer nothin' but you don't always know. Pull them prisoners out so these fellers can see if they are part of them they is lookin' to catch."

Tom groaned, "Oh no, Larry. That tall one is someone that challenged us from the porch at Grover's place. Those two look dead on their feet. We could take them on but the shape they're in, they would never survive."

Tom then yelled back to Marty, "Yep, they look like they are some of them. It this all you caught?"

"There were three but one tried to run. He was short and fast but not as fast as Howard's musket ball. If you're thinkin' of takin' them off our hands, keep on goin' unless you got reward money. We don't want script, neither."

"You are fresh out of luck. Guess you'll have to hold them till we can get the money. We can come back this way. You need to feed them up some, or they won't make it back to camp. They need to be alive when we bet back."

One of the prisoners looked up to see who spoke, and Larry recognized him and winked. The prisoner either didn't recognize Larry or was too tired to care.

Tom approached and asked, "Are you the leader of this Home Guard?"

"Yep. They call me Marty." Marty stuck out his hand to shake Tom's.

Tom grabbed the old man's hand and looked him in the eye and smiled.

Marty continued, "We been lookin' for deserters and them that is dodgin' conscription. When we got notices there's escaped Yankees comin' this way we gave up on everything else. How much further are you goin' to track this bunch before you head back and let the Home Guard or troops go after them?"

"We'll go on into Wilkes County I expect, but we need to be on our way since we got hours of daylight left. Our wounded are not too bad off. I think this is as far as they wanted to come since they're with kin. So we'll fill our canteens and continue the search."

Dick walked up to where Marty and Tom were talking. He began to stand on first one foot then the other. Both men turned to Dick and expected him to say something. Dick cleared his throat uncomfortably.

"Tom, since they're fewer prisoners, I figured to stay with the women."

Having made the statement about staying with the women his face turned red.

"My game leg is startin' to give me misery. Don't think I can march much further without several days rest."

Tom could easily see Dick was embarrassed, but he couldn't help teasing a bit. At the same time he needed to be serious ... to a degree.

"Dick Roundtree, you want Preacher to marry you and Grace before we march off? We could delay long enough for that."

"Tom, I appreciate that but it's too soon. There has to be another preacher here bouts. Me and the boy need to see what can be done to help these women folks while I get better acquainted with Grace."

Larry sauntered over to where Tom and Dick stood. He had heard enough of the conversation to grasp the purpose.

"Dick, I'll trade you my musket and a pistol for that rifle musket."

"Nothin' doin'. Grover is a dead shot with it and we need it to gather meat, if we can find any. Me and the boy plan to do some huntin'. I might take a notion to join this Home Guard."

He gave Larry a wink and started for the house. "If you come back this a-way, drop by. Don't like sayin' goodbyes."

Tom had failed to notice Marty was still in hearing distance. He was in a conversation with one of his people. On impulse Tom spoke to his former antagonist.

"Marty, you might have a new recruit. He is a good man, fair and honest. You can't do better. We need to be on the hunt.

"Larry, call them together and let's see what we can find up the road."

Now there were only ten men since Dick and Grover joined the three women at Aunt Frances' place. Tom considered Company-A. He would have preferred fewer people.

He thought, *I don't like being responsible for so many in this uncertain country. The next Home Guard we come across might not be so easily fooled. There wasn't a time limit on how long we could search for prisoners. But if it occurs to some at the prison we might try to desert, it won't take long for word to get ahead of us. Wish I knew how far the telegraph lines go west.*

Tom hung back to let Larry catch up. "Do you remember how many of those that escaped through the tunnel are still loose, the ones we saw at Grover's old home? I don't know if they are ahead or behind us. They could draw cavalry down on us."

"I figure only six or seven. There was a bunch of them … might be more like eight. I'm wonderin' where that guard's territory ends we left behind, and where the next guard outfit begins. I guess they could overlap right smart if money's involved."

"Larry, we've got to consider lawless renegades as well. There are too many looking for revenge or ways to make a profit off the back of unprotected folk. The closer to Wilkesboro we get the more dangerous it will get.

I considered dividing the men into two groups again. We're still stronger in numbers the closer we get to the mountains. The journey of one man will attract less attention, so Lambert and Lem can take turns to walk ahead and look for safe ways to move. They can signal like before but with more caution. If we all bunch up like we have when tired, it will look suspicious. The documents we got from the Major might not help us forever."

"I'll see to it Tom."

Larry trotted ahead and soon could be seen an animated conversation with Lambert and Lem, the most physically fit of the travelers. There was plenty of brush and new growth pine but also many open fields. Some fields had been plowed but many had been neglected for lack of workers.

Near dark Lambert motioned for them to stay close to a creek bank lined with trees. Lem made a small wave and pointed to a woman and two small children who were picking something off the ground.

Tom peered at them through his field glasses.

"The woman turns to look around. She doesn't want to be seen. I think she is digging potatoes, or is pulling some out of a mound. The mound must have been covered with that brush to the side. Larry, do you think you could buy about two potatoes a piece for us, or trade something? We'll make camp in that clump of trees ahead."

After everyone had found a spot that suited them, they plopped down to rest and search through their packs for what food was left. There were a few hard crackers and used coffee grounds between them. Elmo pulled out a big chunk of pork he had been carrying. He held it up and grinned from ear to ear. Without a word, preacher sliced off a small piece for each of them.

Preacher spread his arms and pronounced, "The Lord provides. Now there should be enough for another meal if used sparingly. The rest goes back in Elmo's pack."

Nate and Adam started to build a small fire in a spot that had previously been used by travelers. It would soon be dark enough that smoke would not be seen, and light would not filter through the trees.

Larry came panting into the little clearing. "I nearly went by you boys. I smelled the smoke and here I am with about twenty potatoes. Some are sweet potatoes. I surely scared that poor lady half to death ... and her youngsters. She didn't want my money but took some powder and shot ... and glad to get it too. Where'd you get that cookin' pot Lambert? We been needin' one from the start?"

"Flo slipped it to me before we left her aunts. Had a little corn meal in it too. Said she was sorry for all the trouble. I told her she shouldn't be carryin' that heavy pot with her hurt arm but she just smiled. I want to come back this way after this is all over." Lambert smiled at Tom and Larry. Then added, "We better be sparing with the food we got."

It was cold and damp the next morning. They ate a cold breakfast and started tracking for the distant mountains. There was little conversation. The company started down a rather steep hill toward a creek ... not too happy about a climb up the hill beyond. It was plain to them that travel was going to be tougher.

No one spoke of the fields opening up around them. Everyone felt exposed to whoever might be watching. Their one comfort was the knowledge that their numbers could make a difference. To stay hidden among the forests was taking too much time and too much of their strength. It was much easier to go straight ahead. Being this tired and hungry would lead to carelessness.

Preacher and Larry looked at Tom with worry in their eyes. It was apparent they were too exposed.

Tom spoke just loud enough for closest to hear. "Lambert is ahead, to avoid trouble. We need to spread out a bit. I will take the right about three hundred paces and Larry can take the other side the same distance. Nate, take the rear. The rest stay with Adam and Preacher. We don't want to be caught unaware. This way it will look like we are searching for something. Should have thought of this before, so the Adam and Preacher can spread out more. We can meet at the top of that hill on the other side of that cabin."

Tom began to wish he were back at the prison where things were much simpler. *You obey orders and do the same thing every day and night ... go hungry and smell as bad as the prisoners.* He had a wry smile at that thought.

To conserve strength, we should slow down. There is no need to be in such hurry this far from the prison, except for who or what we can't see. I should remember what Preacher said about how the good Lord has provided for us thus far. Wish I knew what day it is. We should have a Sunday service with Preacher to build us up. I been neglecting my spiritual life and took little notice of the others needs.

"What have I been doing with my life and the responsibilities I have for these men?" he asked aloud.

Matt coughed when he tried to speak. "What did you say Tom?"

"I'll tell you later. I need to talk with Preacher when we get to that cabin across the creek. You need to catch up with Preacher and the rest, Matt. You look worn out.

Take your time. We are going to rest for the night at that cabin. A rest for a spell would do us all good."

Although the roof of the cabin where Company-A gathered was sagging, three of the men found a place to rest inside.

The others expected Tom or Larry would soon have them moving again. Lambert and Lem had already posted themselves as lookouts. Tom walked to where Preacher stood. "Anybody know what day it is?"

Someone mumbled just loud enough to be heard. "We left on Monday; the escape was on a Sunday. How many days ... it's got to be Saturday."

Tom studied the tired company. "I had thought we would rest up here for the rest of the day but tomorrow will be Sunday, so we'll keep going till dark. Sunday we could rest half a day. Preacher, you reckon you could come up with a sermon or something?"

* * *

After a meager breakfast, Preacher brought out his worn Bible. "To think we put so many miles behind us and the prison and finally come to this. I have neglected my job as a servant of the Lord. I don't know how many of you claim to be Christians or were brought up in church. None of us can argue the fact we have come safely this far. I have prayed that we would be under the watchful eye of the Lord, and I believe we truly have been. We have been preserved for a reason, from sickness and starvation. Let our lives count for something to honor the Lord.

"I heard one of the other preachers at the prison say that this war had one redeeming quality. Don't know if the thought was his or he quoted someone else but here it is: that it had brought many men to their knees before their God. I'm sure this is true. You boys remember your own experience. You are not here by chance. Perhaps the Lord brought you here today to hear this little sermon from a tired preacher that had just about given up. But the good Lord is not finished with any of us yet.

"That dark cloud you see that comes this way, can't work that into this sermon, but it prompts me make this short so I will read from the 3rd Psalm.

Lord, how are they increased that trouble me.

Many there be which say of my soul, there is no help from God.

But Thou, O Lord, art a shield for me; my glory and a lifter up of mine head.

I cried unto the Lord with my voice, and he heard me out of his holy hill.

I lay me down and slept; I awakened; for the Lord sustained me.

I will not be afraid of ten thousands of people that have set themselves against me round about.

Arise, O Lord; save O my God; for thou hast smitten all mine enemies upon the cheek bone; thou hast broken the teeth of the ungodly.

Salvation belongeth unto the Lord; thy blessing is upon thy people.

"Now pray with me. We thank thee O Lord for your protecting hand; we pray you will continue to lead us and spare us from our enemies. We wish to arrive safely in the hands of our friends and family, and to live lives that's honoring to our God. Amen!"

There followed another "amen" from most of the men.

Fellow travelers know this: Hopefully we all are, or soon want to travel, to a better land. We first must repent of our sins. My Bible tells me God doesn't ask us or invite us, He commands us to repent. Only through Christ can we find forgiveness. You do not want to fall into the hands of an angry God, because you rejected his Son who was tortured and hung on a cross in our place. True, God is good and loving. He would not be good if he didn't judge and punish evil.

If any of you have questions about Christianity, I'll be happy to talk with you on an individual basis. Now I've said enough.

Let's take our rest here unless these tracks warn us of possible discovery.

Preacher packed his Bible in his pack and fastened concerned eyes on Tom.

"I think we are ready to rest here for the day but lookin' at these tracks, this is a regular place to camp. Travelers have used these stones for a campfire right regular. That old cabin doesn't appeal as a resting place now when you see these tracks in the light ... and that threatenin' cloud means an uncomfortable walk. I know we are admonished in the Scriptures to not work on the Lord's Day, but our Lord did say that if an ox is in the ditch on the Sabbath, we should get it out. Boys, I'd say that the ox is in the ditch. What do you think?"

"I think you're right. It would be better to move into that wooded area ahead. In the woods we can maintain a leisurely pace to rest our weary bones but shouldn't tarry as you say. And not when we're exposed in open fields."

Company-A soon discovered that riders had used the path through the woods. The men followed fresh tracks in places. After crossing a small field of old corn shocks, they skirted a thick forest. This offered some protection.

With the fact of increased traffic, the leisurely pace was soon forgotten. At the top of a hill the forest made a turn to the south. A broad, open field grown up in weeds lay before them. It was obvious some of the field had been used the previous summer.

Although Lambert was out of the vision of the company, Adam was tall enough to see his signal to stop.

A rider emerged from the trees ahead followed by several others. Company-A squatted in the weeds, as if by command, to make themselves smaller.

Tom looked over his company. Everyone hunched over ready to rise with weapons at the ready.

"Fellers, that was too close. We're not out of danger yet. Stay cautious. Now I hear dogs. Would you listen to that?"

A large number of dogs began their mournful baying. Company-A froze as if turned into statues. From a short distance men began to shout and curse. The entire company crouched even lower to the ground and took whatever cover was available.

"Now I know why they call them blood hounds," mumbled Lem in a low voice. "That hounds carryin' on so makes my blood run cold."

Everyone winced at the sound of two gunshots.

Someone shouted, "Don't shoot, don't shoot. We give up!"

More shouts and curses tormented their senses. The sounds came from about a hundred yards behind them and to their right ... from the stream where they waded and drank only a few minutes before.

They looked at each other with a mixture of fear, shock and surprise. But then the commotion seemed to move away from their hiding place.

Tom tried to peer over the brush without being seen, and groaned, "I half expected this. They got two more of the other prisoners. Surprised they got this far. That might make all of them ... poor devils."

"They were warned ...," Matt started to say more but had to stifle another cough, holding his mouth and turned red. Finally he was able to breathe, still strained to suppress a cough.

Adam patted Matt on the back. "Brother Matt, you're in a bad way. We need to get you to a doctor. You hear that, Preacher and Tom?"

Adam couldn't hide his concern for his old friend.

Preacher looked at Adam with a look of utter despair. "I hear, but how am I to get him to a doctor out here? Even if I could, it would expose our intentions to reach freedom."

More coughing followed. Someone's stomach growled. It reminded them all how hungry they were. One of the men crept forward to get a better view of their surroundings.

Larry stood up and pointed toward a clearing. "I think the present danger is over. We better move while we can. I see those beautiful mountains and freedom from war and the smells of that ole stockade. You know, I still smell the place at this distance."

"I'll never get tired of the thought of the beautiful mountains and freedom. That's what keep me going," retorted Tom, "about the mountains naturally."

Tom adjusted his pack and moved his musket to his shoulder before he moved. "I'll take the lead the rest of the way. I should know this country. We traveled this way to my uncle's place. That was more than four years ago."

He picked up the spare musket and shifted his load again and then stepped out into the clearing. The others followed in single file.

The further west they traveled the rougher the terrain. They thought there would be fewer eyes to look on them with suspicion. No one could fault people for being suspicious during these times. Who could they trust ... neighbor against neighbor, brother against brother were common discussions. Small gangs of deserters and the Home Guard were threats to travelers and local farmers. Some in the Home Guard were true patriots while others were thieves and murderers. They often took advantage of the war situation to line their pockets at the expense of innocent folk. Tom's little band didn't want to fall into the hands of this last group ... criminals without regard to life or property.

Darkness began to approach. Tom and Larry began to look for a place to camp.

Farm buildings were fewer and further apart. The ones they saw were too risky to approach. Farm fowl and animals were not far from their minds. Their weary minds conceived the possibility there might be some left in the state. Hope of survival and possible game kept them trudging through briars and thickets.

Preacher stopped abruptly as though he just discovered something. Tom turned to see why his friend stopped.

"Tom, you know each step we take fools us into thinking we escaped our conscience. Each one of us has something from which to escape ... the horror of war, smells of the prison, hunger, lost friends, responsibilities ..." He then took up his regular pace and rambled on. "We've had to look for our comfort, whatever it might be, to keep our sanity ... hope and peace with our conscience. We shouldn't feel guilty if we face the demons for what they are and ask help from above."

Tom continued to trudge ahead. "Preacher, I think you're right. But that's too much for this tired old mine to consider. Would you pass this extra musket back to Adam. I hope your boots are in better shape than mine. Larry already strapped a piece of leather on one boot and a strip from his pack on the other. Look at Lem march on bare feet. Adam's boots, new when we left, are almost gone. The rest don't fare much better. Still most of us have part of a uniform that would identify us as Confederate. Now there are only three canteens and a jug between us."

Tom reminded himself that most still carry a pack and a weapon of some sort. He patted his Navy Colt that his brother had returned. It comforted him to know he had six loads. To give up his small single shot pistol was unthinkable. It remained in his pocket even though it chafed his leg when he stepped over a log or brush.

Lem mumbled loud enough for the closest could hear. "There's another clearin' down a ways but I reckon we better scatter a bit amongst these trees so we kin keep an eye on the road yonder."

For some reason Lem dropped to his knees between some scrub pine and stared through the branches. The land had been burned over several years back judging from blackened snags and new growth. There was little to hide them above their chest. Those that followed close were alerted to a problem when Lem caught his breath.

"They're goin' to shoot them fellers ... I do declare!."

Tom crawled up behind Lem to see for himself. "Oh No!"

Two shots followed.

"That's murder, pure and simple. I think Adam and Holtsclaw were right to advise we stay together, safety in numbers and such. We will never give up now. Men, we go down fighting when it comes to that. You all agree?"

Adam agreed, "Especially when dealing with the likes of those. Think most of those shooters were local Home Guard?" Adam looked quizzically at the others for reinforcement in regards his observation.

"Could be," Preacher answered. "Can't tell decent folks from murderers, has been since the beginning of this war ... last few years anyway."

Everyone was morose and made no further comments. Tom started to move away from the area and the others followed silently. He decided to wave his usual signal for them to follow several paces back in case he came across game. There was no help for the mood that permeated the group, not feeling too well himself. Even after the ordeals at the prison, they felt saddened at the loss of the others and still connected by past experiences.

Tom stepped into a small clearing surrounded by stunted hard wood, brush and pine. A deer snorted and bounded off.

"Hear that deer blow?" He whispered to no one in particular. Even though it was too late for the deer, Tom peeled off his bow with the intent to string it and pick an arrow. Then a second deer bounded past followed by a yearling.

The yearling stopped to look back. It gave Tom time to string the bow and fit an arrow. He held his breath, as he made sure he had fitted the arrow-notch on the string at the right place. The deer would see him when he stood above the brush to shoot. Even cool as it was, perspiration trickled down his back. It could mean food.

The men behind him realized there was possible game and froze where they were ... everyone, one by one down the line to the last man, as a stack of cards that fell against each other. Not having eaten for days sharpened their instincts.

Tom had to take a chance ... moved very slowly to position himself for a shot. The deer seemed to be momentarily confused. He anticipated its' move to join the others, moved his aim ahead of the animal and released the arrow in one motion. Luck and skill moved it in the path of the arrow. It didn't run far before it dropped out of sight.

Tom said, "That was as tense as any battle."

His companions agreed.

"Man oh Man, we eat tonight," exclaimed Adam.

Someone else sprang forward with a hunting knife. "It's bigger than I thought. That's good."

The rest gathered wood or formed a ring with stones.

Lem's face was covered with a huge smile as he produced several sweet potatoes and turnips from his pack. "Look what somebody missed back in that field we came through."

Company-A ate their fill. Little was left to carry for another meal. The men soon spread out to find a place to bed down. A shower had left everything wet, and wet leaves made it easier for someone to sneak up on them.

Adam took the first watch. He would like for the leaves to have been dry. The snap of a twig or someone brush against a tree or bush might be the only warning.

MORE BATTLES TO FIGHT

Tom, in the lead, stopped when he saw trees sway. A new threat emerged from the trees a half-mile away. He studied the threat with his field glasses. The first three horses were too fine for anyone other than outlaws. He studied these three too long to get a picture of the other three on horses. The riders disappeared in a forest of hardwood going south.

"Glad they're not coming this way, fellows. If they saw us, they pretended they didn't."

It was time to make their way through the open field, uphill most of the way. On reaching the forest where they first saw the horsemen, no one spoke. Though relieved, they were too tired, sore and thirsty, even after stopping at the stream at the bottom of the hill. Fear of exposure limited their time to get their fill, so while they filled their canteens, they drank in haste.

Once in the cover of the trees, they stopped to take a swig from their canteens. After several minutes they came to a small clearing of scattered boulders from a landslide. There was enough brush, fallen logs and small pines to offer additional concealment. Tom and Preacher flopped where they were without a word. The climb and presence of a possible enemy made them perspire. Cold winds began to chill the group.

Larry started to build a fire.

"Lem, if'n you was any account, you'd rustle us up some grub out of this woody place."

"Well now Larry. I reckon if you got a taste for piney cones, that won't be no problem."

Tom grinned, in spite of his current concerns, glad for the easy banter among the men.

"That barn and house we saw back yonder west of the open field looked kind of deserted, what do you think Matt … Lem?" Larry said.

After a pause Lem responded. "Like we always say, Mr. Tom, in a situation like this it's too risky."

"Why you still call him Mr. Tom after all we've been through?" questioned Nate.

"Cuz it's better we keep on bein' Mr. Tom or master and servant to stay in practice in case we meet up with more nosey folks, right Mr. Tom?"

"If you think so.

"Take cover! I hear horses."

Larry peered at Tom with a half grin. "Them fellers is goin' right by us. If they find our tracks and bring dogs, we might have to use some of Lem's turpentine."

Adam had to ask. "Remind me one more time why we don't ask food from some of these small farms?"

Tom spat out a twig he held in his mouth. "You must not have heard me or Larry relate how some of the prisoners were returned to us. It was because they stopped to beg for food, stole a hog, chicken or something. They didn't know which person to trust for assistance. Some people would help but not many."

Breakfast the next morning was quiet. The men finished what was left over from the evening before. Each rose with few words as they assumed their regular morning activities.

Nate mentioned, "I had to chase a coon off of me during the night. Couldn't risk shooting it and alerting some unfriendly person, or we'd have it for breakfast.

Tom was still a sleep since he had the last watch, which probably lent to the unusual quiet morning activities. The last person on guard always appreciated the quiet early morning.

To stay under cover was more difficult even as the forest became denser. It made the march in single file a necessity, and spread them out too far at times to skirmish. The rag-tag group found the hills steeper and too frequent to be comfortable, even in the cool morning. They found a deer trail that lead through rhododendron. It offered only crawl space in places

Around noon they came upon a chestnut tree with a few nuts on the ground. Everyone was too tired to talk at first. They sat down while they gathered a few nuts to lunch on. They removed their packs and weapons, placing them within easy reach. They took their knives and began to peel the outer layer of nuts. Adam and Larry briefly considered throwing nuts at each other. A look from Preacher put a quick halt to their play.

"It would be a beautiful thing to build a fire and roast a few," commented Larry. "Could find a few more the further we go." He stopped munching long enough to study Adam.

"Adam, when I look at you at times, I feel like a big brother. If I left you in that prison I would be no better than a murderer. No better than them that shot the two prisoners. My conscience pulls me first one way than the other. Don't matter the war is lost for me except my pride. I suppose all my pride was replaced by anger at the prison."

Tom cut in. "We are all in the same boat. You realize we're all prisoners of our consciences … or should be. I look at it as character building and good for our souls. So to the immediate situation, it would be prudent for us to move out and cover as much ground this morning as possible."

The march west continued. Tom debated with himself whether to strike out for Boone or continue to the Asheville area.

"Going around Asheville by way of Boone might be best … safer," he mentioned aloud. "We can make that decision as we approach the mountains and see what's on our path … adjust as the situation determines."

Adam caught up with Tom. "What did you say just now?"

"I was just talking to myself. I think we will stick to our original plan, even if it takes longer."

Matt patted Adam on the shoulder. "Adam, just think …" Matt had to pause, catch his breath and cough again. "… Tom here is in a hurry to see if that pretty Indian girl still fancies him. That is what I think. Talked to her in his sleep last night."

A few chuckles followed the comment.

Despite their hunger, the company had become stronger physically. With the exception of Matt, who coughed almost constantly, the men were stronger for their hardships.

The group came to a halt at the edge of another open field about three hundred fifty feet across. Tom looked both ways. He saw no one and moved to cross the field, exercising his usual caution with the company close behind.

They were startled when a black man and his woman stepped out of the woods to their left. Neither the couple nor the men had seen each other until that moment. The man and women each carried a sack across their back. They smiled at first but their demeanor changed when they noted the Confederate buckles on Tom and Larry.

"You white folks goin' far?" questioned the man. He and the woman sat their sacks down and eyed the seven ragged men suspiciously. The men stopped but made no attempt to answer.

Rather than running off, the black man offered Company-A some food. "We got us some corn and some beans. You want some?"

"To answer your first question," Tom motioned toward the mountains, "we are on assignment to look for escaped Yankee's from Salisbury. Have you seen any suspicious white people this way?"

Adam spoke before the man could answer. "As to the second question, we could use some of your food, if you can spare any."

Adams polite Yankee accent gave him away, judging from the expression on the strangers face.

"Well, I reckon we'uns could spare a meal. You'd have to grind this here corn or boil it. And I seed some fellers a-horse back yonder along the creek. Figured them to be bushwhackers."

As he spoke he eyed Adam boldly and opened his eyes wide as a warning.

Preacher asked, "To whom do you belong and what do they call you?"

"They calls me Uncle Mort and this is Millie, my wife. Right now we belongs to ourselves. Master done got himself kilt in this terrible war and the Missus we still helps is Miz Wilson. She been helpless since her man got kilt."

Millie moved in front of Mort, held up her hand and spoke for the first time. "Now Mort, Miz Wilson is improvin' most every day now. She ain't all that bad, so don' down her none. She still got hopes her boy'll come home sound of soul and body. I been wid her more'n you"

Uncle Mort took hold of his bag and stomped out on a well-worn path. The path led in the direction of a trail of smoke they noticed.

"You-all jus' follow ole Uncle Mort and we can fix up some vittles to et on … even if'n they be short a belly full."

Company-A followed Uncle Mort and Millie in single file, as if Uncle Mort were in command. The thought of food threw caution to the wind for the moment.

When they entered a patch of forest, Lem turned to speak to Adam. "Sure could use some of those turkeys I heard earlier. Must have been a big gobbler. It would go well with the food we got."

He was about to ask Millie what they had in the way of food, when his eye caught the sight of smoke from a house up ahead.

At that point a hand and arm shot out from some short pines. The hand held two turkeys by the neck. The big birds swayed back and forth from the thrust momentum. Uncle Mort froze in his tracks with a loud gulp enough to be hard at the end of the line. The hand held still while the turkeys continued to sway long enough to get every ones attention. The buckskin sleeve caused some consternation to the closest travelers.

Tom started laughing and almost doubled over. Then slapped his leg and continued to chuckle.

"If that isn't Johnny Running Bear Adams, my name isn't Tom Gentry. What are you doing here?"

Johnny Running Deer Adams stepped out of his hiding place. He held a third turkey with his other hand.

"How did you know it was me skinny white boy? And you're not so skinny any more … filled out some. Have to call you something else."

"I recognized the scar on your wrist and the way the sleeves are made. It's your mothers' art work. It gave you away. You say I've filled out? I don't feel filled out … feel skinny as I was before I left home. I'm hungry too, we all are."

Tom turned to his company. "Fellers, this is Johnny Adams or Running Deer. He's got the prettiest sister you ever laid eyes on, and Johnny takes real good care of her, just like his paw and ma told him."

Johnny moved out of the woods and stood with two of the men.

"In answer to your question, I was wounded and able to get medical leave to go get my sister. I was to bring her home. And I see you remember Kate. We must have passed each other because she had already left for home. Sorry I missed her. Anyway, I'm glad to get back in these deer skins. I was on the way back home when you men crossed a clearing some miles east. I thought I recognized Tom's walk and decided to investigate. Besides, the way some of you were dragging, I knew that you needed food."

Larry looked at the turkeys and got excited again and had to restrain himself to keep from jumping up and down.

"This here's unbelievable. What a peck of good luck."

"Not luck, Larry," responded Preacher. "The good Lord provided, it is an answer to prayer."

"I know, I know. We're blessed beyond measure, makin' it this far and all. And just short of them mountains and now provided for like this."

After the scare, Mort found his voice. "I needs to warn you all. Miz Wilson done turned crazy since all her trouble but she's harmless."

"There you goes again. She's crazy like a fox. You just don' see it," argued Millie.

"I heard you talkin'." The group turned to see a lean woman in her late 30's or early 40's. She wore a simple faded brown dress. The woman could have been younger. Hard life in the mountains plus her loss could age a person beyond their years.

"Well, come on to the house, if you can call it that. My man could keep this place up but I can't. Cow and hogs been gone. All my critters went the way all the farm stock did around these parts. And it wasn't all Yankees that got um either. Lots of hungry folks around."

The woman wore no shoes and a faded dress. The rag on her head must have passed for a scarf months before. The weeds that grew beside the path brushed against the file of travelers as they headed toward the small trail of smoke, but paid little attention to their surroundings. Their hungry eyes followed the turkeys in Johnny's hands.

Widow Wilson led them into a clearing in front of the cabin. The yard was swept clean of any vegetation, despite the two big oaks in the yard. The cabin appeared sound but the roof looked in need of repair. A porch ran the length of the front of the cabin. The stock of wood filled one end of the porch and hid most of one window. And an old rocker occupied the other end of the porch. A large stone was all that was needed as a step to reach the porch. It appeared an extra room had been added to the right side of the house.

The fenced in pig lot was filled with weeds. If she had had chickens they must have been free ranging like most folks did with their hogs. There was a well-cultivated garden at the back that stopped short of a slope. What appeared to be a stream-fed pool contained crockery of light brown baked clay. About twenty paces from the house past the garden stood an outhouse that had a door that hung on leather hinges. Not far from the house stood what remained of a partially burned barn.

Preacher said, "I'll take the first watch while you all eat and rest. We can share what we have with the widow. Don't want to put her out none."

"You always do, Preacher. I mean take the first watch," responded Adam. "You live by your convictions, to be a real servant."

Widow Wilson walked into the house while the men sat on the ground or the porch. Shortly after the men settled down to rest, the widow appeared at the door. She wore an apron around her waist made out of an old towel. It was held in place by a string.

As her smile rested on the men, it had a peaceful and calming effect on men who had seen little of females of late

"Looks like we have company, Millie. You want to help me get things ready?"

The widow acted as if she was seeing them for the first time and that she had expected company.

The thought of a woman that wanted to cook and serve them was new ... a real comfort. Most of their food, including the turkeys that had been dressed, was presented to Mrs. Wilson.

Tom and Running Deer exchanged news while they ate. It was a time to get reacquainted. Tom wanted to hear more about Kate but didn't want to appear too eager. Adam, impressed with Johnny Running Deer, joined the two out of curiosity.

"Johnny, this is Adam McFarland, my future brother in law. He's to marry my sister." The two shook hands. Johnny was overcome by Adams size and big smile.

The widow stared at Adam. "I detect Yankees amongst us ... that big feller and you." She pointed to Tom.

Tom chewed for a moment to give the remark some thought. The remark was not hostile. It was more of a statement of fact.

"I spent some valuable time in Philadelphia where I studied before the war. I think brother Adam did also, that right Adam?"

"As a matter of fact that is true. You can pick up an accent too easy after a few years in that area. We are on assignment from the prison in Salisbury to look for escaped prisoners. Have you seen any signs of strangers pass near here, Mrs. Wilson?"

"Home Guard or bushwhackers don't bother me none. Don't think they know about this place."

Her response surprised the men. It was as if she had not heard Adam's explanation and regarded Tom and Adam as Yankees.

Tom glanced at Adam and Larry and wondered if she had put the pieces together. Had she recognized the situation? Tom recalled Millie saying she was crazy like a fox ... smarter than one would expect.

"If I was to escape," cautioned the widow, "I'd head for that ridge of mountains yonder and look for a barn in good shape. The door on the right half is open if it's safe

to go in. If the one on the left … your left you know …
it means it won't be safe. There's talk of a mystery man,
Dan Ellis, what can lead folks safe across the mountains
into Tennessee that passes that way. That barn might be a
meetin' place."

It was obvious the widow was trying to tell Adam and
Tom that if he wanted to get through the mountains past
Home Guard that he should watch the barn and its doors.
She had given them the general direction with a nod of
her head while she talked.

Adam sighed, "It would be worth an investigation."

Preacher stood and rubbed his stomach. "The turkey
breasts couldn't go far without adding them to that soup
mixture of potatoes and such. It was just what we needed,
and I thank you Mrs. Wilson, we all do. Think I would like
to look at that barn you mentioned. And I think we better scatter a bit and bed down to we can get an early start
before the sun's up."

THE BARN

"How far is it, Mrs. Wilson, to that barn?" Larry asked.

"Hit's bout two or two in a half hours yonder ways."

This time the widow pointed in a North Western direction the way she had nodded previously.

"And call me Lois. That's what my maw and paw called me. My man called me 'Love'."

With the last comment she seemed to be lost in thought and gazed out the window. Her face was peaceful and began to bloom into a dreamy sweet half smile.

Larry gave her an understanding smile.

"I reckon we would feel all shut in if'n we was to stay in a cabin by our lonesome most the time," ventured Lem.

The tired company soon spread out to find secure places to rest for the night. There was little talk. Tom heard an occasional word or two as the men settled down for the night. He noticed that the black man, Uncle Mort, rested with his back against the wall next to the door.

When Uncle Mort saw Tom look at him, he motioned to a bucket on the porch rail and held up a big rock. "That'll wake you up, or I'll just roll the rock across these here boards."

Tom nodded. He's guarding the door. That's good.

They awoke with the smell of bacon and wondered where it might have come from. Some early risers stretched and eyed the coming dawn.

Tom wondered where the widow got the meat. *None of us had any left.* Tom started for the door as did some of the others.

When he entered, Mrs. Wilson handed Tom a tin plate with a strip of thick bacon and eggs.

"Thank you kindly."

Tom relished every mouth full. Little was left when Nate Melville rushed up. Tom realized something was wrong so he wolfed down the last few bites. Nate was too hurried for so early in the morning ... not like Nate. His face portrayed deep alarm.

"Tom! Preacher! Matt is cold as an icicle. I shook him and almost yelled at him but he don't move. That's when he felt cold. I fear Matt is dead."

"Lead the way Nate," Tom spoke gently and pushed Nate in the direction he had come. It was light enough that they had no trouble as they viewed Matt Holtsclaw. He lay on his back with his arms folded across his chest as if everything was now settled.

Tom knelt down near the head and tried to listen for breathing.

Mrs. Wilson must have followed the men. She stooped down on the other side of Matt and held a mirror under his nose. No sign of life.

Tom put his ear on Matt's chest. "No heartbeat and he's cold to the touch."

The men stood around to take a last look at Matt. Their old friend looked peaceful and content ... no longer troubled by his cough. The group looked to Tom and Preacher for resolution ... what to do next.

Mrs. Wilson took a deep breath and let out a sigh. She said, "You fellers better go finish your breakfast so you'll be strong for the trail. Uncle Mort and me will take care of this poor feller. Preacher, you say a few short words over your friend and be gone. Wouldn't be good for you to burn up too much daylight here."

The widow then led the group back to the house.

The men finished their meal in silence, picked up their gear and shuffled to the spot where Matt lay. Preacher was there with his worn Bible.

Company-A stood with hats off as Preacher read familiar verses.

Tom thought, "Dust to dust and ashes to ashes."

Nate said, "Poor Matt. We will all miss him."

Preacher turned to Widow Wilson. "We thank you for your hospitality and appreciate all you're doin' for us. I know I speak for all of us. We'll be on our way now."

All Company-A thanked her and each waved goodbye as the remaining men moved toward the mountains.

For the first time that morning Tom realized that Running Dear was not among them. Preacher had taken the lead as Adam followed behind. For some reason Tom found himself in the rear about three paces behind Lem.

The trail would only allow them to proceed in single file.

Tom thought: *the guide we hope to meet will meet us at the barn of two doors.*

Tom hurried to catch up with Adam. He wanted to discuss what the possibilities would be if they found Dan Ellis, the mystery man. Adam watched two crows circling lazily over the next hill. The crows made an attempt to light in a large tree near the tip of the hill, but they abruptly wheeled to the left and flew away.

Tom and Adam stopped and looked at each other.

Adam gave the warning birdcall.

Lem was the only one that heard. The other four continued on into a barnyard.

"Those crows were scared off for some reason," whispered Tom.

"I think we have someone that waits our arrival," ventured Adam. "I think we better separate and scout ahead. What do you think Tom?"

While they formulated a plan in their minds, a voice from beside the barn shouted. "Hold hit right thar!"

And another voice, "Drop them weapons."

Tom peeped through the brush and saw several rough men. Three were on Preacher's right and five on the left.

The four men, who didn't hear Adam's warning, stood where they were. They were caught.

Then Preacher held out his hands as if he were trying to explain their presence. At the same time he cocked his head to one side as to listen. The others in the company pretended not to be concerned.

"We might be able to sound like a bigger company?" ventured Tom.

Adam and Lem nodded. Lem made a crouched run to the right and Adam did the same to the Left.

The rest of Company-A and their captors were a few paces from the barn.

Tom considered the situation. The barn is too big and not an impressive target.

He strung his bow as he crept closer, selected a fence post and let fly an arrow. At almost the same time another arrow hit the same post from a different direction.

"Rest easy out there. No need for anyone to die today." It was Running Deer's voice. "What the preacher said is true. We need to be about our business, and you need to be about yours. Leave those people alone."

The leader, a tall rawboned, red-headed, sharp-nosed man, better dressed than the rest of his men spoke, "We got your people under our guns. Show yourselves and we can talk."

During the stalemate the man closest to his leader mumbled, "Can't be more than four or five or they would show themselves. Remember them tracks we studied?"

The red-headed leader shouted again, "We know how many is out there. Hurry up. I'm losin' my patience ... come out or this man dies."

Red shoved his musket at the trembling Elmo. And then he growled and shoved the musket once more. This time the musket fired. The shot knocked little Elmo on his back.

The rest of the captives fell to the ground as if they, too, had been shot. Two arrows flew into two men on the right. One man on the left fell to Lambert's shot. Two other men on the left spotted Lambert, shot at him and charged the spot where they last saw him. Red hid behind an old feed trough and pulled out his pistol. Tom fired his musket at the two that crouched near Red. One man on Red's right was hit in the shoulder, and that made him fire his weapon into the ground.

Red fired his pistol. He was partially hid by gun smoke, so he bounded for the woods.

Lambert saw the two men charge him. He turned to lunge for the thicket but stopped behind a big oak. He hoped they would run past ... they did. His pursuers stopped just past the tree. One turned in time to get a gun but in the face. The second man, despite his size, was quick ... swung his musket up with a beefy arm, struck

Lambert's musket to the side which struck him on the head and stunned him. Lambert staggered against the big oak … tried to clear his vision.

"Now, by jabbers, I'm goin' to skin you alive and you'll know when Ole Rob is near finished." Huge Rob pulled a large blade knife from his boot and started for Lambert.

Nate had risen from where he had fallen when the first shots were fired, grabbed the closest musket. It was too warm. He threw down the musket.

"It's been fired. Find another one. The man with the arrow in his chest won't need his." Nate made sure it had not been fired, looked around to see where he could help.

It was then that he heard Rob threaten Lambert, spotted the big man, and prayed he would not hit his friend. He fired at the big man. The shot hit Rob on the left side below his rib cage. It made him take a step to the right and gave Lambert time to gain his balance and senses. Rob looked at his side. Lambert grabbed his musket off the ground, held it over his head for protection and ducked behind the tree.

Rob growled angrily, "I'm kilt but still goin' to skin you."

Tom heard the commotion, took his musket by the barrel to use as a club.

Before Tom could reach them, two more deafening shots were fired. Rob was knocked to the ground. This time it was Larry and Lem that came to the rescue.

Lambert loaded his musket as fast as he could and looked around the tree, but his assailant was down. When he viewed the battle scene, the smoke had blown away and all was quiet.

"Didn't know this would turn into be a killing field … a real slaughter." Preacher shook his head in disbelief. "I had hoped to leave all this behind. Poor Elmo ... never had a chance. We don't even know what his real name was. Don't think anyone ever heard him speak."

The company approached Preacher and the bodies cautiously. Some viewed the barn suspiciously. Others searched the trees and bushes even though they were certain the battle was over.

"Appears like the leader got away. Might be one or two more went with him," Preacher mumbled, and kicked a weapon away from one of the bodies that still looked alive.

Tom stared at Running Bear's bow.

"I'm glad you're still close. When did you start to carry two weapons ... start using a bow? I thought you favored gun powder over arrows."

"You carry bow and arrow, and I'm not going to let a white boy best an Indian. Like you, I carry both when I can."

"I didn't see it back at the widow's cabin?"

"That's because I had it back at ... let's say it was at my temporary camp."

"Those were real killers. We thank you for your help. You've make a habit of showing up at the right time. Why don't you travel with us? Your company is more than welcome."

"If I'm to help, I need to be free of this group and allowed to scout as well as I know how." Running Deer smiled, waved at the men and trotted off toward the mountains.

Tom glanced over the bodies and spoke to the company. "These people are better shod and equipped than any we've seen ... especially us." Tom pointed to one of the men with boots and a wide leather belt. "Might as well relieve them of their foot wear and anything else that we might find useful. But don't load yourselves down … don't want to carry but what is needed."

Lem clapped Tom on the back. "Well, Mr. Tom. I would just as soon be satisfied with what I got. Don't feel right takin' from the dead."

Lambert stepped back toward the barn. He was repulsed by the scene before them. Larry and Lem looked sick and didn't want to move at first.

"Tom's suggestion appeals to me. I'm nearly bare-footed." Adam immediately started comparing sizes. No one seemed interested in the clothes except the belts. Nate and Lem gathered all the weapons, powder and cap pouches. When they took inventory of the weapons, they found enough minié balls to fight a small battle. They stored the extra weapons in the barn.

Lem gave a pleading look at Lambert. "There should be two more muskets and a big knife back beside that big oak where you tussled with them two. I'll go back and fetch what I can."

He started to walk rather slowly back to where Lambert had narrowly escaped death. "You want to come help, Lem?"

"No, I'll help right here, thank you."

Tom spoke up. "You play the scared part well Lem. You're not that scared. I'll come." Lem changed his mind and joined them.

Tom asked, "Lambert, do you still plan to lose yourself among the Cherokee when we get there?"

"Yes, I'm ready to get acquainted with my cousins again. Here is the big man that was going to skin me alive."

Tom stopped and looked around. "But where is the one I hit with the end of my musket?"

"It looks like he crawled off that way. You be careful if you want to follow that trail," cautioned Tom. "I only see one musket. We should load up and get out of here."

"I thought he was hit harder than that." Lambert complained. "But he'll have a headache. Ha."

Lem decided to follow the trail a short distance. When he rejoined Tom and Lambert, he told them, "The missing man crawled until he was out of sight, and then he staggered west."

Lambert walked back to where he first fired at the men near the barn. "Oh my, Lem, do you see what I see?" Lem caught up with Lambert to see what held his attention. James Mathews lay on the ground. There was a small amount of blood on his chest. "Lem, James took a ball that was meant for me." Lem leaned down to examine their friend.

"He ain't goin to march no more, Lambert. We better drag him over near that mud bank and pull some dirt on top. That's the best we're goin to do for him. Can't stay near hear after all that musketry. Preacher, you want to say a kind word over our old travelin' companion?"

* * *

Red made his way to where the horses had been tied and stopped short when he realized they were gone. Only three mules remained. He stomped and cursed. "Why did I leave that fool youngster to handle the teams? He should have been too scared of what I'd do it he ran the horses off on his own."

A man with two black eyes and a swollen nose staggered into the mules.

"Bruce, where've you been? You look bad. Your eyes almost swelled shut. Anybody come with you? Are we all that's left?"

"I reckon, Red. The others must be all dead or hurt bad. Rob got three holes in him. He's real dead. What are we goin' to do now Red? Where are the horses?"

"It had to be that dad blamed Dan Ellis. Who else likes horses like him and leaves us to ride raw boned cursed mules? Answer me that?"

Red started to stomp and curse again. "We better saddle up the mules. You take that one and I'll take this one. That other'ns too wore out."

"How we goin' to saddle up. They done took the saddles too. My poor head hurts somethin' fierce. Ridin' that mule won't help none."

They growled and grumbled and climbed on the mules that were disposed to be self-willed.

"They got all our baggage," mumbled Bruce.

Red complained, "These mules are cantankerous, they are. I got to figure an ambush and get even with those back at the barn."

Bruce didn't answer. His head hurt and his eyes were almost swollen shut. He shook his head in a regrettable attempt to clear his vision. His eyes didn't want to focus like they should. Noting Red's awful mood, he decided it was better to stay out of his way.

"How we two goin' to ambush that bunch anyways?"

* * *

In order to hasten their departure, Tom and Adam moved Elmo's body under an embankment and caved it in on top of the body beside James. Preacher said a few words, and they left the rest of the bodies where they were.

Nate wanted to talk while they marched. "Elmo knew what was happening when we crawled to escaped ... followed us through the tunnel. He couldn't be persuaded to go back until it was too late. Even if Elmo was out of his head he helped carry his share of the burden when asked. Elmo, or whatever his name be, would shake and whimper if near the guards, even if they didn't look at him. It's strange how he accepted me, Tom and Lem. It bothers me that the red headed leader singled out Elmo."

Tom interjected a thought. "Survivors nearly always feel guilty for their survived after a death, accident or battle."

With Running Deer gone, Company-A followed Tom over hills and descended hills to climb others. Tiresome as it was, the group was happy to find the abandoned mule. They tied most of their gear to its back.

They were about an hour and a half past the barn when they stopped to rest the mule. The spot they chose was at the crest of a hill, which was not too smart. It outlined them against the sky and made them too visible. Tom was about to scold them and not too kindly.

"You should know the danger by now. The whole world can see us."

Without a word, Lambert pointed to three figures on horseback at the top of a hill they had crossed in less than half an hour before.

Tom and company sat where they were and observed the three on horseback. It was too late to hide. The men on horses started to move in their direction.

Lambert said, "They're leadin' some more horses."

One of the men waved. "Look at that," observed Preacher. "What do you figure they want? From here they appear to be friendly and we sure outnumber them."

Tom stood and waved back. He didn't want to appear unfriendly.

"You think they might be the horses that made all those tracks where we found the mule?"

"Could be the same animals. Take a look with your glasses, Tom. I doubt it would be that red head and the one that crawled off. Looks like a youngster on one of the horses. You remember we saw smaller tracks where the animals had been tied?"

Tom replaced his glass. "There's a half grown boy and neither one has red hair, as you might expect. They carry pistols, though."

The approach of the strangers created no small amount of excitement. There was much speculation about what would settle the questions. The men settled into a relaxed "wait and see" mood, since there appeared to be no immediate danger. Tom was pleased to see that his men held their weapons … always on guard.

The man waved again. "Hello, the travelers' camp!"

From the inflection in his strong voice he appeared to be very friendly. His smile made the wrinkles almost close his eye. The friendly speaker wore worn striped pants, a brown shirt, brown suspenders and a wide belt that held a leather pistol holster. He wore a worn brown cap and low-cut boots. The other gent was dressed similarly but with a higher boot. The boy was hatless, wore a torn blue faded shirt, dark brown pants and suspenders that appeared to be new, in contrast to the rest of his dress. The horses could use a few good meals but were in fair shape.

"This here is Ned Turner and I'm Dan Ellis. What's your name again boy?"

"Walter, they call me Walt for short. Don't got no last name I knows of."

Dan eased off his mount rather stiffly, as did Ned. The boy stayed mounted until the men moved to shake hands.

"Widder Wilson told us we might catch up with you fellers. She allowed you was headin' for east Tennessee and could use help. She calls me the Mystery Man. I been helpin' folks cross over for a while now. You-all look Confederate enough so most of the people here in Wilkes County might shy off. Some folks here are Unionists. They stick close together. There are enough others to cause trouble but the way this war is goin' they're not as brave as they use to be. The Unionists, when they're together, don't take nothin' off the others."

Tom introduced the others then shook Dan's hand. "Aren't you taking a chance, Dan, to reveal your name to strangers like that? Suppose we were still Confederate sympathizers?"

"Well, Widder Wilson is a good judge of character and so am I. Besides, those bodies you left behind and Walt here's witness to the character of the men you fought makes me feel plumb safe. Wish you had drug those bodies off, though. I had to and the horses got spooked at the smell of blood. But you done me a big favor. That bunch has been layin' for me some while ... wanted to collect the bounty the Confederates got on me. Didn't want to take sides in the beginnin' but when they started the conscription, well, you know ... pullin' these mountain men out of their homes."

"I don't have to be skeered of them no more neither."
At his statement, everyone looked at the boy. "Fetch this,
fetch that. We feeds you well, boy."

Ned had only smiled and shook hands up to that
point. Now he spoke for the first time. "They left him holdin' the horses whilst they did their devilment. Me and
Dan done relieved them of their horses, which we is good
at. That's how we send a few folks over the mountains."

"Yep, Ned. And we better stay off the main road. Folks
might recognize these horses. You men follow us. You
weaker fellers can mount on the spare horses. When we
get to our meetin' house, we'll try to dig up some kind of
meal, get some rest and take you on your way west."

There was some good-natured grumbling about who
should ride or walk. It was easy and pleasant to follow Dan,
Ned, and the boy. The humor in Company-A improved
and their burdens lightened. The mule was easier to control since it now was with familiar animals.

They soon could smell smoke and dreamed of a warm
bath, bed and meal. Tom considered Wilkesboro a good
place to rest after a meal. He could then see his party off
with Dan while he made for the Boone or Waynesville area.

*I might join up with Running Deer. Would like to take Lem
with me but it might be better to let him stay with them.*

The party had to take the main road for several miles.
After a time, they followed Dan off the road into a side
trail that looked to be a sled trail. There were no wheel
marks but plenty of sled marks and mule tracks. Tom
judged from the sled's skid marks, the last one carried a
heavy load ... possibly logs.

A small trail of smoke rose above a hill. The smoke would
spread out and vanish as the wind came down the opposite hill. After they crossed the little hill they saw a weather

beaten, but sturdy house and barn, alone with other out-buildings. As the tree line to their left drew back at their approach, they could see another much larger house across the knoll. It set a shouting distance from the house they approached. The larger house was painted a bright white and appeared to be at least two stories. Dormers revealed space above the second floor. The barn that came into view behind the large house spoke of a well-maintained farm.

Dan noticed their interest in the white house, smiled and explained. "Those are good neighbors of ... I'll say the Smiths, who live in the older home. The Jones, who own the white house, might will help us on our way with some extra horses."

A large dog came out to meet them. It barked and stopped to look back at the Smith house.

"Quiet down old dog. We bring friends."

The dog recognized Dan's voice and began to wag his tail furiously.

Tom laughed with amusement and said, "I don't know if the dog wags his tail, or the tail wags the dog."

An elderly lady stepped out the front door followed by a man with a cane. Both raise a hand in greeting. Smiles revealed friendly faces. The women said something to the man before the reentered the house. It seemed strange that they should disappear when guests arrived. That was until Dan and Ned led them to the barn.

Ned pointed to some stalls with a nod. "Put the horses in those stalls. We might need them come dark.

"Three of you can follow us to the house, while the rest can climb up to the hayloft to rest a spell.

"When we finish eatin' we will swap places. These good folks usually have enough to share. They have good friends that look out for them, if you know what I mean."

Tom, Preacher, and Adam followed Ned. They could smell coffee and bacon when they entered the house. Dan met them and introduced the elderly couple as only Mom and Pop.

Pop motioned for them to have a seat at the table. That was all it took for the hungry men. Preacher said a brief prayer of thanks, not only for the food but also for safe travel. And then the three hungry men dived into the food like starving dogs.

Tom noted a bookshelf next to the cabinet that held dinnerware. The books looked to have been handled many times. A pair of spectacles rested on a small desk just visible in the next room and a well-worn chair with equally worn cushions next to the desk.

This is a well read family and probably educated.

An ashtray sat on a slim single pedestal with a twist of tobacco and a long-stemmed pipe.

Tom thought: *I had to be distracted by food smells not to notice pipe smells ... reminds me of granddad.*

The couple hovered over the five while they ate. There was little talk between gulps of coffee.

When offered coffee, Tom politely declined. "Thank you but I seldom drink coffee. Water will do just fine."

Pop handed Tom a pitcher. "Try some buttermilk and Mom's cornbread."

"Think I will. Haven't had buttermilk and cornbread since I was at home."

Dan leaned back satisfied. "Before we send for the others we need to bring you up on our usual way of how to get you across into East Tennessee. Naturally we might have to change plans accordin' to how things go. Hope you don't mind using a sack of corn for a saddle? Be prepared to ride hard at times. We'll take four or five days of food. We got the usual tin plates Mom?" Mom gave him a nod so Dan proceeded. I will guide you the rest of the way. Ned will scout this trip for more horses. Tom, I think you decided to try for the high mountains by yourself. You goin' by your lonesome?"

"I'll start out on my lonesome, but hope to hook up with Johnny Running Deer somewhere along the trail."

Tom studied Adam a bit longer than usual, trying to read his thoughts. Adam downed the last of his coffee and saw he was watched.

"Adam, I guess we are even now ... or am I ahead? You saved my life and I led you into good company going west. Got you closer to home anyway. The next time we meet we might be enemies again."

"How you figure you're ahead? And are we to be enemies after I get away from the southland?"

Adam wore a hurt expression as he sat back in his chair. He stroked his beard and waited for Tom's answer.

Tom, noting Adams heartfelt hurt and dour features, burst out laughing. The others looked first at Adam then Tom and joined in the laughter. Adam's face transformed from hurt to a grim tightlipped study of hard-determined concentration ... with a twinkle in his eye. He finally grinned and glanced at the others.

"I suppose you want to know why I'm ahead, Adam."

Adam placed is napkin next to the plate. "That was going to be my next question, friend. How are you ahead?"

"Well, I look at it this way. My sister nursed you back to health so you could make this trip, and she and the family risked much to save your hide."

Tom regretted the last statement. *That would really hurt.*

"Please forget what I said about the family, I went too far." Now it was Tom's turn to look distressed.

"Just for that, when this war is over, I'm coming back and marry your sister and make a brother in law out of you."

"It was hard enough facing my neighbors as a guard instead of fighting, now to have a Yankee as a brother in law?"

Tom stopped to listen. He heard a horseshoe strike a rock.

And then everyone in the room heard horses walk into the yard and a shout.

"Pop! Mom! We smell food. Could use a bite."

Adam didn't have to move from his chair to see through the window.

"It's that redhead from the barn fight. How many does he have with him? Anybody see."

Pop moved to the window and held up five fingers.

"We need to scare them off without a fight. It might bring half the county down on us. Red and three of the others just got off their mounts."

"Pop, you're to be our prisoner for a time. Look like you're mad as a hornet."

"No, let me." Adam took Tom's pistol. He then took Pop by the arm and stepped toward the door. "You'll be by yourself and don't need to be seen by these men, Tom. I will be gone over the hills in a little while. Open the door, Pop, and be a mad prisoner."

Adam pushed Pop out the door and let them see the pistol. The new arrivals stopped in their tracks.

"We got you outnumbered, so mount up and go back the way you came."

With that remark two windows raised and muskets stuck out.

Mom shouted, "Don't you-all hurt my man, you hear?"

Red retorted, "You gotta know you ain't seen the last of us."

As Red and his cronies backed up to their horses, he looked around to see if there were others.

"I only see you and two muskets. What if we call your bluff?"

Adam took a bead on Red and calmly replied, "You forget too easily. You want to forget the fight now?"

At that point he pushed Pop back in the house.

Red growled and mounted his horse. Two more muskets appeared at the windows as if on drill. After that, there was no more grumbling but a retreat just short of a gallop.

Adam backed into the house, handed the pistol back to Tom, and glanced at Mom. He half expected her to scold him, but she seemed completely unconcerned. She had gone along with the prisoner act, but now the act was history.

Dan motioned toward the retreating men. "That tall black bearded man in the rear has been dying to get his hands on me … and anybody that helps. I'm surprised he let Red lead that bunch. Could be Red ran into them because he hasn't maneuvered in this area much. We all better watch our step with them. When it gets dark we better move out of here. They won't go far without puttin' somebody to watch for us. Hope this won't cause you more problems Pop, or Mom."

"Don't you worry about us none. We got many friends in spite of them troublemakers."

Mom hurried to clear the table and gave Dan a playful poke on the arm when she passed and said, "Now you can send in the other men from the barn."

"Before we leave our good hosts this evening, I better scout around and see if some of them are watching. The rest of you get some rest. Dan, they might expect us to leave after dark. What if we delay until after midnight? It will take them longer than that to collect more men."

"You're probably right. We can delay until you find how many they left to watch us, and how we can dodge them."

"Can that bunch recruit more of their own kind?" Adam asked as he glanced at Dan.

Pop was the one to answer. "Don't really think they can before you leave, unless they luck up."

When it was dark enough Tom slipped out a window on the dark side of the house. He ran toward one of the outbuildings, stood for a time, and listened. Fortunately a cloud covered the sliver of a moon. It was cool but he still perspired. Feeling exposed he slunk down and ran toward the trees in back of the buildings. The feel of the New Navy pistol made him feel more secure. Damp leaves helped muffle his steps but a broken twig made his hair want to crawl.

Ah ... It's my own foot.

Tom circled back toward the road where the unwanted visitors retreated ... the most likely place they would post a lookout or two. He moved fast in places where he felt exposed, and moved more quietly. When he saw nothing and heard only an owl, it calmed his nerves. The cloud that hid the moon moved. Finally he had to stretch to see better ... get a view of the road that approached the house.

A horse nickered. He stood still a second, and determined that the sound came from his left. He dropped down on all fours. He had the pistol in his hand and didn't realize he had removed it from his belt.

I'm discovered. Make the best of it Tom. I'll crawl toward the horse.

He heard someone snore. On closer examination, a horse was tied to a sapling.

If there were more, the horses would be together. Judging from the snoring, there's only one man.

Tom moved where he could see the man in the moonlight, about five paces from the horse.

From the sound of him, he won't wake when we move out. When Tom started to move back the way he came, something stuck him on his left leg. He reached down and found a bur, and a second bur.

These are good size. I hate to do this to you old hoss, but you'll get over it.

Tom removed the burs, moved to the horse, and then lifted the horse blanket. The cinch was too tight to slip the burs under the saddle. He stuck the cockleburs on his shirt till he could loosen the cinch, and then placed them under the blanket.

Tom whispered to the horse, "Wish I could be around to see the fun, fellow."

Tom crawled into the hayloft but couldn't sleep. He could hear the others deep breathing. Time to leave and separate from friends would come too soon.

After midnight Dan entered the barn followed by the others from the house.

"Time to get up and ride, fellers. Mom sent a little breakfast … cold corn fritters wrapped in old newspapers.

Didn't want to take them but she don't know the meaning of no."

Mom stepped in the doorway. "Don't worry yourself about Mom and Pop none. The good Lord took good care of us this far. I know He will continue to. You people go with God and just trust. He will see you through." She spoke just loud enough for those that crowded together to hear her.

Preacher whispered a hoarse "Amen, sister."

Preacher turned to observe Tom and Adam embrace. All must have been said before.

Then it was Larry's turn. "Larry, ole son, come look me up around Cherokee when this is over."

"Tom, me old friend, from the news that's about, it's over and we're soon be at the mercy of the Yankees."

Preacher waved at Tom and swung astride a horse. The others soon did the same. Dan led the group out of the barn into the night.

OLD AND NEW TRAILS

Tom decided to take the seldom-used trails rather than risk being spotted as a lone traveler. He stepped off in the general direction they had taken, and then chose to take another trail. The trail wasn't easy, especially in the dark. Trees hid most of the moonlight.

This looks like the trail Uncle Casper and I went on back in '55 when we looked for Uncle Abner's store, he thought. Should get there in a couple days if all goes well.

As it became lighter Tom began to recognize familiar landmarks.

I've covered more ground than I thought. The meals and rest were what I needed to prepare me for the walk. But I better slow down. The climb to the store might be steep and don't need to be too tired ... if I can find it.

Tom stopped beside a stream, pulled off his pack and decided to eat the meal Mom had packed for the trail. After he ate, it was time for a drink. The creek made pleasant sounds. Cool clear water flowed over a rocky bed.

This is what I've been longing for. Mom's well water was good, but nothing compares to mountain streams.

After corking the canteen, he noticed the stream had gotten muddy.

"That's strange! It hasn't rained ... not that much. If someone crossed the stream it wouldn't cause that much mud? Could be a cave in at a crossing close by? I'll have to be more cautious."

Tom climbed a trail parallel to the stream.

Well, here are footprints of a small barefoot person that walked ahead of me. Track cold ... a day or two old ... not recent.

A fallen tree required him to climb over. In the process he glanced at the stream.

Hum ... no longer muddy. "Strange indeed."

To his right he observed a deer trail someone had used recently.

None of my concern, I hope. Drat! There's a stone in my shoe. That stump will do.

Tom sat down to remove his shoe and shook out a small stone. Constantly on guard, he quickly studied the area.

Uncle always said to be aware of your surroundings, especially in hostile lands. I'm glad he taught me well how to survive in the woods.

A movement to his left caught his attention. It appeared as if a clump of brush or fallen limbs moved. They did. Tom purposely stared at a nearby tree as if unconcerned. He picked one that would allow him to watch the brush out of the corner of his eye. After a time that satisfied him, nothing appeared unusual; he started to resume the climb.

"There is the deer trail to my right and brush that moves to my left. I'm followed by ghost," Tom chuckled to himself.

He stopped again to adjust what was left of his sock that bothered him.

Socks, you've served me well, but no more.

The discarded socks were stored in the pack. When he stood up, he saw an emaciated little man dressed in rags. His cap was similar to Tom's, and his trousers still had traces of Confederate gray. Even from a hundred yards you could tell the shirt had been patched many times. The laurel thicket concealed Tom well enough so he could watch the strange figure of a man.

Poor fellow's bare foot, but his feet are too big to make the tracks I saw.

When the man reached the stream, he emptied his bucket. Tom was surprised. He spoke softly, "The bucket's full of dirt. That accounts for the muddy water I saw."

The man straightened up with a hand on his back, stretched, and looked around before he retraced his steps. One limb was all it took to lift the brush over his hiding place.

Tom, me boy, that was pretty clever. If I had not seen it I wouldn't have believed it.

Tom adjusted his pack straps again before started to climb. He needed to climb around another dead fall, and as he did, he came face to face with a too-thin gray haired woman. She stopped in her tracks and gasped. Her eyes showed fear and shock.

Her gasp startled Tom as much as her sudden appearance.

Tom couldn't determine her age, but her face suggested she might be as young as late thirties. The gray hair suggested an older woman. Tom thought, Might be the result of a hard life.

"Excuse me Miss, didn't mean to startle you."

Tom stepped aside to let her pass. The woman did a little curtsy and quickly stepped past. She seemed nervous

and avoided eye contact with Tom. He assumed she was
with the man under the brush.

*Must be taking food to the man under the brush. This is too
good to let go by.*

"Ma'am," Tom yelled to be heard over the sounds of
the stream, "I think he's home."

Couldn't resist could you Tom? He chided himself.

The woman stopped in mid stride. Her mouth
dropped open, and she looked back at Tom in confusion.

Brush began to move. Tom waved and yelled again.
"Your secret is safe with me."

He turned and started back up the trail.

Couldn't resist. You still have to be the jokester.

"Wait, mister, come share with us." The woman looked
frail but her voice was strong.

I'm sure these good people have little for themselves.

"Thank you kindly. I just ate."

Perhaps these folks know about Uncle Abner and
Aunt Dorcas.

Tom stopped to shout once more. "I would like to ask
about the folks around here, and the trail ahead. It's been
years since I was close to this place."

The strange man was out of the hole by now. "Come
sit a spell. We'll tell you what we can. It's not likely we get
much company."

The man from the hole appeared to be more interested in conversation rather than hiding his new abode.
"If anybody comes along while we talk, we can try tell a
whopper and might get by."

Tom backtracked. He soon discovered the woman had
spread their meager meal on top of a cloth covered flat
rock. Their eating-place had a good view of the trail from
both directions. The location was a good choice.

I wonder how long they've been doing this. The couple seems happy with their circumstances. Their happy countenance is a wonder to behold.

The couple bowed their heads before the man said a brief prayer of thanksgiving. Tom took a seat on a fallen tree and watched the couple begin their meal.

I would bet they're glad I've eaten.

"How long have you been here like this? And you can call me Tom."

"Several months back, best I can recall. Mister, I'm not a coward. Me and the two others that left had just too much of this war ... worried about our women folk, no one left to raise crops, don't you see."

The man stopped to suck on what appeared to be a rabbit leg.

"Tom ..." It was apparent he wanted to tell his story. "My name is John Joseph ... John Joseph Boyd. The first two is what my maw called me. This here is my Julie. We've been together for near fifteen year. No man could have a better woman."

Julie blushed ... put her arm around his slim shoulders.

"Too many boys had to leave their families to care for themselves as best they could. Then some of us mountain boys were made to go off to save our state ... and from what? We're far worse off.

"Sometimes I wonder who the real enemy is here in these mountains. But when you end up ... have to shoot your own brother's son ..."

John began to choke, sob and shake.

Julie hugged him close. "The boy was just ..."

John held up his hand to quiet her. He wanted to finish ... wiped his eyes with the sleeves of his ragged shirt.

After he composed himself, he continued. "The boy's father, my brother, didn't care. He was so mad at his boy he would've shot him himself.

"Tom, the three of us that left ... deserted you might say ... Tim is up the trail a ways, I reckon. He had too much of this marchin' and shootin', got too old. Ben, he was the last of us three, went on into Jackson County. He was with the 21st North Carolina. Was afraid one of his musket balls might have hit Jackson ... Stonewall himself. The shame of it almost put him under. I heard tell it was somebody else, but he wouldn't listen. Said he was goin' home to die. We all met on the trail."

"We all wanted to get away from that kin-killin' war. We was all three wounded so it was easy to pass guards and pickets. Ben made out like he was out of his head when we got stopped once."

Tom would have liked to have heard more, but he felt pressed for time and wanted to be on his way. Before he went, he asked, "What about the folks in these parts? Are they friendly or hostile along the trail? I need to travel."

Julie turned on the log where she sat. "People from around here mostly moved to Georgia and most of the folks west of Wilkesboro did too. Some went to Wilkesboro. The ones that stayed like us are too stubborn to leave. Our nearest neighbor was about two miles west. Now there's this store in a valley just off the trail up a ways. Don't know how they're doin' since all the folks moved away?"

When she saw Tom's interest, she added, "It's about a half day's walk from here."

"That would be my Uncle Abner's store."

"They're good people, God fearin' folks ... always fair with us."

Tom stood, tipped his hat to Julie and shook hands with John. No words were spoken and he started his journey once again.

About dusk Tom found a weather-beaten sign that pointed down a side trail. He could just make out "Coffee – Salt" painted on the thing. After a few steps down this side trail Tom spotted the store. The clearing around the store grew tall weeds, except for a beaten path to the open door. A shed behind the store still held hay in the loft. He began to have a bad feeling about the place, yet he hurried toward the store.

Can't stay long. That mountain behind the place will be a chore to climb.

Tom stopped for a moment to study the store. Curiosity got the better of him. When he approached the store, smells of burnt grease and smoke offended his nose.

Must be someone stays at the place. The door is open and in good repair.

He stepped into the interior to be greeted by stale grease and unwashed body smells. As his eyes became accustomed to the dark, he saw the windows had been boarded up and few shelves remained.

A voice from the corner startled him. "Come in and sit a spell."

"No thanks, I'm just passing ..." something poked Tom in the back.

"Yes ... you're goin' to sit, move on in! Just look-a here. He's wearin' a bow just like a Injun. Think he had a hand in that shoot-out you was tellin' about back at the barn, Red?"

"Could be. Let's see what else he's got?"

They removed his bow, knife and pistol. Red pushed him into the wall, grabbed his arms and tied his hands with a rough rope. Red kicked Tom's feet out from under him.

"Tie his feet too, Simple."

Someone kicked him and yelled as if he were the one kicked. Three other voices laughed. "What's wrong Bruce? Might be you should kick your horse instead."

There was more laughter. Another man kicked Tom in the ribs, and a man on the opposite side kicked him in the rear.

"It might be him what put burs under your saddle blanket."

Laughter again. It was apparent the jug had been passed around more than once. The smell of stale liquor added to the body smells.

Someone added, "Bruce, if you'd treated your hosses' sore back to start with, he might not of took on so. Then you wouldn't have a stove up shoulder and ribs. Tried to tell you he had a tender back."

The speaker picked up Tom by his jacket front. His liquor breath was strong enough to curl Tom's whiskers.

"Now where are them other fellers? You talk right fast like or I'll try your own knife on some of your parts."

Tom took a deep breath when the man inhaled to avoid his breath. It hurt his ribs to breath.

"They rode off and left me when I was asleep." *Might be able to gain some time and make some kind of deal.* "They must have thought there wouldn't be enough food or horses to last. I've got an idea where they plan to stop."

"Don't he sound nice now. Talks like an educated Yankee."

Red interrupted the interrogation.

"Leave him be. All right Yankee, or whatever you are. Where are they goin' to stop next?"

Tom winced when he took a breath to answer.

"It's some place this side of Boone. We can catch them if we hurry … get in front and cut them off."

"What do you mean we? And by the by, how many we talkin' about?"

"No more than four, unless they picked up somebody else."

"Try again. I know Dan Ellis and his partner is with them. Oh, almost forgot. Bruce, you and Monty here watch this feller while we scout ahead and see if we can pick up their trail. Since we caught this dandy, the others can't be far ahead. We need to pick up the rest of our boys before we try to catch Dan. That's your job, Short Leg. You fetch the others."

Monty puffed out his chest. "We-uns will watch him real good, and if he's lyin', what you want us to do with him?"

Red shook his fist at Monty. "Just don't let him get away."

Tom heard them argue who was to get the horses. A command was given and soon he heard them mount and ride.

He looked around the room and noticed what looked like words written on the wall. He moved on his side to read the writing.

Has to be a message for any member of the family that might pass this way. O river by C. Must be the Oconaluftee River in Cherokee.

"Hey Simple. I'll watch the door. Cook us up some bacon."

"Uh, Bruce. You know how I cook. Build us a fire and I'll burn us some food."

Bruce walked away from the door to build a fire.

Tom moved against the wall in an attempt to stand. He felt a cloth stuck to the wall.

There has to be a nail that cloth hangs on. Hope it's not too high.

A closer examination did reveal a nail.

If I could reach the nail, it might loosen the knots ... but it's too high. Think Tom think. Leaning against a log wall isn't a good place to think. Oh yes. I faced a wood box after that first kick. How do I get it closer to the wall? How do I get on top with my feet tied and stand so I could reach the nail with hands and feet tied?

To move the box with his shoulder and head was no easy task. If there had been a guard at the door it would have been in possible.

Now, to stand on the box, it has to be done. Is the box strong enough?

He used his elbows to pull himself onto a sitting position on the box.

Now what? Lord, I need help. ... Tuck my legs against my chest and push my back against the wall. I should be standing. Where did that come from? Is that answer to prayer?

It started out well until Tom had slid half way up the wall. His weight made the box tilt and his feet slipped off the box ... down he sat with a bang.

"What's he doin', Simple. Go see right now."

"Aw Bruce, the bacon will burn. I don't like it burnt. And stop callin' me Simple. I'm Monty."

He stuck his head in the doorway. Tom remained seated on the box. It hurt too much to move.

"So you decided to sit a spell. Why was you wearin' that bow. You a Yankee Indian?"

"I had to sit a spell, I was getting cramped on the dirt floor. It sure was hard getting up on this box. Monty, these ropes are too tight and I'm not a Yankee. I'm on my way to catch some escaped Yankees when I got left. I was on special assignment. How about loosening these ropes a bit so I can get some circulation in my hands."

"Them ropes will have to do till Red gets back. You can't trick me. I'm simple but not that simple. Sit easy and I might have some bacon left over. Now where did that dog go? He should smell the food by now. There he comes. You know when it's time to eat, dog."

Bruce growled at his partner. "That dog is eatin' better than we are. You notice his ribs ain't showin' like yours. If you're goin' to make a search dog and watch dog, you got to train him."

Tom took his eyes off the doorway to accustom his eyes to the dark room again. After further examination, he could see another box that looked heavier. There was a stump someone had brought in for a seat. He then slid off his box and decided to push it against the one where he had been sitting.

That should hold the first box from tipping.

He elbowed his way back to the sitting position once more, than had to rest because of pain in his side.

A FOUR LEGGED FRIEND

Tom took his eyes off the doorway to accustom his eyes to the dark room again. After further examination of the room, he could see another box that looked to be heavier than the first. Next to it was a log on end. *They're short on seats.*

He slid off his seat to move the heavier box. I need to use my time wisely. He pushed the heavier box against the one under the nail. That should keep the first box from tipping ... if I balance well. Once more he elbowed his way back on the box. And once more he rested to relieve the pain in his side.

The ropes are too thick to cut ... and with what? If I can get untied, I need to warn the others. Oh my, what if I inadvertently put these murderers onto Preacher and the others? With a price on Dan's head they will make a strong attempt to capture them. Don't know which way or how they planned to go, but they could have chosen the way I suggested to Red. I have to get out of here somehow.'

His ribs hurt, he was thirsty and he could smell the bacon, which didn't help his hunger.

Got to stand. That second box has to hold so I don't slip again.

He tucked his legs under himself once more and placed his feet on the edge of the box where the cross pieces were stronger. Tom pressed his back against the wall slowly and carefully pushed himself up to stand.

It was a painful strain to bend forward so he could reach the nail, and not fall forward on his face. On the first attempt to reach the nail, he moved to far forward and almost fell. The second attempt made his arms cramp and he nearly pushed himself off the box.

If I slide my feet to the second box it would put me further from the nail and an unbearable strain.

He reached again … tried not to grunt as most of his body complained. This time he succeeded. The first knot caught on the nail.

God, I could sure use help right now. The first knot came loose easily. Did I hear one of the men mention a double knot? That means there are two and it feels like it.

After resting a mere moment, he tried for the second knot. To lift his arms again meant even more pain. But his desire to escape increased his determination. This knot was tighter but with a purpose born out of desperation, it too came loose.

"Thank you Lord," Tom whispered.

With more twists, he was able to get the rest of the rope off. He sat down on the box to untie his feet. It took longer than he liked. His fingers were numb and felt like useless clubs. When the feeling started to return, his fingers tingled. Now he was completely free.

Now how do I get out of here without getting shot?

I need to get one of them to the door. "How about some food for me. You need to keep your prisoner healthy if I'm to be any use to you."

"Hesh up in thar."

"I will if you get me some food."

"Simple, stuff a piece of that there chunk of bacon in his mouth to shut him up."

Tom listened to footsteps approach ... stood at the side of the door. He tried to decide what would be his next move. Simple stepped into the room. Tom grabbed the bacon with his left hand, took hold of the man's neck with his right hand and stuffed the bacon in his pocket. He got a grip on the man's belt and shoved him into the back of the room.

Tom started out the door and was quickly spotted by Bruce. He ran in the opposite direction ... into the weeds ... and looked back to see Bruce throw a hatchet. He dived into the weeds. It gave plenty of room for the hatchet to miss. Moving weeds gave away his location, so Tom decided to run a crooked course as fast as his legs would carry him. There was one shot but he didn't hear the ball. That worried him a second.

He felt nothing but except his pocket pistol bang against his leg. "My little pistol, they missed it. Couldn't help much against two."

Tom reached a wooded area and paused to catch his breath and chew on the bacon. The pup ran up to him, sat down several paces from him and slowly thumped his tail. Tom threw him the rest of the bacon.

"Good dog, you like to play games. You run after people that run, eh?"

I better backtrack down the trail. They will expect me to go higher.

As he trotted down the trail he thought, *I regret I have to leave my pack and pistol, especially my bow and arrows. That's the second time I've lost my Colt pistol.*

What was that?

He began to hear shouts and horses. They're coming this way.

His escape became a desperate run. As the sound of horses got closer, Tom started to look for a thicket or brush. I will need to rest soon.

He heard a man call, "Go get him, Dog! Show us what you're made of Dog."

Tom dived into a rhododendron thicket. The dog ran past and didn't catch his scent. He peeked through the leaves and recognized the brush pile that hid John.

Good thing the wind didn't blow toward the dog.

Tom ran up to the brush pile and asked in a low voice. "Got room in there for one more, friend? I'm chased by bushwhackers."

"No!" came a nervous reply. "Go straight up the hill from here. You'll see a hollow tree ... my old hiding place. It served me for a while ... too exposed in winter."

"Thanks John."

Tom sprinted up the hill hoping he wouldn't be spotted. There was a barely discernable trail that led to a large tree. When he passed the tree, a glance back revealed a hole toward the bottom big enough to hide someone.

It looks rotten and full of spiders. Hope spiders remember how cold it's been. The one thing I hate and dread is spiders ... might hate snakes more.

He picked up a stick to clean the hole before he decided to enter. Hesitation ended when he heard someone yell from horseback. Before he entered the hole, a quick glance down the hill didn't reveal anyone.

Don't want to go in if I'm seen.

The dog sniffed around the thicket where Tom had left the trail. A man on horseback watched the dog.

Tom thought, *Oh no, I've led them to that poor worn out soldier.*

Backing into the hole was not easy. John had been smaller. He could have stood up part way but would not have been able to look out.

John must have pulled brush against the hole but I don't have time. Impossible to relax on my haunches, especially after such a tense run.

It wasn't long before he could hear the dog sniff through the leaves.

Simple trained the dog well, too good for my sake.

Occasionally there was the sound of horse and leather squeak as well. Then Tom saw the dog's feet. It decided to sit and thump its tail. Tom peered out of a crack above the hole. The dog sat on the ground and stared at him.

Tom managed to get out his pocket pistol.

"You look friendly enough … just sit there please, and they might overlook us."

"What you got, dawg … a polecat? Hee, hee."

Tom realized one of the chasers had gotten off his horse.

"Well stupid, go get him out of there if he is in there."

The man took a swing at the dog with his pistol, but the dog jumped away as if he expected it. The dog had become accustomed to the rough company he kept.

Tom had spread his legs as far as he could but it would be impossible to hide if his pursuers chanced to look in the hole.

The man stooped down looked in the hole and began to curse.

"Well, look what we have here." The pursuer cocked his pistol.

Tom cocked the hammer while he held the trigger back. The enemy would not hear Tom's weapon until too late.

The man yelled, "You cause too much trouble I'm goin' to shoot you dead."

Tom pushed his pistol into the hole opening, released the hammer and fired into the man's chest. Tom's weapon fired a second before his opponent's weapon fired. The wood split in front of him and threw wood chunk against his chest.

He jumped out of the hole in time to dive beneath another shot. The man had fallen in a sitting position. Tom took hold of the man's feet, and twisted him on his stomach so he couldn't fire again. Going for the man's pistol, he realized it had been dropped. The handle stuck out from under his left leg. He took hold of the man's pistol. His enemy no longer moved. The other horsemen were now closer.

As he looked back at the tree hole, he saw a flattened ball that bounced off his chest and was slowed by the tree.

Tom took a closer look at the pistol he had acquired. It was heavy and had a shotgun barrel in the middle.

The second man spotted him and came fast, waving a big pistol.

Not used to this weapon, I might not hit him with a regular ball. I'll use the shotgun ... just hope it's loaded.

A split second after Tom shot, the fellow yelled, and his horse shied away.

Tom made a run for it under some low limbs, and knocked the man to the ground.

Hope I don't have to shoot this man again.

The man rolled over and came up on his knees. Tom thought this was one of the men who kicked him.

Before the fellow could get a bead on him, Tom fired and the man bell backwards.

The horses were too spooked to catch, but the dog just stood and took in the action as if it were an everyday occurrence. Tom searched the first man for shot, caps and powder. He ran to the second assailant and was able to add one more pistol to his belt. Tom still held one pistol in his fist when he stopped by John's brush pile. He was about to speak when two more shots came from up the trail.

"I got the other gent's pistol as well. Sleep good down there, John."

John only grunted.

Tom checked his pocket to be sure he had his little pistol. Satisfied, he started walking slowly up the trail. Well armed as he was, the last two shots disturbed him. He was as mad as he could ever remember.

"Been kicked, shot at, and tied up ... enough is enough. Careful, Tom. Self defense and war is one thing. Revenge should not be on your mind, despite the pain."

He had not gone far when a horse moved beyond a large rhododendron. Tom moved closer and found the reins hung loose. The horse was cropping something close to the stream. There appeared to be a small patch of blood on the saddle. He wondered if the horse had belonged to a Confederate officer by the looks of the saddle and blanket. When Tom moved closer the horse's head jerked up, but he remained still.

A curse from a short distance up the trail and a moan added to the mystery. Ignoring the horse, Tom proceeded cautiously to get closer to the moan he had heard. Peering around a clump of laurel he saw, much to his surprise, a dead horse. The dead horse had Red pinned to a tree on the left side of the trail. On the right side of the trail, Bruce leaned against a tree and held his bloody side. It was Bruce that had moaned.

Red was startled to see Tom. He studied Tom for a moment before speaking.

"Well hello there Yank. If you're a Christian, you'll pull this here horse off me. You ain't goin' to leave me here are you?"

"I ain't ... I'm not a Yankee, but I'm a professing Christian, though I don't feel like it right now. I better look to Bruce first."

He approached Bruce to see how serious his wound might be.

"You two run into a bigger bunch of bushwhackers or did you have a misunderstanding?"

"Ask the hothead Bruce. It was more than a little misunderstandin'."

"Red slapped me on my sore ribs. I ain't takin' that no more."

"I was tryin' to get your attention hothead, that's all."

"Let me see your wound Bruce ... and the both of you throw your weapons out of reach if you want my help."

Both men threw their pistols some distance. They were anxious for Tom's help. Bruce gingerly pulled his shirt open to reveal a long gash along his side above his belt. The bleeding had all but stopped.

"You aren't hurt bad. You'll be sore for a few days. Your legs look good. Are they hurt? Did you fall from the horse too?"

"I took a fall when my horse jumped. Landed hard, too."

"That probably saved your soul for a time. What about you Red? You hurt under that horse?"

"Don't know exactly."

Bruce moved to a better sitting position.

"Mister, you must be a tough mean man. Tougher than Red over there, even. But you got a good heart too."

Tom nodded and decided to pick up the weapons to eliminate temptation.

Red stared at Bruce.

"When I get out from under this here horse, you go your way and I'll go mine."

Tom removed the pistols from his belt and realized the one with the shotgun barrel was a Confederate make ... a copy of the French La Matt. The second was none other than his own Navy Colt they had removed at the old store.

That means there is another pistol near that second man. He can keep it. Now how to get the horse off Red.

Tom stepped back to the horse that was still grazed and tried to lead it near the dead horse. The live horse wouldn't get close to the dead one. Smell of blood spooked him. He removed a short rope from the dead horse and tied it to the saddle of the standing horse. He then took Red's knife, cut a length of grape vine, threaded it through the cinch strap on the dead horse, and tied the loose end of the rope to both ends of the vine.

"I've now got doubled vine tied to the rope ... should take care of it. You better pray this doesn't hurt you more than it already does."

"You know I don't know how to pray."

"Now is a good a time to learn. If not, when you get out of this you better learn how. Find a minister who can show you. I'm not a good teacher and having to learn myself."

It didn't take much encouragement for the live horse to pull. The makeshift rope held, and gravity on the hillside and loose gravel helped. Red grunted when the dead horse came off. Tom wisely kept an eye on both men.

"I would say Bruce here should use the horse. Can you stand Red?"

Red groaned as he used the tree to stand. "I reckon. Should be another horse behind the old store. You're welcome to it. Tell Simple I said so. Bruce, I'll get one of those horses for you from down where most of the shootin' took place, if I can get back on this horse. And Indian, or whatever you are, I didn't shoot the feller back at the barn a purpose. Blasted musket just went off. I'll take Bruce down there."

Bruce soon returned with an extra horse. Tom held up a hand to get their attention.

"Let me have a ride back to the store so I can get my pack and bow. And don't get into your heads to cause me any more trouble. When we part I don't want to see either one of you again. I can't forget what happened at the barn fight. You want to be a better man, then work on it."

"You have my word as a former gentleman and teacher."

Tom looked at Bruce in surprise.

"It's been better to appear to be uneducated after more or less captured by this group. I fell into bad habits to survive."

It pained Bruce to mount and he continued to talk after they mounted and started for the store. "I better go somewhere else than Wilkesboro, and I'm not sure where?"

Tom figured Bruce would be good to have with him when they faced Simple. He said to Bruce, "When you leave the old store you could head for Asheville or West Asheville and start over."

He must have had chances to escape bad company before this. I wonder how much truth there is to what he said, probably well practiced in the art of deception. I'll trust him in front of me until we part.

Bruce hesitated before he moved the horses into the trail. "I know it's easier to say, don't think too hard of me and my situation, but please ..."

"Are you trying to say, forgive me? That's not easy since you took part in the barn fight that got men killed. Most of them were friends of yours too. I would have to do more than think on this learn to pray better."

"Mister, you did bust us up considerably. Red told us later he had not intended to shoot. He carried a strange musket that had a hair trigger. When he threatened the man, his finger hit the trigger. I'll make you and myself a promise. No more bad company and no more fights, war or not. I did what I did out of desperation for preservation and survival, if you will. Now I'm ashamed."

Tom nodded, slipped from his mount and looked around. "I'll pick up my belongings and be on my way. Remember your promise, and let your conscience be your guide. It would be good to find a minister."

Bruce raised a hand, pulled the reins toward the path and rode away. Tom watched him for a moment then looked for his pack and bow. He added food to his pack since the renegades would have no further use for it. It angered him when he found one end of his bow in the ashes of the cook fire. The bow was blackened a bit, and he would need a different string.

Before he entered the barn to search for other useful items, he slapped his mount on the rump.

"I hope you know the way home, horse. No need for me to be caught riding a stolen horse. I'll walk first."

Tom spied some strong twine. "It's just the thing for a new bow string. I'll double twist it to make sure."

He pulled Bees wax from his pack and laid it aside while he twisted the twine. He watched for Simple while he waxed the string.

The fellow disappeared ... must have gotten tired of the company he kept. Perhaps he isn't as simple as they thought.

His ribs were sore but it still felt food to travel again ... and alone with his thoughts.

Better to be alone than in their company. That sounds Biblical somehow ... still have my Bible. It's extra weight but Ma would never forgive me if I didn't have it.

The climb was now more difficult and the path steeper. Each step brought pain. Tom mumbled, "I need to take shorter steps and not breathe so deep."

When he took a deep breath it expanded his rib cage. Deep breaths were too painful. The slower pace was not to his liking but his leg muscles were sore from the running.

I'll have to walk the soreness out. When I think on the abuse I took it makes me angry. It wasn't revenge when I shot those two men. To borrow Bruce's words, it was self preservation ... I call it self defense.

Tripping over a stone brought a stab of pain. He began to fuss with himself.

"Tom you should have taken the horse for a distance more. The risk would have been worth the danger. I'm worn out ... plumb wore out, Paw would say. Time to rest."

Tom crawled under a large clump of rhododendron and found a ground cover of leaves. He lay on his back and observed other lifeless bushes with small finches flitting between branches. Their chirping, the breeze through the rustling leaves, and the sound of a brook lulled him into a peaceful sleep.

It was the smell of a dog that woke him. The dog sniffed him in the face but jumped back when Tom opened his eyes. He stopped about five paces distance, sat and looked at Tom. It was the same dog he had thrown the meat and the dog that had given him away at the tree.

"Dog, you sure favor Unk's old dog. Could you be one of his pups?" This one is not full grown ... a young dog, but looks more like a wolf.

"Do you look for human company dog?"

The dog cocked his head to one side and stared at Tom.

"You didn't bring any of your old friends did you?"

Tom listened and looked around. He neither heard nor saw anything unusual ... decided it was safe. Dog moved out of the way.

That wild bunch expects too much out of this pup. Who would follow you, dog? Who would be left that's a threat? "Well dog, it's getting on to dark. Come along if you're a mind to. We might find something to eat later."

He was reminded just how sore he is when crawling out from under the bush.

"Got to keep going anyhow, dog. I've got to walk out some of this soreness before dark."

Dog moved out of Tom's way and watched as the man-creature tried to stand straight before he walked. Tom considered a deer trail that led off into the trees. He gave it up for the worn trail. That deer trail would tire us even more."

When Tom would stop after a few yards and look back, the dog would stop too.

"Come on, I'm not going to hurt you. I'm too sore to swing a pistol barrel at you like your old friends. Then consider I like your company."

They marched on. Tom could hear a stream again and decided to follow it in the fading light as far as he could. He glanced back and was amused when the dog stopped.

"Don't believe me do you? I wouldn't hurt a traveling companion."

Dark came quickly in the mountains. The tree canopy made it even harder to see the trail. He often stumbled on rocks and tree roots. Tom wished for a full moon but there was none. Dog could be heard splashing in the steam.

"Try this well worn path, dog. I judge from the lack of brush it'll be easier to travel."

It was getting colder but the climb kept them warm.

"I'm hungry, dog. I'll share a biscuit with you."

Tom sat on a log beside the trail, took out the last of his two remaining biscuits and tossed one to the dog.

"Don't break your teeth on it, dog. I'll bet you'll have to hold it between your paws to chew on it. I could have soaked it in water like I'm going to do mine."

Tom moved to the stream and held his biscuit under the water. He could hear the dog in the stream below him.

"Don't think we have time for this bread to get soft, dog. Smart dog … figured to do the same."

He decided to press on since it was getting colder. Tom adjusted his pack strap and felt an unfamiliar lump. When the lump was removed from the pack, two strips of thick bacon and a clump of damp left over coffee grounds greeted his nose. He glanced at the dog and noted the dog watched with increased interest.

"It looks like we got some of Red's used coffee and a bit of bacon. It's been cooked too. I'll give you half of mine. It might be days before we find food but we need the strength now."

TRAVEL COMPANIONS
AND NEW FRIENDS?

"Let's decide on a name for you, if we're to be traveling companions, or partners. How about 'Cautious'. Nah ... doesn't sound right for a good lookin' dog like you. You have a reason to be cautious. By the time we get to where we're going you might learn to trust me."

Tom walked the trail cautiously himself. Dog followed for a time but soon ran past to take up the lead. "I was thinking of calling you 'Jack'. How would you like that?"

Tom followed the white underbelly of the dog in the semi darkness. The dog kept a steady pace not too far ahead of Tom.

"Jack it is then. I do believe you have wolf in you, more wolf than dog. You don't have full growth or you've been starved."

The two new companions rose before daylight. Tom noticed the sky was getting lighter. "It's downright cold Jack. I wish you were friendlier and kept me warm last night."

They had not gone far when the dog stopped ... froze in mid stride. Tom strode forward cautiously. They could see a trail of smoke against the morning sky. It was too far to attract the dog's interest.

In a low voice Tom asked, "What do you see, Jack? A rabbit?"

Jack watched something to their southwest. Tom walked in the direction Jack watched. Two figures rested on their haunches. They appeared to be watching the trail of smoke Tom had seen. There was a musket or shotgun that leaned against a tree.

Tom and the dog climbed a hill north of the two. This would allow him to observe them and see what their interest might be in the smoke.

I see what aroused their curiosity. They're watching a man partially hidden by new-growth pines.

Tom spoke to the dog in a low voice. "That man's hat looks familiar ... like Preacher's. He walks like Preacher. If it is, they should be further west. The rest of them must be further down the hill near the smoke. Didn't figure to catch them. They must have been delayed. I haven't traveled that fast."

The two strangers moved away from their observation place. One was an old man of over sixty and the other couldn't be more than twelve.

They must want to get around Preacher and the rest. Think I'll find out.

Tom moved to intercept them. They soon came out of a patch of woods. Tom stepped out in order to be seen ... pretended to be surprised.

The strangers were startled. It was obvious they missed Tom and the dog behind them.

"Howdy, folks. You headin' for Boone?"

"Naw, we're headin' for Jefferson Town ... if we can get by that bunch down there."

The man suddenly gave Tom a look that told him he was suspicious. He first appeared friendly but now he was cautious. The man must have been napping in the early morning sun and let the boy watch.

"You lookin' for the Home Guard, mister?"

"Nope, tryin' to catch up with some relatives. You might know them, happen to come across a couple about forty to fifty? They would be my aunt and uncle. Gentry's the last name. Had a little store between here and Wilkesboro."

"No, but now that I think on hit, about two year ago they was not doin' good at the store. Couldn't get supplies like they usta. They was goin' to head fer Injun country, Cherokee country or Georgia."

"Hit was not more'n a year when they left, Pap." The boy spoke for the first time. "We better get, Pap. Them fellers down there is beginnin' to pack up."

"Stranger, we'uns hope you find your kin. We don't have many left our own selves. This here boy ain't goin' the way his brothers done. He's too young, only one left. This war done tore this country up somethin' pitiful."

"You folks hungry?" The three of them were startled by a new voice. They turned around to look into Preacher smiling face. He must have been listening at the edge of the woods.

"Come on to the fire. We got enough to share. Tom, I thought you would be further south?"

"I ran afoul of that red-head from the barn fight and his bad men. That bushwhacker bunch was going to try and catch you. Won't have to worry about him now unless he's able to round up more like himself. He didn't have as many with him as he did in Wilkesboro. I think he's had enough of us. Why aren't you further along?"

"We've been playing cat and mouse with the Home Guard. Don't think they know it. Every time we try to go one way or another, they are there ... have a picket posted."

"You might have to trick your way through. Let me borrow a horse. I might lead them on a false trail. It might give you a chance to slip past."

The boy pointed to the bush and spoke excitedly. "Look Pap. See that young wolf laying at the edge of the woods? He just watches us. Don't suppose that's one of Babe's pups do you?"

"Well ... most likely. It ain't afeared of us, just cautious. Fellers, if that animal takes a likin' to any of you'uns, you got a loyal friend fer life. My brother tried to raise wolf-dogs. He wanted mostly wolf, not as mean. Some pups got stole."

The three newcomers approached the fire.

Dan was the first to speak. "Fill your plates boys."

"Dan, I plan to leave Company-A and branch off to Cherokee on my own."

"Tom, your plan might work, but what if they catch you?"

"I know these parts almost as well as the Guard." *Wish I was confident as I sound.* "If I let the horse go at one point, the guard might rather ride than chase me in the woods. They should follow the horse when I let it go. It's worth the risk."

"Life's a risk these days. If that's what you want to do Tom, may the good Lord go with you. We might help out some. Come with me and pick out a horse."

"Dan, no need to give me a good horse if I'm to let it go. This nag will do fine. What's this you're handing me?"

Without a word, Dan handed Tom three days food supply for his pack. Tom then mounted quickly, waved and rode for Boone.

After he had ridden a short distance, he turned in the saddle and shouted, "Farewell, fellers. See you in Tennessee."

Jack bounded out of the bushes to ran behind the horse. Dan and Company-A started their ride toward Boone. They intended to skirt the edge of the community and local farms.

Tom rode as long as he could, going southwest. He neither tried to conceal himself nor make an effort to be too visible. At one point a farmer and a black man glanced at him but went back to splitting wood.

"Sure glad for this horse in these steep places. I'm saddle sore and not used to it anymore, and I'll be glad when it's time to let you go, horse. Rather hike any day. I've got Cherokee on the brain."

"Fresh horse and mule tracks in the mud, Jack."

Tom stopped the horse and studied the tracks. "Wonder what this might lead us into? I have a gut feeling that it's not right."

The dog walked a few paces ahead and stopped, then stared up the trail. The horse's ears told him something or somebody was around the bend. From a short distance a horse whinnied.

"It's time for horse to go home or join those ahead."

Tom removed his pack and left the horse standing. "Whatever that is around the bend is not in the path of our little company. Company 'A' should be safe if they avoid this road. I don't know of a path or trail that would be safe for the guard to chase me like I planned."

A walk through the brush and trees was too difficult to make travel fast. Two horses became visible below him. He soon determined there were three or four men hidden off the trail. Tom crept past the men, thirty yards above them. Tobacco smoke occasionally wafted up the hill.

"Dog, you've got to do a better job of warning us. I'm glad to get by that bunch. Could have been trouble."

"They were guards for this trail that goes by Grandfather Mountain. Must be where they anticipate travelers, Jack."

Back on the road, Tom felt jittery, but he was determined to make better progress.

"I still have a copy of the papers that charge me with the capture of escaped prisoners. Hope that will help if needed."

The day was almost spent and the two travelers were tired and gotten careless. Fortunately Jack stopped ... spotted or smelled trouble ahead and to their right. At the same time a small bird about to light in a tree, abruptly changed course and went in another direction. *There is something behind that big tree or boulder ... scared the bird. Jack's cautious too.*

Before Tom could see through the brush, he could smell unwashed body, wood smoke, and damp clothes. In an attempt to crawl closer a twig snapped, a man wheeled around, and Jack growled.

The man's weapon rested between two saplings. It pointed toward the trail while the musket butt shined at Tom. It was impossible for the man to swing around in time to do harm.

The man Tom saw before him was literally a bag of bones, he was so emaciated. Fear stood out in his eyes as he stared at Tom and Jack.

Tom couldn't help grinning because of the situation.

"Did you plan to bushwhack me stranger? You notice I'm not hostile or I would have you under my pistol. I just want to get into Cherokee country without trouble, my dog Jack, and me. Please let your weapon lie where it is and walk away about, say, a hundred paces so we can be on our way."

"That's all right with me stranger. I ain't no bushwhacker, just cautious like. We'uns up here on the mountain got plenty to be cautious about. We been hunted, bushwhacked our own selves. Don't pay to be too trustin' any more. You'uns not be spyin' on us'ins. If you air, that's bein' brave or awful foolish, one or t'other."

"I'm Tom, and like I said, we're on our way to the Cherokees. Who would be spyin' on you in this lonesome country?"

The skinny man countered. "Like I said, we done been hunted down like critters and murdered. When we got the signal from on top you was comin', we was bound to be curious like. We are hidin' out from … I'll just say them that aims to do us harm. You got to be runnin' your own self. If in you air, you'll find more of your own kind goin' down into the next valley. Better watch out for copperheads and rattlers. Now I'm a tellin' you the gospel about bein' hunted and such."

Jack growled. Tom glanced at the dog and saw the dog look behind them. The hair on Tom's neck stood up. There's someone behind me and this man's eyes says so.

A female voice spoke from behind, "He's tellin' the gospel truth, mister. What brought you into these hills? You aim to go back and tell what you found or you goin' to that Injun country? If you're plannin' to go back you kin tell them they failed two times and will fail again."

Without looking back, Tom answered, "You can watch me and Jack here walk on our way over the mountain.

That should be proof enough … and do I have a pistol pointed at this man?"

"Nope, you don't. You an' that dog ought to turn up this hill to a clump of rocks and rest for the night. It's getting' too dark an' some of our kind might take you to be a spy. Wait until mornin' and we'uns will signal. Then you can pass unharmed."

"I take kindly to your advice. Jack and I will start for the rocks. We got a little food to share."

"T'wont be necessary. Be careful goin' down that valley. Thar's some folks that air plumb touchy."

* * *

The next morning Tom and the dog were able to pass Grandfather Mountain without incident. They did see a figure on a large boulder within yelling distance. Tom waved but the man didn't respond.

"I know he sees me. He'll tend to his business and I'm expected to tend to mine."

By afternoon they were on their way into the valley. They were able to travel faster. Tom no longer feared the guard.

"I remember someone told me about a cave or cavern where I could rest or hide. There could be more conscripts that hid there. They could tell me what it's like ahead and if my people passed. I hear water. Jack, we'll walk down to the stream, get a drink and fill my canteen."

They jumped from stone to stone. It was so exhilarating he ignored the pain in his side. Jack seemed to enjoy Tom's antics as a sort of game.

Tom stopped to catch his breath and examine his surroundings. He looked at the dog for any sign of trouble and the dog looked away. Tom glanced at trees near a stream and back at the dog who looked away ... then back at Tom. He had taken off his gloves Dan Ellis had given him to remove his hat. Out of the corner of his eye he noticed the dog would look at him but when he turned to look at Jack, the dog would look away again.

"Jack, you are acting strange. How come you are playful now? Time to get some water."

Before replacing his hat, Tom smoothed down his hair. All of a sudden Jack rushed by, and snatched the gloves out of Tom's hand. Jack pranced about several feet in front of Tom, then stopped as if to say get them if you can.

"So you want to play. You know I can't catch you."

Jack pranced to the edge of the stream, looked down stream, walked back a step or two and dropped the gloves. The dog looked at Tom and then downstream. His ears indicated he had seen something.

"You have my attention. What did you see Jack?"

After several steps Tom could see a man in ragged trousers and shirt, if you could call it a shirt. It was more like a rag hanging on a large frame.

The figure saw Tom about the same time. He continued to fish as Tom approached. The fisherman was short of statue and stocky. His Confederate kepi was too small for his large head and his gray pants were almost worn through the seat. His shirt had been white at one time. The jacket hung on a bush nearby was not military cut.

"Catch anything?"

The man gave Tom a careful look-over.

Doesn't look friendly ... takes too much interest in my knap sack and doesn't answer my question. Don't think I'm going to like this boy ... figures me for easy picking, I'll bet.

Tom was beginning to get irritated. "I asked you if are catching anything?"

The fellow acknowledged the anger in Tom's voice and decided to answer. "Nope, don't look like it does it? Deepest hole in this creek for miles and can't catch fish. You got any grub in that there pack?"

"I had hopes you had some at the cave." *The cavern should be around here somewhere … didn't tell a lie, just avoided the question.*

"You know our hidin' place." It was more of a statement than a question. "We're short on food but aim to correct that shortly."

"How are you going to do that?"

"There are some farmers south of here."

Jack growled. Tom stepped back to be out of reach of the man's pole … looked where the dog stared. Jack had his eyes on another man. This man held a cavalry saber and didn't look friendly.

DIFFERENCES BETWEEN FRIENDS AND ENEMIES

The new arrival froze in his tracks. His eyes opened wide and his jaw dropped a couple inches. It was then Tom realized he had drawn his revolver. It gave him confidence to realize his reflexes responded to the situation.

Strange, I don't recall reaching for the pistol. Some of the practice paid for itself.

"Hold on down there!" It came from higher on the ridge and from Tom's right, not more than fifty yards away.

Tom knew from the voice he was probably safe or trouble was late to come.

"You boys leave the traveler alone. No need to get hostile, stranger. And no need to get defensive boys. Stranger, these boys have reason to be mistrusting. You can join us if you're a mind too. We have plenty of room."

Tom moved to put a tree between him and the voice. *Hope I made the right move.*

"Thank you but I'll just be on my way. There's a place I need to be."

He took a closer look at the man with the saber. The fellow was better shod than his friend. His boots were neither too old nor his trousers. His shirt was worn but not patched, but too small for him.

It appears like he ran into someones' clothes line ... thus the small shirt. Bet he's a good scrounger.

The one with the pole spread his arms. "We don't mean nobody harm. You-all come join us ... your wolf too. We got plenty of room. Come see for yourself."

The man stared at Tom's pack as he spoke.

"I'll just move on down the creek, boys. Thanks anyway. The wolf and I need to cover much ground today."

If I joined you two I might wake up in the morning dead. Now Tom ... if you could do that, you'd scare them to death.

"If you've a mind to keep goin', watch your back. There are a few friendly folks in the valley below but stay on your guard."

The hidden voice hasn't moved. That's comforting. These are desperate men in desperate times.

Without further words, Tom left the two ... and the unseen third man. He chose the path that sometimes ran beside the stream. Jack gave the men and the saber a wide berth, circled around him and joined Tom.

"Jack, I think we made the right decision to keep going. You might have ended up on a stick over a fire. I'm not sure why you chose me for a companion but I'm glad you did. You probably saved my bacon. That feller called you a wolf. The way you pranced back there with my glove sure made you look like a wolf. I'll bet you're mostly wolf ... gray and black on top with white on the belly, and that face. I've been too busy to notice. Always wanted a pup like you when I was a boy."

Although the sound of a stream had a comforting and calming effect on Tom, he realized the noise made it difficult to hear other sounds. This prompted them to take a higher route above the stream.

It was late in the day when the two travelers decided to get away from the worn path and find a place for the night. They had to work their way through brush and across the creek again. It was then that he saw another path leading toward a group of tall evergreens.

"Jack, that clump of trees looks like a good place to spend the night." When they reached the trees they could see a partially burned house. Most of the roof was gone. Behind the place where the house had been, stood a barn.

"That barn looks fairly decent."

The faint path to the barn had been used recently.

Wonder is someone uses it. Chances are someone might live there. If it were me, I wouldn't want a worn path showing. Think we will pass ... don't want a repeat of Unk's old store and end up a captive again.

Tom started to turn. His leg got in Jack's way, and the dog wheeled around to face the way they had come. It was the second time Jack had been this close. The hair on Tom's neck wanted to crawl. He felt someone behind him.

Not twice in one day?

"If you be a friendly passerby, you're welcome. If not, you can join that cemetery yonder. You can't see it but it's there. What's your name, and what's your business here, stranger?"

Tom turned his head slowly to see who talked. A glance at Jack revealed he wasn't particularly bothered by the man's presence.

I think Jack has become a judge of character.

"I'm friendly most the time, and my name is Tom. I'm just traveling through these parts."

Tom completed his turn to face the man and realized he held a shotgun leveled at his middle.

"I'll just keep on traveling – march or get on my way."

"You a deserter?"

"I didn't desert. Who do I have the pleasure of addressing?"

"My friends, what's left, call me Zeke ... Zeke Trivette. What's your family name?"

"I'm Sergeant Tom Gentry. I've been trying to catch deserters, least ways that's what my papers say. Spread out from my men going west in the search. I'm also looking for my Uncle Abner and Aunt Dorcas Gentry. Have you heard or seen of them in the last few months?"

"I know them. I heard talk your uncle changed his mind about settlin' round here when he got to the top of Linville Gorge. Too much trouble near the caverns and not enough folks still live near. Come on to the barn. That's home to me and my missus ... and grandson."

The shotgun was now pointed to the ground. Tom followed the old man to the barn. The roof and sides that faced the burned out house looked like it could use more boards and shingles.

Tom thought the appearance of the barn would discourage the most curious from trespassing.

What I saw from the trees didn't look that bad but when you get closer, a person might change their mind ... unless they searched for tender to start a fire.

"Mr. Trivette, you know which way my uncle went?"

"Nope, can't say I do. My woman told me about him. Might be she would know. Come on in the barn and rest up. It's comin' on to dark you know."

An elderly woman, curious to see to whom her husband spoke, opened a door that had been cut in the side of the barn.

"We got company, Dad?"

"Yep. This here is my wife Bess. That's our grandson Porky. That's what his paw called him when he was a little'n."

Porky wore shoes too large for him; his trousers and shirt had been cut to fit. The galluses were made from strips of old leather that made him appear neater than the adults. Bess wore a faded blue dress, and the toes of old work shoes stuck out from under her dress. Tom took note of Zeke's patched black trousers, a faded red shirt and frayed galluses. The boots were worn down on the outside.

Zeke must be bowlegged.

"My real name is Peter, but I like Porky just fine. My paw must've got himself kilt in the war. My maw's buried out back. When I get bigger I'm goin' to fight for Robert E. Lee."

Porky looked Tom over. "You be a deserter?"

"Watch your manners, young man," his grandfather admonished.

Both grandparents could scowl with the best.

"Have a seat. We'll have somethin' to eat directly," the grandmother offered.

Tom glanced around the room. There was a plow and some tackle in one corner. The plow didn't have much rust, indicated that it had seen recent use. There was another door that suggested another room.

Bess noticed Tom's curiosity. "We built this barn over my Pa's old cabin. We got a right comfortable place to live, hid right here inside this barn. Got some food we can share. We don't get many visitors. Porky, get us some firewood please."

Porky opened the door and stopped.

"Mister, that your dog? He looks like a wolf. He stands there and stares at me."

"He's still young and not very trusting. He'll get out of your way."

When Porky returned he looked back at the Jack and asked, "Can he come in?"

"Don't think he will. I'll throw him some scraps after we eat."

At one point while they ate, Zeke looked at Tom like he just remembered something. "Why, I think your uncle went back up the mountain. Told one of the neighbors that was coon huntin' that he was headin' for Trade. It was about two years ago or less. Don't think he got as far as the caverns comin' this way. Never made it into the valley. Might have heard about the men hidin' in the caverns. Can't be that many men, though. Not much way to get food. Don't think he ran into trouble."

Bess said, "After you've et, you can bed down on the straw in the barn. Sorry we ain't got no room in here."

Tom mulled over the prospect of a straw bed. *The barn feels confined after my travel experience thus far ... don't want to leave Jack out there. And this couple doesn't truly know which way Uncle Abner went. Suppose I still have Cherokee in mind.*

"I appreciate the food and thank you most kindly for the offer to sleep on the hay, but I better be on my way. I'll feel more at home sleeping out in the open. You don't need to put yourselves out to feed me. I'm sure you need your supplies."

Bess reached over to hold Tom's arm. "Don't fret yourself on our account. We got it better than most folks around here. There's hid behind us ground where we grow stuff. It's behind them tall pines. We got fixed up with other kin and friends ... sort of a group to trade and help each other. It works good. We don't let on about this group to outsiders. Since you'll be movin' on, tellin' you don't matter."

Zeke continued telling about the group. "Reason we joined with the others was fear of them boys what hide out in caves and hills you came through. They've tried to rob neighbors a time or two, stealin' clothes off lines, fence posts, and food out of storage. If a body is hungry and asks, we try to help. We don't take to thievery.

"My good woman and me try to be Christian and pray for our enemies like the Good Book says. You got any idea how we can handle them rascals from up the gap. I know they get hungry and tired of war, but we got a right to protect our own."

Tom thought for a moment. He wanted to be helpful because of their generosity but was reluctant to pose a solution.

"You could post a sign somewhere that you could supply flour and salt in exchange for deer or bear meat and hides. Why not establish a spot where you could trade? You wouldn't have to see each other."

"That sounds like a likely idea ... would work as long as deer held out up there and food lasted down here. I don't write none too well but Porky is a hand at it. You do it Porky boy. But be sure and add we'll be watchin' for trickery."

While they ate, Tom stuffed a ham biscuit in his pocket. Bess noticed and motioned for him to take another. Grinning, he helped himself to another and stuffed in the other pocket.

Tom moved to the door and tried to avoid an awkward farewell.

"I thank you for your generous hospitality. It will be remembered the rest of my life."

His pack was adjusted to his back before he hung the bow over his shoulder.

"Noticed you carry a bow. You might have need of a new string soon. A part Indian dropped off some deer meat, left some string and bees wax and arrow makings. They're yours if you can use 'em."

"Well, thank you again. I probably know that Indian."

Running Deer probably knew I would have lost or broken mine. Now I have two strings.

In a hurry to depart, he smiled, made a short bow and made his exit.

More conversation would cut in to what daylight remains. After Tom shut the barn door he handed Jack a ham biscuit.

"Dog, we're still headin' for Cherokee country."

The two travelers had not gone more than ten paces when a dinner bell clanged. Someone banged on a triangle with a piece of metal. There was a pause, than it rang three times more.

"That sounds like a signal, Jack."

The barn door flew open. Tom and his dog both turned to see Zeke and Porky run out, each carrying a weapon. They glanced at Tom and Jack when they ran past.

"Zeke, does that signal mean trouble? Jack, the dog, and I would be glad to help if we can."

It could be a fire but not with weapons unless they take them out of habit. I think it is more defensive.

"That bell ringer means he got a signal from up the mountain. We got company comin' we don't want. You can help if you're a mind to. Could be shootin'."

If Tom hadn't been tired from his walk off the mountain, it would be easy to keep up with the old man and his grandson. Zeke and Porky set a good pace. It was almost dark when they reached their destination. Zeke and his grandson stopped behind a rock fence. A short distance away a man lit his pipe. Tom didn't think that was wise until someone on their left did the same thing. Neighbors were setting up a preplanned defense.

"Them mountain boys most likely will wait until almost daylight to move in on us. Get some sleep Tom. We got a few more of our friends comin', if they can make it. Pick a spot near them small trees. You'll know when it's time."

Tom scraped together a pile of leaves for a bed, placing the bow within easy reach and the pack against a small sapling. It didn't take long to get comfortable. Jack lay beside him and began to sniff Tom's pocket with the remaining biscuit.

"All right fellow, I'll split it with you. It might be a long time before we get another."

In a matter of seconds the companions were asleep

Tom dreamed of another encounter with Slim the mountain man. It began to disturb his restless sleep. Half awake, Tom thought he could even smell Slim.

A low growl from Jack brought him to full awake. He rested his hand on Jack to quiet him … raised his head to see. The sky was now lighter, not long before daylight. A movement revealed a slight figure crouched low. It moved between his resting place and the rock wall.

That's not a friend. How did he get past the pickets … or lookouts?

The figure suddenly stood next to the wall, facing the old man. "Mister, I got a big knife on this boy. Put down your musket and step away. We aim to get us some food, and might get me a coat and shoes."

Tom rose out of his bed of leaves … cocked his pistol as he stood. The figure turned to face him. It gave Porky a chance to jump away from the threat.

"I think a ball from this pistol is faster than your knife. It's your turn to put it down."

He moved toward the figure with the knife. Tom felt a jab in his right side.

"You drop the pistol. This musket makes a right sizable hole."

Tom's pistol dropped to the ground as the second voice raised his musket to strike Tom on the head.

Tom dodged, and the barrel glanced off his right arm.

To Tom's surprise the assailant yelled in pain. Jack had him by the arm close to the shoulder and carried him to the ground. Tom quickly retrieved his pistol to face the first man who had his hands in the air. Zeke had a shotgun in the man's back.

"Turn loose Jack, come to me. Good dog. It's all fine, we've got them now."

I sure didn't expect that kind of response from the dog.

"You on the ground, why were you going to hit me on the head? You had us prisoners with your musket."

"I couldn't shoot you without alerting the rest of your people and you have us outnumbered. It would be pure murder to shoot you. Besides, we don't have that much powder."

He held his arm and whined, "That dog bit me good. I'm bleedin', can I get some help? You got us fair and square. All we wanted was to get some food and clothes. Didn't expect to run into this kind of defense."

Zeke pushed his captive to the ground.

"How many more are out there?"

His captive held up three fingers.

"We don't got much law and no place to lock you up. See this here stone fence? When you're desperate for food and such, one man come down, leave a note. We'll trade for deer or turkey meat when you got it. You can owe us the meat and deerskin, and we can drop off food for you. We'll share what we got. Don't have to be any bloodshed. Up to now there's none been shed. If you hurt one of ours it will be war, and we could come up there and smoke you out. We only lost a ham or two and some shirts. When you aim to trade, beat on that hollow log to get our attention. What do you say?"

One of the attackers sat on the ground through the lecture, looked briefly at his partner before answering.

"That's more than fair. I reckon we all heard. I'll speak for all of us. Now can somebody help me with my arm?"

Zeke motioned for Porky to help. The boy then tore away the sleeve, pulled out a flask and poured whiskey over the wound. The injured man gritted his teeth.

"It's time we all went to our homes or hiding places. We thank you for your Christian hospitality, helped us like this when we don't deserve it."

Zeke helped the injured man to his feet.

"You come on to the spring house where my missus can look at that dog bite. We can give you a little food to take back. There might be an extra shirt. Porky, run ahead and have grandma meet us at the springhouse with her doctorin' fixin's. She might have some apple vinegar to put on it. That there looks like a deep bite."

Tom reached down to pet the dog.

"Zeke, it's long past time for me and the dog to be traveling. I'll bid you farewell once again."

"Drop by the spring-house. Should be some ham and biscuits left from last night. Take some with you, and thanks for helpin' last night. If you come this way again, stop for a visit. You're welcome any time ... you and Jack."

* * *

Tom noticed the dog wasn't as fearful around him as at first. Jack would walk ahead much of the time, stop and look back occasionally to see if Tom followed. One evening when food ran low, Jack dropped a rabbit at Tom's feet.

"What a surprise, thank you Jack. I suppose you prefer it cooked, like me. What a tale to tell Running Deer.'

One night west of Asheville there came a late winter snow. Tom picked a large pine for shelter, made a lean-to and pulled Jack next to himself for warmth.

"I could use two of you tonight, Jack"

Early in the cool mornings Jack would be playful. Tom would romp with him to get warm. They made a game of catch or retrieve a ball made of bound cloth. It took much of the boredom out of travel when the path allowed.

"You're still a young dog, and you keep getting bigger. No wonder you were able to take down that man by the arm, even if he was skin and bones. When you jump and prance around, it's like a wolf playing I saw once. Jack, you're bound to be part or most wolf."

It was a painful effort to dodge farms and small settlements, and more difficult around Asheville. Tom made a compromise between the windy high peaks where they could be easily seen against the sky and the lower more traveled routes. There were times when he craved human contact and thought often of Larry and Adam and wondered where they were.

He dreamed often of Kate ... dreamed of making her his wife and starting a family. It would not be surprising to the family, especially sister Sue. Tom talked through different ways he would tell his family.

"Which is the better way to tell them I intend to make Kate my wife? 'Brothers, meet my fiancé.' What a thing to anticipate! Will the family approve? Is she still single? Her parents will probably approve, and her brother. He'll probably tease the both of us unmercifully."

Being caught up in such day-dreaming tended to become a distraction, when he knew he needed to watch for trouble.

Returning to more appropriate thoughts, he said, "I remember several prisoners returned to the prison, after they made contact with farmers for food. Got to avoid contact with others even this far from the prison."

And then it was back to other thoughts.

"The last letter from my uncle and aunt said they might settle south of Bird Town. They planned to build a small store north of the first one. I've got an idea exactly where they'll put the new store ... not too far from the river. I'll spend Christmas with them if all goes well. I'll miss spending Christmas with Maw, Paw, Sis, and Uncle Casper and Aunt Jane. As a guard, I was close enough to spend part of Christmas with them. Why am I thinking on Christmas? It's almost spring. Wonder where my brothers might be now?"

LIKE GOING HOME

Scattered farms and homes around Waynesville were not easy to bypass. Tom observed folks from a distance. Their angry mood made him want to stay clear. But fate brought him into contact with an elderly gent in farmer's clothes. They startled each other in a curve of the trail and felt forced to speak.

"Howdy, mister."

The man just glared at Tom and marched past.

"Don't take kindly to strangers do you?"

"Nope ... don't pay. Way this war's gone, don't know who to trust."

The old gent didn't turn when he responded but kept walking.

Over the next hill Tom saw Union troops make a brief appearance at one farm.

This could be the reason for the mood ... far different from the friendly people we encountered the first time Uncle and I came through. I hope it's just this particular area.

Two days later Tom spotted the store, right where he remembered they planned to build. The new store looked to have a small second floor that held a small window almost hid by a large walnut tree with crooked limbs.

One limb of the tree hung out over a shed roof at the rear. There were two outbuildings that appeared to be much older.

An old mule was carelessly tied to a new hitch rail. Voices could be heard from inside the store. There appeared to be several customers in the building. Tom moved to get a better view. A second mule was harnessed to a sled. This mule showed its age as well. It was a bit muddy in front of the store since the snow had melted.

"Jack, that type of sled isn't meant for snow, just rough roads and trails. That sled will probably be used for years to come for supplies, rocks, wood and such. I don't recall those outbuildings before. Probably didn't pay that much attention. Think we will wait until dark Jack, or when the customers leave. We don't want to cause trouble for Uncle Art and Aunt Eleanor. There's folks who'd sell us for a reward like your old friend Bruce."

Man and dog found a sunny spot behind laurel bushes and settled down to wait. As long as the sunshine was on them, they were satisfied to sit and relax. Jack rested at Tom's feet with his head on his paws. The two kept a wary eye on the store.

"This is like going home, Jack … almost. We could walk in the store when they finish their chatter. I wonder where uncle gets the stuff he sells and how much he has? He must have connections or very good friends."

By dusk it appeared there would no more customers or visitors. Venturing down the hill to the store created excitement too difficult to suppress.

"I think I'll see if they recognize me … see how long it takes."

Jack took the lead and seemed to know where they were going. Lamps had been lit. The soft light cast by the lamps against a fir tree created a peaceful, homey atmosphere … deceptive for the times.

"Hope they didn't bar the door yet."

Tom pulled on the latch and slipped in. Jack followed cautiously and stood behind his trusted friend. Aunt Eleanor had started toward the door and stopped. She looked suspiciously at this new visitor.

Uncle Art stepped behind the counter made of a broad board placed over two barrels with the space below the boards filled with boxes. His shotgun rested on the wall behind him. Uncle paid more attention to a coat pocket near his right hand.

Tom snickered. *That's where he keeps his little pistol.*

"Kind of late to be out for a feller and his dog, ain't it? Anything we can do for you? We're usually closed by this time."

Tom stood for a moment and looked at each of them. *Must be the beard.*

"Well?" he responded, trying to disguise his voice. "I'm travelin' a great deal, could you put me and the dog up for the night? It's not safe in the woods durin' these times. You got room?"

Poor Aunt Eleanor looks so uncomfortable.

She shook her head no.

Uncle Art looked at Tom closer, then at the dog. It must have been the crooked grin on Tom's face the beard couldn't hide. "Why sure we can. We got that room we made for Howard Crow above. Don't suppose you want to be without your dog?"

His aunt's mouth dropped open, as she looked at her husband in disbelief.

"Yes young man, we can put you up for as long as you like. Ain't that right, Mama?" He looked sideways at his wife whose mouth still hung open.

Finally she shut her mouth and frowned crossly at her husband.

Aunt Eleanor began to suspect she had become the brunt of a joke. Tom and Uncle Art couldn't contain themselves any longer and began to laugh at the same time. Aunt Eleanor squealed and ran to throw her arms around Tom. The dog growled, Tom placed his hand on the dog and moved to meet his aunt.

After the embrace, she withdrew an arm's length.

"Tom ... my Tom, how you have grown and filled out. We got to put a stone on your head to keep you from growin' any taller. I do believe you've growed a foot."

Tom looked down. "No, the same two feet I reckon. But I'll answer to anything to sample some of your chicken and dumplings. It sure is good to see you folks again. This store is pretty much like the other one. What happened to it?"

"There was a fire," responded Art. "The roof and upper part were damaged some. We added on back and repaired. It's much the same. Only stock we lost was from thieves when we ain't lookin'. We know who to watch for."

Tom reached down to stroke Jack's head. "Can I be of help to you and the store? If I'm caught by surprise by customers, I will pretend to be out of my head. I did have a head injury. You probably know from mother's letters. People here that know me shouldn't be a problem. It's the strangers and the Goins family I'll have to watch. If you think my presence would be a liability, Jack and I can take off after a day or two."

Art nodded his head to indicate he understood. He then dropped a heavy crossbeam into two strong wooden supports. The supports were fastened to the wall on each side of the door.

"Stay as long as you want. You spoke of the Goins, the only reason they didn't rob me blind and burn me out is cuz they don't want to put me out of business. I suspect they are the reason supplies get here from Georgia. This is a good meetin' place for them to trade off their hides, whiskey and such. We kind of need each other like. Sad, ain't it. You've not forgotten them I'm sure."

"Not likely," Tom frowned. "Thought they'd be further south. They like that country best. The law couldn't find them there. I hoped they would. Don't look forward to meeting Slim and his big knife, or his brothers."

"Well," chimed in Eleanor, "them boys and their paw like to trade with the Cherokee and so they pass through once in a while. We think they have a camp close by. The Indians don't trust them much, and they behave themselves around them.

Tom sat down in a chair that had been converted from an old barrel.

"Don't they live up in the mountains about twenty five or so miles from here?"

"That's what I hear. Nobody goes up into their holler. Eleanor, you reckon you could see to fixin' a place in Howard Crow's old room in the loft?"

"No fixin' necessary. It's just like I got it ready for when Howard Crow gets back from followin' Chief Will Thomas. You're probably tired. Before you go up, are you hungry?"

"That boy's always hungry, Mom. Don't you remember?"

"Don't want to impose; it's been a spell since we ate, dog and me."

"Come on to the back room. You and paw can talk while I scratch up something to eat. We put in a wood floor back there so watch the step-up. We aim to put in a wood floor in the store part, one day. The dirt floor does fine until it gets wet outside."

Art and Eleanor wanted to hear all the news at once. Tom told of his travel experience between chewing and bits of food. He thought of how Ma would disapprove of his manners, but the couple was captivated by his tales. Tom felt relieved that they accepted his explanation for his part in his company's trip to east Tennessee. They were very hungry for news of the family back home. It didn't matter they themselves had more news through letters.

The aunt decided the dog would be family too. It was clear that Tom and the dog had become inseparable friends. She would not separate them for the night.

"We can catch up on the rest in the morning. Go up the steps Tom. If your dog can make it, he is free to try. Looks like he's attached to you."

Tom awoke the next morning to the smell of real coffee and bacon. When he raised his head, Jack noticed. He had momentarily forgotten about Jack until he heard his toenails on the floor. Jack nuzzled hi to get his attention and received scratches behind his ears. A look around the room in daylight revealed a much smaller room than he realized. The one small window looked out over the shed roof in back. His interest turned to a tree limb that came close to the shed roof.

I could climb onto that limb from the roof; step down to two other limbs and onto that shallow bank of grass and leaves. Then get lost in the rhododendron and laurel where it grows thick behind the shed. If I had approached the store from that direction, I wouldn't have seen the shed until almost bumping into it. This might prove to be important someday.

Tom looked back to watch Jack carefully descend the steps. It was amusing and amazing at the same time.

"Good morning Uncle Art and Aunt Eleanor. I must have been tired to sleep till daylight.'

"Papa, you ever remember Tom not sleepin' till the sun was well up?"

"Only when he was hungry, or by his workin' around the store in hopes he might get a good look at that pretty Cherokee gal."

Eleanor motioned for Tom and Art to have a seat at the table.

Art said, "I'll join you directly. I haven't had time till now. Got in some goods smuggled from Savannah … thanks to your brothers. It sure cost me a heap."

Tom tried to be casual as he asked, "Have you seen Running Deer or is sister lately?"

"As a matter of fact, Kate gave me several letter to mail to Salisbury the day before yesterday, mailed them the same day. She stopped askin' for your letters, though."

Art cut his eyes to the side at Tom. "Guess you ain't interested, eh?"

"I haven't gotten letters lately, not since I left the prison. Been on the move up to now. Suppose I could have posted one on the way but it might have put you in danger. It could have put the company I led in danger too."

Tom stood up, stretched a bit, picked up his plate and cup, and placed them on the cabinet beside the sink.

"I got letters from her more frequently when I became a guard. They dropped off to two or three a year sometime in sixty-three. Figured it to be hard times."

There must have been not more than three people in the store that first day. It gave Tom time to tell what had happened around him since his last Christmas letter of 1863. Art and Eleanor had received letters that informed them of Tom's wounds and prison assignment. The last letter from Tom's ma told of his job to find escaped prisoners.

While they talked, Tom removed an Indian bow from its pegs.

"This bow could use a new string. I've got an extra, so I'll put bees wax on it."

He took some thread from his shirt and 'dressed' the string to better hold the arrow knock.

"I don't like my arrows falling off the string before I can release the thing."

Art stood up from the table, stretched with a grunt and a sigh. He moved into the store section from the living quarters, and decided to say what was on his mind.

"It's about time them Goins come down from the mountains. I always dread them comin'. My shotgun ain't much against five of them if they decide this place is no more use to them. If they didn't have need of this stop for a meetin' place, I reckon we'd been robbed, burned out and worse."

Tom looked puzzled. "I thought you said … how come there are now five instead of three sons and their old man?" His voice revealed alarm.

"They got a no account cousin that's runnin' with them. There use to be seven or eight of them. Either Junior or Slim stole a gal, west of here about twenty miles or so. Then they headed to their place south of here, aimin' for the high mountains. Her paw and her two brothers along with one or two others took off after them, so the story goes. The paw and his two boys must have caught up with them. Nobody has seen the girl's paw or his two sons since. Now we only see the Goins and that cousin. Reckon they had a war of their own. We hear tell the gal's mother hasn't been in her right mind since."

Art began to stoke his pipe. "I'm inclined to believe the story. Too much evidence to prove the story is made-up. Overheard them talkin' outside some time after. Somethin' like, 'Nobody is ready to mess with us on the mountain no more, lessen they want to be buried next to them. Sure sounded like what they said."

Tom joined his uncle in the store. "It's evident they want to be known about as bad apples. Slim was bad enough when I tripped him with a broom before I left. Later he came close to slicing me across the middle with his big knife. I had nightmares for a long time after that. He threatened to cut me up you remember, and might try it given the chance. Is there any place without troubles?"

* * *

After lunch Tom decided to take another look at the window in his room.

An escape route would be a prudent thing to consider. There's nothing so pressing that it requires my attention this afternoon. Opportunities to complete such a plan might be scarce in days to come.

Tom first shaved off the window so that it fit loosely on the sides of the frame. Next he made hinges out of two small pieces of leather. To find the right size drill bit was more difficult. One hole for a large nail or peg was all he needed to complete the task. When he wanted to open the window, it only required a pull on the nail from the windowsill.

The only problem I see is the nerve-wrecking squeak when I open the window. Gotta shave more wood from the window. If I lift up just enough on the window, it makes very little sound. Damp weather could be another problem. So I'll correct with wax or tallow.

The evening turned into another pleasant chat beside the large wood stove.

Eleanor asked, "What was all that noise in your room about."

"I fixed the window so I can climb out. I might be suspected as a deserter and tempt some people for a reward. That could bring trouble. It doesn't matter even if the war is going bad for the south. We got more news from new prisoners than from the Raleigh paper. Greed and revenge is the rule of the day. I can't say that enough. It's everywhere.

"Horror stories of killings and robbery are bad enough. To the mind of some in the Home Guard and bushwhackers, if they saw anything they wanted, anyone who had it was subject to beating or murder. Over near Boone, they shot a man because he wouldn't give up his horse. Fair or not the blame falls on the guard. And then another one-legged Confederate was murdered because he fought for what he believed. These are not unusual tales. The Unionists take revenge on the helpless Confederates, and I see the Confederates do the same thing on their enemy ... any neighbor they didn't agree with. There are not many clean hands."

Aunt Eleanor proceeded to sew while the men talked. It had been a busy day. Tom, under his uncle's instruction, was becoming proficient with the adze in hewing out timbers. After he had stacked boards, Tom split wood until dark. They were relieved with they were called to supper.

Eleanor stopped her sewing for a moment to look at Jack.

"Tom, you should call your dog Wolf. He has to be part wolf. You said so yourself and I think it fits. I don't think Jack or whatever you sometimes call him fits. To call him plain old dog don't do him justice ... does it Wolf? I'm glad Art didn't make them steps any steeper or Wolf would have trouble getting' down. As it is he comes down pretty fast. Never seen the like."

"I agree with my wife. That's a handsome animal."

Tom reached down to stroke Wolf. "Hear ye, hear ye, from this moment forward you will be known as Wolf."

* * *

One evening the last of March, Wolf growled a warning. A glance out the window confirmed their suspicion. It was the so-called Home Guard. Wolf's alarm would give Tom time to escape.

"Aunt Eleanor, Wolf and I are going out the back."

Eleanor picked up a cloth and scrapped crumbs onto a plate.

"Let me look first. It will look like I'm throwing out scraps. There might be one of them out back."

She made a quick exit, threw the scraps, looked around and was back inside before the front door could have opened. Tom heard footsteps approach the store. He and Wolf started up the steps to his room. Eleanor looked at Tom, frowned and shook her head.

He and the dog were up the stairs in half the time, but now he felt trapped.

From upstairs he heard several heavy footsteps enter the store.

A harsh voice demanded, "We got word you people been hidin' a deserter. We come to fetch him back where he kin do some good. You know the penalty fer hidin' such. Where is he?"

The couple looked at each other in surprise. Art and Eleanor played innocent, but they hoped Tom would escape through the window in time.

"Come on now. Give him up now, and it will be easier on you. If'n you be hidin' him, you'd be committin' treason. What would people around here think of a traitor? Don't care about your politics right now. I want that deserter, you hear. One of your neighbors done seed him."

The man moved menacingly toward Eleanor but quickly changed his course when he saw the stairs.

"One of you climb up that there stairs."

"Wolf", Tom whispered, "if I can escape the family will be saved."

They're trying to bluff. What neighbor saw me? I'll lift on the window ... won't squeak as loud.

There was a bit of a scrape when he gently pulled up on the window. He motioned with his hand for Wolf to wait.

"Stay Wolf, I'll be back."

Tom pulled the backpack through the window behind him, closed the window and moved to the side in time.

Wolf growled when the intruder stuck his head above the floor. The growl was enough to cover the window squeak. It also distracted the man from his purpose.

"Good dog, I'm only lookin' around."

For fear of his leader, the man climbed one more round of the ladder to give a quick look, and then backed down. Wolf didn't take his eyes off the man.

"Only a big dog up there. Didn't find him again. That old man don't know what he was talkin about."

"We're right sorry to trouble you folks. Got a job to do, you know. You got any whiskey to sell? We got a long way to travel and need to warm up a bit."

Eleanor was about to reply with disgust. Art rose from his seat, uncrossed his arms before he spoke.

"I'm sorry, we ran out. Anything else we can do for the Home Guard?"

"Nope, we'll be headin' west I reckon. Don't think the Indians like us much."

Eleanor looked at Art. She couldn't suppress a grin, as if to say, I wonder why.

The three men left the store without another word. A fourth man waited outside with one horse and three mules. He had walked the animals from their hiding place to the store after the element of surprise had passed.

The retreating riders eased Tom's mind. Do I descend by the tree or go back through the window. I better use daylight to try the tree for the first time.

The window opened with a loud squeak, but it no longer mattered. He was happy and amused to see Wolf watch him come through the window.

And there's the peg for the window on the bed ... have to remember to take it with me next time.'

Tom decided to talk to the folks about the possibility of him going into east Tennessee.

"My presence is a danger to you-all. Uncle Art ... Aunt Eleanor, I think it better if I go west. It's too risky for me to stay, and it puts all of us at risk. I would like to find out if my friend Adam and the others made it. They had a good, experienced guide, but I would still like to know."

Aunt Eleanor protested, "It will be four to six months before that guard swings around here again. That old man that likely saw you won't be back till the fall of the year. You said you could fake bein' out of your head if you got cornered. Hadn't mentioned it before, but Art suffers from rheumatism and it has about got him down sawin' and planin' them planks. We could use your help. Besides, you haven't seen that pretty gal yet, and she's still not married. Then them Goins are due most any time. You need to protect her from them, since her paw and brother are away fightin'."

"You're very convincing. Doesn't sound like I have a choice. I'll have to find out later what happened to Preacher, Adam and the rest."

The next morning they were awakened by a knock on the store door. The folks down stairs had been up and built a fire. Art could be heard striding to the door.

"Who's there this time of mornin'?"

He was answered by a girl's voice. "It's Kate, Mr. Art."

"You're just in time for breakfast. Let me get this log off the door and get a look at you."

Art pulled the heavy timber aside so the girl could enter.

"Welcome to our humble home Kate. Sure is good to see you again. How come you're out this early?" Art spoke louder than necessary to notify Tom of her arrival.

"I figure there would be fewer travelers about, especially certain mountain men ... the Goins or 'Wents', as Johnny and I call them. My uncle's been down with his leg for weeks now and hasn't been able to come with me to the store.

"Do you have any mail for me or brother?"

"We can do better than that."

The couple looked to the stairs where Wolf had started down the steps, followed by Tom, finger-combing his hair.

Kate sighed, "What a beautiful creature."

Tom chuckled, "Thank you. Always good to know that a girl thinks I'm a beautiful creature."

She can respond, "Silly. You know I mean the dog. But you are a sight for sore eyes, too."

Kate stroked the Wolf while he waited to be let out. She glanced sideways at Tom descending the last two steps. Their eyes met and they both smiled.

She's prettier than I remember … a real handsome woman.

"Brother is right. He can't call you skinny anymore. I haven't called you that since you tripped Slim with the broom."

Everyone laughed at the remark. Art and Eleanor seemed pleased at the reunion.

"Let me get my coat and we can walk to the river if you like."

"You haven't had your breakfast," teased Eleanor.

Uncle Art added his bit of a teasing. "I don't think he needs food right now."

While the two walked to the river, Tom let Kate go first when the path narrowed. He couldn't help notice how gracefully she moved and how her hair moved from side to side. Her skirt trimmed in green and red reached her ankles, and the short brown coat was trimmed in fur.

This I want to remember the rest of my days. Short coats are probably out of style in the east but very practical in the forest.

Kate hummed a tune he remembered from the last time they met. It was a tune that was played when they danced.

When Tom chuckled, Kate turned slightly to give him a knowing smile. The pleasure and excitement he experienced was another moment he would cherish the rest of his life.

"Tom, I haven't gotten a letter from you in months. I was getting worried. If not for brother, I would think you were dead. What has happened?"

"If you mean do I feel the same? Yes I do and more. Why have I not written? I'll cover as much as I can without boring you. Four of us left the prison sometime in February I think. Not sure the date anymore. The stink of death was too much to absorb. Battles I can handle, but the prison was killing me, and about seven others. I've traveled to get here ever since, dodging homesteads and towns. Sorry I didn't have a chance to write. Do you feel differently toward me? From our letters I thought we might get to actually court in person."

Why don't I come right out and propose?

"I knew from your last letter you were not happy at the prison ... that it was like murder ... starved men and sickness. Then when I didn't hear from you for a long time, it did occur to me that you might be on your way. I prayed that you were, and that you were safe. It is truly good to see you again. Perhaps now we can get to know each other. We've had little chance till now."

The two sat on a log most of the morning. They tried to catch each other up on past events as they watched the clear water of the river flow by. Although ice had formed at the edge of the riverbank and the cold wind blew from the west, they hardly noticed the chill. As they enjoyed each other's company, time stood still and breakfast almost forgotten.

After more than an hour, Tom's stomach growled. It reminded them they had not eaten, and their time alone was over for time being. Tom would have liked the moments to last longer, but suddenly they heard loud voices.

Kate peered over some weeds, grabbed Tom by his elbow, and pulled him into a depression near the river-bank.

"Tom, it's the Goins family. Those boys are always bothering me when they come to this place. Slim still talks about cutting you up if he ever catches you again ... stay low."

Tom growled, "Here I am without my pistol for the first time in months. I would sure feel better if I had it now."

"I'm going to slip home. Don't do anything foolish. I will pray for you. You do the same for me."

Kate quickly planted a kiss on his lips, and made her way along the riverbank. After she took several steps, she looked back, smiled and disappeared behind a thicket.

An angry voice shouted, "I tell you, I know for sure she came this-a way goin' to the store. I'd bet my britches."

"She ain't at the store now is she?"

The second voice sounded older, like their paw. There was more loud talk and arguing. Shortly they were heard no more. Tom and Wolf had a chance to reach the store.

Why didn't I go with her? I waited too long; however, she knows the way better than I do.

He looked right and left. Tom spotted the Goins walking south, probably toward their camp.

It would be better for everyone if I disappeared for a few days. Those boys and their father will be in the area for as long as it suits them.

When Tom crossed the path in front of the store, he glanced in the directions the Goins had taken. One of them pointed to him.

Now I know I'll have to make myself scarce.

In the store he didn't take long explaining the situation to his uncle and aunt. The need for a hurried exit was essential. Pack and weapons were retrieved. Wolf got caught up in the excitement. They were going to travel again. His excitement made Tom smile.

Stepping out the back door they were met by a tall, lean, rough man Tom had never seen before. The meanness in the eyes revealed under the edge of his floppy hat made Tom's blood run cold. Transfixed, Tom was momentarily in a frozen state. The stranger flipped out a small pistol, and pointed it at Tom.

Wolf growled and made a step toward the man. There was a quick shot and a yelp. An evil smile spread across the face of the man who pointed the pistol at Wolf for another shot. The dog staggered back, tried to stand. There was another shot.

If Tom had been mad as he'd ever been before in the fight with Red and his cronies, now he was livid ... more angry than he had ever been in his life.

DEEP CHEROKEE COUNTRY

Tom, seething with anger, momentarily froze. His pack was in his left hand and the bow in his right. Without thinking he swung the bow up toward the evil grin, knocked the man's pistol into his face, followed by a swipe at his head with the pack. There was a loud enough thump to tell Tom's pistol in the pack had connected. His assailant crumpled to the ground.

Art ran up to Wolf. "I'll take care of him. There are too many of them."

He saw Tom look at Wolf and hesitated.

"Tom, he is shot through the left shoulder and the mouth … lost some blood. I think he will heal. Now go … go!"

Sprinting off, heavy of heart, Tom heard Art shout, "Me and Mama will take care of Wolf for you."

I don't think they will follow me into Cherokee lands, not where I'm going. There is an old Indian named Hawk Eye. I can go there later with some meat. Perhaps he has room for me if I can bring him some fresh deer. This hunting lodge will have to do for now, if it's still standing.

Tom had to chuckle at the thought of the lodge, made more like a lean-to on the side of a hill, open at the front.

The trail to the so called lodge was still visible after the many years he had hunted.

Tom was pleasantly surprised to find the lodge or small cabin had been improved. There was still a dirt floor, a hole in the roof for smoke, the door hung on loose leather straps and a small window facing south now covered with an old shirt.

The food that his aunt slipped in the pack had taken some abuse against the man's head, but it didn't affect the taste or fail to satisfy his hunger. After Tom ate, he began to realize that he was very tired. The encounter with the stranger and perhaps the loss of Wolf had taken its emotional toll.

That stranger cost me more than the hike up here. And I know it's not good to get so angry. Will I ever have the faith and spiritual strength Ma has? The few times Preacher had preached on the trail, we were too tired or hurried to give it enough thought. I'll see if my Bible is intact and read till dark.

His intentions were good but he fell asleep thinking of the Bible verse he learned as a boy, "All have sinned and come short of the glory of God".

* * *

After a cold night Tom awoke to see a thin layer of snow in front of the cabin.

April is going to be cold this year.

"What am I doing here? I've run away from those no good Goins and Home Guard. To think, the Goins own family ran them off, and some day people will have had enough of the guard. It's time I made life for that Slim and Junior difficult ... hit and run warfare. One night in this lean-to the old man called a cabin is more than enough. Cabin, I'm going to get a deer for the old man and start back.

"What if those crazy brothers and their paw decide to take revenge on my uncle and aunt because of me? They say not to worry because they're useful to those renegades. The stranger that shot Wolf must be the cousin Art talked about. He sure had the family appearance ... mean all the way through. I doubt I killed him ... made him mad. Not mad as I was when he shot Wolf. Sure miss him. Wish he were with me now."

Tom built a small fire to warm his hands, fry a little bacon and soak hardtack in coffee. To prepare for the trail was such a routine that little thought was needed. This time it was different. It wasn't the same without Wolf. He decided it was not like the old days when he used to hunt. Now he craved company.

"Why am I feeling so alone? It's because I don't have Wolf and I've seen Kate. Life is incomplete without them. Man, or boy, is not meant to be alone."

Tom gathered his gear and bow, stepped out of the cabin cautiously and saw nothing unusual.

Small bird tracks in the snow ... no human or animal tracks.

He then stepped off in the direction where he had seen deer tracks. The tracks led to a small stream he had crossed the day before.

"Should have gotten up earlier, but there could still be a deer coming from the stream."

As he stopped to adjust his pack, Tom saw the flicker of a white tail. He strung his bow without taking his eye off the occasional tail flicker ... automatically moved forward down the slope quietly as possible. He drew back the string to touch his jaw like the professor had taught ... took one more step. The deer raised its head. It has been nibbling on rhododendron new growth. Releasing the string sent the arrow to its mark. The deer bounded out of the thicket. Tom ran forward while he fit another arrow on the string.

The deer now ran toward him, and then swerved to its right.

How strange? No matter Mrs. Deer, you're mine.

He shot the deer under the shoulder. It fell ten paces from Tom.

"Where's my first arrow, deer? There should be another."

He caught the movement of something large to his left, and he ducked. A mountain lion sprang at him and took the pack off his back. The blow knocked Tom on his stomach. Seeing the big cat hit the ground, Tom quickly drew his knife out of his boot.

Tom braced himself for a dangerous fight, but instead of another attack, the cat bounded off into the woods to Tom's left.

Only seconds after the cat disappeared he heard excited Cherokee spoken. They chatted too fast for Tom to understand ... too long since he had heard the language. Two Indians about Tom's age walked into the deer trail. They looked Tom over and his equipment. They paid particular attention to the quiver Kate had made for the store years ago. The fur around the top was of particular interest.

Tom replaced his knife, brushed off the dirt and leaves. He pointed to the claw marks on his pack and shook his head. One of the Indians pointed to Tom's right. There lay the deer with his first arrow.

"I shot two deer? What a wonder. And you scared off that big cat. I'm glad you happened by."

"Um, you give-um one to Charlie?"

Tom nodded yes.

"Big white man look for Tom ... you Tom?"

"I'm Tom. What did the big white man look like? Did he have sandy hair and blue eyes?"

I shouldn't have asked the Indian to describe the man. Could it be Adam?

"Him big man, carry big gun. Big black man with him."

"Stop that Jim," spoke the second Indian. "Talk straight English. You make yourself look stupid."

"I was just talking like white men expect me to. And the way they sometimes talk to me."

Tom reasoned, "I think I know who these two men are. I'm glad you happened along when you did. That big cat could have made jerky out of me. Take your choice of the deer. I'm taking some of my meat to Hawk Eye down near the river. Were you looking for me?"

"No," responded Jim, "we were hunting. We'll help you skin and dress the deer. Now I know you. I believe my cousins called you Skinny. We were at the store one time ... doubt you would remember. Now we call you Tom-with-the-fast-broom." Jim expected a response and grinned.

"I'm honored to be called Tom-with-the-fast-broom ... I think? I hope the stories you tell about Skinny are of me tripping Slim and not sweeping the floor."

Tom tried to wear a questionable expression but couldn't help chuckle. The two Indians laughed.

Tom took leave of his two new friends and wasted no time getting to the old man's cabin. Hawk Eye still wasn't at home. He then tied about ten pounds of meat to a tree limb where Hawk Eye would see it. It was time to hurry back to the store. He thought about the meat that would supplement crackers, potatoes and winter squash. It energized him to move faster.

"I can just imagine Aunt's excitement. But Tom my boy, don't let impatience diminish caution."

In a painful flash he once again saw the scenes that made him run. "I can't forget my fast exit and Wolf laying there."

Tom looked around to make sure he was alone before he approached the door. Then ...

I smell horseflesh. Where? I know those horses. We have company.

One horse turned to look at Tom and nickered. Tom cautiously opened the door a crack, peered in and smiled.

Pushing the door open with a rush he exclaimed, "Well, just look what the wind blew in?"

Adam and Lem grinned from ear to ear. Wolf rested beside the fire, raised his head and began to thump his tail.

Adam rose to greet his friend. "You're the one that just blew in. And you've been eating very well, I would say ... wouldn't you Lem?"

"Yes sir, he sure looks good. Mrs. Eleanor been feedin' him real good. That girl of his probably been feedin' him too."

They proceeded to slap each other on the back, laugh and try to talk all at the same time. During the evening meal they tried to bring each other up to what had happened since they parted.

Finally Tom couldn't contain his curiosity any longer. "You didn't come all this way to find me. Why' are you back in North Carolina when you could be safe in Tennessee?"

Adam sat back in a chair and folded his arms. "It appears this war is about over. I got some sick leave and decided to visit your folks near Salisbury. Lem has interest in that area too. You remember that tall pretty maid at your neighbors, the Greens? We thought we would go as far as Waynesville where we have troops, I'm told. We're to wait out the war there. Lee is trapped, or so I hear, and Johnston's Confederates are about to come up against Sherman."

Tom looked at Lem who was grinning again.

"Yes sir, Mr. Tom, I just might get that pretty maid to run away with me and start a small farm. She deserves the likes of me, guidin' them fellers into east Tennessee ... I did help, you know."

They all laughed, as much at his sudden change from the broad smile to a serious face. "We plan on travelin' before daylight. You want to come with us Tom? You could be mah master again ... for a little while. No. I know you've got a lady friend."

Lem looked seriously at their hosts. "Tom never was my master, except to fool nosy folks. He's been a good friend. I'll always remember and be grateful how he helped me. He don't know it, but he's a Christian his ma would be proud of. One of these days the Good Lord is goin' to shake him. And He's goin' to show Tom he belongs to Him and wants Tom to serve him the best way he can. Our travelin' friend Preacher had more time to preach after we got to Tennessee."

Tom looked embarrassed and thoughtful. He shook his head before responding.

"I better stay close to the store for now. You're right; I don't want to leave Kate again. Besides, people near the prison may not feel too friendly toward me."

Aunt Eleanor added a little teasing humor. "Now that Tom got himself interested in his pretty little gal, you couldn't pull him away with your horses. Think he's just about got himself hogtied."

"I thought that might be the end of the story," mumbled Adam. "We should get some rest. It's hard to say farewell again."

* * *

Tom awoke sometime in the early morning to the sound of saddle and tack creaking. He pulled the nail out of the window casing, tried to avoid the window creak to no avail. He extracted himself from the window and slid down the damp shed roof to the tree limb.

"You weren't going to leave without saying goodbye, were you?"

Adam threw his saddle on the horse. "No, we're getting ready. That was our intention until we saw this place is being watched from in front. You be careful Tom. Your uncle told us about the revenge and bitter feelings that hold folks captive all over these mountains. Both sides of the conflict won't put aside their hatred for years to come ... perhaps generations, I'm thinking."

"Give my folks my love and hug my sister for me."

A lump came to Tom's throat when he thought of his sister and the family. Tom pulled the men to himself and gave them a bear hug.

As Adam untied his horse, he said, "I'll be more than happy to oblige you about hugging Sue. She has been on my mind almost constantly since we left."

Adam studied Tom's face in the gathering light. "Do you suppose it would help if I circulated the story that you have bouts of forgetfulness ... that you kept on going after the search became unprofitable? The head wound you know. You could have had another fight that prevented you from returning to duty. That should help set things right with your neighbors."

"That story wouldn't be true, unless you consider I'm love sick."

Tom turned to Lem and said, "Lem, I hope that pretty maid will say yes, and you have a good life. Adam, take good care of my sister."

Someone coughed in front of the store. Tom feared it might be the Goins gang and urged the two friends to leave.

"It's better to walk the horses through the trees some distance before you ride. Watch your back until you go over the mountain."

Tom watched his two friends lead their mounts into the trees and disappear.

When he could no longer hear or see them, he realized he had gotten cold, even though it was spring. His underwear and bare feet were exposed to the morning chill.

I'll go back to bed to get warm. First I'll put on my trousers. Sleep will be impossible.

Tom slipped back through the window, hurried under the covers and curled into a ball. Covers felt good, and if it had not been for his aunt preparing breakfast he would have gone to sleep again.

My hunting trip must have tired me. It's a temptation to stay in bed, but I'm hungry.

* * *

Half-way in and out of a dream state, he thought he heard squirrels on the shed roof.

Scampering around outside my window…Uh oh! Not squirrels. The scraping sounded more like someone on the roof.

He felt for his pistol, rose on his elbows to look out the window … his mouth dropped open. There was Kate, about to knock on the window.

How did she know about my tree?

They both smiled when he started to pull opened the window.

I forgot to replace the nail … no matter now, good thing.

Kate started to crawl through the window and knocked the big nail off the window sill. It hit the floor with a clatter. Tom rose on his knees to help her squeeze her legs threw.

"Tom, they're watching the front of the store … those smelly mountain men. This was the …"

Kate didn't get to finish her statement. Their combined weight snapped a bed rope that supported the straw mattress. It threw them to the floor. Neither of them could suppress a giggle that turned into laughter. Kate kissed him between chuckles, got up from the floor to close the window for fear they might be heard outside. Wolf did a few kisses himself, licked Tom on the nose.

"Come down children and have some breakfast before it gets cold," Aunt Eleanor yelled. "Watch the steps. Don't want anybody to get hurt."

"You go first Kate. I'll be right behind you." Glad I was half dressed. "Give me a chance to put on a clean shirt. I was up earlier to wish friends safe travel."

At the table Tom looked at Kate. He remembered the kiss down by the river and how he cherished it through the last few days.

Wish I could have seen more of her since I returned. Kept thinking about her while I helped Art prepare boards for the cabin. To make an effort to see her might have been dangerous. Now that she is here and my mouth won't work ... except for chewing.

Aunt Eleanor placed another coffee cup in front of Kate.

"It's not real coffee you know, but it will do. It's got old grounds, chicory and beech tree bark. Next time you come to visit, just knock three times, and add one more, and we'll know it's you. Then you won't have to climb that tree."

"Yes ma'am, I will. There's too much open ground at the back door, and the way to the tree was more protected. I hoped Tom would be up and the window would open easily."

Kate looked toward the store door. "We need salt, pepper and corn meal if you have it. Cousin Jim brought some deer meat he said Tom killed. We've run out of corn meal and a few other things. I left some winter squash behind a pile of new lumber. May I use that for trade?"

Eleanor rose from the table, patted Kate on the shoulder, and moved to the shelves that were almost bare.

"Sure you can, dear. We can help each other out you know, because we're all in this together. Sit a spell longer while I see what we got."

Wolf walked to the door, looked at Eleanor expectantly.

"All right boy, out you go. Tom, my hands are full. Open the door."

Tom scooted his chair back and moved to open the door. The heavy beam had to be removed that barred the door.

"It's a relief to see Wolf healthy again. I thank you once again for nursing him back. He's become a real companion to ... us all. Paw would probably say, 'I'm much obliged'."

Kate rose from her chair. "It's time for me to be on my way."

She gave Tom a couple fond pats on the shoulder before she reached the door.

"I'll go out the back way after I peek outside."

The family watched Kate go out the door but not before she turned to give them a smile. She let her eyes dwell a moment longer on Tom. This made his heart swell.

Ma would say how blessed I am and indeed I am. I should tell someone to kick me for not proposing when we were alone by the river. She knows I care and she cares for me.

Uncle Art brought his fist down on the table playfully, hard enough to get their attention. "How long are we to sit here when there's work to do? Tom, you starin' at that door ain't goin' to make her come back in. Why don't we ...?"

A shot and a scream interrupted uncle's remark followed by a minié ball thump against the house. Tom bounded for the door.

"That was Kate yelling."

REVENGE OR SELF DEFENSE

Tom banged open the door, sprung to his left and took cover behind a woodpile under the overhang.

I didn't bring a weapon ... foolish. Doesn't seem to be any present danger.

He could see Kate standing a short distance away with her hands to her throat, where she gazed to her right. Tom rushed to Kate.

I fear to find her hurt, even though I think it's not the Goins idea to harm her.

When he reached her, Tom could see what held her attention. A pair of boots protruded from between rhododendron bushes.

Kate rushed to Tom, threw her arms around him tightly. She didn't cry or sob, but trembled all over. When he looked closer at the boots, Wolf looked back at him. Next to Wolf lay a body.

The boots and the man look too familiar. It's Slim's and Junior's cousin of ... the one who tried to kill me and Wolf.

He moved his hands to hold her face and looked into her eyes. There was perhaps a mixture of fear and sadness.

"What happened, Kate?" *I got an idea but better let her tell.*

Neither Tom nor Kate was conscious that Art and Eleanor had joined them.

Aunt Eleanor took Tom and Kate by the arm. "You better come inside where it's safer. You can tell us what happened in there."

It was a solemn procession that entered the living quarters of the store, each dealt with their particular emotion.

Kate stopped before they could be seated. "I don't want the Goins to find me here. I'll tell what happened and start for home. Wolf was resting under his favorite bush as usual. He got up when he saw me, but stopped when this awful smelly man started toward me ... grinning so awful evil. He didn't see Wolf until it was too late. And when he threatened me and made a move toward me, Wolf jumped and knocked him down. The man got his pistol out, but by then Wolf had him by the throat. The shot missed both me and Wolf ... went wild. That's it."

She shivered with the horror, and said, "I better go."

Art went to the door. "Let me check outside first."

It was the first time Tom noticed Art carried his shotgun.

"If he's dead ... and I suspect he is ... me and Tom will take care of the body. Kate, you take this double barreled pistol as a precaution."

They watched Kate go out the door the second time that day. She managed a weak smile before closing the door. This made Tom's heart burst with adoration.

Ma would say, "How could you be so blessed?" *And she would also get on to me for not taking her home.*

"Why am I standing here? I'm not thinking clearly. I'll take the other double barrel and take her home. Be back soon."

Tom had to run hard to catch her since she was running. Kate turned to look back, saw Tom and slowed to walk.

"You don't have to do this. But I'm thankful you chose to do so. You can return when we see Hawk Eyes cabin. Those mountain boys wouldn't dare go further in daylight. Tom, I need to get away from these beloved hills. But I don't know where to go. It's not safe for you either. There's my uncle. You can go home now."

Tom felt she would now be safe, but at the same time he regretted the uncle's presence.

I would like to assure her but it will have to wait.

"Kate, we'll talk of this again later."

* * *

No one at the store felt like they wanted to eat that evening. Tom and Art were emotionally drained having to bury the man they assumed was the Goins cousin. There wasn't a thing on the body to tell who he was, not that it mattered since the grave would have to remain hidden like so many in the mountains.

Uncle Art chose the floor of an old shed that had seen better days. Old boards and sacks were thrown on the grave much as the floor had been before the burial. Art didn't intend to use the shed any longer.

Art said a word and a prayer for those that would miss him, adding, "I hope his disappearance will have some positive effect on kin and friends.

* * *

A few days later Tom decided to find Little Fawn.

It's a fine sunny day ... no reason to prevent me. I'm glad she likes both of her names ... Kate and Little Fawn. Sometimes I prefer to remember her as Little Fawn and think of the first time I saw her. I had never quite felt that way before ... not even about Mary Ellen. My! How she could run!

Tom stopped at Hawk Eye's cabin. He was home this time. He inquired of Hawk Eye about her cabin's location and learned that it was easy to find the trail to where she lived. When he rounded a bend he saw her picking up sticks. Her back was to him. He decided to approach quietly and surprise her.

Tom was the one to be surprised. A big arm grabbed him around the head and a big knife flashed to his throat. Kate wheeled around at the sound, and screamed loud enough to be heard in Knoxville. She dropped the sticks on the ground, her hands and arms frozen ... pleading. "It's Skinny, Uncle Luke ... it's Skinny! Not any of the Goins."

Releasing Tom, Uncle Luke growled, "How could I know? He's not skinny any more ... not from the back anyhow. Sorry son. Them Goins, or 'Wents' as she calls them, been pesterin' something fierce, the one called Slim.

"I wasn't goin' to cut his throat, just scare him so he would get it in his head it's dangerous to bother my niece. I'm talkin' about Slim, not Skinny, here."

Kate, still shaky, started to pick up the sticks again.

"Let me get rid of these sticks and I'll walk you to the store or my folk's cabin."

She held the sticks close and stopped to look into Tom's eyes. "It doesn't look like he scared you?"

"It happened so fast I didn't have time to get scared ... figured my time had come. Your scream finally scared me. Is that your folks place?"

"Yes, that's our cabin. My paw and brother should be back any time. Did you hear how they scared the Yankees in Waynesville? They hit them with a good punch. Chief Will Thomas and the rest sure fooled them ... campfires all around the hills. It made us look more numerous. The plan had to come from the story of Gideon in the Bible."

Kate saw confusion in Tom's expression. "Oh, you haven't heard about what happened in Waynesville ... or maybe you don't remember the story of Gideon."

Tom waited for her to tell the rest of the story. He decided he had to drag the story out of Kate.

"All right, what happened, Kate? All I know is what you tell me. When I traveled past Waynesville, I tried to avoid the people."

Kate smiled with pride and came closer to Tom.

"Chief Will Thomas, with the Cherokees and some of our white neighbors, surrounded Waynesville. They built fires on the mountain ridges around the town. It looked like there were hundreds of us. Chief Thomas demanded the Yankees surrender or leave town, I don't recall which. The Yankee leader told Will the war was practically over, but they left town anyway. Even if they returned it's a great victory and a morale boost."

Uncle Luke touched Tom on the shoulder. "I see smoke coming from the store direction. You don't suppose them Goins is up to more mischief?"

Tom studied the smoke for a second.

"I better go see. Kate, if you don't see me in a day or two, you'll know all is right. I'll try to get back soon to see you."

He raced to the clearing to find everything as he left it, except for bad smelling smoke.

Smells like somebody tried to burn wet wood. Strange, wonder what happened. Someone tried to burn ...

It was then that he noticed the two outbuildings burned to the ground. They had also tried to burn the new lumber but it was too green and wet.

Aunt Eleanor opened the back door to toss out a basin of water. Tom was greatly relieved when he saw her.

At least she is safe.

"Oh Tom, I'm glad you're back. That old mountain man and his boys been around askin' questions about their cousin. All we told them is we didn't know. We really didn't know which way he went when he died. That last part was true enough."

She smiled a bit at the last statement.

His aunt motioned for Tom to follow her into the store. "Of course, they're not convinced. Since he was to watch the store, naturally they assume we had something to do with him being gone. They need this store or it would be burned down too. And that Slim is bound and determined to catch Kate. They watch this place since they're not brave enough to go near her cabin. Slim wants revenge and so did the cousin. Tom, you better take that gal out of these parts or keep her hid amongst the Cherokees.

"Oh, I almost forgot, Tom, your maw sent us a letter. Said if you got here to tell you the second murder is solved. You would know what she meant. You're paw went to put flowers on his mother's grave and heard some sniffling. On the other side of a stone was this man sayin' over and over I didn't mean it. It was an accident. Your paw said the man confessed to a fight with Buttons, whoever he was, and Buttons fell against a stump and broke his neck. Didn't mention the other man's name but you would know. Mystery solved?"

"Glad you told me, mystery solved."

"Another mystery that bothers me, what happened to the dog that followed us from Old Fort? Every time I think to ask it's not the right time or I'm busy here or there."

"It disappeared the next day after you left on that old mule."

* * *

Two days later when Tom didn't return to the forest, Kate walked to the store and Wolf met her. The door was partially open. Wolf pawed it open the rest of the way. Kate looked around for signs of Tom. She didn't see Tom, but Aunt Eleanor was behind the counter.

"Aunt Eleanor, it appears the men have worked hard on the cabin." Eleanor was chewing and didn't attempt to answer right away. "I thought Tom would have come by our cabin by now. Is he working awful hard?"

"He did go by yesterday, honey. Said nobody was there."

"Ma and I must have gone down to Uncle Luke's and Aunt Zena's. It looked like someone tried to leave a note, but it must have blown loose from the hook on the door … just left a scrap. Must have been Tom."

Heavy footsteps could be heard outside. Tom and his uncle each entered with an armload of firewood. Aunt Eleanor put her hands on her hips and stared at the men.

"I know why you two came in, and carryin' firewood. You ain't foolin' us. Art is hungry and Tom saw Kate. Ain't that so?"

Tom dropped his load in the wood box. "Yep. The only reason Wolf would leave me and Unk would be if Auntie called, 'come and get it' or Kate was around. I'm hungry too. Can I help fix something?"

Kate joined Eleanor at the table. "You men rest. I'll help Eleanor get things together, even though it early."

Wolf leaned against Kate's leg and looked at Tom. It pleased him that Wolf liked Kate. While Tom observed the two, Wolf averted his attention to the back door and made a low growl.

Eleanor grabbed Wolf by the leather collar. "Help me hold him Art. We don't want him shot up again."

Bang! The front door of the store was violently shoved open. Slim Goins rushed into the store and started for the living quarters in back.

"Junior, I told you I heard that gal's voice! Come here Injun. I waited for you long enough."

Kate lunged for the back door ... ran through and bumped into Roscoe, the bigger of the Goins boys. Before he could get his big arms around her, Kate dodged and ran for the trail.

Slim started after her but Tom kicked one of the barrel chairs in front of Slim. It made him stumble. Slim's momentum brought him head first into Tom which forced them over another chair and against a wall. Tom was off balance, made it easy for Slim to push him aside.

"I'll get you for that, Skinny, I'll get you good."

Slim was not about to lose his chance to catch Kate and bounded for the door. Slim gained a good ten paces before Tom regained his balance.

Slim yelled again as he ran. "I'll fix you later, Skinny, this time for good."

Tom started after Slim, but Uncle Art stopped him.

"There are too many of them, Tom. Besides Slim, you got Junior, Roscoe, and the old man. I know you're determined. Kate is fast. She can outrun them boys, unless they got a trap set up to catch her. At least add the mate to that over-and-under-pistol[1] to your boot. I've kept them loaded for a time like this. You got another pistol in your room. Get it too. They've been drinkin'."

"Not enough time for my pistol, Uncle. I'll take the extra double barrel and that Cherokee bow and some arrows. Those Cherokee arrows will be real justice. Kate can't keep runnin', and my best defense is to make the first move."

Tom stuffed the first pistol in his belt, the extra pistol in his boot top, and grabbed the bow and arrows off the wall. He was out the door on the run.

Kate can run faster than anyone I know. If she gets by the old man and Junior she should be safe for now.

"This has to end today, Lord. Protect Kate I pray."

I'm not going to give Slim the chance to cut me or grab Kate. Uncle Art and Aunt Eleanor are in danger now. They know what is happening. Their knowledge of Slim's attempt to possess Kate puts them in real danger.

Tom got just a glimpse of Slim just before he disappeared on the wooded trail. In order to intercept Slim, Tom took a short cut to Kate's cabin. He knew it would be close.

Where are the others? This is not good. Where are those other brothers?'

* * *

---

1 Over and under Pistol: double barrel pistol with one barrel over the other instead of side by side.

Aunt Eleanor spoke sharply at Art, "You're not goin' to let that boy fight this battle alone. I see you're takin' your rifle musket. That's good. Be careful ... real careful, and come back to me with that boy."

"I will Mama, and I'm takin' the shotgun too. Pray Mama, like you never prayed before."

Art ran out the door with both weapons and ran as fast as his old legs would carry him. "Hope I'm not too far behind Tom. Which way did they go?"

* * *

Tom reached a curve in the short cut ... heard Kate give an angry yell.

One of the brothers ambushed her. It would have to be Junior. I'll bet they set a trap.

Tom stopped long enough to string the bow and fit an arrow. The nerve-racking moments it took to string the bow seemed like ages. He could hear curses, laughing, and Kate's angry protests. With all the shouting, Tom didn't have to be too concerned that they would hear him. There was movement behind him, and when he looked around he saw Roscoe, plodding along to catch up.

Did I pass him, or did he get lost? Don't think he sees me.

Tom found a good vantage place without revealing his position too early. The old man leaned against a tree, held his musket loosely in the crook of his arm and looked bored. Junior jumped up and down and giggled foolishly.

Tom moved closer to see why Junior was so excited. He saw Slim and Kate. Slim, with a wicked grin, tried to grab the top of Kate's dress and received a scratch across his face for his trouble. Slim hit her on the head with his fist and knocked her to the ground.

Slim dropped to his knees and tried to pin Kate down, but she fought like a wild cat. Her arms flailed to ward off Slims hands. Slim only toyed with her hands by slapping them around. Then he started to rough her up.

Junior started to jump up and down and yelled like a cornered hog.

Old man Yandel shouted, "You goin' to kill her like you done that gal from down Macon County way? Tie her up and bring her along."

"I ain't goin' to kill her, Paw ... just teach her a lesson."

It was difficult for Tom to get a clear shot through the brush. He wanted to shoot Slim but was afraid he might hit Kate.

Wish this was my bow. Take them one at a time as fast as I can and give Kate a chance to run. Lord, be with us now ... please.

Since Junior quit jumping when he thought the 'fun' was over, he would be the first target. Tom took a quick aim at Junior and released the string. In his determination he didn't make an allowance for the twigs, which deflected the arrow enough to make it glance off Junior's shoulder blade and bury in the old man's arm. Yandal's musket dropped to the ground, while both Junior and the old man yelled in pain.

Old Yandel spotted Tom and yelled at the boys, "Get that feller Tom. He done crippled my shootin' wing."

Now that he had been spotted, Tom could move to get better shots. Junior stood on one foot to rub his shoulder and look for Tom. When he saw Tom he picked up his musket ... only to receive an arrow in the chest. Slim, tried to tie Kate's ever-moving hands and was unaware of what had happened behind him until Junior fell on his legs. Slim cursed at his brother, turned his head around long enough to see the arrow that stuck several inches out Junior's back.

Old man Goins managed to pull the arrow from the tree where his arm had been pinned. "I said get him. Get him Roscoe. Leave her be, Slim, and help."

The old man picked up his rifle-musket with his good arm.

Roscoe spotted Tom and charged him like a mad bull. The brush kept getting in the way of Tom's bow so he dropped it, drew his belt pistol and fired at the charging Roscoe.

The mad bull kept coming, only several feet away. Tom fired the second barrel into the man's chest. The last shot stopped Roscoe in his tracks. He looked dumfounded at the two holes in his shirt were it began to turn red, fell on his knees, and rolled over on his back.

Slim released Kate to grab Junior's musket and rose to take aim. Now that a tree protected Kate from Tom's arrows, he untangled his bow and let fly another arrow. The arrow glanced off the musket barrel and buried in Slim's hip. The musket fired harmlessly.

Another movement alerted Tom to duck instinctively … in time to avoid a minié ball from the old man.

Old man Yandel Goins charged up the hill after Tom with a pistol in his hand. "You kilt my boys. I'm goin' to skin you alive."

He was fast for an old man. Tom ran down the hill to meet the man and to finish his business with Slim.

Yandel fired first. The ball hit Tom in the mid-section and caused him to bend forward from the impact. This made it easier to pull his second pistol from his boot.

The ball knocked the breath out of me but not the fight.

Slim reached for his pistol only to find it had fallen somewhere. He then pulled Junior's pistol from the body's belt, and took aim with both hands.

Kate kicked Slim to spoil his aim. The shot went wild.

Slim gave Kate little attention but cocked the pistol for another shot. She then pulled Slim's hunting knife out of his boot and sprang on him with all her pent up anger and strength. The knife sunk in Slims back. The pistol fired a second time into the air.

Tom tried to catch his breath after the ball had hit his stomach.

I got to finish this.

The old man dropped his pistol and drew his big knife … charged once more.

Tom fired the first barrel upward into the old man's chest and set him back a step. He then cocked and fired the second barrel. Old man Yandel fell back and rolled across Junior's legs.

"If I hadn't been running at him, I believe the ball would have knocked me back a step or two. I can breathe easy now, but it doesn't hurt as much as I expected. Strange."

Kate ran up to him, "Lie down and let me look at you."

Fear showed in her eyes. Anxiety was written on her face. She looked with concern at the blood, and then gently tore the shirt loose to examine the wound. Tom didn't know what to expect in Kate's features after their experience. He saw the fear on her face, but he also saw her contrasting strength.

"Don't you die on me; don't you dare die on me now. Dear God, don't let him die."

Tears came to her eyes when she stripped away the bloody shirt. Cleaning away some of the blood revealed a long gash along his left side.

"I think I see a rib. The lead cut your side and didn't enter you anywhere I can see.

"What's this?" Kate saw the buckle Tom had fastened to the belt that held the quiver for his arrows.

"The ball hit your buckle and then made a cut along your side. It must not have hit you straight on. I don't think it's bad, not bad at all. I can stop the bleeding and sew you up. Maw is better with sewing up wounds than I am. We should get you to our cabin."

Tom breathed easier and without pain. He decided it was time to take stock of Kate's health.

"Are you hurt? I see a knot on the side of your head."

Kate forced a smile despite the recent battle. "My shoulder hurts more than my head. I'll be sore all over tomorrow."

Kate tore off a piece of her petticoat and placed it against his wound.

"Hold that tight. It might stop the bleeding. That piece of lead must have been jagged to cut your side. Let's get you to the cabin. No one will see us there like they would at the store. My maw can sew you up but first ..."

Kate left him and ran behind a tree. Tom could hear her getting sick.

Tom stood for a moment, felt weak and had to sit.

Poor girl, strong as she is, this was war, and war's enough to make anyone sick. I wanted revenge some day but didn't realize how terrible it can be and how it affects others. I'll tell myself ... others this was war.

Kate returned quickly, looking pale but determined.

"Kate, you'll have to help me some. The battle and the wound have left me a bit out of sorts."

"Stand up slowly and put your arm around my neck." She stooped a bit to allow Tom to stand.

Tom couldn't help grinning. "I had to get myself shot so I could put my arm around your neck."

Kate smiled, "You want another punch in your breadbasket?"

"Not today, ma'am."

To chuckle hurt his ribs, but he couldn't stop. Battle excitement made them both giddy. Their laughter was finally reduced to giggles.

"I might risk another punch when this wound heals."

Uncle Art rested his weapons against a tree and watched Tom and Kate. "I'm too late for their little war. All that shootin, only way I could find them. They don't need me now ... never did. Thank you Lord, thank you. I'll leave them be ... still in good hands."

Their movement and her closeness helped him forget some of the stress they had experienced. Tom began to feel stronger but was not about to tell Kate.

Kate's mother must have seen them coming. She was out the door as soon as they entered the clearing. Before Mrs. Adams stepped off the porch she turned to speak to someone in the house. A man came out of the cabin with his left arm in a sling and joined Mrs. Adams to meet the wounded. From his appearance he had to be Kate and Johnny's father. This was the first time Tom had seen Mr. Adams.

Her father looked on the two with concern. His daughter looked disheveled, and she supported a young man with blood on his shirt. Mr. Adams obviously heard the shots and had an idea what took place. Mrs. Adams, without a word, motioned for Tom to take a seat on a stool near the front stoop.

"And who might this boy be, daughter? He must be a mighty good friend for you to hang on to him like that. Looks like you two been in a scrape. You don't have to wound a feller to catch them Kate."

"You know better, Paw. We've been in a scrape alright. We had us a last war with the Goins boys and their paw. You remember how Johnny and I talked about Skinny? This is Skinny, or used to be. Tom Gentry showed up at the right moment and saved me. He didn't come ridin' up on a white horse in shining armor but might as well have."

Mr. Adams decided to sound out this new fellow. "Tom, what are your plans now that the war is over. You still want to study law? Kate said once that was what you wanted. We have kin in both Sevierville and Jonesboro who could name a lawyer you could study under. Why not give Tennessee a look?"

"I had thought on Raleigh but Tennessee might be the better choice right now. As my Paw would often say, 'I'm much obliged', and appreciate the suggestion."

Tom looked at his surroundings. He saw the snug, well-built cabin was nestled in a small clearing. There was a porch that extended across the front; a large chimney at one end and a window on each side of the front door. The cabin faced south so it could catch the winter sun. Trees in back kept it cool in the summer. He heard a stream nearby that eliminated the need for a well.

Tom relaxed as Mr. Adams was listening to what Kate was saying.

Kate explained to her parents what has transpired on the trail while Mrs. Adams attended to the wound. She gave an almost step by step description of what she saw.

While she talked she held Tom's arm high to enable her mother to work on the wound. The bleeding had almost stopped.

Mr. Adams pulled a jug from under the porch and sat it by his wife. The whiskey was used to wash the wound. It burned like fire. Tom tried his best not to show pain. It was a good attempt to impress her parents. The father looked on Tom with admiration.

Mother finished with a wide bandage, turned and smiled at Tom. "That should hold long enough."

No one noticed Running Deer who leaned against a porch support until he spoke. "Well Tom, it's good to see you're still alive. Now I'll have to share some of the meat Jim sent to pay a debt, if I saw you."

"He didn't have to repay a thing but it's appreciated. I might just be hungry after all that excitement."

"When have you not been able to eat since I've known you?"

Tom only grinned. He remembered not to laugh and irritate his wound.

Kate looked at Tom intently while she helped her mother replace his shirt. She moved her head to better see his eyes.

"Tom, we Cherokees have a custom. If you save a girl's life or her honor, you are bound to marry and take care of her the rest of your life. And she is to honor and obey her husband for the care and concern he has shown her."

Kate's face blushed with her boldness.

Tom's mouth dropped open and his eyes showed mock surprise. He pretended to look for support from Johnny Running Dear.

Her father tried to suppress a smile, but there was a twinkle in his eye. Johnny shrugged his shoulders and looked grim. He moved away from the porch support to place his hand on Tom's shoulder.

"Tom, old friend, my sister knows more about these things than I do. It appears you're hooked like that old trout we used to try catch."

Johnny cut his eyes to look at Kate's smug expression. He almost laughed.

"There's another matter to consider. Kate, since you're only one quarter Cherokee and Maw is half, I don't know how strong a hold this new custom will have. You better come up with another plan in case this one backfires."

Kate placed her hands on her hips in an expression of annoyance.

Tom saw her frustration and decided the teasing had gone far enough ... almost. On the other hand, he couldn't resist a bit more.

"Well ..." He let out a sigh of resignation, "... I wouldn't want to offend any tradition or custom like Kate has brought to our attention. So it looks like I'm caught. It doesn't look like Johnny will come up with a plan to get me out of this."

"Oh You! This is supposed to be serious." Kate sputtered. She dropped Tom's arm and drew back her fist as if to hit him.

"Wait Kate!" Johnny almost yelled and then chuckled. "You're supposed to kiss an injured man, not hit him, sister."

"Kate," Tom stood from where he sat on the stool. "I have a question I've wanted to ask from the first time I saw you. Will you marry me?"

He didn't wait for an answer but placed his right hand behind her head and drew her to his lips.

"Son ..." Kate's father addressed Tom, having gotten into the spirit of the game. "Unless there's a reason you shouldn't get married ..." He looked around at the others with a smile and continued, "... times, what they are, we got to get these two married. It seems to be a bright spot of sunshine now shines through this terrible war. I pray it will spread to the top of these peaks."

It was Tom's time to shrug his shoulders. "The circuit rider for these parts left not long ago ... for how long I don't know. How long do we wait?"

Mr. Adams held up his hand to get their attention. "Don't concern yourself on that account, I'm the sometimes Chaplain in Will Thomas' outfit, especially since I got my wing clipped. Tom, you're a Christian are you not?"

Tom smiled and nodded. "Yes Sir. The good Lord came to my ... our rescue today. He must have plans for us."

"I was sure you were and I would be pleased and honored to marry you and my daughter right here in front of this cabin or anywhere. Go back to your uncle and aunt. Bring them back with you first thing in the morning and we'll do this thing right."